"I suspect that you should hurry," Marrow suggested.

"Why?" Dolph squeaked.

"Because a harpy is coming," Marrow concluded.

Oops! Harpies were bad news. Not only were they female, they were ugly, and nasty, and hungry. A harpy would snatch up a dormouse just like that and gobble it down instantly. Dolph made it to the end just as her dirty glistening talons snatched at him. He flung his arms around the trunk of the tree to which Marrow's hand attached, and changed from a mouse into an ogre. "Me think she stink!" he growled.

"Oops! Didn't see you pretty-face!" she screeched. "Where's the mouse?"

"Me mouse, she louse!" Dolph retorted. Evidently she did not realize that he was a form changer.

"You took my mouse, I'll take your bones!" she screeched.

Dolph became a small flying dragon. This gave him room enough to fly well and also gave him fighting strength. He launched himself at the harpy.

She saw him and did a messy double take. "A dragon?" she screeched. "Where did that come from? Help, sisters!"

Immediately there was an answering chorus of shrieks. The other harpies were coming!

TOR BOOKS BY PIERS ANTHONY

PIERS ANTHONY

HEAVEN CENT

TOR®
fantasy

A TOM DOHERTY ASSOCIATES BOOK
NEW YORK

This is a work of fiction. All the characters and events portrayed in this book are either products of the author's imagination or are used fictitiously.

HEAVEN CENT

Copyright © 1988 by Piers Anthony Jacob

A Tor Book
Published by Tom Doherty Associates, LLC
175 Fifth Avenue
New York, NY 10010

www.tor.com

Tor® is a registered trademark of Tom Doherty Associates, LLC.

ISBN: 0-812-57498-2

First Tor edition: May 2000

Printed in the United States of America

0 9 8 7 6 5 4 3 2

For Cam—my wife of 32 years, and counting

CONTENTS

MYSTERY

Dolph made himself comfortable on Ivy's bed and watched the Tapestry. The things its moving pictures showed were always so much more interesting than his dull life at Castle Roogna! Ivy was off at a tutoring session with Chem Centaur, so he had the Tapestry all to himself. That was best, because big sisters were a pain in the tail.

With that thought, he changed form, becoming the wolfen aspect of a werewolf. He curled around, with his four legs tucked under him and his tail just touching his black nose. Animals generally had better bodies than human folk, being both fiercer and more relaxed. Of course he couldn't see the Tapestry as well, because his eyes could not focus sharply, but that hardly mattered because he had seen just about everything before. Everything interesting, anyway: the big battle scenes, the horrendous magical events, and the strange monsters. After the first couple of times it wasn't much fun watching an ogre squeeze the juice from a boulder or twist a tree into a pretzel, or seeing yet another herd of centaurs playing people-shoes. But here and there a mystery remained, and that could be moderately intriguing.

For example, there was the question of what had happened to Grandma Iris' talent. She was a Sorceress of Illusion, who could on her better days make anything seem like anything else, and sound and smell and feel like it too, so that it was almost impossible to tell what was what. That could be a lot of fun! But in the last month she had lost a significant part of it—the visual aspect, as she put it—so that while she could still make something sound like something it wasn't, she could no longer make it look that way. Grandma Iris was old, of course, but Dolph could understand how such a thing could be bothersome even so. Where had her Illusion gone? He had used the Tapestry to look for the missing talent but had been unable to find it.

Then there was the matter of the roses. They grew in a special courtyard, a gift to his father King Dor: five bright colors of them, signifying indifference, friendship, romance, love, and death. One person stood in the center, surrounded by the bushes, and another plucked a rose, only of the color that signified his or her attitude toward the other. The wrong color brought a terrible scratch from the thorns. Dolph understood that much; the mystery was why anyone bothered. Young men and young women came all the time to pick roses for each other—to prove their love, they said. What was the point? What, for that matter, was love? All Dolph knew was that it related in some devious way to the secret of summoning the stork so that it would bring a baby. He had tried to trace the storks with the Tapestry, but though he had spotted them carrying babies, he had never managed to discover how anyone signaled the stork in the first place. What was the big secret?

This time he tuned the Tapestry in on the major mystery of all time: the disappearance of Good Magician Humfrey. This had been discovered when Esk Ogre, Chex Centaur, and Volney Vole came together to ask Questions, and had discovered the castle empty. They had looked at the Book of Answers, but it turned out to be too technical for any normal person to understand; only the Good Magician could interpret it, and he was gone. After that, King Dor had gone and taken the Book and locked it up, so that it could come to no mischief while the Good Magician was absent. Everyone had tried to find the Magician, but no one had succeeded. So for the past three years, the mystery had prevailed. It seemed that no one but the Good Magician could solve the question of his disappearance with his family. Meanwhile, there were no Answers to be had, and that was a great frustration to many people and creatures of Xanth.

Dolph worried the riddle back and forth, like the wolf cub he was at the moment. Where could the Good Magician have gone so abruptly, leaving behind his castle and everything in it? It seemed to have happened just before the trio came, because challenges had been set up for each of them. Normally there were three barriers opposing the entry of anyone who came to ask a Question, and only those who won through could have the privilege of giving up a year's service to the Good Magician for the Answer. His reputation was notorious. Once the Gorgon had come to ask the Magician if he would marry her, and he had made her serve a year before Answering. Once Smash Ogre had come, but had forgotten his Question; the Magician made him serve as a guardian to another querent, Tandy Nymph, anyway. In due course the two of them fell in love and got married, and it seemed that was sufficient Answer for each. They were Esk's parents. The Magician had lucked out again.

Now there were no barriers, no challenges, and the castle was deserted. Everybody agreed that the Good Magician had to be found, but nobody knew how to do that. Any number of adventurers had set out to locate him, and some of them had gotten lost themselves. It was a bad situation.

Wouldn't it be great if a mere nine-year-old boy solved the riddle of the age? What fun, to make all the adults look stupid!

Dolph concentrated on the Tapestry. He could tune it in

to any time and any place just by thinking what he wanted.
Most folk couldn't affect the pictures one way or the other,
but he and Ivy were Magicians (well, she was actually a
Sorceress, which was vaguely inferior) and it obeyed them
with alacrity. He tuned it in to the day before Esk's arrival.
If he could spot the Good Magician actually leaving—

After some joggling around, he found the Good Magician's castle on the last day of the Magician's presence.
There was Humfrey in his study, looking about a century
old (which he was) poring over his tome. Once he had
overdosed on Fountain of Youth elixir and become a young
child; Dolph had laughed at that, seeing it in the Tapestry.
But then he had found out how to revert to his regular age,
and that wasn't much fun to watch. There was the Gorgon
downstairs making gorgon-zola cheese by staring at milk
through her veil. There was their son Hugo, about fifteen
or sixteen years old, supervising the placement of a cage
of dragons on the bridge over the moat: one of the challenges for the approaching querents. Everything seemed
quite in order.

Dolph moved it forward, orienting on the precise time
of departure. Was he the first to use the Tapestry this way?
Surely his father had thought to do this! Yet maybe not,
because the mystery had never been unriddled. Adults were
sort of stupid, as a class. That was why they needed Answers. Maybe that was why they so rigorously guarded the
secret of summoning the stork: otherwise the children
would do that better, too.

Abruptly the image disappeared. Had something gone
wrong with the Tapestry? Ivy would murder him if that
were the case! Hastily Dolph backed it up—and the image
returned. It wasn't the Tapestry, it was something in it that
blocked out the pictures.

He played it forward slowly, checking simultaneously on
Humfrey, the Gorgon, and Hugo. It was possible to do that,
because the Tapestry had many pictures going at once; it
would not tune in on different times or places simultaneously, but it would show several scenes relating to a single

place and time. This was the group of the castle, its various rooms open like those of a doll house. Humfrey was still poring over his tome—he never seemed to leave it!—while the Gorgon was making up a petrified cheese salad in the kitchen, and Hugo was conjuring assorted fruits in his bedroom. That was his talent, but he wasn't very good at it; the fruits tended to be misshapen and oddly colored. Meanwhile, an elf was setting up some kind of device in a workroom, evidently on Humfrey's orders. There were usually assorted creatures around the premises, working off their years of service for their Answers, so that Humfrey had never lacked for assistants.

But something went wrong with the elf's project. Smoke started pouring from it. The elf retreated, coughing. The smoke expanded, filling the chamber. Now the Gorgon perked up, sniffing; she cried out to Humfrey (the Tapestry conveyed no sound, but Dolph could see her chest inflate, her mouth open, and he saw the reactions of the others as they heard), who roused himself reluctantly from his tome and trundled downstairs. Hugo also came down, carrying a blue-speckled bunch of bananas he had just conjured. They converged on the smoke.

But the smoke did not wait for them. It doubled its effort and quickly filled several chambers. The elf gesticulated, explaining, but the smoke was hot on his trail. More than that: it was circling around them, forming an enclosure so that they could not escape it. Dolph realized that it was no ordinary vapor; it was holy smoke! There was no telling what a big cloud of that would do.

Magician Humfrey looked annoyed. He gestured, and the four of them hurried to one more chamber. The smoke roiled up avidly, pursuing them. The stuff was out of control! As they squeezed through the door, so did it, closing in. In a moment the chamber was filled, and the picture of that region blotted out.

This time Dolph played it on through. In a few minutes the smoke thinned and dissipated. But Humfrey, Gorgon, and Hugo were gone. Only the elf remained, plainly distressed. He had evidently lost track of the others in the smoke and did not know where they were.

When they did not reappear, the elf proceeded to shut down the castle, perhaps operating on standard emergency instructions. He opened the cage and released the dragons at the moat, who took off down the enchanted path with all the speed they could muster. That was a blunder; Dolph knew that dragons weren't supposed to be on that path. When things were wrapped up, the elf departed himself; apparently his own tour of duty was done now.

That was it, until the three querents arrived the next day. The Magician and his family had simply gone up in smoke! Holy smoke!

Dolph played it back to the smoke, trying to find some angle that would penetrate the obscurity at the key moment. Now he understood why the adults had not solved the mystery through the Tapestry; the smoke had stopped them. But if his sharp eyes managed to see what theirs could not—

Dolph changed to griffin form. As a griffin he had excellent vision. Now—

"What are you doing in my room!?" Ivy demanded, bursting in upon him. "You brat of a brother—you aren't supposed to be in here!!" Half her anger was real, half pretense; he could tell by the doubled punctuation.

Dolph reverted to human form. What a stew of a picklement he was in now! He had gotten so absorbed that he never heard her returning. "I was just watching the Tapestry! If you'd let it hang in my room for a while—"

"Never!!" she exclaimed. She was fourteen, and at the very total height of her bossiness; Dolph knew that nothing, repeat NOTHING, was worse than a big sister that age. Her talent was Enhancing, and it certainly enhanced her nature. It was futile even to attempt to reason with a creature like that.

Therefore he didn't try. He changed into a giant poisonous spider and stood over her, mandibles dripping.

Ivy screamed and retreated. "What utter ick!!" she cried

in simulated horror. "He's finally reverted to his true form!! I always knew he was creepy!!"

Somehow he was still getting the worst of this! She always managed to do it to him. He reverted to boy form. "You think you're so smart! I'm going to do something to make you look like harpy guano!" He tried, but he just couldn't manage doubled exclamation points, unfortunately.

"Yeah? What, you little twerp!?"

"I'm going to go find the Good Magician and rescue him!"

She did not retort. She was too sneaky for that. She simply burst out laughing. She fell on her bed, supposedly overcome by the mirth—and abruptly sobered. "There's werewolf hair on my bed!!" she exclaimed, outraged. Her moods could shift from horror to sardonic mirth to outrage with incredible velocity.

Dolph realized that there was valor in judicious retreat. He changed into a mouse and scurried out, leaving the screams of sisterly ire behind.

But the notion of searching out the Good Magician would not leave him. He had said it in the spirit of a dare, to daunt his imperious sister, but now he could not retreat from it without getting horribly razzed. Besides that, he was fed up with being the younger sibling, and wanted to get out to make his own mark. Why *not* seek Good Magician Humfrey? He was as well equipped to search as anyone; he was young, but he was a full Magician. If anything threatened him, he could change into something to stop it in its tracks.

So he decided: he would do it. He would go to the Good Magician's castle and see whether there was not some hint in that chamber that would show him where the Magician had gone. Then he could follow.

There was, however, one small problem: his parents. They thought he was too young. Their answer to anything ambitious was always that. While this was merely another proof of the opacity of adults, it did need to be handled. After all, his father was King of Xanth, so could not be completely ignored.

"Perhaps in a few years," King Dor suggested diplomatically. He was always the more liberal of the two, but that counted for little in the face of Queen Irene's certainty.

"But the Good Magician needs to be found *now*!" Dolph exclaimed. "Everyone knows that!"

"I don't," his chair said.

"Shut up, wood-brain!" Dolph hissed.

"Don't call *me* names, smart-bottom!" the chair retorted, louder. "I'll run a splinter into you."

Dolph decided not to argue further. His father's talent was conversation with the inanimate, and the inanimate wasn't very smart. In King Dor's presence anything was apt to talk, even when not asked.

King Dor exchanged a glance with Queen Irene. Dolph knew that meant trouble. They were looking for some way to keep him home without hurting his feelings. Parents were experts at stifling adventure without seeming unreasonable.

"Perhaps if you had a suitable adult companion," Irene said. She was actually just as bossy as Ivy, but she masked it expertly. Her suggestions, however mildly phrased, had the force of law.

Ouch! That was worse than a splinter! An adult companion would ruin everything. Especially the kind his mother would favor: a centaur. Centaurs were entirely too disciplined and reasonable, and they always wanted to educate children. Dolph had had more than enough tutoring for a lifetime.

Still, his mother had spoken. She knew he didn't want a companion, certainly not an adult. She figured that would turn him off the Quest. But perhaps he could get around her by getting a companion who wouldn't be too obnoxious. It could be a real art—getting around parents—but it was possible if one truly put his mind to it.

"All right," he said. "But I get to choose him."

King Dor kept a straight face, which meant he was trying not to smile. That was a good sign. They both knew that Queen Irene would want a female centaur; if Dolph got this past her, he would win half the battle at the outset.

"Very well," she said after a significant pause. "But we must approve him."

Um. That could be a devastating qualification. She would not approve anyone he really liked, only someone *she* liked. How could he get around that?

Dolph had a quick, juvenile mind. In only three seconds he had figured out a way. "Done," he said. "I'll make my choice tomorrow."

"Certainly," Queen Irene agreed with one of her smooth masked smiles. She thought she had him.

"This'll be fun, twerp," the chair remarked insolently.

King Dor said nothing. He knew better than to get in the way of a contest of wills like this. That was why he was King.

Back in his room, Dolph pondered names. His strategy was simple: he would make a series of suggestions so awful that his mother would reject them with queenly outrage. She was good at that. Then he would slip in the one he wanted, and it would seem so sensible by comparison that she would agree before she really thought about it. She might regret it later, but she would be committed. A Queen never went back on her word; it looked bad, and she was very conscious of her appearance.

The one he had in mind was Grundy Golem. Grundy was an obnoxious, loudmouthed little creature, fashioned from wood and string and rag and later made real by the Demon X(A/N)th. He had an insult for every occasion. Therefore he could be a lot of fun. He also spoke every language that existed, both animal and plant, and that could be handy on a trip into the wilds of Xanth. He was married to Rapunzel, who was a sickeningly nice little woman at all times except when she got a snarl in her hair. That was because her hair was endlessly long. Then she could speak almost as interestingly as Grundy as she fought with the tangle. Grundy was devoted to her, but he liked adventure too, so would probably agree to travel with Dolph.

Now all he needed was a suitably awful list of names. Who would really turn off his mother? Well, there was Brontes the Cyclops, the huge one-eyed monster who lived in a cave and ate people. There was the Gerrymander, who was continually dividing and conquering, changing his shape into the most grotesque configurations. And Pook, the ghost horse. But he needed more names, in case his mother was too canny to be fooled by only three.

Dolph jumped on his bed, bounced a couple of times, then swung his legs over the side. A cold hand shot out from the shadow under the bed and grabbed his ankle.

"Hey!" he cried. "You aren't Handy!" Handy was his regular bed monster.

"How can you tell?" a voice inquired from under the bed.

"His hand is big and hairy. Yours is skinny."

The hand let go. There was a scramble and clatter under the bed. "I resent that! My hands have no skin. They are skeletal." Then the thing under the bed crawled out. It was a walking skeleton.

"What are you doing under there, Marrow?" Dolph asked. "Where's Handicraft?" He now used his bed monster's full name, because he was alarmed; he inherited that from his mother.

"He went to visit Snortimer. I agreed to fill in while he was gone. We thought you wouldn't notice."

"Not notice!" Dolph exclaimed. "Your hand isn't anything like his! And you only have two of them!"

"True," Marrow agreed, disgruntled. "I suppose it was a foolish attempt. But he did so want to see Snortimer again, and I had nothing to do, so—" He shrugged, his bones rattling apologetically.

"Why should he care about Snortimer?" That was Ivy's monster under the bed, who had departed for the realm of the fauns and nymphs, taking Ivy's bed with him. Ivy never had gotten over her snit about that, even though a bed-bug had moved in that was twice as big and soft as the bed she had lost. She had declared herself to be grown up, so that she no longer believed in bed monsters. It was Dolph's private opinion that Snortimer had gotten out just in time. It was doom for monsters when children stopped believing in them. Dolph intended never to do that to Handy.

"It wasn't Snortimer so much as his situation," Marrow said. "The news circulated that he had more nymphly ankles to grab than he could possibly keep up with, and was liable to perish from sheer delight. Handy thought he should investigate the situation, in case Snort needed help."

"What's wrong with the ankles around here?" Dolph demanded.

"Oh, nothing, nothing, I'm sure," Marrow said quickly. "But it just would not do to have poor Snortimer expire from overwork."

"Any monster who would rather grab a nymphly ankle than mine is a jerk!" Dolph declared righteously. "What could he possibly see in them?"

"I admit to being baffled," Marrow said. "Full-fleshed ankles and legs—no appeal at all." Then, diplomatically, he added: "Present company excepted, of course."

Dolph decided that Marrow was all right. The skeleton had arrived after Esk Ogre and Chex Centaur restored the Kiss-Mee River to its curvaceous state, making it affectionate again. Marrow had been rescued from the Lost Path in the gourd, and now served as a general helper around the castle. He was especially good in the dungeon, because he didn't mind cobwebs or rats. In fact, he normally rested his bones there, lending excellent atmosphere. Visitors not in the know could be quite startled. He even had a convenient hollow finger bone, with which he could whistle for his friend Chex when he needed a lift.

"Maybe I'll add you to the list," Dolph said.

"List?"

Dolph explained about his campaign to trick his mother into agreeing to let Grundy Golem be his companion for the Quest. "You're adult, aren't you? You should qualify. You'd give her a real fit!"

"Excellent notion," Marrow agreed. "Perhaps I can suggest some additional names. What about Cumulo Fracto Nimbus?"

"Terrific!" Dolph exclaimed. "That will really dampen her!" Fracto was the King of Clouds, and was a foul-weather friend. One could never tell when he was going to throw a storm and tear things up with lightning bolts. The very notion of Fracto hovering over her carpets would send Queen Irene into a femalish frenzy.

"Then there's Hardy Harpy, and Xap Hippogryph," Marrow said. "Not to mention Stanley Steamer."

"Great!" Dolph agreed enthusiastically. "Those will drive her crazy! She won't know what she's doing!"

So it was decided. Marrow crawled back under the bed, which was as comfortable a place for his bones as any, and Dolph tuned his magic mirror in on the Tapestry in Ivy's room. Unfortunately she was letting it run random; there was nothing interesting on. That was the problem with big sisters; they had no taste in viewing.

Next day he started his program. "Marrow Bones," he said. "I want him for my companion."

Irene nodded. "Yes, I think that is an excellent choice."

"Well, then, how about Cumulo Fracto Nim—what?"

"Marrow is adult, mature, and experienced," Irene said. "He has a good skull on his shoulders. I understand he was a great help to Chex Centaur. There is also no problem about feeding him. I commend you for your perspicacity in selecting him."

Dolph didn't know what "perspicacity" meant, but he knew he didn't like it. How could she agree to the first foolish name he had named? It wasn't fair! Now he was stuck with the walking skeleton! "Uh, yeah," he said. Maybe Marrow wouldn't want to go.

But by the time he got back to his room, he decided that maybe it was better to stick with what he had. Marrow *was* a decent sort; for one thing, not only did he believe in the monster under the bed, he helped him. That made him childlike in a way that counted. He would do anything for anyone, and he could keep a secret.

So it was arranged: Dolph would go on his Quest to solve the mystery of the Good Magician's disappearance, and Marrow Bones would be his companion. The Adventure would Begin.

2
MESSAGE

They set off next morning, walking east along the enchanted path. It was a two day trek at normal human pace, so Irene had made Dolph wear a knapsack filled with sandwiches, spare socks, a small magic mirror, and other such motherly inconveniences. "Be sure to wash your face every morning," she had admonished him. "And don't forget behind the ears." Dolph had almost died of disgust right there.

Marrow carried nothing, for he had need of neither food nor clothing. He was a magical creature, for whom the rules were different. As Dolph's legs began to tire from the long walk, he envied the skeleton increasingly.

"What makes you go?" he inquired.

"Magic. And you?"

So much for that conversation! Evidently skeletons were not strong on imagination. That wasn't surprising, considering their empty skulls.

"I'm hungry," Dolph said.

"That's why your mother packed sandwiches."

That reminder did not thrill him either. "I could change into a dragon and catch myself something to eat."

"I have never understood why living folk like torn flesh," Marrow remarked.

Suddenly Dolph wasn't hungry. He continued walking in his human form.

"If I may inquire . . ." the skeleton said.

"Who's stopping you?"

"Why are we walking?"

How stupid could a creature get? "How else can we get to the Good Magician's castle?"

"I thought you might change into a bird and fly there."

"Mother said I have to have adult company," Dolph said witheringly. "And you can't fly."

"Can you change into a big bird?"

"Sure. Any size. Even a roc. So what?"

"I thought you might become such a bird, and carry me directly to the castle."

Now there was an idea! Dolph stopped, removed his pack, then hesitated. "I have to get out of my clothes because they don't change."

"I shall be happy to hold your pack and your clothes," Marrow said.

"But Mother doesn't like me to run around naked."

"That's odd. I don't see your mother here."

"Of course she isn't here, numbskull! She's back at Castle Roogna!" Then Dolph made a connection. "You mean— she can't say no?"

"That had occurred to me."

Maybe the skeleton wasn't so stupid after all. Dolph scrambled out of his clothes, bundled them up, and handed them to Marrow with the knapsack. Then he changed to a roc.

Now he was monstrously hugely big! He clucked with satisfaction. Rocs couldn't talk in human fashion, but they hardly needed to. Nobody backtalked a roc!

"But perhaps—" Marrow began.

Was he chickening out now? Well, it was too late.

Dolph picked up the skeleton with one claw, spread his wings—and whacked his feathers into the trees on either side. Ouch!

"—we should look for a suitable clearing first," Marrow concluded.

Good point. Dolph reverted to human form, recovered his clothes, dressed, and resumed motion down the path. Why did things always have to get complicated?

In due course they came to a glade that seemed big enough. Dolph changed again, spread his wings cautiously, and verified that there was room.

"Still—" Marrow said.

Dolph picked up the skeleton again, pumped his wings— and sailed into the trees at the edge of the glade. He suffered a horrendous crash, and the trees seemed hardly more pleased than he. A small shower of leaves came down.

"—we should look for a longer runway," Marrow concluded.

Dolph reverted to boy form and picked himself up. His left little finger was hurting. Then he saw a broken feather on the ground, and realized that he had lost it in the crash. Part of his fingernail was missing. The injuries suffered in one form carried over into the other. He stuck his finger in his mouth, displeased.

They marched on, and before long came to a broad expanse of fields. Dolph changed again, spread his wings, sighted ahead to make sure he had sufficient runway, and picked up the skeleton.

"Yet—" Marrow said.

This time Dolph paused.

"—perhaps we should check for the wind," Marrow concluded.

The wind? Dolph lifted his beak. He felt a nice stiff breeze blowing in exactly the direction he wanted to fly. No problem there! He began to flap his wings.

"Because—" Marrow said.

Dolph pumped harder, and hopped into the air. Immediately he was moving, borne by the breeze. But though he flapped hard, somehow he could not rise very far. In a moment a low hill came up and scraped his legs, throwing him out of control. He skidded to a stop, losing another feather.

"—a tailwind can make it difficult to gain elevation," the skeleton concluded.

Dolph resumed boy form. There was a gash on his right thigh that smarted something awful. "Have you any other remarks to make?" he asked acidly.

"Me? Of course not," Marrow said.

"Well, then, how can I get into the air when everything always goes wrong?"

"Perhaps if you take off into a headwind, it will be more effective."

"But the wind will push me back!"

"I confess that it seems nonsensical, but I have seen birds do it that way."

"Well, okay, but if I crash again, it's your fault!"

"Naturally," Marrow agreed without rancor. His blood never got riled, because he had none.

They walked downwind until they had plenty of runway. Then Dolph changed yet again, oriented, spread his wings, picked up the skeleton, and paused.

Sure enough, Marrow had a thought. "Yet—"

This time Dolph waited for the conclusion.

"—perhaps you should eat first."

Eat? He was hungry, but that could wait. He was eager to get on to the Good Magician's castle and get on with the adventure!

He pumped his wings and jumped into the air. The headwind caught him immediately, giving him excellent lift. There was no question about his ability to fly high now! He was on his way!

Then he furled his wings somewhat and glided back to ground. He made a pretty good landing, then changed back to boy form. "Why?"

"Because I understand that flying requires a lot of energy, and energy for living creatures comes from the food they ingest," Marrow explained.

Dolph thought about what would happen if he ran out of energy over some deep ocean or where a dragon was lurking nearby. "Okay, I'll eat. Give me my knapsack."

"I wonder—"

Dolph impatiently grabbed the knapsack. He fished out a sandwich, then paused.

"—whether energy is relative or absolute," Marrow finished.

"What are you talking about?"

"It occurs to me that you have sandwiches for only a few meals. They might go farther if—"

Dolph opened his mouth to take a huge bite, but paused again, bite untaken. He waited.

"—you consumed them in smaller size."

Dolph thought about that. "You know, when I'm in a big form, like a sphinx, I can eat an awful lot, but I get hungry again the same time even if I turn small. When I'm small, and I eat, then I turn big and I still get hungry in the same time. I never thought about it before."

"So if you ate a crumb in ant form, it might last you as long as a whole sandwich in boy form, or a whole carcass in roc form," Marrow said.

"I guess so." Dolph looked at the sandwich. "But if I became an ant, someone might step on me."

Marrow picked a bit of bread from the sandwich and held it in his bone-fingered hand. "I will not step on you."

And of course he would not; Marrow never hurt anyone. Dolph realized that this was one excellent use of a companion: to protect him when for some reason he was in a vulnerable state. Of course, he would not go so far as to concede that his mother might have had a point about the need for a companion, but certainly there could be an advantage.

He reached out and took hold of the end of Marrow's bone finger with two of his own flesh fingers. Then he became an ant. Suddenly he was clinging by the hairs of one leg to that huge white bone. But in the small form he weighed so little that it was easy to cling, and indeed, if he fell he would not be hurt. He climbed up to the top of the finger, then walked along it to the network of bones that was the hand. There perched the crumb. He bit into it, and it was delicious, the ideal ant food.

Soon he was full, and the crumb was only partly gone. He walked to the end of a finger and jumped off. As he fell he changed back to boy form. He still felt full. "Let's go!" he said. "I'm full of energy now!"

Marrow gathered up the pack and clothing again, and Dolph turned into the roc again, and picked up the skeleton. He spread his wings.

"I suspect—" Marrow began.

Dolph waited. He had learned to pay attention. His mother would have approved of that!

"—that we are ready to proceed," Marrow concluded.

Good enough! Dolph jumped and pumped, and they were airborne. The wind helped him rise, though he did not make much forward progress. Soon he was above the trees. Then he circled, getting his bearings. Rocs had good eyesight. He forged into the wind.

"But it is possible—"

What now? Dor cocked his head and listened.

"—that the wind might shift, above."

Good notion. He resumed his climbing. Sure enough, at a higher elevation the wind changed, and a cold current bore directly toward the Good Magician's castle. Now that he was airborne and satisfied to fly level, he did not need its lift; he could fly with it, and make better speed with less effort.

He flew, pleased with himself. His belly was full, and he had plenty of energy, thanks to the skeleton's timely advice. It wasn't so bad having an adult along! Dolph still stopped short of the notion that his mother might actually have been right, however; there were limits.

As evening approached, and the sun ducked down to hide behind the horizon so that it wouldn't be caught by the dark, Dolph glided down toward the Good Magician's castle. He couldn't land right in it because he was too big, but there was a nice field a short distance from it. He coasted to an almost perfect landing. They had saved a whole day!

But now it was dusk, and he was tired. Marrow's caution had been good; he was hungry again, and would have been horribly famished if he had not eaten before flying.

"I think—" Marrow began.

"We had better spend the night here," Dolph concluded.

The skeleton nodded. "You may sleep; I have no need of it. Would you like shelter?"

Dolph looked around. The trees that had seemed so pretty by sunlight seemed sinister in shadow. Odd, unfriendly sounds were starting up. He had not thought about this. He did not relish the notion of sleeping out on bare ground, not even in animal form. He was accustomed to his warm, safe bed in Castle Roogna, with Handicraft, the monster under the bed, lurking guard. He was, after all, only nine years old. "Uh, yes," he agreed pensively.

"Kick me in the tailbone."

"What?"

"Give me a good kick. I require that initial impetus."

"Well, okay, if you say so." Dolph stood back, swung his foot, and delivered a wonderful kick to the skeleton's posterior.

Marrow flew apart. His bones exploded, flying in every direction. Then they came down—and landed in a pattern. When the last one fell into place, there was the shape of a small house, fashioned of bones. The skull was the front door, upside down.

"Pull me open," the skull said. "Crawl in, and pull me closed. No one will bother you in here."

Dolph could believe that. He paused for a call of nature (nature called in an almost inaudible but most persistent voice, until there was nothing to do but answer her), then hefted his knapsack and approached the house of bones. He got on his hands and knees and hooked one finger into the nose socket. The door swung open, supported by a neck-bone that was now mounted on the top. Dolph wriggled in feet first, finding the interior snug but just big enough. He hauled his pack in after him and set it up as a headrest. He swung the skull down, and it clicked into place. The square eye sockets looked out, watching for any danger in the night.

It was dark in here, and comfortably warm. He felt quite secure. Marrow was really quite a fellow!

He had wanted to travel with Grundy Golem. It had always seemed to him that Grundy should be considered a Magician, because he could speak to any living thing. After all, King Dor couldn't do that; he could only speak to dead things. But Ivy had explained (not that he had asked her) that *anybody* could talk another language if he just took the trouble to learn it, while *nobody* could speak the language of the inanimate except King Dor, so Dor was a Magician and Grundy was not, dummy! That last word had really griped him, but he had had no effective retort.

But though Grundy could be a fascinating character, he wasn't much for building houses. Not only had Marrow given some pretty fair advice, he was now protecting Dolph in a pretty neat way. Maybe Dolph really was better off with the skeleton, just as his mother had judged—no, there were bound to be catches!

In the morning Dolph got up, kicked the house, and it reformed into the walking skeleton. Marrow explained that in the early days he had had to be reassembled by hand, bone by bone, but that with practice he had mastered instant reassembly from any configuration. That was good, because Dolph would have had little patience with connecting a pile of bones individually. Then he changed into the ant and ate part of another crumb. Then he reverted to boy form and they walked to the castle.

They intersected the enchanted path and followed it right to the main entrance. Even in its desertion, the castle was imposing. It had a good-sized moat half-filled with slimy water, and a rickety drawbridge covered with cobwebs; and the stones of its walls were green with mildew. It looked perfectly haunted: a real delight.

"Perhaps—" Marrow began.

Dolph paused in mid-stride toward the drawbridge. He still had the sore places from damaged feathers to remind him about heeding adult advice.

"—I should enter first, to be sure there is nothing dangerous lurking inside," the skeleton concluded.

"But wouldn't it be dangerous for you too?"

"What could be dangerous to me?"

Dolph was at a loss to answer that, so he didn't try. Anything that liked to bite legs would have trouble with Marrow's bones, and anything that liked to scare the living would have trouble scaring the dead.

Marrow crossed the moat first, stomping his bone feet on the old wooden planking of the drawbridge. Nothing gave way beneath him. He reached the huge open gate, and looked around. Nothing stirred. He tapped the stone of the archway leading into the castle proper. The hollow sound echoed and expired. The castle seemed empty.

Dolph walked across, a little embarrassed at his caution. How did it look for an adventurer to enter a deserted castle so hesitantly? He should have charged in, sword waving! If he had a sword. If anybody had been watching. If it mattered.

Did it matter? Had his mother let him go because she knew that the Quest was harmless, that there was nothing to find? That all he could do was come here, look through the empty castle, and go home again? With Marrow along to be sure he didn't get lost? Some adventure that would be! Ivy was probably snickering in her insufferable big-sister way.

Dolph resolved not to return home until he found the Good Magician. That would show them!

Now all he had to do was figure out *how* to show them.

They walked through the entire castle, finding nothing but deserted chambers festooned with cobwebs. The Magician's personal effects had been cleaned up and put away by folk from Castle Roogna shortly after the disaster had been discovered. Anything that remained to be discovered would have been found at that time. There was nothing left for Dolph. As Queen Irene had surely known.

"There does not appear to be much here," Marrow observed.

What else was new? Dolph stared at the floor in deep disgust. He knew that he had no choice but to go home, unless he could find something that no one else had been able to find.

"However—" Marrow began.

What possible qualification could the skeleton have now? Dolph had no confidence, but he waited, just in case.

"—the perceptions of some other type of creature might detect something we cannot," Marrow concluded.

Dolph shrugged. He became a potato and peered around with his sharp eyes. All he saw was dust and desertion. He became a dogwood tree, and sniffed with his sensitive canine noses. All he smelled was dust and desertion. He became a shock of corn, and listened with his finely-tassled ears. All he heard was nothing.

"Yet—"

Dolph returned to boy form, waiting.

"—there may be other modes of assessment, other means of measurement, that some other type of creature might use to discover the undiscovered," Marrow concluded.

Had the skeleton lost what little wits he had in his hollow cranium? That was gibberish! But Dolph refrained from making the proper retort, still hoping against hope that there might be a good idea hiding somewhere. "What do you mean?"

"I am accustomed to the various devious chambers of the realm of the gourd," Marrow explained. "It seems to me that if there is anything remaining to be found here, it must be in such a chamber of the castle, undiscoverable by normal means."

"A secret chamber?" This intrigued Dolph. "Where?"

Marrow shrugged. "Wherever no one has looked before, assuming it exists."

"But how could we find it? We looked everywhere there is to look."

"I'm not sure. I thought perhaps one of your alternate forms could measure and discover whether—"

Dolph became a huge measuring worm. He traversed the castle, measuring every step. And discovered that the measurements did not add up.

They discussed it, and concluded that there was indeed a discrepancy in the middle of the castle. The rooms and stairs and walls formed a complex mosaic, so that it was almost impossible to tell what added up to what, but the measuring worm found the difference. There was room for a small hidden chamber. It might be merely a solid foundation of stones, but it could be a secret room.

Dolph was elated. They had made a discovery that no one else had made! Now all they had to do was get into the chamber and see what was there.

The stones of the castle were big and heavy: far too much so for a nine-year-old boy or a walking skeleton to move. But Dolph could handle that. "I'll become an ogre and bash my way in!" he said zestfully.

"I am not certain—"

"Yeah, you're right," Dolph agreed reluctantly. "Mustn't damage someone else's castle. But maybe if you could become a pry bar, the ogre could use it to move just a few blocks out of the way, and put them back after."

"Kick me," Marrow said.

Dolph gave him a good swift kick in the rear. Marrow flew apart, and fell together as a long, solid bar of bones with the skull forming a knob on the end.

Dolph became an ogre. Now he was so big he hardly fit in the room, and he had monstrously hairy muscles. He gazed dully around, and spied a small spider spinning a web; the spider took one look at his ugly puss and fainted. Ogres were the strongest, ugliest, and stupidest creatures of Xanth, which was why they were so much fun.

He reached for the bone pole—and another ogre tromped into the room. Dolph paused, surprised. "Who you?" he demanded in typical ogre style.

"Who you?" the other responded in the same tone.

"Me ask he mask," Dolph said. Ogres typically spoke in inane rhymes, which was pretty limiting for anybody but an ogre. What he meant was that he had asked first: that the other should unmask himself.

"Me ask he mask," the other repeated.

"Me bash he ash!" Dolph declared, angry at this mimicry. He raised a huge hamfist.

"Me bash he ash," the other said, raising a similar hamfist.

"Perhaps—" the skull-knob began

Suddenly there was a second bone pole. "Perhaps—" its skull-knob said.

Dolph reverted to boy form. "What's going on?"

Another boy appeared before him. "What's going on?"

"—we have another challenge," Marrow's skull said.

"—we have another challenge," the second skull said, reappearing as the boy vanished.

"This thing is copying whatever we do!" Dolph exclaimed.

The boy reappeared. "This thing is copying whatever we do!"

"A mimic-dog, I think," Marrow's skull said, immediately echoed by the other.

"What's that?" Dolph and the creature asked.

"A creature who mimics whatever it sees and hears," Marrow and the creature replied. "It has no intelligence of its own; it merely copies."

"Maybe it will help us get in to the chamber, then," Dolph and the creature said. He reached for the bone pole.

So did the mimic-dog. Their two hands closed on it together.

Dolph changed back to the ogre. So did the other. This was getting nowhere.

Now he remembered what Marrow had said about the

challenge. In olden times, when the Good Magician was home, there had always been three challenges to those who sought to ask him a Question. Could there be some challenges left over? In that case, the first would have been to find the hidden chamber, and this could be the second. The mimic-dog could have been summoned by their finding of the chamber; the Good Magician could have set this up long ago for some other purpose. Now Dolph had blundered into it. How was he to get out of it?

Well, if this thing was a dog, maybe it liked doggy things. Dogs were mainly Mundanian creatures, but some had strayed into Xanth. They liked dog biscuits.

"Talk to it, Marrow," he said, reverting to his normal shape.

"Talk to it, Marrow," the creature echoed.

"As you wish," the skeleton agreed.

While the two bone poles chatted idly in duplicate, Dolph quietly fetched his knapsack. It seemed that the mimic-dog only mimicked the one who was doing the important talking or acting. Dolph took out his partly-eaten sandwich and squeezed it into the shape of a biscuit.

He held the biscuit aloft. "I have a delicious big dog biscuit," he announced. "Does anyone want to eat it?"

The other boy appeared. "Does anyone want to eat it?" he repeated, his mouth watering.

"But nobody can eat it who is doing something else," Dolph said. He set the biscuit down and walked toward the wall. "I am doing something else."

"I am doing something else," the other said. But his gaze lingered on the biscuit. He was tempted, all right!

Dolph picked up the bone pole. "I have a long, hard job ahead," he said. "I don't know when I'm ever going to have time to eat a delicious sandwich-flavored big dog biscuit!"

"...delicious sandwich-flavored big dog biscuit!" the other repeated, moving toward it as if drawn by a magic magnet.

Dolph started prying at the largest stone. The mimic-dog

did not interfere. When Dolph looked, the dog was gone. So was the biscuit.

That was the way of dogs, he thought with satisfaction. When they got hold of something good to eat, they carried it away to a private place so they could consume it without interference. The mimic-dog had been unable to resist its basic nature.

"You handled that very well," Marrow's skull remarked.

"Well, when you said it was a challenge, I knew I had to get around it," Dolph said. "But does that mean there is one more challenge coming?"

"It may," Marrow agreed. "We do not seem to be making much headway here."

Indeed they were not. The stone seemed absolutely immovable. Dolph resumed ogre form and strained at it, but it would not budge.

"This appears to be one solid mass," Marrow said. "What resemble individual stones are in fact merely projections of a single stone."

"How do you know?" Dolph asked, reverting to boy form.

"I have a certain feel for the inanimate, particularly in this form. I very much fear that we can not force an entry without destroying the castle."

"The third challenge!" Dolph exclaimed. "How to get into a perfectly sealed chamber!"

"So it would seem."

Dolph kicked the bone pole and it fell back into the skeleton's normal shape. They pondered the problem. "Maybe we could make it perm—perm—"

"Permeable?"

"Soft. By using magic or something. Then we could cut a hole in it and get in."

"Perhaps so. If there is something inside, there must be a way to enter."

"Right. We just have to figure out what it is."

Neither one of them had much idea. Finally Dolph tried random spells. "Stone, turn soft!" he ordered it.

The stone changed color. It now looked like boiled mush. Dolph stared. "It worked!" he exclaimed, amazed.

Marrow poked a bone finger at it. "It remains very hard," he said.

Dolph touched it. The rock was absolutely solid. It looked so soft it should sag at any moment and crawl across the floor, but that was not the case.

"The perversity of the inanimate," Marrow said. "I say it as should not."

Dolph knew what perversity meant, because his big sister Ivy liked to use it on him. It meant doing the opposite of what he was supposed to. "Well, maybe the other way, then." He faced the rock. "Stone, turn hard!"

The rock assumed a complexion like polished steel. It looked so hard he was almost afraid to touch it. Marrow poked it instead.

"It has not changed," the skeleton reported regretfully. "It appears that we can affect only its appearance, not its reality."

Indeed that seemed to be the case. The wall changed color freely, but never its hardness. They still could not get in.

"But this must be the way," Dolph said. "The Good Magician wouldn't set up something like this just to look pretty!"

"So it would seem."

But they remained stumped. The wall would assume any color they asked, either by name or by description, but would not change in any other way. They could not get through it.

Then Dolph had a bright idea. "Maybe we don't have to get in to it!"

"Do you mean there is nothing worthwhile inside?"

"No! Maybe we can see what's in it instead of touching it!"

"What good would that do?"

"Let's find out!" Dolph addressed the wall: "Stone, be no color!"

The wall became transparent. It looked like colorless gel, completely transparent.

Now they could see through to the center. There *was* a small chamber there, and in the chamber was a piece of paper.

"Very interesting," Marrow said. "You have penetrated the secret. But I cannot read what is on the paper."

"Neither can I," Dolph said. "But I do know how to read; that horsey centaur Chem made me learn. Maybe if I can see it from above—"

They went upstairs. They lifted the tiles from the floor of the room above and swept away the dust. There was the transparent stone. They could see the paper flat-on!

Dolph put his eye to the stone and peered down, but the paper was too far away; all he saw was black markings.

"Perhaps—" Marrow began.

"If I became an eagle, with sharp eyes," Dolph finished. "But then I might not be able to understand the writing I see."

"But perhaps you could trace it with your claw, and then—"

"Gotcha!" Dolph became the eagle, and peered down through the stone. Now he could make out the writing on the paper.

He made a mental note of the first of the lines, then moved over and scratched similar lines in the dirt they had moved. He returned for another peek at the paper, then scratched a few more lines in the dirt. After several such exchanges, he had it all.

He returned to boy form and looked at what he had scratched. It said:

SKELETON KEY TO HEAVEN CENT

It was certainly a message! But what did it mean? Neither one of them could make any sense of it.

It was now getting late. They had spent all day on this. But Dolph was pleased because he knew he had made more

progress than his mother had expected, and more than anyone had before. This was a message left by the Good Magician himself, and surely it told where to find him. All
they had to do was figure it out.

"Skeleton key," Dolph said. "Does that have something
to do with you?"

Marrow's tone indicated that he was smiling. "No, a
skeleton key is a magic key that fits any lock. Obviously
only such a key can fit the lock of the Heaven Cent, whatever that may be."

"So first we need to find the skeleton key. But that could
be anywhere!"

"It occurs to me—"

"Ha! You have an idea! I can tell!"

"—that there could be a pun on the term 'key.' That also
means a small island."

"An island that's a skeleton?"

"I understand that some islands are fashioned magically
by the skeletons of creatures of the sea called corals."

"Like the Brain Coral? I don't think—"

"Other kinds of corals. They aren't smart, they merely
form reefs or islands. Such an island might be termed a—"

"A skeleton key!" Dolph exclaimed, catching on.

"So perhaps we have merely to look on such a key to
find the Heaven Cent."

"Great! Let's go there!"

"Unfortunately—"

Dolph waited. The skeleton's inability to formulate a
complete thought in one effort might be because his head
was hollow. Dolph was discovering that a certain tolerance
made things easier.

"—there are a number of such skeletal keys off the coats
of Xanth," Marrow concluded. "We may have trouble as-
certaining which one is correct."

Dolph considered. "Well, the message reads from west
to east, so if I kept on reading east, that must be where the
Heaven Cent is."

"I am not certain that makes sense."

"It makes Heaven Cents!" Dolph said. "What key is east of here?"

"Well, in very general way, there is the Isle of Illusion—"

"Then we'll go there!" Dolph exclaimed.

"But we don't even know that the message is for us!" Marrow protested. "The Heaven Cent may relate to something entirely different!"

"Non-cents," Dolph said. "The Good Magician Humfrey always knew exactly what he was doing." Though he wondered as he spoke how Humfrey could have been caught unawares by the holy smoke, if that were the case.

"But such an obscure message, so well hidden—"

"He did that so that only the right person could find it or understand it," Dolph said confidently. "I am obviously that person. Tomorrow we'll go to the Isle of Illusion. Oh, my mother will have a fit!"

"She certainly will," Marrow agreed with resignation. It was evident that the skeleton, like Queen Irene, had not anticipated this development. That delighted Dolph; now at last he could make the Quest his own, forging into uncharted territory. Sheer adventure!

3

VILA

In the morning they set out for the Isle of Illusion. Dolph had planned to fly there, but when he became the roc he discovered that his wing muscles were quite sore from the prior day's exertion. He wasn't a real roc, and lacked the stamina of practice; also, his flight was relatively clumsy. If he worked at it he knew he could get better, but it wasn't worth it; it was easier to walk for a while.

They followed the enchanted path north and then east when they came to an intersection. This was the path that Esk and Chex had used; he had seen them in the Magic Tapestry. Esk had seemed like a great guy, with his quarter-ogre ancestry. Then he got involved with that brass girl Bria and turned all mushy. Dolph knew that *he* would never get mushy about any stupid girl; he knew what they were like. Like his arrogant big sister! No boy in his right mind would have anything to do with any girl like that! Just because Irene bossed Dor around unmercifully, Ivy figured she had a duty to boss Dolph around. No, as far as he was concerned, the only good girl was one who was far away.

"You knew Esk," Dolph said after a bit. "Why did he stop adventuring and take up with that creature from the gourd?"

"I was part of his adventure," Marrow said somewhat stiffly. "I see no call to disparage my origin."

"I didn't mean *you*, bonehead! I meant Bria Brassy."

"We are both creatures of the gourd," Marrow said, unmollified. It was not easy to hurt the feelings of someone as hardheaded as a walking skeleton, but evidently Dolph had managed it. He realized that he had been undiplomatic. Marrow was basically a good guy, and there was no reason to get him upset.

Dolph pondered, and finally came to a very awkward conclusion: he would have to apologize. That was one of the stupid things adults did, and Marrow was an adult. Sometimes it was necessary to cater to the foibles of adults, no matter how pointless it seemed.

"Marrow, I'm sorry if I insulted you," Dolph said. "I know you're from the gourd, and you're okay. I meant to say that the brassy girl was the dumb one, and Esk was dumb for taking up with her. She probably bosses him around as bad as Ivy does me."

The hollow eye sockets of the skull turned to glance at him. "You are sensitive to being told what to do?"

"Well sure! Nobody likes having dumb girls boss him around all the time!"

"Then I think I misunderstood the thrust of your remark," Marrow said. "I may have taken offense erroneously, and I apologize to you for that."

"Hey, you can't apologize to me! I was apologizing to you!"

"Sometimes it is possible to exchange apologies. But let me explain something about the gourd, and about women. There are many creatures of the gourd, and they are unlike the creatures of regular Xanth because they are animated by magic, but they do have duties and feelings too. It is not fair to dismiss them merely because they reside in a world that is unlike yours."

"Yeah, I guess so," Dolph said contritely.

"Similarly, women are in certain respects like another species, and men can have difficulty understanding them. But they too have duties and feelings, and should not be lightly dismissed. Bria Brassy is a fine woman, and an excellent match for Esk Ogre, and he is a better man because he recognized that."

"But that mush stuff—ugh! I saw him in the Tapestry, kissing her."

"In time you will understand why adults derive pleasure from such activity."

"Never!" Dolph swore.

Marrow did not reply, but he seemed to be smiling.

"Would *you* kiss a girl?" Dolph asked challengingly.

"I fear a living girl would not appreciate such a gesture on my part."

"Well, a bone girl, then?"

"Oh, yes, if she liked me, though we of the skeletal persuasion have other ways to interact. However, that is academic, as I am the only one of my kind out here in the outer realm."

Dolph realized that Marrow, though he was an interesting fellow, was nevertheless still an adult, with those peculiar adult attitudes. He refused to condemn mushy stuff. It was a good thing there were no female skeletons here!

After a time, Dolph got tired of walking. But he realized that he would be just as tired in animal form too. He had been able to fly before because only his legs had been tired, but now his arms were sore. This was an aspect of adventuring he hadn't thought about, when he watched the Tapestry.

"Perhaps—" Marrow started.

"Yeah, maybe it's time to rest," Dolph agreed.

"—I could carry you. I do not tire, and if you were to assume a small form—"

"Great!" Dolph became a dormouse. Marrow put down his hand, and Dolph scrambled up to his bony shoulder.

Marrow bent to pick up Dolph's pack of belongings. It was much better traveling this way; now he could rest while still making progress toward the Isle of Illusion.

In due course the enchanted path petered out. It seemed that very few folk cared to travel this far. Progress slowed, because although Marrow's bones were tireless, it was slower to forge through the encroaching wilderness than along a cleared path. Now they had to weave around the more dangerous plants, such as tangle trees, and to watch out for dragons' lairs. Dolph wasn't really afraid of such things, because he knew he could transform into something to fight off any obnoxious plant or animal. But it was better to stay out of trouble and save his magic for true emergencies.

They came to a river. Marrow merely started to forge through it, but then he hesitated. "Something is gnawing at my leg bones," he said. Sure enough, there were dogfish under the surface, and more coming. Marrow quickly retreated to the shore. He did not suffer pain, but it would have been inconvenient for him to lose a leg bone, and the slowness of his motion in deep water would give the fish plenty of time to work at it. Dogfish liked to carry away their bones and bury them in deep muck.

Back on shore, Dolph assumed boy form. "I'll become the roc and carry you across," he said. "My flying muscles are stiff, but I can do that much."

"The flying room is limited," Marrow pointed out. "You would have trouble both taking off and landing, because the trees come right up to the edge of the water."

All too true. "I could become a big fish—"

"I fear the pack of dogfish would attack you. No, I think I shall have to facilitate my own crossing. Kick me, and I shall become a bone line that anchors to a branch on the far side. Then you may fly across in small bird form and haul me in from that side."

That seemed sensible to Dolph. He became the ogre, and delivered a tremendous kick to the skeleton's hipbone. Marrow flew apart, and reformed as a string of bones that extended across the river. One bone hand at the end caught and grasped the branch of a tree, while the other caught the projecting root of a tree on the near side.

Dolph, about to change to bird form, remembered his sore wing muscles. It didn't matter what size bird he was; those same muscles would hurt. He looked at the bone line, and had a notion. He could cross on that!

He became the dormouse and scrambled up along the line of bones. He was surefooted in this form, and had no fear of falling. If he did fall, he would simply change to bird form and fly; better a sore muscle than a dunking in the river!

"I suspect—" the skull in the center began as he approached it.

"I'll be across in a moment," Dolph replied. Because he was in mouse form, this emerged as a series of squeaks that the skeleton probably couldn't understand. All human languages were the same in Xanth, but each species had its own language, and few creatures spoke the languages of other species. Marrow, being a human skeleton, spoke human, and most of the human variants, such as elves, goblins, nymphs, and centaurs spoke it too. Ogres also spoke it, but piers tended to be so gruff that they could not be understood, except for those who had direct human ancestry.

"—that you should hurry," Marrow continued.

Dolph was in no trouble, but he couldn't actually run on the bone line; he had to keep careful hold on the bones. "Why?" he squeaked.

"Because a harpy is coming," Marrow concluded.

Oops! Harpies were bad news. Not only were they female, they were ugly, and nasty, and hungry. A harpy would snatch up a dormouse just like that, and gobble it down instantly.

Could he make it across before the harpy arrived? Dolph paused to look, and saw the foul creature coming. She was flapping heavily with her gross wings, a clumsy flier; he could outrace her to the forest, where he could change. He didn't want to have to change in midstream; that could get complicated, and he might wind up yanking Marrow apart.

He scooted for the end of the line. The harpy definitely saw him; she veered to intercept him. Her foul odor preceded her; what an awful stench!

"I'll get you, you fine feculent mouse!" she screeched. Her voice was as unpleasant as her smell.

He made it to the end just as her dirty glistening talons snatched at him. He flung his arms around the trunk of the tree to which Marrow's hand attached, and became the ogre. "Me think she stink!" he growled.

"Oops! Didn't see you, pretty-face!" she screeched. "Where's the mouse?"

"Me mouse, she louse!" Dolph retorted. Evidently she did not realize that he was a form changer.

"You took my mouse, I'll take your bones!" she screeched. Her talons closed on the bone line, and she gave a tremendous yank. Marrow's fingers were wrenched from the branch they had clung to. His hand swung down to touch the water, dangling helplessly. The members of the pack of dogfish forged toward it. "Oh no you don't, fish-face!" the harpy screeched as a dogfish snapped at a bone finger. "These bones are mine to crack open!" She flapped upward, hauling the bone line after her.

Crack open? Marrow was in trouble! He could not reassemble himself; he had to be helped, and the harpy certainly wouldn't do that. It was up to Dolph to save him.

He became a small flying dragon. This gave him room enough to fly well, because he was not nearly as big as the roc, but also gave him fighting strength, because dragons were about as savage as anything. He launched himself at the harpy.

She saw him and did a messy double take. "A dragon!" she screeched. "Where did *that* come from? Help, sisters!"

Immediately there was an answering chorus of shrieks. The other harpies were coming! He had to get the bone line away from this one before they arrived.

He flew at the harpy, but she would not let go of the

line. Harpies were very good at snatching, but no good at letting go. He sent a jet of fire at her, but she ducked it and kept flying. A real dragon probably could have speared her with a single lance of fire, but Dolph was clumsy at it, and his fire wasn't very hot anyway.

He closed his own talons on the middle of the line where the skull was. He pulled back on it, trying to snap the end out of the harpy's grasp. Still she would not let go.

"I fear you will pull me apart," Marrow said. "That would be unfortunate, for if I lost some of my bones—"

Dolph was sure it would be bad. Meanwhile, the other harpies were arriving, each worse than the others. They would soon pull Marrow apart! What could he do?

"Perhaps some smoke," Marrow's skull said.

Smoke! Dolph became a flying smoker dragon. It was a rare species, but he could become anything, rare or common. He inhaled, building up a bellyful of smoke. Then he breathed out a smoke screen that would have done credit to a real smoker. It formed a cloud that enveloped the bone line and the harpy at its end. He heard her coughing; she did not like the smoke. It was probably too clean for her.

"She has let go," Marrow's skull said. "Haul me away!"

Dolph clung to the line and took off into the sky. But this carried him away from the cloud of smoke. The flock of harpies spied him and wheeled in the air to commence the pursuit. They wanted those bones! They screeched curses at him as they flew. Dolph was glad that his dragon form did not properly understand the human language, because his metallic ears were flushing. Those flappers had fowl mouths!

"Sticks and stones will break my bones," Marrow's skull remarked philosophically, "but names will never hurt me." Nevertheless, there seemed to be a slight flush even on the bone.

Dolph flew as fast as he could, the line dangling down and back. Marrow could not change back until kicked, and Dolph couldn't do that until he landed and changed form. He had to get away from the dirty birds!

But that seemed impossible. The harpies were ranged behind, not catching up but not falling back either. They would close the gap the moment Dolph tried to land, and might snatch away the flying bones when he kicked them. That was no good!

Maybe he could lose them in the deep forest. He veered to the east, where a forested mountain rose.

And the harpies fell back. Dolph had to glance back several times to be sure that his dragon's eyes weren't getting confused, but there was no doubt: they were no longer following. They were hovering in the air above an invisible line.

"You'll be soo-ry!" they screeched in unison.

Dolph made a questioning growl. Marrow understood his query. "Evidently something bars them from this region," he said. "But this forest seems harmless, and certainly better than getting my bones cracked by those awful creatures. Find a landing place, and we can resume our trek on foot."

Dolph angled down. He searched, but found no suitable place for a dragon to land.

"You may drop me, then change to a smaller form," Marrow said. "The fall should not damage me."

Dolph located a small clearing, let go the line, then changed to hawk form and dived down after them. They reached the ground together. Then he resumed ogre form, picked up the line, bunched it together, and gave a big kick.

The bones flew up and out, and landed back in Marrow's familiar skeleton form. "That is a relief!" he said. "I can not be harmed by many things, but bone chewing and bone cracking will do it. The harpies would have eaten out my essence."

"That's what I thought," Dolph said. He was more shaken by the experience than he cared to admit. Those harpies were vicious creatures, so full of malevolence. Their example even made him inclined to wash behind his ears, because the harpies had ears almost as dirty as their mouths.

They decided to proceed afoot over the mountain, so that

the watching harpies could not intercept them in the air. At least they were across the river!

Except for one thing: Dolph's knapsack with his clothing and supplies was on the far side. He chose not to speak of this inconvenience, because he knew it was pointless to face the harpies again.

Dolph remained in ogre form, because this was a strange region and he believed this form was safer. Hardly anyone in his right mind ever bothered an ogre, and even those in their wrong minds were apt to regret it. There were stories about foolish goblins attacking ogres and getting hurled so far that some were still lost behind the sun, getting terribly hot from its flames. Sometimes a large tangle tree would tackle one; there were still some twisted stumps with their tentacles tied in massive ogre knots. Dolph couldn't do such things, of course, because he wasn't a real ogre, but who else would know that?

He looked around. For a wilderness area, this was amazingly nice. The ground was even under the trees, and there were no bad bramble bushes. They stopped for a drink at a lovely little brook whose water was sparklingly clear. It was like a park—where no park should be.

Dolph lay down and put his ogre snoot to the water. But just then there was a horrendous scream from upstream. Startled, he jumped up, and Marrow cocked an ear hole.

The forest was silent. Dolph shrugged and lay down again, ready to drink—and again the scream sounded, worse than before, and closer. It sounded vaguely female, and less vaguely menacing. But nothing appeared, and the forest was undisturbed.

Dolph decided that he had better get his drink before the thing reached them and attacked, forcing them to fight or flee. A real ogre wouldn't know how to flee, of course, which was apt to make things awkward: if Dolph had to flee, his masquerade would be exposed. He got down a third time and put his ugly ogre puss to the water.

This time the scream was almost on top of them. A huge bear burst into view, its fur wild. "That's my water!" it screamed. "You can't have it! Get out, get out, get out!"

A talking bear? Dolph scrambled back to his feet. An ogre could smash a bear, but he was not a real ogre and hesitated to try violence. So he tried to reason with it. "Me want drink; what he think?" Ogres had trouble with pronouns, so me, he and she were about the number they could manage.

The bear pointed to the brook. Instantly the water turned color, becoming smoky. "You drink, ogre, you die! Now it is poison!"

How could a bear poison a brook without touching it? But the water certainly looked dangerous now!

Marrow poked a bone finger into the water. The bone changed color. "Yes, it is poison," he said. "This must be a vila in bear form."

Dolph wanted to ask what a vila was, but to do that he had either to figure out a suitable rhyme, or change to boy form. He couldn't do the first at the moment, and hesitated to do the second while facing a dangerous animal. So he just stood there stupidly, which was easy to do in ogre form.

"Yes, I am Vida Vila, and this is my forest!" the bear said. "You are intruders! No ogres or skeletons allowed here! Get out before I do something to you."

Vida? That sounded female. But it still sounded vile— or vila, as the case might be.

"We are merely passing through," Marrow said. "My companion only wants one drink; then we shall cross on out of your territory."

"Get out! Get out! Get out!" the bear screamed.

"Well, if you feel that way," Marrow said. He turned to Dolph. "How do you feel about it?"

Dolph would have been glad to get out. But he didn't want to go back to where the harpies lurked, and he did not want to move straight on to the Isle of Illusion, which was farther in the direction they had been going. Also, he was very thirsty; even the thought of not having a drink made him crave it more. "Me think me drink," he said.

"You drink, you stink!" the bear screamed. "You'll die and I'll use your corpse for fertilizer for my flowers!"

That notion did not appeal either. Dolph looked at Marrow for help.

"I suspect—" the skeleton began.

"Get out! Get out! Get out!" the bear screamed.

"—that we shall have to chop her tree down," Marrow concluded.

The bear screamed, the same way as originally, but more so. Evidently Marrow's threat really bothered it. It strode toward the skeleton, but Marrow merely ran uphill, eluding it.

"The tree should be at the top of the mountain," the skeleton called back to Dolph. "When we find it, I shall assume the configuration of an axe, and you can use me to chop it."

"You win! You win! You win!" the bear screamed. "Spare my tree!"

Marrow paused. "You will unpoison the water and let my friend Prince Dolph drink safely?"

"*Prince* Dolph?" the bear asked, amazed.

"Yes. He is on a Quest, and I am his companion. We never did intend any harm to you; we just want to drink and move on."

The bear disappeared. In its place stood a lovely young woman whose curly reddish-brown hair fell in waves to her feet. Her clothing was fashioned from green leaves magically fastened together. "Why didn't you say so before?" she asked.

"You didn't ask," Marrow said. He tended to be literal. "Now the water, if you please."

"Of course." Vida Vila pointed at the brook, and the water cleared. "Drink all you want, Prince." But then she frowned. "Are you sure?" she said aside to Marrow. "He doesn't look much like a prince."

"He's a form changer," Marrow explained. "For forest travel he assumes the form of an ogre. He can assume another form if you promise not to try to hurt him."

"I promise!" Vida exclaimed, her hair shimmering in her excitement. "I've always wanted a prince!"

Dolph reverted to boy form. He got down next to the brook. The water certainly seemed good. If Marrow believed it was safe, it surely was; adults had good instincts about such things. He drank deeply, and it was the finest water he had ever tasted.

Then, as he got up, he remembered that he was no longer alone with Marrow. There was a woman present, and he was naked. Now he missed his bag of belongings back on the other side of the river; the situation with the harpies had caused him to forget the problem of nakedness. So he had no clothes to change into anyway. It was too late to change to some other form; she had already seen him. He felt a blush developing.

"You must introduce us," Vida said to Marrow.

The skeleton shrugged. "Prince Dolph, this is Vida, the vila of this forest. Vida, this is Dolph, the son of King Dor."

"Uh, glad to meet you," Dolph said doubtfully, extending his hand. He reminded himself that this was not really a human woman, but some kind of forest creature who could change forms, just as he could. That in itself was surprising, but—

Vida avoided the hand, stepped in close, and embraced him. Her body was marvelously cushiony. He opened his mouth in surprise, only to have it covered by hers. She gave him a deep kiss that practically smothered him.

"Now wasn't that nice?" she inquired as she let him up for air. "There is much, much more where that came from, after we are married."

Dolph had been about to close his mouth, but this locked it open. What had she said?

"I fear there has been a misunderstanding," Marrow said. "Dolph is not—"

"Not interested in marriage yet?" the woman finished. "Well, maybe that is understandable. This is fairly sudden, I confess. I had not been thinking of it either, until I learned his identity. Suppose I remove my clothing?"

"I—" Dolph began.

The leaves shimmered on her torso, and faded out. Now she was a voluptuous naked nymph whose hair played about her ample curves. "Now isn't this a body fit for a prince?" she inquired. "I assure you, it's fully functional, for it is my natural form. Now if you will just assume your own natural form so that you can react in manly fashion, I'm sure you will be satisfied."

"But—" Dolph said.

"Let me encourage you," Vida said. "I normally don't give samples before marriage, but in this case I can make an exception. Just let me get really close to you—" As she spoke, she took him in her arms again, this time lifting him off his feet and bearing him down to the ground so that she could wrap her legs around him as well as her arms. "Now change, Prince," she whispered huskily. "I am ready for you!"

"Help!" Dolph cried.

Marrow stepped in. "This is his natural form," he informed the vila. "Dolph is a *young* prince, just nine years old. He is not ready for marriage."

It took a moment for that to sink in, for Vida was in the process of capturing Dolph's mouth for another thorough kiss. "How old?" she asked.

"Nine!" Dolph answered.

She pondered. "Well, maybe in a few more years." She released him. "Too bad; I have so much to offer right now."

"Indubitably the case," Marrow agreed smoothly. "We regret the confusion."

"So you are a child," Vida said, readjusting. "We vila are very protective toward children. Come, you must eat; a growing boy needs nourishment."

"Uh—"

"And you really shouldn't be going around without clothing; you'll catch your death of a cold!" She made a gesture with her hands, and suddenly Dolph was wearing a cloak of green leaves.

"Perhaps some food would be good for him," Marrow agreed.

"Yes." A huge green salad appeared in her hands. "Now eat it all, and brush your teeth after," she admonished Dolph. "Then you will have to wash up, especially behind the ears."

It occurred to Dolph that he might have been better off as a man. Her wrestling would have been more fun than this salad! Now she was acting just like a mother.

But it seemed he was stuck for it, because Marrow, though he did not have to eat himself, knew that living folk had to do it. Like so many adults, Marrow thought that yucky salad was better than candy corn on the cob.

But it wasn't all bad. After the meal, Vida changed into a fine big horse so that Dolph could ride in style, and carried him up the mountain to her tree. This was a huge old beech, with white sand all around it and the sound of ocean breakers in its branches. She invited them to spend the night here, and Marrow approved. "No one bothers anyone under the protection of a vila," Marrow said.

They talked, for Vida was eager to impress Dolph with her virtue as a prospective bride, for the time when he should be ready for one. He learned that the vily were the guardians of mountain forests, like hamadryads, only far more powerful. They could assume a number of forms, and could cause and cure illness in those who intruded on their forests. That was why the harpies had stopped at the border; they feared the local vila. But this power came at a price: the vily were forever tied to their trees, and if the tree died, so did its vila. Thus Marrow's threat to cut down her tree had completely unnerved her; she could have made a living creature sicken and die before ever reaching her tree, but Marrow was not alive in that sense. A vila could wander far from her tree, and remain away from it as long as she wished, unlike the hamadryad who had to stay quite close. But if Vida wandered too far, someone might sneak in and harm her tree, and she could not afford to risk that. So she maintained a nice forest as far out as she deemed proper, and that was it. She was sorry to have threatened Dolph, but he had looked just like an ogre, and ogres were notorious for damaging trees. Had she known at the outset that he was a prince—

"You know, it is true that you are young," she said, thinking of something. "But perhaps if you assumed the form of a grown man, we could do something interesting together."

"Oh? What?" Dolph asked, intrigued. He had never been able to assume the form of anything older than himself, but this talent improved as he grew, so maybe he could be a man now.

"I think not," Marrow said quickly.

"But—" Dolph and Vida said together.

"She is not thinking of wrestling or handball," the skeleton explained. "She is thinking of mushy stuff."

"Ugh!" Dolph exclaimed, appalled.

"Well, perhaps wrestling—" Vida said.

But Dolph demurred. He did not trust her not to throw in a kiss. He was glad Marrow had warned him. Adults simply were not to be trusted.

Vida sighed. "Well, when you do get interested in mush, Prince, you will know where to find me. I will be glad to show you varieties of mush you never dreamed of, and that's a promise."

Promise? Dolph was onto that kind of language. It meant a threat. He would never fall for it!

In the morning she made him eat a big bowl of mush, getting even with him for being young (or whatever), and resumed horse form to carry him to the coast. Dolph kicked Marrow, who became a bone blanket that Dolph wrapped around his body for warmth.

First they went back to the river to recover the lost bag. They were lucky; the harpies had not thought to look for that, and it was still sitting by the bank. Dolph became a buzzard, found that his wing soreness had eased, and flew across to fetch the bag back. Then he reverted to boy form, dressed, and the horse carried them back over the mountain and on to the east. It was indeed a nice way to travel!

Dusk was looming as they reached the shore. "I really would like to stay the night with you," the horse said. "But I fear for my tree. Unless you would like to—"

"In a few years," Dolph said. It wasn't right to fib, he knew, but he didn't think it was wise to tell her the truth: that he would never be interested in mush no matter how fancy she made it. With luck, he would not encounter her again.

"Just so." The horse became a hawk, which flew swiftly back west.

"How can she change forms, the way I can, but she's not a Magician?" Dolph asked. "Also, how can she do different kinds of magic? I thought each person could have only one magic talent."

"She is not a person, she is a vila," Marrow explained, "a magical creature whose natural form only happens to be human. You have noted that I can do a number of magical things related to my body; similarly she can do a number of things related to her nature. These are not multiple talents but aspects of her single talent: to protect her tree. She protects it, and it sustains her, giving her life as long as it lives."

"I guess so," Dolph said, though he found this explanation confusing. "But that tree looks a lot older than she does." In fact, now that she was safely gone, it occurred to him that her body had been sort of interesting. Like a nymph's, only more so. He regretted that he hadn't wrestled with her.

"They are the same age," Marrow assured him. "Perhaps two hundred years."

"Two hundred years! What did she want with me, then?"

"Only a human man can give her children; she cannot reproduce with her own kind, for there are no male vily. She hoped you would reproduce with her; not only would her offspring be vily like herself, they would be related to the royalty of Xanth, and have special prestige. She is most eager for that."

"I guess so," Dolph agreed. "But how did she expect to get children from me? I mean, what is the exact process of summoning the stork?"

"That is part of the Adult Conspiracy," Marrow said. "I am not permitted to inform you of that. It is something you will have to discover for yourself, or with a knowledgeable partner, when you are of age."

And with that frustrating answer Dolph had to be satisfied. He had hoped that Marrow would not remember the Adult Conspiracy against Children. He knew, of course, that babies were brought by storks; the secret was how adults managed to signal the storks so as to order the babies. Storks answered only to very particular directives, and absolutely refused to deliver babies otherwise. No child had ever figured out the secret; if children ever did, they would be able to order babies for themselves and bypass the adults entirely. What a dream that was!

Now that it was too late, he also realized that Vida Vila might have told him the secret, if he had thought to ask, because she was so eager to please him. Well, maybe he would return this way after all, after his Quest was done, and ask her. The trick would be to get the answer and get away before she could set up for any more mush.

But meanwhile the Isle of Illusion was there across the water; soon they would find the Heaven Cent!

4
GRACE'L

I n the morning they gazed at the isle. "I'll become a roc
and carry you across," Dolph said.

"Perhaps—"

Dolph was coming to dread that opening! But he knew
he'd better hear it. "What?"

"—it would be better to cross by boat."

"We don't have a boat!"

"I can assume that configuration, if you can find a paddle."

"You can be a boat? Why didn't you tell me that back
at the river?"

"You didn't ask."

There were times when adults could be very trying! "All
right, we can do it by boat. But what's wrong with flying
across?"

"We do not know precisely what we will encounter there
and may not wish to advertise our approach. An air approach could lead to complications about landing, and if
harpies happen to be nesting there—"

"Good point." Dolph wanted no further business with harpies! He searched around the shore until he found a flat branch that would do for a paddle.

He kicked the skeleton. The bones flew out, and splashed on the water in the form of a small boat. Dolph climbed in, finding that there was just room for him. It was amazing how many shapes Marrow could assume! The bones were set slightly apart, but seemed to keep the water out anyway, so that the boat floated without difficulty.

"What keeps the water from leaking in?" he inquired as he paddled.

"Connective magic," the skull he was using as a seat replied. "I consist of bones and cartilage; the bones are visible, but the cartilage can become very fine, and its webbing holds the water at bay. A similar effect enables me to speak to you; that invisible webbing captures air and pushes it past my mouth bones in such a way as to make sound."

"You're quite a creature!" Dolph said admiringly.

"Thank you."

Dolph was not the best paddler, but the craft was well designed and the distance was short, and a gentle wind from behind helped. He made decent progress.

As they neared the isle, its outline became stranger. It was not the wilderness Dolph had anticipated; instead it seemed to be an elaborate city. He saw golden domes and silver turrets and flying buttresses and waving banners. The morning sunlight glinted from its shiny surfaces, and an intriguing network of avenues showed below. Where had this come from?

"I thought the Isle of Illusion was empty!" Dolph panted as he paddled. "Where did that city come from?"

"The isle has been uninhabited by man since your grandmother Iris left it, generations ago," the skull said. "Perhaps you see a mirage."

"What's a mirage?"

"Something that is not really there. When you get close to it, it is gone."

"It sure is pretty!" Dolph continued paddling, drawing slowly closer. "I hope it doesn't go soon!"

The closer he got to the isle, the larger and clearer the fabulous city looked. The elegant buildings cast shadows, and the exotic plants growing around them waved in the breeze.

"It sure looks real," Dolph said.

"It should be fading out very soon."

But it didn't fade. Finally Dolph squatted in the boat and lifted the skull, drawing it up with its trailing neck bones, so that Marrow could look. "Amazing!" the skull agreed.

Finally they landed. The city loomed over them, looking realer than ever. It was huge and clean and bright, every part of it clean and polished.

Dolph kicked the boat, and it reformed into the skeleton. "I am beginning to suspect this is something other than a mirage," Marrow remarked. "But it was certainly my understanding that the isle was deserted."

"Do you think there is any danger?" After the business with the harpies, Dolph was more alert for danger. Back at Castle Roogna things had always been safe. He had seen much danger in the Tapestry, but that wasn't real. Rather, it was real, but it was somewhere else, so didn't threaten him. To have things actually come after him—that was unnerving.

"There should not be any we cannot handle. But perhaps—"

Dolph waited patiently. Apparently, skeletons could be disconnected in their speech as well as in their bodies.

"—we should contact Castle Roogna, just in case."

"Contact Castle Roogna?"

"With your magic mirror."

"Oh." For a moment Dolph had feared this was a pretext to go back to Castle Roogna, from which he might never again escape. He dug in his pack for the mirror.

He held it up. "Castle Roogna," he said.

The reflection of the isle disappeared. Momentary static played across the glass. Then a new reflection appeared:

Dolph and Marrow standing before the strange city.

"What's this?" Dolph asked. "I said 'Castle Roogna' not 'Isle of Illusion'! Why are you back here?"

"Try turning around," Marrow suggested.

Dolph saw no point in this, but didn't argue. He turned slowly, until he was facing the opposite way.

"It's no good; the picture hasn't changed."

"Precisely," Marrow said. "It is not a local reflection."

"Sure it is! There's the two of us and the city!"

"But you are not facing the city. The local reflection would show the ocean behind you."

Dolph glanced back. There was the ocean behind him. He peered again into the mirror. There was the bright city.

He turned again, so that now he held the mirror between him and Marrow. The reflection remained: the two of them standing before the city. Now as he peered more closely he saw that the Dolph figure was holding something between the two of them. The mirror! How could the mirror show a reflection of itself?

"Enlarge the scene," Marrow suggested.

Dolph had the mirror do that. The image contracted as the scope of it expanded. A border appeared. "It's the Tapestry!" Dolph exclaimed.

"Which is oriented on us," Marrow said. "It would thus appear that they are already aware of our situation."

"They're spying on me!" Dolph said angrily.

"Perhaps it is just your sister," the skeleton said.

"Um, yes. Maybe she's jealous of my adventure!" Suddenly Dolph felt much better.

"So if there is danger here, your parents will know of it, and take what action is required. We may rest easier now."

Dolph put away the mirror with mixed emotions. He was glad that there might not be real danger, but he didn't like being spied on. He wished there were some way he could stop it. But the Tapestry could be tuned to just about anything in Xanth. At least it meant that they knew he was solving the mystery of the Good Magician's disappearance.

He was a genuine adventurer, instead of a dumb boy. That was a big consolation!

They walked into the city. The domed buildings were huge, and just as pretty up close as from afar. The streets between them were narrow but sparkling with bright multicolored tiles and polished copper borders. Now it was evident that the plants and flowers growing around the buildings were not real, but cunningly crafted to look genuine.

"This reminds me somewhat of a setting within the gourd," Marrow remarked. "The City of Brass, for example."

"A city in the gourd? Are we in the gourd?"

"No, we seem to be in your world still, and this is not identical; it merely reminds me of the way the gourd is set up. That is where the substance of dreams is fashioned; there are many settings that are used as models for the dreams. This could be such a setting."

"A setting for a dream!" Dolph said. "This could be fun!"

"I do not dream, of course," Marrow said, "because I am from the realm of dreams. But I know that many dreams are unpleasant. Let us hope that this setting is not for a dream borne by a night mare."

"Yes," Dolph agreed, realizing that this adventure could become just as nasty as it could become fun.

"Also, we must remember our mission. We are here to find the Heaven Cent. That may not be easy."

"Maybe it's in one of these domes," Dolph said, glancing at his friend for the first time since entering the fascinating city.

He stopped, amazed. Marrow Bones was gone; in his place stood a handsome living human man in a white suit.

The man glanced back at him. "Is something wrong?" he asked with Marrow's voice.

Was it Marrow, or was it some stranger imitating his voice? Dolph didn't know how to judge. If it was Marrow, he should tell the skeleton right away. But if it was a stranger, maybe he should pretend not to notice the difference, so that the man would think he had succeeded in fooling him. "Uh—" he said.

"You look as if you'd seen a ghost," the man said. "And not a friendly one. What is the matter?"

He had to say something—but *what?* Dolph wished he had some adult judgment so that he would know what to do. "Uh—" he repeated.

The man extended a hand to him. "You seem about ready to faint; let me help—"

Then the man's gaze fell on his own hand. His eyes seemed to bulge. "Uh—" he said.

"Yeah," Dolph agreed.

"*Something's happened to my hand!*" the man cried, horrified. "It's all covered with meat!"

"Right," Dolph said. At least this was solving his problem of what to say.

"My arm too! And my legs! I think I'm going to be sick!"

"Sickening," Dolph agreed, reassured.

The man touched his own arm. "But it's not real!" he exclaimed with vast relief. "My bones are still there!"

"Not real?"

"Feel my arm!" the man said, reaching for Dolph.

Dolph retreated, then realized that it was better not to show fear. Gingerly he touched the arm.

His fingers passed through the arm and touched cold bone. "It *is* you!" he cried joyfully.

"Of course it's me!" Marrow replied. "Who else would it be!"

"But you look just like a living man! It's awful!"

Marrow went to stand facing a mirrorlike wall. "Appalling!" he agreed. "This *is* a dream brought by a night mare! How can you stand to look at me?"

"It isn't easy," Dolph said. "But I think I can hold my breakfast down."

"But at least it isn't real!" Marrow's hands were feeling his head. "There's no hairy skin on my skull, no loathsome eyeballs in my sockets, no grotesque tongue in my jaw. No fat clings to my body. I only *look* grotesque; I'm not really that way."

"That's great," Dolph said, conscious of his own hairy head, loathsome eyeballs, and grotesque tongue. What was he doing with all that stupid flesh on him?

"It is all right for you, of course," Marrow said. "You're supposed to be that way. You would even look a bit strange in bare bones. But for me—what a horror!"

"What a horror," Dolph said, feeling better.

"I wonder—" Marrow stepped closer to the mirror wall and poked a fleshed finger at it. "—whether this too is illusory." The finger passed through the wall. "It is! That explains it! This whole city must be illusory!"

Dolph touched a wall. His questing hand found nothing. Sure enough, it wasn't there. That explained how there could be a great fancy city on a deserted isle.

"But am I changed?" he asked. He looked at his own hands. "I don't look different to me."

"No, you are exactly as you were," Marrow reassured him.

"But if you've changed the way you look, how come I haven't? I should look like a skeleton or something, shouldn't I?"

"That is odd," Marrow agreed. "I can only conjecture that you are a Magician, so it has no power over you. But it is possible that it clothes all living things with flesh, and you are already fleshed, so it has no further effect. Perhaps it would be the same with genuine buildings, leaving them alone."

"Some of these illusions may be real? We'd better watch how we walk into them, then."

"Yes. Fortunately, we can stay on the streets and use the apparent doors to enter. That way we won't risk banging into anything solid."

"But suppose the Heaven Cent is covered over by some illusion? How could we ever find it?"

Marrow made a remarkably human type frown, lips and all. "I fear we shall have to do some very tedious checking, unless we can discover a way to abolish the illusion."

That was what Dolph had been afraid of. "Then I guess we'd better get started. I sure wonder what all this illusion is doing here, though, when Grandma Iris is so long gone from here."

Then they both stopped short. "Her missing talent!" Marrow exclaimed. "It came back here!"

"It missed the old Isle of Illusion!" Dolph agreed. "This is where it feels at home!"

"I had not realized that talents could do that," Marrow confessed.

"Well, she's pretty old. Maybe she lost her grip on it."

"That may be the case. I am surprised she has not acted to recover it."

Dolph considered. "Maybe she doesn't know it's here. I mean, it could be just about anywhere, and she didn't think to look here. If it's just my stupid sister watching the Tapestry, and not even watching now, 'cause she never sticks to anything long except bossiness, she wouldn't've told anyone, so they don't know."

"Perhaps so," Marrow said. "I suppose it could become tedious watching another person's adventure constantly. Still, we ought to draw attention to the matter. I wonder if we could alert them?"

"You mean, call on the mirror?"

"That does not seem to differentiate sufficiently, at this range. It merely focuses on one site in Castle Roogna, which is the Tapestry."

"Yeah, it's a small mirror, and I never was too good at tuning them in. If I messed with it, I might lose Castle Roogna entirely. But how else can we call in?"

"Perhaps—"

Dolph wished he had a speed-up spell, to quicken that hollow skull's thinking process. He waited.

"—if we set up a message," Marrow concluded.

"Like a note on a piece of paper? They'd never see it because it would be too small."

"A big note."

"Oh."

They got to work at the fringe of the region of illusion, collecting sticks and stones. Marrow's body changed oddly as he passed in and out of the illusion, one moment reverting to his normal bare bones, then becoming fleshed. At times he was part bones and part flesh.

In due course they had laid out objects in a big pattern on the small beach, spelling out words: TELL IRIS. Actually it should have been Grandma Iris, but they didn't have enough material for a big word like that. When Ivy saw that in the Tapestry, she would surely tell someone, and when Grandma Iris learned of the phenomenal city back at her old haunts, she would understand. Then she could reclaim her magic talent, and all would be well again. Dolph had not yet found the Good Magician or even the Heaven Cent, but already he was accomplishing something!

They paused for lunch. Dolph's sandwiches were gone, but he didn't really need them; he simply changed to an ant and consumed a segment of a leaf. He did not like green salad in ant form much better than he did in boy form, but anything would do when he was hungry enough. That was another thing he was learning during this adventure: there were times when it just wasn't worthwhile to be too fussy about food.

Then they commenced their search for the Heaven Cent. They were not sure exactly what it looked like, but hoped they would know it when they found it. Dolph knew that in Mundania there was a small magic copper coin called a cent; it wasn't supposed to be worth much, but it was pretty when shined. He thought the Heaven Cent might be a very big, bright cent. Just how it would help him find the Good Magician he wasn't sure, but he would figure that out when he got hold of it. The Magician's message made it clear that he needed the cent: SKELETON KEY TO HEAVEN CENT. This was the key made of a skeleton, so the cent had to be here. He hoped.

The vast illusion covered the isle. They did not know in what building the cent might be, so they had to check each

in turn until they found it. Because it might be covered by
a wall, they had to poke their hands through the walls too,
feeling for anything round. Mostly what they found was
weeds: without the fantasy city, this island would be just a
weed-ridden lump.

The job soon became tedious. Dolph wished there were
a faster, easier way to do it, but he couldn't think of any.
He tried changing to hound form, so that his superior nose
could sniff out the cent, but he didn't know what it smelled
like, so that didn't help. He assumed eagle form, in the
hope that his sharp eyes would pierce the illusion, but they
only made its detail clearer. It was easiest to keep his own
form, so that he could use his hands to check for what he
could not see.

He stepped through one more wall—and spied a woman.
She was tall and well proportioned in the adult fashion,
with hair as black as midnight and skin as white as midday.

Dolph jumped back through the wall. He remembered
his experience with Vida Vila, who really wasn't bad once
he had gotten to know her, but that threat of mushy stuff
had really turned him off. This new woman looked like the
kind who was good at mush, so he was wary of her. Fortunately, she had been facing away from him, so had not
seen him.

He hurried across to where Marrow was working.
"There's a woman!" he whispered to the living man that
Marrow appeared to be. "Between the buildings!"

Marrow considered. "Is she a real woman or an illusory
woman?"

Dolph hadn't thought of that. "I—don't really know. She
looked real, but—" He shrugged.

"She might be a monster, made to look human. I had
better investigate."

"Yes," Dolph said, relieved.

They went to the region where Dolph had seen the
woman, and poked their heads cautiously through the wall.
There she was, moving along the wall further along, her

hands poking into it. She seemed to be looking for something.

"I shall approach her," Marrow said. "But I shall not divulge very much about myself until I know her nature. She could be dangerous."

Dolph nodded agreement. The illusion made everything uncertain.

Marrow stepped through, while Dolph watched from the wall. Marrow approached the woman. "Hello," he said.

"Eeeek!" the woman cried, jumping.

"Who are you?" Marrow asked.

The woman backed away from him. "I didn't know anyone else was here! You alarmed me."

"Or perhaps I should inquire *what* are you," Marrow said. "Are you what you seem to be?"

"No. Are you what *you* seem to be?"

"Not exactly. What is your name?"

"Tell me yours."

Marrow paused. "I am trying to ascertain whether you are dangerous. If you do not cooperate, I shall have to assume that you are."

"That is exactly the way I feel about you," the woman said.

"Then answer my questions, and I shall answer yours. What is your name?"

"Gracile Ossein. Grace'l for short. What is yours?"

"Marrow Bones. What is your nature?"

"I am a skeleton. What is yours?"

"I am a skeleton. Where—"

"Now I know you are trying to fool me!" she exclaimed. "You are pretending to be what I am!"

"I suspect it is the other way around," Marrow said stiffly. "There are no female skeletons in Xanth."

"There weren't until I stepped out of the gourd. I am the only skeleton stranded out here. Now what is your nature, really?"

"Let us clasp hands, and we shall quickly verify each other's natures," Marrow suggested.

"No! You may be a bone-crunching monster!"

"As you may be," Marrow retorted. "If I had been that, I would have pounced on you from behind."

She nodded. "True. Very well, we shall touch hands."

They extended their hands. Slowly the two approached. Then they touched. Then they clasped.

"You *are* skeletal!" they exclaimed together.

Dolph decided it was safe to emerge from hiding. "She really is like you?" he asked.

"Is this another of our kind?" Grace'l asked.

"No," Marrow said. "He is human. The illusion does not affect him."

Then they were happily talking. Dolph was immensely relieved to know that Grace'l was neither a monster nor a mushy woman. They explained what they were doing here, and Grace'l explained how she was looking for the gourd that she had stepped out from. "It was an accident; I only meant to travel to another setting, but I took the wrong exit and found myself in this strange place. At first I thought it was merely a new setting, and I walked through it, but then I realized it was not what it seemed, and I tried to go back—but I had lost the gourd. I have been here for days, trying to find it."

"It's hard to find anything under all this illusion," Dolph agreed. "I don't know how long it will take us to find the Heaven Cent."

"What does it look like? I may have felt it in my search."

"We don't know. But maybe like a big bright copper mundane penny."

"Mundane? What's that?"

She had never before been outside the gourd; she had never heard of Mundania. They tried to explain, but she could not grasp it; it was too strange for her.

Then, abruptly, the illusion vanished. The three of them were standing on the weedy island.

"Grandma Iris took her talent back!" Dolph exclaimed.

Indeed it was so. The two skeletons were revealed in their bare bones; each had spoken truly. Marrow was taller, but Grace'l more rounded. Still, Dolph wasn't certain he could tell them apart, if he were to see them singly. "How can you tell boy from girl?" he asked.

The skeletons exchanged eyeless glances. "That is a trifle delicate to discuss," Marrow said.

"Still, it is no secret," Grace'l said. "I have more graceful bones and one more rib than he does."

"One more rib?" Dolph asked, surprised.

"High G, the grace note," she said.

Dolph remained baffled. "High gee?"

"Prince Dolph has not been exposed to skeletal history," Marrow said. "Perhaps we should start from the beginning."

"Very well," she said. "If you will help me look for the gourd, I will tell the tale."

"We can look for the Heaven Cent too!" Dolph said. He had the feeling that the skeletons were about to get into a long and dull discussion of some kind, and he didn't want to waste all that time.

"We shall all search for both," Marrow agreed. "With the illusion gone, it should not be difficult to find whatever we want."

So they started the search, walking three abreast, with Dolph in the middle, and the two skeletons took turns explaining about the G rib.

It seemed that long, long ago, when magic was new, the Demon X(A/N)th (or someone; Dolph wasn't quite clear about that) made the ordinary Land of Xanth for the ordinary creatures, and the gourd for the extraordinary creatures that the others could only dream about, and left the refuse to drear, unmagical Mundania. He put a kind of barrier around Xanth to keep the Mundanes mostly out, and sealed off the gourd realm by making it difficult for any ordinary creature to bring its body inside. In the very center of the gourd he made a fine cemetery, and there he put the first skeleton.

But this skeleton got lonely, for there were no others of his kind. So the Demon took one of his ribs and broke it into pieces, and the pieces grew and became the first female skeleton, complete in every detail. However, the male was no longer complete, because he was missing that one rib. Thus the female had one more rib than he, and so it was ever since.

The first two skeletons made beautiful music together, for their bones resonated each to a different key. Marrow could play over 200 notes, and Grace'l could play over 201 notes. It was the first skeleton's smallest rib that was missing, the one that played the highest note. From that time on, the female always had the higher range, and could always top the male by one note. The male missed that note, but was satisfied to have the female play it for him, which she did when appropriate.

"When is that?" Dolph asked.

Now they were silent. "Uh," Marrow said at last, "when they want to reproduce."

"You mean they play music to signal the stork?" Dolph asked, suddenly very interested. Maybe he could get a line on how flesh folk did it, too! If it was just a matter of playing a tune or singing a song, maybe a mushy (ugh!) love song—

"Not exactly," Grace'l said, as diffident as Marrow. "We don't use storks; they are reserved for the living folk."

"Oh? Then how do skeletons do it?"

"You would not care to know," Marrow said.

Now Dolph was sure that the process was similar to the one living folk used that was secret from children. "Sure I would!"

"It involves—mushy stuff."

"Oh." What a wet blanket! Just when it was getting interesting, too. But he had sort of known it would be something like that, because adults were entirely too interested in mush. Maybe age turned their brains mushy. What a fate!

They continued searching the isle, but neither gourd nor cent showed up. "I fear the gourd has rotted," Marrow said. "None remain on the isle. But there should be many on the mainland."

"The mainland?" Grace'l asked. "You mean there's more?"

Dolph managed not to laugh. She really was innocent!

"Yes, this is but one island, and not the largest," Marrow said. "Normal Xanth is actually a fairly extensive place, having perhaps as much room as the gourd."

"Amazing!" she exclaimed. "I had no idea!" Then she turned to him. "How did you come to be here in Xanth?"

"I got on the Lost Path, so of course was lost. A man from Xanth found me, and brought me from the gourd. I confess it was a strange realm out here, but once I came to know it I found it interesting, and decided to stay. Certainly it is better than returning to the Lost Path."

Her skull nodded. "I suppose so. But you should be able to avoid the Lost Path now, if you return in the company of one who is not lost."

"That is true," Marrow said. "But I have a duty here."

"What duty is that?"

"I am the adult companion for Prince Dolph. I must see that he does not get into too much trouble, and help him find the Heaven Cent."

She did not reply. They kept on searching, but as the sun dropped low, getting ready to set the distant trees on fire, they knew that neither gourd nor cent was to be found on the isle.

"It seems this was a false lead," Marrow said with regret.

"But the Good Magician would not make a mistake!" Dolph protested. "His note said—"

"But it is possible that we erred in interpreting his note. I understand that his Answers could be at times obscure."

"What was the message?" Grace'l asked.

" 'Skeleton Key to Heaven Cent,' " Dolph said. "And it read this way, toward the Isle of Illusion, so I thought this must be the right key, made from the skeleton of a coral."

"That does seem to make sense. Are there other such keys?"

"A number," Marrow said.

"Where are they?"

"To the south, all around the peninsula of Xanth."

"So this is the end of a line of keys?"

"In a way," Marrow agreed.

"Then maybe the Magician meant you should start here, and keep going until you found the right one," she said.

"Say, maybe so!" Dolph agreed. He was getting to like Grace'l.

"But to search them all—" Marrow protested. "That could take a long time. I am not certain—"

"Perhaps there is another gourd on one of them," Grace'l said.

Marrow glanced at her. The notion of traveling with her did not seem to bother him unduly.

"We could go by boat," Dolph said. "Can you become a boat, Grace'l?"

"Of course," she said. "Anybody can do that!"

So it was decided: they would travel together for a while, looking now for two things: cent and gourd. They were bound to find one of them. Dolph liked this development, because he felt more secure with two companions than with one.

5
MELA

In the morning they set off for the southern keys. There was a fairly brisk sea wind blowing in toward land, and that helped because Grace'l volunteered to become a sail. She said she could help them tack against that wind.

"Tacky?" Dolph asked.

"Tack. It is a way of sailing slantwise against the wind, even into the wind. I have done it on Castor Lake."

Dolph felt a bad taste in his mouth. Castor oil was the stuff that leaked from castors when they rolled too far, and it tasted absolutely awful, which was why adults made children eat it. "There's a whole *lake* of that stuff?"

"Indeed there is," she agreed. "It is used as the setting for the bad dreams of children."

"I've had those dreams," Dolph said grimly. "I don't think I'd like it in the gourd."

"You aren't supposed to. Bad dreams are no good if people like them. No reputable night mare would carry a good dream."

"Mare Imbri carried good dreams!" he said stoutly.

"You know Mare Imbri? She was a good mare, until she got half of someone's soul and kept it instead of turning it in. That ruined her, and she washed out of the business."

"She's a day mare now," Dolph said.

"Well, they don't have much substance. But I suppose if you like that type—"

"I sure like it better than what the night mares carry!"

"Kick me in the tailbone," she invited him.

"Gladly!" He delivered a perfect kick. She exploded and fell into the form of a triangular outline of bones, with her skull at the base.

"Now kick me," Marrow said.

Dolph did so. Marrow became the little craft he had been before. "Now lift the sail to the craft," his skull said.

Dolph heaved up Grace'l's sail, staggered to the boat, and clunked it down. Her skull opened its jaws and grabbed onto a crossbone. This anchored her form upright. Now the sail was in place.

"Haul us to the water," Marrow's skull said. "Then jump in quickly, because when that wind catches us, we'll move well."

Dolph hauled. A single skeleton did not weigh much, but the two together were all he could handle. He managed to get the boat to the water, which wasn't far distant. Then, as it bobbled, he grabbed his paddle and jumped in.

Just in time! The sail swung about of its own volition and caught the wind, and suddenly they were moving swiftly across the water. Dolph did not have to paddle at all; he just hung on to the bone rim and enjoyed it. He removed his knapsack and set it on the floor of the boat between the skull-seat and the sail pole; it should be safe there.

For a while he reveled in the sensation of motion across the water without effort, and watched the passing scenery. The Isle of Illusion fell behind, and the beach to the west moved resolutely to the rear, its sands and trees marching at an even pace. Closer in, the surface of the sea rippled, forming fringes of bubbly white froth at the cutting edges of the waves. The water was greenish where the morning sunbeams lighted it, and deepening gray and black below. What, he wondered, was down under there, that could not be seen from here?

The wind shifted, so that now it was coming from the southeast. Grace'l's sail changed orientation, and the Marrow boat continued south.

Dolph looked at the sail. He was used to the magic of the skeletons, that enabled them to form useful alternate shapes and to hold out the water or the air as if the porous networks of bones were solid. But this magic of tacking—how could that be? They were moving almost toward the wind, and that did not make sense. Unless the tackiness caused the boat to be drawn in toward the wind, instead of being pushed away from it. Yes, that had to be it!

But that would represent another kind of talent. Marrow had said that the seemingly different talents of Vida Vila were actually merely aspects of a single talent, and maybe that was so, but this new type of magic of the skeletons seemed different.

"Are you sure you don't have two magic talents?" he asked Marrow. "Shape change and tacking?"

"Tacking is not skeleton magic," the skull Dolph was sitting on responded. "Anyone can do it, if he knows how. I have heard that even the Mundanes can do it, though I confess I suspect that is an exaggeration. Certainly you could do it, with practice."

"But my talent is form changing!"

"Some magic is independent, available to anyone who invokes it properly. Indeed, I understand that the Good Magician Humfrey, for whom we search, has no evident talent except the ability to locate other types of magic that he can use. If some other person could locate the same types of magic, that person could hold the same office."

"He's the Magician of Information! No one else can do that!"

"Well, I am a creature of the gourd. Perhaps I have overlooked some aspect of the situation."

"But if someone else could do it, what would happen to Humfrey?"

"I wouldn't know. But we must face the possibility that we may not find him."

"Never!" Dolph said.

"But certainly we have not yet exhausted our options. We shall search every key until we find the Heaven Cent."

"The Heaven Cent?" a voice called from the side.

Dolph looked. There was a woman in the water, swimming beside them. He could see her face with its halo of hair, that was blinding yellow in the sunlight but seaweed green in the water. "Are you in trouble?" he called. "Do you need to get in the boat?"

She laughed merrily, and her shoulders rose out of the water, showing her breasts. Dolph really wasn't interested in such things, but he couldn't help staring; she was, as his mother would have put it, extremely well endowed. "I have no need of boats! Come join me in the water."

"That sounds like a merwoman," Marrow's skull remarked.

"It's sure a woman!" Dolph agreed.

"I would advise—"

"What's your name?" the woman called.

"Prince Dolph. What's yours?"

"—caution," the skull concluded.

"Mela. Melantha for long. You're a prince?"

Now Dolph remembered the problem he had had with Vida Vila in the forest, who had been really taken with the notion of a prince. "Uh, well—"

"Let me get a look at you." She swam close, and now he saw that below the waist her body was that of a fish. This was indeed a merwoman! "Why so you are! What a fortunate day for me!"

Dolph hesitated to ask her what she meant, so he changed the subject. "Do you know something about the Heaven Cent?"

Now she was going through her hair with a bright coral comb in her right hand, and holding a small ornate mirror up with her left. Dolph had not seen where these devices came from; they just seemed to have appeared. "Why certainly! Who wants to know?"

"I do! I'm looking for it."

She gazed at him, cocking her head so that her golden hair fell lustrously to the side. Her mirror and comb sparkled; he thought for a moment that both were encrusted with jewels, but then saw that they were barnacles. "Perhaps if you join me in the water, I will tell you."

"Do not go in the water!" the skull warned.

Dolph had already decided that this was not the time to swim. "Why don't you come in the boat and tell me?"

She grimaced prettily. "If you insist, Prince. But you will have to help me, for I can't climb very well." Her comb and mirror disappeared. She flashed her flukes, sending up a considerable spray.

"Don't—" the skull began.

The merwoman swam close. "Is there someone in the boat with you?"

"Not exactly. It's—"

She lifted her arms. Her impressive breasts came out of the water too, causing him to gawk. "No matter. Take hold."

"—let her get hold of you," Marrow concluded.

Too late. Mela put her arms around his neck and hauled. Dolph tried to help lift her up, but she weighed more than he, and her arms were surprisingly strong, and she was instead pulling him down. He was trying to hold on to the boat with his legs, but the position wasn't good. In a moment he knew he would be in the water.

"Tack!" the skull cried.

The sail swung around suddenly, and the boat lurched. Mela was drawing Dolph's head and shoulders into her bosom, almost smothering him. The bottom of the sail collided with the merwoman's back, giving her a hard smack. She made an exclamation of pain and let go.

Dolph got himself back in the boat, out of harm's way. "You tried to pull me into the water!" he cried.

Mela shook her head, her hair throwing off yellow glints. "I've been knocked before, but never quite that way," she said angrily.

"You wanted to drown me!" Dolph accused her.

She laughed, not as merrily as before. "Hardly that, Prince! I can enable you to breathe water. I want you with me. Come on in; your hair's all mussed. I'll comb it for you." The barnacled comb reappeared in her hand.

"You said you knew about the Heaven Cent!"

"I do. Enough. I just prefer to tell you in my own domain. It is not comfortable for me out of the water."

Dolph could believe that. He had not seen many fish that liked dry land, and she was a fish below.

"We must get away from her," Marrow's skull warned.

"Let's go!" Dolph agreed. He had had quite enough of the merwoman's deception.

The sail swung around again and caught the wind. The craft resumed speed.

"Prince Dolph, I'm sorry!" Mela called, swimming alongside. "I'll tell you about the Heaven Cent, if you'll only listen."

"I'll listen while I travel," Dolph said grimly. He was developing a healthy aversion to women of all types, to match the aversion for girls that his big bossy sister had inculcated in him.

"Very well," she agreed, having no trouble keeping up. Her tail was very good for swimming, so that she hardly needed to use her hands, and her pillowy breasts enabled her to float without effort. "The Heaven Cent in the past has cent folk to whomever it makes cents for them to meet, anywhere under the heavens. That's what it's for."

It was an illumination. "That does make cents!" Dolph cried. "We want to find the Good Magician!"

"The Good Magician is missing?" she asked, interested.

"Yes, that's why we're looking for him. We will find the Heaven Cent on the Skeleton Key."

"I doubt it."

"Why?"

"Because there is no Heaven Cent."

"But you just said—"

"Silly boy! I told you how it has been used in the past. The effort of its great magic melts it down, and so it no longer exists after it has performed its function."

"But—"

"So it has to be forged anew each time. That is the skeletal key to its use."

"The—"

She laughed again. "How little you have understood your mission! Did you really think the skeleton key was a place?"

"I—" Dolph felt very foolish.

"She may have a point," the skull said, disgruntled.

"But how can we make the Heaven Cent!" Dolph asked. "We don't know anything about that!"

"I do have one bit of information about that," Mela said.

"You do? Tell us!"

"Come down to my abode below, and I will tell you, sweet Prince."

"No!"

"I assure you I shall not mistreat you, Prince. I only want your company for a while."

Again Dolph remembered the vila, whose interest turned out to be mushy. "I'm not good company."

"Well, perhaps not right at the moment. But in time you will be excellent company, I'm sure. I'm willing to wait."

Now Dolph was sure he wanted to get away from her. "No!"

"I can't cajole you?" Mela asked, frowning.

"No! Go away!"

"I will even sing you a nice song."

"No!"

Now she frowned. "Then I will sing a song that is not so nice. You are making me unreasonable, Prince Dolph. That is not wise."

"I'm not a wise person!" he retorted. "I'm just a boy!"

"And I am a merwoman. You have something to learn about my type."

"I don't want to learn it!"

"I have set my sights on you, and I shall have you, delicious Prince."

Dolph wasn't certain how she meant that, but none of the interpretations he could think of were very appealing. "Can we move faster?" he asked Marrow.

"Only if the wind picks up," the skull replied.

But now the wind was dying. They were in a calm, at just the wrong time.

Melantha began to sing. Her voice was eerie. It sounded more like ghosts being blown by a gale than like music, yet it had a certain compelling quality. Dolph found himself wanting to be with her, despite his aversion to the notion.

But then the wind did pick up. In fact it became quite gusty. A shadow fell across the boat. Dolph looked up, and saw to his dismay that a storm was brewing.

"Of all the times for bad weather!" he exclaimed.

"It isn't exactly coincidence, you know," Mela called from the heightening waves to the side.

"That's right!" the skull muttered. "They can summon storms."

"We certainly can," Mela called over the rising roar of wind and sea. "We have a deal with King Fracto, a mutual assistance pact."

"I've heard of him," the skull said. "He's the worst of clouds. Cumulo Fracto Nimbus. Always looking for mischief."

"I'll tell him to go away, if you come to me," Mela called.

"Don't deal with her!" the skull said. "We'll cut in to land, where we can escape her."

The boat turned, angling for the beach.

Mela resumed her song. Immediately the storm intensified. The wind caught the sail and whipped it about. The boat tilted scarily.

"I don't like this," the skull said. "We had better furl our sail."

"I don't like it either," Dolph said. "I'm getting seasick!"

"Not in my waters you don't!" Mela protested.

"I can't help it," Dolph said, leaning over the side.

"If you do, you'll clean it up!" she cried, swimming close.

Dolph jerked back. He didn't want her to grab him again.

"Kick the sail!" the skull said.

Dolph realized that this was the only way Grace'l could change form. He stood up.

A sudden gust caught them. The boat was blown over on its side. Dolph, rising precariously to his feet, was pitched into the heaving sea.

He opened his mouth to scream, but his stomach was roiling so violently that what came out was no scream. It was a retch.

Then the merwoman caught him. "Now you are mine, you precious boy!" she said. "Kiss me!" She put her face to his.

The contents of Dolph's stomach spewed out, splashing against her nose and soaking her hair.

"Yuck!" she exclaimed. "I thought you were housebroken!" But she did not let go of him. She hauled him under the water, and in a moment it was much calmer.

Dolph inhaled. He thought he would drown, but he took in a full breath of water and it was just like air. She was right: she had enabled him to breathe the water.

He watched the vomit being carried out of her green hair by the water as she swam. Her tail stroked back and forth, and her body undulated, and she moved with considerable grace. She hauled him along, her grip on his arm so strong that he knew he could not break free. And if he did, what would happen? The moment he broke contact with her, the sea might change back to water for him, and he would drown.

He was her captive, without doubt. What was going to happen to him?

*   *   *

Mela deposited him in a cave garden at the bottom of the ocean. Treelike seaweeds surrounded it, arching up overhead to form a canopy. He could breathe, but knew it was water, because he was able to swim in it.

The ground was covered with pretty colored stones. Some of them glowed, their gentle green, red, blue, and yellow radiance lighting the region so that he could see. Here and there there were floating masses of fine seaweed that looked like cushions. Between the sea trees and the stones was a rough circle of shiny metals.

"Do not go beyond the canopy," Mela told him. "My enchantment extends only within it, and you will not be able to breathe the water beyond unless you are in contact with me. We are far down; you would surely drown."

Dolph swam over and poked his head beyond the sea trees. The water seemed thicker here, and the farther he went, the worse it got, until he was choking. She was right: he could not swim away.

In the middle of the garden she had a fireplace. She put some waterlogs on it, and the fire blazed up warmly.

"But how can there be fire under water?" Dolph asked, amazed.

"It is mermagic, of course," she explained. "We are excellent housewives, managing the hearth and land until our husbands return." Then she turned away.

"Husbands?" Dolph asked. "If you have a husband, why—"

"I *had* a husband, Merwin Merman. But he is gone."

"Gone? Where?"

She turned to face him, her flukes twitching. "You are young, and I brought you here against your will, so I must forgive you your inadequate social grace. I spoke euphemistically. Merwin is dead."

"Oh." Dolph had indeed failed to understand her manner. He wanted to ask more questions, such as what that big word "euphemistically" meant, but realized that this might not be smart. "I'm sorry." He was getting better at apologizing in the adult fashion.

And she reacted in the adult fashion. "No, you could not know. I apologize to you for what I have done. But let me explain."

That was exactly what he wanted. Adults had funny, indirect ways of doing things sometimes, but they generally got there in the end. He kept his mouth shut and listened.

"We merfolk live a long time," Mela said. "The males get old and grizzled, while the females remain young in appearance. This has to do with hormones—well, no need to get technical. But Merwin had a fine charm that helped him stay young. It was a large, brilliant firewater opal that sparkled with its internal energy. We merfolk collect pretty gems and rare metals, as you may have noted; we like them for our homes and gardens. But Merwin had only this one, and he valued it above all others. He wore it on a chain about his neck.

"One day he was aloft at the surface of the sea, generating a truly fine storm with the cooperation of the clouds that were on duty then. A flying dragon came and offered to help by breathing fire and smoke and thickening the mists. But then it saw Merwin's opal and coveted it. While Merwin was concentrating on the storm, that fell dragon turned its fire on him and toasted him. We merfolk are vulnerable to fire, which is why we stay in the water. Merwin was stunned and fell senseless in the water. The dragon scooped up the firewater opal, breaking the chain that held it, and flew away to his lair somewhere on the land.

"Merwin, deprived of the protection of the gem, died. I was a widow. It was hard for me to manage after that, because a merwoman does not like to live alone. We had been building up our property so we could raise a family; our property was just about good enough, but now there could be no family. I did not want to share our estate with a strange merman, but that was academic; without the firewater opal it was not a sufficient estate to attract another merman. My only chance at recovering some share of my hopes was to recover the firewater opal, and the chance of that seemed remote indeed.

"That is why I was interested when I heard you mention the Heaven Cent. With that I might get to the opal." She shrugged. "But it was a foolish passing notion. That dragon lives on land, and I am a creature of the sea; if I went to that dragon's lair I would only get myself killed. I cannot use the Heaven Cent, because it would take me only to my death. But even as I realized this, I realized that you were a pretty boy who might do instead. The fact that you are a prince made it even better. So I captured you, and I regret it if this makes you unhappy."

"I don't want to stay here," Dolph said. "Will you let me go?"

"No."

"But I'm only a boy! I can't—do what you want."

"Oh, I am sure you can, once you mature. Your kind and mine can interbreed, and merfolk often make it with captive sailors. The storkfish brings halflings, who may choose either the land or the sea. This will take time, of course, but I will treat you well as you grow up, and I am sure you will come to like it here."

"I don't even know how to—whatever. The secret has been kept from me by the Adult Conspiracy."

She laughed. "Is that what they call it on land? We consider it to be mere discretion. I would not be concerned about it."

"Well, you're an adult," he retorted. "You already know!"

"And I will gladly show you—when the time comes. You should find it interesting."

"Never!"

She smiled tolerantly, just like an adult. They were all so smug about this! "You will see."

"But I have other things to do!" Dolph protested.

"You may do them after I am through with you," she said firmly.

"I'll escape!"

"You are welcome to try."

Dolph changed form to a fish and swam for the edge of the canopy. But as he passed outside, he began to choke. His gills couldn't handle the water!

He had to back off. He had done a little fish swimming in the past, but evidently not enough; something wasn't working.

"I had not realized that you were a form changer," Mela said. "But I see you are not an experienced one. Your body is attuned to my enchantment, so that you can breathe the water. When you try to adapt to normal fish breathing, you cannot; your magic and mine interfere with each other, and you choke."

Dolph returned to boy form. "I'll learn how!"

"Surely you will—in time. All it takes is a good deal of practice. Meanwhile, I hope to persuade you that your best interests lie with me."

Dolph doubted that she would succeed in that, but thought it best not to argue the point. "What about the Heaven Cent? You said you'd tell me one more thing about it if I came down here."

She smiled. "But you did not come here voluntarily. I am not certain that counts."

"You didn't say it had to be voluntary!"

She tilted her head, and her halo of green hair swirled around her torso. "Perhaps there is room for interpretation. Let me make you a proposition."

"Nuh-uh! That sounds mushy!"

"Not necessarily. This is merely an agreement we both shall honor. Because you are a form changer, you could be a threat to me, so that I might be concerned about sleeping in your company. That would be inconvenient. So let's agree that I will tell you the rest of what I know about the Heaven Cent, and you will not try to harm me. You will not become a swordfish and slice me up, for example. You may do anything else you wish, but you will not offer me any violence or other harm."

"I can try to breathe water and escape?"

"Yes. You just may not attack me, or try to hurt me otherwise."

The truth was that Dolph really did not want to hurt her; she was a reasonably nice person, once allowances were made for her adult nature. He just wanted to get away from her. It seemed a fair deal. Except—

"Will you also tell me how folk summon the—"

"No. Not while you are a child. You know that."

Dolph grimaced. It was infuriating the way all adults hung together; not one of them would break the Conspiracy. But he hadn't really expected to succeed. "All right. You tell me about the Heaven Cent, and I won't try to hurt you."

"Agreed." She extended her hand, and after a moment he realized that he was supposed to shake it to seal the deal. He did so. Her fingers were webbed, but her hand was marvelously soft, and she squeezed his fingers in a way that sent a small tingle through him. More magic, of course, but not really objectionable.

She moved to the fireplace. "Now I will fix you something to eat. You're a growing boy; you need good food."

Dolph didn't like the sound of that. It seemed to be another adult conspiracy: to make all children eat yucky stuff. What—?"

"Seaweed soup. Plenty of vitamins and minerals and proteins. As sure as water douses fire, a growing boy needs them."

His worst fear had just been realized! Why hadn't he thought to make that part of the deal: no yucky food! Now he was stuck with it.

As they ate the soup, she explained about the forging of the Heaven Cent. "It cannot be crafted by ordinary means; it requires a very special magic called electricity. This is used to plate the copper on it: electroplating. Only when it is done just so will it function properly. So you will need someone with that kind of magic, and time."

"Time?"

"I understand it is a very slow process. I believe it took two years to make the last one."

"Two years!"

"I agreed to tell you about the cent; I did not say you would like that information."

"Well, I agreed not to try to hurt you," Dolph said, annoyed. "I did not say I wouldn't insult you, fish-rear."

She laughed, her merriness returning. "Beautiful, Prince Dolph! We shall get along famously, as sure as sand displaces water."

"You aren't mad?" he asked, disgruntled.

"Of course not. My rear *is* fishy. But that it merely an option; I, like all my kind, can change." And abruptly her tail fuzzed, and reformed as a pair of well-fleshed human legs.

"Oh." He should have realized. "But then you can go on land. You said—"

"I said I was a creature of the sea, as indeed I am. Certainly I can go on land when I have to. But I don't like it; the weight on my feet is burdensome, and the dryness intolerable. If I went to the dragon's nest and were lucky enough to get the firewater opal, I would still have to walk back to the sea, and I doubt I could make it. No, these legs are mostly for show and for certain specialized applications; otherwise I prefer the tail." The legs fuzzed, and the tail reformed.

Dolph was almost disappointed. He seldom got a good look at bare woman legs; usually all he saw were those of nymphs as they ran away. Nymphs were great teases. It wasn't that legs were special, but that for some reason children weren't supposed to see them too close, and that of course made him curious.

Then Mela swam out to tend her estate. She had, she explained, a herd of sea cows and a sea horse, which she maintained on sea oats. Also a nice patch of sea cucumbers, which she had to protect from the mischief of sea urchins. She offered to take him out to see them, but he declined; he had had enough experiences for one day.

"Tomorrow, then," she said. "You can join me in searching the sea floor for shells and gems. Wouldn't it be nice if we found another firewater opal!"

"Would that mean that another merman would marry you?" he inquired.

"Yes, probably."

"Then you wouldn't need to keep me!"

"Oh, but I like you better," she said. "It isn't often that a girl gets to raise a genuine prince."

So much for that notion.

In the evening Mela fed him disgustingly wholesome seafood and dolphin milk, with—sure enough—slices of her homegrown sea cucumber. She put him to bed at the unreasonably early hour adults insisted on, and gave him several floating pillows that reminded him alarmingly of her bare bosom. Ugh! There was a seaweed-cloaked cubby for natural functions; the seaweed snatched the stuff away as if it were a great prize and used it for fertilizer. Dolph had hoped that Nature would not be able to find him down here, but her call came as insistently as ever. Nature was evidently another adult. Mela even provided him with a nightshirt of woven sea grass fiber. He had to admit that her garden and her care were comfortable; she was not mistreating him at all, by adult definitions. She even gave him a tasty piece of saltwater taffy, then insisted that he brush his teeth with a toothbrush she had salvaged from a sunken ship, and wash behind his ears.

As he drifted to sleep he pondered the events of the day. He was not happy about his captivity, but he had to admit that Mela's position was reasonable by her reckoning. She was simply making the best of her situation and her opportunities.

Obviously the Heaven Cent would not do her much good. He could now appreciate why she would settle for a human man. She probably didn't like it any better than the man would, but it was a way to have her family without the firewater opal. It was just his misfortune that she had captured Dolph, and planned to keep him until he became an adult.

He would just have to learn how to handle those overlapping magics, so that he could become a fish and breathe the water naturally. He hoped he could do it before Mela managed to convince him that it was better to stay with her. Already he feared that he did not have an awful lot of time.

Then, just before he slept, he remembered: the Tapestry was oriented on him. The folk at Castle Roogna would know where he was! They would rescue him! He had nothing to worry about!

Why, then, did he feel a certain tinge of disappointment?

6

SKELETON CREW

"Hang on, Dolph!" Marrow cried as the sudden gust of wind blew the boat over.

But it was too late; Dolph was pitched into the heaving sea. Marrow was unable to help him, because his skull was set inside the craft and could not see out and the craft was now capsized. All he could see, as the waves turned them around, was the flash of a fluke as the merwoman moved.

She had done this, he knew. She had summoned Fracto, who had been glad to make mischief, and now she had what she wanted. She would haul Dolph to the bottom of the sea and keep him there forever.

Marrow knew it was his responsibility, for he was Dolph's adult companion. He should have anticipated this disaster and taken precautions. If they had just crossed directly to land, the merwoman never could have interfered. If he had even told Dolph to become a sea bird or a fish, at the last moment, it would have helped. But his hollow skull had not thought fast enough, and so had come up with an empty warning. Naturally, the boy had been too distracted to think of changing form himself; the merwoman had acted with too much dispatch.

He would have to do something to help Dolph. But first, he realized, he had to help himself. He had to regain his normal form, and Grace'l had to regain hers. At the moment she could not even speak, because her teeth were locked onto his shinbone that made the bar across the boat. If she let go, she would be washed away. Fortunately, she was aware of this and kept her teeth clamped tight.

The savage winds continued to howl, and the waves did their best to smash the craft to bits. If they succeeded, both skeletons would be lost, for they could not survive dismemberment. Not in a situation like this. If it occurred on land, friends could collect the bones and put them back together, but here in the sea there were no friends and the bones would be completely scattered.

"We are in trouble," he called over the roar and splash. "Don't let go, Grace'l, until I figure out what to do. Maybe we can ride out the storm!"

But that seemed less likely with every moment that passed. Mean Fracto was concentrating on the craft, trying to buffet it apart. Fracto loved to destroy things; his reputation was notorious. Whenever rain was not wanted, Fracto would float over to bring a deluge, and whenever calm weather was needed, Fracto would be there to disturb it. Now the mean cloud had a helpless victim, and intended to demolish it completely.

In addition, the waves were washing the craft farther out to sea. Fracto intended to see that no bone got back to shore!

Neither Marrow nor Grace'l could change form until some other party booted them apart. The action of the waves wouldn't do it; it had to be a swift kick in the tailbone. If one recovered the natural form, he or she could kick the other—but how could either of them change now? There had to be someone else—and how could there be, here on the heaving surface of the ocean, here in the heart of the storm?

"You're a terrible person, Fracto!" Marrow cried in frustration. But the winds only laughed. Fracto was really enjoying himself.

Then Marrow thought of a way. His arm bones were part of the bracing of the sides of the boat, and his hand bones gripped the ends of it together, and his finger bones formed the topmost rim. If he could just raise his hollow finger—

It was a struggle, because he was not in his natural form, but he managed to lift that finger so that it stood at right angles to the rest of the rim. Now to get Fracto to do his part.

"Hey, you fuzzy cloud!" he called with his jawbones. "I am contemptuous of you! I present my finger to you!"

There were many types of magic in Xanth, and few in Mundania, but some aspects of it were so universal and fundamental that they were to be found everywhere. One of these was insult magic, especially of the simplest variety. A single elevated finger represented one of the most potent of all; anyone who saw it was immediately insulted and driven to fury. There was no practical reason for this; it was just the nature of the spell.

Fracto saw the finger and of course reacted. He blew the most horrendous gust at it, trying to destroy it. The wind was so strong that the air passed right through the finger and activated its whistle.

The sound was piercing. It struck right through the dull roar of the waves and the mixed swish of the air. It was Marrow's cry for help. He had succeeded in sounding it!

"Now all we have to do is survive until help comes," he called to Grace'l. "Just hang on."

They hung on. The angry winds continued, but were unable to do more than shove the craft farther out to sea. Fracto's rage was impressive, but inevitably it blew over; the cloud just did not have much staying power.

Then a form loomed in the air. Marrow could see only

its fleeting, vague shadow, but he knew what it was. "Chex!" he cried. "Here!"

Too late he realized that Chex would have little way to help. She was a winged centaur, and could not land on the water, and her hands could not reach to the ground. She would not be able to pick up the craft and carry it out of the storm. Had he summoned her for nothing?

Then a net slapped the water beside him. The edge of it sank, and was pulled up—and the craft was caught in it. Chex had come prepared!

Fracto howled with renewed fury, but it was too late; by the time the cloud could organize his second wind for a real blow, Chex had hauled the netful of bones into the air. At first it was too heavy for her, but she flicked it twice with her tail, and it became lighter. This was an aspect of her magic: her tail made what it flicked lose weight. When she flicked herself, she became light, so that her wings could carry her aloft; when she flicked something else, that thing became similarly light.

Stronger gusts came at them, but Chex merely used those winds to buoy her flight, and made better progress. She was not afraid to fly out to sea; she could fly wherever she wanted. Soon she left the turbulent storm behind and flew into clear air. She had rescued them.

It required some time to reach land, because they had to go around the storm, but in due course Chex settled on the beach and opened the net. "Kick me," Marrow told her. "And kick the sail."

Chex understood; she was an old friend of Marrow's. They had met when Esk brought Marrow from the gourd, and had traveled together when she went to talk with her sire, Xap, at the top of the mountain of winged monsters. She booted the side of the boat with a forehoof, then booted the fallen sail.

Marrow and Grace'l landed, reformed, almost together, Dolph's knapsack between them. "Well," Chex said, "I see you have a lady friend, and she has really nice bones."

It was of course impossible for skeletons to blush, but both Marrow and Grace'l gave it their best effort. Marrow hastily introduced skeleton to centaur and explained about their mission to find the Heaven Cent and a viable gourd for Grace'l's return. "But a merwoman abducted Dolph," he concluded. "Now we must rescue Dolph. His mother would never speak to me again if I let him be permanently lost."

"You could be correct," Chex agreed, with a quarter smile. She was a fine figure of a centaur filly, with full bare breasts, and great gray wings, and flowing brown hair and tail. Even her eyes were esthetic, being the same shade of gray as her wings, which were almost the color of bone. Marrow found that flesh was not hideous when it was where it obviously belonged.

"So we must rescue him," Dolph concluded.

"Are you sure he needs it?" Chex asked.

Both Marrow and Grace'l looked at her with surprise. "Of course he needs it!" Marrow said. "He's captive!"

"But I think not in danger."

"Of course he's in danger! Why would you think otherwise?"

"Because his mother and sister are surely keeping track of him via the Tapestry, and they will act the moment they believe he is in serious peril. Since they appear not to have acted, we can assume that he is not in peril."

Marrow had not thought of that, but it did make sense. Of course, centaurs always made more sense than other folk did. "But wouldn't they act to prevent him from remaining captive?" he asked. "Surely they don't want a prince of Xanth held forever under the sea!"

"I think they would not act quickly," Chex said. "They would prefer either to leave him in a safe place where he could not stray until he became thoroughly bored with his adventure and was quite ready to return home without complaint, or to have him make his own escape, so that he could gain necessary experience and prestige as a prince."

"Oh—and then help him if he got in trouble while trying to escape?"

"Yes. But of course he may not try."

"May not try! Why wouldn't he try?"

"Let me explain," she said in the practical manner of one who has evidently thought a matter through more thoroughly than others had. This manner was another centaur trait, the more maddening because it was usually justified. "Merwomen keep their youthful appearance much longer than do mermen, and while the men become very little interested in romance, the women retain what is said to be a very lively libido. Thus they are all too often in search of extramarital affairs of the heart. Since they are uncomfortable on land, though they do have the ability to shape legs and go ashore, they seek solace mainly from the men of the sea: sailors, fishermen, and visitors. Once one of them fixes on a particular man, she will not rest until she has him. When she does get him, she treats him very well. They are highly proficient in the arts that please men. Indeed, it is said that there is hardly a better fate than for a man to be captured by one of these, and that many reported drownings are nothing of the kind; the man simply does not want to leave his lover in the sea. Now, since you know that Prince Dolph was taken by such a creature, how can you be sure he is not quite satisfied to remain where he is?"

"He is only nine years old," Marrow said succinctly.

"Merwomen are kind to children, too; many wilderness nymphs are. Children have been known to mature surprisingly quickly, in the company of such creatures. In the interim, she could give him many things he likes, such as toys and candy and uncritical attention. She could show him a side of the female persuasion that he has not before appreciated. No, children are not immune to such blandishments; they are more receptive to them than are adults."

"But Dolph was on a mission!" Marrow protested. "He was in quest of the Heaven Cent!"

"The what?" she inquired, frowning.

Marrow explained about the cent. "So you see, he would not want to leave that unfinished."

"I suppose that's true," Chex agreed, not entirely pleased to have had to learn something from a noncentaur person. "So he should have motivation to continue his search. Perhaps it would be best simply to wait and see what happens."

Marrow pondered. His hollow skull was ill-equipped to debate policy with the sharp mind of a centaur, yet he was not satisfied to accept her suggestion. Why wasn't he?

Finally he got it straight. "I don't think so. I must go to rescue Dolph."

Chex arched an eyebrow at him. "Oh? Why?"

"Because he is a child, and is not expected to make mature judgments on things. I am his adult companion; it is my job to provide the judgment he lacks. If he does not have the sense to try to escape from the merwoman, I must exercise that sense for him. Otherwise there is no point in my presence."

"Even if he does not want to escape?"

"Especially if he does not want to escape! That would mean the merwoman has corrupted him, and it is my duty to counter that corruption. When he is an adult, he may stay with a merwoman if he wants to, but as a child this an option I must deny him."

Chex looked at Grace'l, who had not said a word during this discussion. "How do you feel about it?"

"It is not my business to interfere," Grace'l said. "I am only along until we find a gourd, so I can go home."

"As it happens, I saw a gourd as we were coming in for a landing here," Chex said. "It should be quite close; let me check." She spread her wings, flicked herself with her tail, and took off.

Marrow had mixed emotions. This was a rare experience, for skeletons were not phenomenally emotional, and seldom had more than one emotion at a time. On the one bone hand, he was glad that Grace'l would have her wish; on the other, he would have liked to have her company longer. He had not been aware of how much he missed the companionship of his own kind until he met her.

"How are you going to rescue Dolph?" Grace'l inquired.

"I had not thought about that. I suppose I shall have to walk under the sea and search for the merwoman's lair, and take him out."

"That may not be easy."

"I must at least make the effort."

She nodded. She seemed to be thinking her own hollow thoughts.

Soon Chex returned. "Yes, I found it. We can reach it very quickly. At least one problem can be readily solved."

"No," Grace'l said.

"What?" Marrow asked.

"I have changed my mind. I will take another gourd home."

"Why?" Chex asked.

"Because if Marrow is responsible for Prince Dolph, then I am responsible too. They were helping me look for a gourd, and I was helping them look for the Heaven Cent. I was part of the craft on the water that let Dolph get captured by the merwoman. I must at least help rescue Dolph, so that he can continue his mission. Then I can return to my realm."

"So the two of you are going to attempt to rescue Dolph, no matter what I say?" Chex asked.

"Yes," Marrow said, and Grace'l nodded agreement.

Chex smiled. "I am glad to hear it. Let me help you plan the rescue."

"But you are against the rescue!" Marrow protested.

Chex laughed. "Hardly! There was no way I was going to let Prince Dolph remain in the clutches of that merwoman."

"But you argued—"

"The other side. Of course. It is always best to be conversant with both sides of an issue before taking action. It was also important that I ascertain the extent of your commitment to the rescue, as it may be difficult and will require close coordination."

Marrow's skull seemed filled with fuzz. "You have no obligation to rescue Dolph! You came to rescue me!"

"I know the royal family," Chex said. "I took Princess Ivy on a trip to Centaur Isle, not long after I met you. I became responsible for helping Dolph the moment I learned about his predicament. I am sure that one reason his parents delayed their action was because they knew I was on the way. I suspect they are watching us now, via the Tapestry, to be sure that we are not leaving Dolph to his fate."

Marrow realized that was true. If the Tapestry had been oriented on Dolph before, it must still be watching him, and another part of it would be watching Marrow. Queen Irene had not expected Dolph to get beyond the Good Magician's castle, but had insisted on an adult companion, just in case. That "in case" had happened. Now she was surely keeping nervous track, just in case worse happened. She was trying to allow her son as much freedom and adventure as he was competent to handle, and not half a whit more.

"But you said the Queen would not rescue Dolph unless he was in real danger," Grace'l said.

"She would naturally prefer him to make his own escape, in the princely way," Chex said. "But failing that, she would want him rescued by his friends. If that also failed, then she would have to take action and make the King do something. Certainly she will not let him be lost to a mer-woman. The fact that she has not yet taken action only means that Dolph is in no immediate danger; that allows time for him or the rest of us to do something."

Marrow thought about Queen Irene. He concluded that Chex was right. That was the way the Queen operated. She would stay in the background if she could, just as she did when King Dor was making policy, but she would see that things worked out. It would be better to make sure that she never had to act.

"We had better get started, then," he said. "What was wrong with my prior plan?"

"I did not criticize it," Chex protested.

"But you are a centaur. Your analytical mind criticizes everything."

"True. But I did not hear it, so I could not have critiqued it."

Now he remembered: he had mentioned his plan to Grace'l while Chex was looking for the gourd. "I intend to walk under the sea, search for the merwoman's lair, and take Dolph out. What is wrong with that?"

"Everything!" the centaur exclaimed. "First, your walk under the sea will be very slow, because of the resistance of the water. Second, it will take you forever to locate the merwoman's lair, because it could be anywhere in this vicinity of the sea. Third, if you do locate it, the merwoman will surely see you coming and will act to prevent you from approaching. She would send dogfish against you to chew your bones, or a kraken to pull them asunder. Fourth, if you did reach her lair, you would not be able to take Dolph from it without drowning him, because merfolk have water-breathing magic that operates only in their presence or in their lairs. Fifth, if you managed to get around that, he still might not want to go, and might refuse to go with you. You could not make him go against his will, because he would change into some monstrous form you could not budge. Thus your effort would be doomed."

Marrow pondered. Those seemed like pretty good objections. But he knew how to get around them. "How can we counter these things?" For a centaur seldom posed questions to which that centaur did not already know the answers. That quality derived from their generations of experience as tutors.

"I'm so glad you asked," Chex said with a half smile. "The first and second problems may be tackled together. You must locate the lair from above the water, then descend quickly to it. That also minimizes the third problem, because it provides the merwoman very little time to spot you or to act against you. You can alleviate the fourth problem by taking air down with you, for Dolph to breathe. I believe there should be some air plants growing in this area; one or two of them should do nicely. The fifth problem will depend on your verbal skills: you may have to persuade Dolph to leave. I hope you are up to it."

"I think you would be better at that," Marrow said.

"Indubitably. But I cannot go below the water. The pressure of the deep water would crush me, if I were able to get down there at all. Only you, with your tough bare bones, can do it."

"How can we locate the lair?" Grace'l asked.

"I thought I might fly over the water, as the weather clears, and see what I can see. Certainly I can carry you to the site, if we locate it."

"I got a look at that water, when we capsized," Grace'l said. "Even below the roiling surface, it was dark; I could not see to the bottom."

Chex nodded. "I am afraid I had not thought that aspect through. Certainly the merwoman would not have her lair in any obvious place, anyway; she would adapt a cave or use other concealment. We shall have to devise some other way."

Marrow picked up Dolph's knapsack. "Maybe the magic mirror will help."

"You have a magic mirror?" Chex asked. "That should be just what we need!"

Marrow brought out the little hand mirror. "I am not sure. Few mirrors can actually locate things; they must communicate with known sites."

"That is true," Chex said. "But it is my thought that with this one we can communicate with Castle Roogna, where they will know Dolph's location—" She broke off.

"And they won't want to get involved," Marrow concluded, remembering. "Because they want Dolph to make his own escape, or at least to have his friends help him. Still, we might look at the Tapestry."

He directed the mirror to tune in on Castle Roogna. Sure enough, there was the Tapestry, and there was Dolph with the merwoman. They were eating a meal, and by the distasteful expression on the boy's face, it was a nutritious one. She was evidently not plying him with sea candy, which might be a tactical error on her part.

"How pretty!" Grace'l exclaimed, noting the colored stones and circles of gold. "She has excellent taste."

Marrow's gaze was on the merwoman. He had not seen her at all well during the storm, but now it was clear that she was as robustly endowed as Vida Vila. Were he a mortal man, he would be quite impressed. Dolph was a child, but it might not be wise to leave him too long to the blandishments of such a creature. It had been evident that Vida Vila was beginning to make an impression on him, and the merwoman seemed to have similar potential.

"That is under a canopy," Chex said. "See, the sea trees arch up to close overhead. That lair will be invisible from above, even if the water is absolutely clear."

"And there seem to be no hints as to its location," Grace'l said. "We shall have to find another way."

Chex considered. "Perhaps we could use one of the local plants to help us orient. If there is some witch hazel—"

"But we can't speak the language of plants," Marrow protested.

"Even so, we can learn something from them. If we give the witch hazel something of Prince Dolph's to smell, its leaves will orient on him, and we can tell the direction from that."

"How clever!" Grace'l exclaimed. "But how can we tell how far in that direction the lair is?"

Chex glanced appreciatively at her. "I can tell you weren't constructed yesterday. We shall have to find two witch hazels, set some distance apart, and use the generalized magic of triangulation to find the distance."

Marrow knew of that. Triangulation was another fundamental type of magic that was said to extend even to Mundania, in the manner of insult magic or rainbows. It was odd how some magic was everywhere, and some was only in Xanth; the rules seemed to be inconsistent.

They explored the region, and finally managed to find a witch hazel plant. They gave it the pack to sniff, and sure enough, soon its leaves twisted about to orient toward the sea, as if the sun were shining from that region. Marrow drew a line in the dirt and sand, showing the direction.

Then they looked for another witch hazel plant—and could not find it. They searched both north and south, as far as was feasible: no other plants. This was most frustrating. Was their effort to founder on this mischance?

They looked in the mirror again, as darkness closed, and saw that Dolph was still being well treated. The merwoman had made him a floating bed of pillows, and he was sleeping comfortably among them. At least they knew that he wasn't in any immediate trouble—but that itself was another kind of trouble, because it would make him increasingly satisfied to remain with the merwoman. He was at an impressionable age.

"We shall simply have to resume our search in the morning," Chex said unhappily. "I had hoped to handle this more expeditiously."

"What else have you to do?" Grace'l inquired.

"The Monsters of the Air are going to have a ceremony atop Mount Rushmost, and I don't want to be late."

"Isn't Prince Dolph's welfare more important than a ceremony?" Marrow inquired.

"Yes, of course it is," she replied, flushing passingly. The color passed across her face and breasts and disappeared into her equine hide, like a cloud casting its shadow briefly across the landscape. "Still, I hope we can effect the rescue in the morning."

Chex foraged for some fruit, while the two skeletons simply lay on the ground, needing no food. They did not need rest either, but since Chex did, it seemed only courteous to do it.

The centaur slept on her feet, her wings furled, one ear cocked to the wind. Obviously no one would sneak up on her during the night.

Then it occurred to Marrow that he could put the nocturnal hours to better use by searching for that second witch hazel plant. So he lifted his bones quietly—and discovered

Grace'l doing the same thing. She had had the same thought!

Wordlessly they separated, searching north and south. They could see fairly well in the dark, because they did not use inefficient living eyeballs.

As dawn approached, Marrow returned, having found nothing. Soon Grace'l appeared. She touched his arm bone and tapped once: she had found something! Then they both lay down in the places they had left, so as to be there undisturbed when Chex woke.

In due course she stirred. She plucked some more fruit, ate it, attended to the other natural functions that living creatures were afflicted with, and was ready to resume the search. "There must be something!" she said.

"Perhaps there is," Grace'l said. "Does the second plant have to be a witch hazel?"

"Well, we do need two plants, or the triangulation magic doesn't work. I'm not sure what else—"

"Would an arrowroot do?"

"Why yes, it would! But I didn't see any of them, either."

"I seem to remember seeing one," Grace'l said. "Perhaps I am mistaken."

That was possible, Marrow realized. She had not been in this realm long, and would not know all the plants. Yet there was vegetation in the gourd realm too, and arrowroot was part of it; they used the arrows for barbs in bad dreams.

They followed her to the plant, and it was an arrowroot. They let it smell the knapsack, then waited while its roots adjusted. One arrowhead poked out of the ground, pointing the direction. They had their second line!

They extended the two lines to the water, and judged where they intersected. That would be where the lair was, under the water. They had the location; now all they needed was the air plant. It took only a moment to fetch that.

"Remember, I cannot help you once you enter the water," Chex warned them. "I will watch you via the mirror, so that I know when to haul you up, but if anything goes wrong, I cannot come after you."

"We can handle it," Marrow said, hoping that was the case. If the merwoman sent big fish to haul them away, their whole plan would be in trouble. But what else was there to do but try?

He and Grace'l climbed into the net, and Chex tucked the mirror into the top of her mane where she could recover it readily. Then she flicked the net with her tail, making it lighter. She grasped the ends of the net in both hands, flicked herself, spread her wings, and took off. She had to struggle to carry them, but there was reason for not making them lighter.

She carried them to the spot where the two lines crossed. She hovered while Marrow and Grace'l climbed out of the net and dropped into the water. Then she winged back to the beach. She would gather some heavy rocks there, that she could use to weight the net and carry it to the bottom, when it was time to pick them up.

Marrow and Grace'l held bone hands as they plunged down. When they had been in the form of a boat and sail, they had floated, because a boat was designed to float, even when capsized. Now they were in normal form, and that did not float. Had Chex flicked them with her tail to make them lighter, they would have floated, and that would have been no good for this. As it was, they were slowed somewhat by the buoyant air plant.

Marrow watched nervously for big fish but saw none. Would they catch the merwoman by surprise? That would be wonderful! But it was as likely that she was merely preparing worse things for them below.

They reached thick seaweed growing at the bottom, and sank through it. Now they were in a forest of the stuff, with sea trees, sea bushes, and sea grass. It could almost be taken for a landside jungle or a setting in the gourd, except for the small fish swimming through it.

They peered around, not bothered by the darkness here any more than by that of night, and in a moment spotted the canopy of the merwoman's lair. The directions had been true, and now they could rescue Dolph—if the merwoman did not stop them.

Grace'l stayed back, and Marrow stepped through the wall, braced for anything. If anything happened to him, she would try to escape. She might be able to accomplish what he could not, if the merwoman did not know of her presence. That was the remainder of the plan. She had the air plant, so that once Marrow knew it was all right, they could get Dolph to the surface without drowning him.

There was the merwoman, hovering without moving. She was staring at something on the sea floor, and she did not even look up as Marrow entered. This was very strange!

Then he saw what she was staring at. It was a hypnogourd! No wonder she did not react to him; no mortal creature reacted to anything, as long as he or she was staring into the peephole of a gourd. Only the gourd folk themselves were immune, because the gourd was their natural habitat. They did not stare into the gourd, they entered it.

But where was Dolph? He was nowhere to be seen. How could he be rescued, if—?

"The gourd!" Grace'l exclaimed, peeking in from beyond. "He is the gourd!"

Of course! How clever of the boy! He had nullified the merwoman by immobilizing her with a gourd.

All they had to do was haul the gourd up to the surface in the net, and it would be done. This was turning out much better than anticipated.

Marrow picked up the gourd, which was halfway floating anyway. But in so doing he made a fatal mistake. His action broke the contact of the merwoman's eye with the peephole.

Suddenly she was alert again. "What's this?" she demanded.

The gourd changed to Dolph. "Mela, meet Marrow Bones," he said. "Marrow, meet Mela Merwoman. Marrow is here to rescue me."

"But I never saw him come in!" Mela exclaimed. "How did he do that?"

"I did it," Dolph said. "I assumed the form of a hypnogourd, so that you could not stop him."

"But you promised not to harm me!"

"I didn't harm you. I only held you for a while, so that I could escape. That's fair, isn't it?"

"No, that isn't fair!" she retorted. "Sure as fire melts sand, it isn't!"

"But I never touched you! I am only escaping."

"All my hopes of having a family again depend on you," she said tearfully. Marrow was not sure how a person could have tears underwater, but she was doing it. That filled him with alarm, for tears were a notorious device used by women against men. Was Dolph young enough to withstand it?

"But you can have a family with someone else," Dolph protested.

"No I can't," she insisted. "It was sheer, sheer luck that I captured you, and it will never happen again in a hundred years! And I can't marry a merman either; I told you about that. All I can do is keep you until you grow up, and then I can have a nice family. You are hurting me by escaping!"

"What does that matter?" Marrow asked. "Prince Dolph has other business. He has a Quest."

"All my hopes, so cruelly dashed to pieces!" she wailed, the tears flowing more copiously.

Dolph looked increasingly uncomfortable. "I *am* hurting her," he muttered. "I promised not to do that."

"But she is hurting you by holding you captive!" Marrow argued. Chex' warning was fresh in his mind: that he might have to persuade the boy to leave. How true, how true!

"She has been very nice to me, really," Dolph said. "She has promised me all the pretty stones I want, and said I could ride her sea horse, and when I get old enough she'll even tell me the secret of summoning the stork. It's pretty nice down here, and she's really pretty, too. I don't want to hurt her."

"Thank you," Mela said, looking pained.

Marrow realized that he was losing the contest. The mer-woman had already made too much of an impression on the boy, despite feeding him nutritious food. He would have to make some kind of deal with her. But what could it be, when all she wanted was a man to make a family with, in due course?

"Why can't she marry a merman?" Grace'l asked, stepping in. There really was no further point in her remaining hidden.

"Because she has no firewater opal," Dolph explained.

"No what?" Marrow asked.

"Her husband had a precious gem, but a dragon killed him and took it, and without it her estate isn't worth enough to interest another merman," Dolph explained. "So she needs me instead, and I guess it would be wrong for me to leave her."

Mela smiled at Dolph, and he smiled back. Marrow knew that he had to do something right away, for the mer-woman's magic was taking hold already. There seemed to be a spell that fleshly females cast over fleshly males, despite the males' best efforts to escape. He had hoped Dolph was young enough to be immune, but it seemed he was only partially immune. That was unfortunate.

"Maybe if she got that gem back . . ." Grace'l suggested.

The merwoman's gaze snapped up. "Back?"

Marrow grasped that opening. "Suppose you recovered the firewater opal?" he asked. "Then you would not have to keep Dolph, for you could catch a merman."

"Why, yes, that is true," Mela said. "But I cannot go that far on land. I am not used to using legs that much." Her tail became a pair of quite well-formed bare human legs.

"Yes, you can't," Dolph agreed, staring at the legs as they scissored smoothly in the water.

"But *we* could," Marrow said. "We could fetch it back for you, because we are comfortable on land."

Mela's mouth watered. "*Would* you? Oh, how wonderful

that would be! But the dragon is so fierce—"

"Prince Dolph is a form changer. He can become a larger dragon and make the other dragon give it up. Then we can return it to you, and you won't need Dolph anymore."

"But—" Dolph said, still watching the legs.

"But it would be a challenge for a hero," Marrow said quickly. "A real adventure! Everyone would be impressed."

"Say, yeah," Dolph agreed.

"And then you could continue on your Quest to find the Good Magician Humfrey," Marrow added.

"Yes!" Dolph agreed, remembering his adventure. Then his eye caught another flexing of the merwoman's legs. "Still—"

"By all means, you must follow up your Quest!" Mela said, her legs converting back into the tail. "If you can't recover the firewater opal, then you can return to me." It was evident that she really preferred the gem, if she could have it.

"But how could you be sure I would return?" Dolph asked. "I mean, I might just keep the opal and go home."

"This is not the princely way," Marrow said quickly. "A prince has honor. He always does what he says he will do."

"Oh," Dolph said. Marrow realized that he was not totally committed to the notion of escaping the clutches of the merwoman. "But I haven't learned about honor yet, so—"

"You haven't?" Mela said, frowning. "You mean your word not to hurt me was not good? Had I but known—"

"Oh, no, I wouldn't hurt you!" Dolph protested, glancing where he seemed to hope her legs would reappear. "But—"

"Then it seems I do need a guarantee. Maybe this is not such a good idea!"

Ouch! It was falling apart, just when he had it put together! Marrow struggled to get another good notion in his skull.

"A hostage," Grace'l said. "You must leave a hostage, to guarantee your return."

"But we have no one to do that!" Marrow protested.

"Yes we do," Grace'l said. "I will serve as hostage. You won't need me on the visit to the dragon."

"But would Dolph come back for you?" Mela asked doubtfully.

"Not Dolph, perhaps," Grace'l said. "But—" she glanced at Marrow.

"Of course I would come back for you!" Marrow said, more vehemently than he would have thought

"I thought you might," Grace'l said.

The merwoman considered. "Yes, he might. Certainly it's worth the gamble. Very well; I'll accept you as a hostage. But if you try to escape, I'll turn loose my pack of dogfish."

"I won't try to escape. I don't know my way around this realm."

So it was agreed. Mela told them where the dragon was reported to reside. They agreed to leave the magic mirror with Grace'l so that she and the merwoman could watch their progress. The mirror could not locate an unknown thing, but it could follow a particular person if tuned to that person at the outset. Marrow took the air plant and guided Dolph out to where the weighted net came down. They emptied out its cargo of stones and climbed in. It rose through the water, being lifted as Chex flew higher in the sky.

They emerged from the choppy waves and swung into the air. Marrow knew that it was hard for Chex to carry their weight, for Dolph was more solid than Grace'l despite his youth, but she could not get low enough to flick them with her tail. Marrow could have jumped out and walked to land on the bottom, but this would have taken time, and Dolph would have been left alone for that period. So they swung just over the water, their arcs just brushing the waves.

They swung to shore and climbed out of the net. Chex came down, her bosom heaving. "That was—(pant)—a job!" she said. "But where's Grace'l?"

Marrow explained about the deal and the hostage. She

arched an eyebrow but did not object. She turned over the mirror, so that they could drop it in the sea for Grace'l and Mela. "I would stay with you longer, but I really must get to that ceremony," she said. "Just be very careful when dealing with that dragon; they aren't all ignorant brutes, you know. In fact, some winged monsters can be quite intelligent. I'm one myself."

Dolph laughed, thinking that a joke; obviously he did not think of the lovely flying centaur filly as a monster.

"We shall exercise due caution," Marrow assured her. He did not relish the prospect of confronting a dragon, regardless of the creature's intellect, but it was better than leaving Dolph to the wiles of the merwoman. Even now, the boy was casting glances back toward the sea, as if regretting leaving it. That had been too close a call; he could only hope that they did not encounter any more predatory females on this Quest!

"Well, I wish you the best," Chex said. She spread her wings, flicked herself, and took off, leaving the net behind. Marrow wondered what ceremony it was that she was so eager to attend there at Mount Rushmost with the winged monsters. Well, it really was not his business. His business was to get Prince Dolph through this Quest unscathed.

Mela showed up soon thereafter, sitting in the bubbling surf. Marrow gave her the mirror and talked to her, getting the details straight.

7

DRACO

Dolph watched Chex Centaur disappear in the distant sky. He had known that she was Marrow's friend but had not realized that she would come to help him. She had enabled Marrow to rescue Dolph, which was lucky for him.

He turned his gaze to the sea as the merwoman swam away. It was true that he needed to get on with his Quest; yet Mela had been sort of nice. If—

"We must plan our campaign," Marrow said briskly, interrupting Dolph's thought. "According to the merwoman, it was Draco Dragon who killed her husband and stole the firewater opal, and he resides at Mount Etamin, which is one of a constellation of peaks in dragon country, near the Region of Air. Chex inherited some knowledge of geography from her dam, Chem, and says we should be able to recognize it from above; the range is in the form of a giant dragon."

Dolph had not been paying very good attention to the skeleton's discussions with Mela or Chex, having been dis-

tracted by the merwoman's legs. He had never really noticed legs before, but each time he saw these he found them
oddly interesting. In fact—

"So you must assume the form of a roc and carry me
northeast to the Region of Air, where we shall survey the
situation. The sooner we get there, the sooner we can recover the opal and exchange it for Grace'l."

"I wonder what it is about her limbs," Dolph mused.

"Well, she does have nice bones," Marrow said. "Very
nice bones, in fact. But this is not the time to think about
Grace'l; it is the time to get moving."

Dolph had not been thinking about Grace'l's limbs, but
he decided not to clarify that. He became the roc, picked
up the skeleton, and took off for the northwest. Marrow
hastily grabbed Dolph's knapsack; the skeleton was good
at remembering such details. Perhaps it was because there
was extra room for memories in that hollow skull.

This time he flew more strongly, because of the practice
he had had in this form before. He could assume any living
form, and assume the attributes of that form, including its
language and special talents, but it did take practice to use
them effectively. He knew that each time he became the
roc he would be better at it, though he would never be as
good at it as the natural rocs were. He tended to specialize
for this reason; it was no use being bad at a hundred kinds
of creature, when he could be adequate at a dozen or good
at three. It was part of his talent that he also retained his
human awareness, no matter what sized creature he became, or what type—even a plant, even a hypnogourd!—
or how long he held that form. But he had not yet decided
which forms were best for specialization. He liked the ogre
for land, because no creature in its right mind bothered an
ogre, and the roc for the air, for similar reason, but he
hadn't figured out a good water form. Maybe a merman;
then he could—

"There's the Gap Chasm!" Marrow exclaimed.

Dolph restrained a shiver of annoyance. How did the
skeleton manage to interrupt a line of thought every time

it got interesting? He peered down. Sure enough, there was the great jagged cleft that traversed the Land of Xanth, separating the top half from the bottom half. Dolph understood that for many years it had appeared on no maps— and still appeared on no Mundane maps, not that that mattered—because there had been a powerful Forget Spell on it. His father Dor had detonated that spell some eight hundred and twenty-seven years ago, give or take a few decades, and since that time no one had been able to remember the chasm when away from it, until the Time of No Magic had severely weakened the Forget Spell. Then it had begun breaking up, and little whorls of it had spun off and made mischief, because anyone caught by one forgot everything. Finally the whorls had cleared, and the only remaining effect was Ivy's pet dragon, Stanley Steamer, who had once been the dread Gap Dragon, and would be again when he got ready. How did Ivy rate? Dolph had never had a pet dragon! Girls got all the good things, because folk thought they were cute and sweet. They ought to ask brothers about that! Girls were neither cute nor sweet, they were pains. Except maybe for some of the non-human ones, like—

"Keep alert," Marrow warned. "We are now passing over dragon country."

Dolph grabbed for the fleeting thought but missed it, and it was gone. Once again the skeleton had interrupted something that promised to get interesting. Adults had a definite talent for that. It seemed to be part of the Adult Conspiracy. What was the big secret about summoning the stork? If only he could figure that out, and be free of adult restrictions—

"Dragon at three o'clock," Marrow announced.

He was right. Dolph took evasive action, climbing above dragon altitude. The best way to handle dragons was to avoid them. If Dolph had had a choice, he would have avoided Draco too. But responsibilities had a way of cropping up and taking over, when adults were involved. It was too bad.

Soon they spied the mountains. A roc flying at cruising velocity covered territory in a hurry! The range looked like a huge mundane bear.

"No, that's the wrong range," Marrow said. "That's a bear named Ursa, who is chasing the dragon range. Just ahead of it we should see the tail of—there it is, at eleven o'clock!"

Dolph really didn't know what the skeleton meant by the o'clocks; there was a huge time-keeping mechanism in the gourd that enabled the night mares to deliver their bad dreams precisely when required, but as far as he knew that had nothing to do with mountains. But ahead and slightly to the left he saw the tail of the mountain range. He swerved to follow it.

It went for several peaks, then curved to the right for several more. At peak number eight it made an abrupt turn left, and then another, heading up into the raised head of the dragon, formed by four peaks. "The tip of the nose is Mount Etamin . . ." Marrow began.

Mount Eat-amin, Dolph thought. But it didn't look very tasty. In fact it looked quite unfriendly.

"But we had better land a bit apart from it, so the dragon won't know we're coming," the skeleton concluded.

Good idea! Dolph made a descending spiral, and touched ground in a field some distance beyond the mountain. There was a cross wind, but he was improving at landings, too, and did not bump too badly.

He returned to his normal form and stood naked. It was cool here, but he didn't grab for his knapsack, which Marrow now wore, because he expected to assume his ogre form in a moment. "How should I tackle him?" he asked. "He can't be too big, since he's a flying dragon."

"But he's a firedrake," Marrow said. "That suggests two difficulties: he breathes fire, and he lives in a cave. If you brace him in the air, he'll be more maneuverable than you, and may scorch you before you get started. But if you brace him in the cave, your size will be limited, and the terrain will be familiar to him and not to you. That could be bad."

Dolph nodded. Suddenly it came home to him that this was serious business! He had never actually fought a dragon before, and he knew they were dangerous. "But maybe I can bluff him out," he said.

"I hope so. But it will be better if he is absent from the nest, so that we don't have to face him at all."

"That's right," Dolph said, realizing. "I don't have to fight him, I just have to get the firewater opal. But how do we know whether's he's in the nest?"

"We may have to wait and watch, and if we see him leave, then we'll know. The accounts say he is a solitary dragon, which means there should be no nestmate to guard the nest during his absence."

"Good idea!" Dolph exclaimed, relieved.

They walked quietly toward Mt. Etamin, guided by its icy pinnacle, which sparkled like a star above the forest. They watched the sky constantly to see whether the dragon either departed or arrived. All was quiet; even the birds avoided this region. No large animals were in evidence; here and there scorched foliage suggested where one might have been toasted by the dragon. Small animals were abundant, because they were not hunted by the dragon, and those who did hunt them had been eaten by the dragon. Draco was evidently an efficient hunter, and that did not make Dolph feel easy.

They came to the base of the mountain. This was a steep slope, scorched bare of vegetation, clifflike in its extent. Some distance up Dolph saw the cave that was the entrance to the dragon's lair. It was not as large as he had expected; was this the wrong cave, belonging to a smaller dragon?

But Marrow seemed certain this was it, so Dolph did not ask. He became a small bird of uncertain species and perched on Marrow's shoulder, watching that cave. They waited silently for an hour, as the sun dropped slowly in the sky. It was important that they keep quiet, for if they made noise and the dragon heard it, the element of surprise would be gone.

In the second hour Dolph's attention weakened, and he

snoozed. He knew, however, that the skeleton would maintain the watch, since he needed no sleep and had little imagination. This was a time when it was a great advantage to be boneheaded.

Marrow moved his shoulder slightly, waking Dolph. For a moment Dolph could not remember where he was. Then he saw the dragon sailing up from the cave. Draco was leaving!

They had waited and won! It was now dusk, and evidently the dragon was going out to hunt for his supper. Dolph would have been getting sleepy by this time, but his snooze invigorated him; he was ready to act now.

"We must try to get in, get the firewater opal, and get away before Draco returns," Marrow said. "It will be dark in there, so perhaps you should assume a lighted form that I can carry in."

That made so much sense that Dolph changed immediately to a glowworm. Marrow picked him up and set him in his left eye socket where his tender body was protected. Then the skeleton stashed the knapsack in the esthetic crook of a small symme tree and walked swiftly to the base of the cliff.

"Uh, I fear . . ." Marrow began.

Dolph couldn't speak human language in this form, so he waited. What was Marrow's problem?

". . . I will need your help for a moment," the skeleton concluded. "This wall is sheer, and too steep for me to climb. Perhaps if you assume bird form—" He paused, reconsidering. "No, you could not be large enough to carry me up, yet small enough to land within that aperture."

Dolph realized that a living human brain was needed. He crawled out of Marrow's socket, dropped to the ground, and converted to human form on the way. "Maybe I could turn ogre, and throw you up there."

"Excellent notion!" Marrow exclaimed.

In a moment it was done. The ogre hurled the skeleton up, then became a small bird and flew up, then turned glowworm again and got back into the eye socket. They were navigating hurdles more readily than before!

Marrow crawled on knucklebones and kneecaps into the cave, Dolph's green light shining ahead. There was just room to pass this way. The walls of the cave were fairly smooth; the dragon must have polished them to prevent any sharp edge from scraping a scale.

Before long the tunnel widened into a regular cave, with stalactites pointing down from the ceiling like—naturally!— dragon's teeth. Some of them even dripped saliva. But stone saliva was not poisonous, Dolph trusted.

Then the cave ended in a black pool.

"This is odd," Marrow said. "Dragons normally have comfortable nests lined with jewels. A water dragon might sleep in a pool, but Draco is a flying dragon, and a fire-breather. This does not seem right. Yet we saw him departing from this cave, and I found no alternate passage. I cannot explain this."

It was time for a living human brain again. Dolph retained his human consciousness in the worm form, but heavy thinking was beyond it. He crawled out and changed. There was room for them both, here, though their toes were in the water and they could not stand.

It was completely black in the cave, and Dolph could not see a thing. But there really was little to see; just the water below and the stalactites above. He could remember those readily enough. At the moment all he needed was his brain.

"If Draco came from this cave, I can think of three reasons," he said, as that brain began to operate. "Maybe he was just visiting, looking for something to eat in here."

"This cave is empty; he would know that," Marrow responded. "In any event, he would not have waited several hours before emerging, unless he was eating something— and there are no bones here."

"They might be at the bottom of the pool," Dolph pointed out.

"True," Marrow agreed, this notion new to him. "So maybe this is the wrong cave."

"Maybe not," Dolph said, his brain percolating. "It could be that he has a spell to let him rest on the water without getting wet. Then he can bring his food in here and eat it, and let the bones sink down below."

"But then where is the firewater opal?"

That was a good question. "Then maybe the third reason is the right one," Dolph said, his brain getting really warmed up. "Maybe this is not the end of the tunnel. Maybe it goes through the water."

"But firedrakes don't go through water!" Marrow protested.

"How do we know that? Maybe they can, only not when we're watching."

"That is true; we should see whether the tunnel continues under the water."

Dolph did not want to be the glowworm for underwater travel; the water would quickly put out the glow. "Maybe I can be a fish."

"I suspect—" Marrow began.

"Or whatever you suggest."

"—that an armored fish would be better," the skeleton concluded.

"Um. Yes. No telling what might be in that water." He considered, but could not think of an armored fish. "*Are* there such things?"

"There are in the gourd. They are fossils, like me and Grace'l. We know them only in their skeletal form, of course, but you could become a living one. Or maybe an armored arthropod."

"Who?"

"A lobster or horseshoe crab, or—try a trilobite. Maybe you'll like it."

"A trilobyte?"

"I suppose that would be satisfactory. That species might have more memory or intelligence than the original."

So Dolph put his feet in the water and became a trilobyte. This turned out to be a flat armored thing like a fish with trailing spines on its head, and two mouth tentacles. It was a pretty interesting creature, and seemed able to take care of itself. It had no trouble swimming in the dark water.

Marrow waded in, needing no change of form for this. He simply dropped to the bottom and walked.

The tunnel did continue under the water. There was dragon scent that Dolph's arthropod senses readily picked up, marking a channel deeper into the mountain. He led, swimming slowly near the bottom, while Marrow forged after. He had never been an arthropod before, whatever it was, but he found he liked this form; for one thing, he was having no trouble breathing the water. Not that he should, but after his experience with Mela, and the way her enchantment interfered with his water breathing, he had been a bit nervous.

Suddenly a host of little fish swarmed in. They circled Dolph and Marrow, eying them. Then the leader of the pack nudged his snout close to Dolph's antennae and demanded in fish talk: "Who art thou, roach-face? I recognize not thy shield of arms."

Dolph was not a fish, so he found it difficult to understand the words, but he got the essence. There was something about the fish's attitude that annoyed him. Therefore he responded more gruffly than he might have. "Get out of my face before I chomp you, fish-eye."

"Only dragons pass here unchallenged, bug-brain," the fish asserted. "I demand of thee again, show thy colors."

"Perhaps—" Marrow began.

"The only color I'll show you is the color of my teeth, fin-foot!" Dolph exclaimed angrily. Then he realized that in this form he didn't exactly have teeth. But he did have an armored mouth, and that was good enough.

The fish swelled up to its full diminutive size. "Know, O miscreant, that thou hast affronted Perrin Piranha, terror of the cave waters! Now shalt thou discover the consequence of thy folly."

"—we should humor them," the skeleton concluded, a bit late. "There is no point in antagonizing natives unnecessarily."

Perrin and his fellow piranhas charged. They swarmed in around both Dolph and Marrow, their big mouths gaping. They chomped whatever they reached.

But Dolph was thoroughly armored, and Marrow was all bone. Dogfish liked to chew bones, and had tough teeth for it, but these were not dogfish. "Ouch!" Perrin cried as he dented a tooth on one of Dolph's head spines. "Oooo!" others wailed as they crunched on Marrow's shins.

Dolph had a number of legs near his face. He used them to grab Perrin. "Now it is our turn," he said, hauling the struggling fish up to his chitinous mouth. "Where would you like me to take the first bite: head or tail?"

He had hoped to cow the obnoxious fish. He was disappointed. "Go ahead, bite my head off, varlet!" Perrin said boldly. "Thou shallst have no satisfaction of me! I spit on thy snoot!" And indeed he did spit, though it was ineffective in the water.

Dolph was young, and had not had a great deal of experience in life. But he had spent many, many hours watching the great events depicted in the Tapestry. He recognized bravery when he saw it. This little fish might be obnoxious, but he had a certain redeeming quality of character.

"It might be better——" Marrow began.

"Right," Dolph said. The Tapestry had educated him in this respect too. "Perrin, you are a worthy enemy. Therefore I release you, that we may oppose each other again with honor, at some future time." He let go.

The fish hovered a moment, not entirely surprised. "What be thy name, then?"

"Prince Dolph of Xanth."

"A prince! Then doth that figure! I bid thee adieu, till that future encounter." The fish swam away, and all his troop went with him.

"That was well handled," Marrow said.

Dolph experienced a surge of pleasure. The skeleton's compliments did not come often, but that was only part of it. Mostly it was because he knew the compliment was deserved. He had for once handled a situation properly.

The cave rose, and they came to another dry section. Dolph swam to the surface of the water and waited. Marrow stepped out, then put down his bone hand and lifted Dolph clear. Then Dolph resumed the glowworm form. Marrow lifted him to the eye socket. They were back in business, afoot and with a light.

Then a host of dark shapes swarmed down at them, much as the fish had. They turned out to be bats.

"Ho, varlet!" the leader bat squeaked. "Halt and be recognized!"

Not again! Naturally the creature spoke in bat language, and Dolph was hard pressed to understand it. But to a degree all animal languages were connected, and as a glowworm he could make out the gist.

He wriggled out of Marrow's eye socket and became a big bat. "I am Prince Dolph of Xanth," he said. "I come on private business, and request that you let me pass." As a bat he had no trouble with the bat language, of course.

"A prince? Don't make me laugh!" And all the hovering bats burst into shrill laughter.

"I have identified myself," Dolph said evenly, following the protocol as he understood it. "Who are you?"

"I am Brick Bat, and this is my battalion," the bat replied. "We don't intend to let you pass, you faker. We rule this roost."

"I suspect—" Marrow began.

"Ah, shut your face, you bag of bones!" Brick snapped.

"Look, we're trying to be polite," Dolph said, wishing he didn't have to be.

"—that these animals are not going to be reasonable," Marrow concluded.

"You bet we aren't, you animated spook!" Brick said. The bats and Marrow didn't seem to have any trouble understanding each other, though they spoke different languages. It occurred to Dolph that the creatures of the gourd might have a special ability to communicate, because they never could tell into what creature's bad dream they might be thrust.

Dolph's juvenile hope flared. "Does that mean we can bash them?"

"Our time is limited," Marrow said. "We had better ignore them. But if they have the temerity to attack—"

Dolph wasn't sure what "temerity" meant, but—

"Attack!" Brick Bat cried. Immediately the battalion swarmed in, biting.

That saved Dolph the trouble of inquiring about the word. He assumed a form he had practiced long before, in the dusky towers of Castle Roogna. He became a vampire bat. He flew at the smaller bats, his fangs gaping. They scattered, terrified; they were not vampires, and the sight of this one affected them in much the way a charging ogre affected ordinary human folk.

Dolph enjoyed flying in the dark cave, using his high-pitched voice to locate the walls. It was just about as good as seeing with eyes and needed no light source. He would keep this form in mind, too; the bat was a good flier. He had forgotten how good!

Now they came to the dragon's nest. It was on a ledge high in the cave; only a flying creature could reach it. There was no way to miss it, for the floor of the cave beneath was mounded with cracked bones. Dolph had no trouble, of course, but Marrow was stuck below. It was hard to pick him out amidst all the inanimate bones.

"I can get the firewater opal," Dolph piped. "Which one is it?" For as he landed on the rim of the great nest, he picked up the echoes of hundreds of gems.

"It should have a fiery and liquid gleam," Marrow said.

"I can't hear the gleam!"

"You had better bring me up there," Marrow said. "I can see in the dark, so should have no problem."

Dolph flew down to the cave floor, assumed ogre form, and heaved the skeleton up and into the nest. He was about to return to bat form, when his gross ogre ears heard something.

"He's coming, he's coming!" the bats were chanting. "He'll crunch your stupid bones to bits, to bits!"

Oops! "I think we're in trouble," Marrow remarked from above. "You had better distract the dragon, while I search for the opal. There are so many gems here, it may take a while."

Distract the dragon! Dolph dreaded the notion. Why had Draco returned so soon? It would have been so much better if they could have escaped quietly with the opal; the dragon might never have noticed that it was missing.

Now he heard a hissing, as the dragon forged through the water. No doubt about it now, flying dragons could swim when they chose to! But how did they keep their fire when they got all wet?

He heard the creature splashing at the surface. His ogre eyes saw Draco's nose glowing. That was it: he held his breath! It surely did not take the dragon long to pass through the water, and the stifled fire would be no problem for that little time.

"Gonna getcha!" the bats chorused. "Gonna getcha, gonna getcha!"

Well, Dolph had planned to bluff the dragon; now was his chance. What form would be best? He decided to make it large but credible; if the dragon saw a figure too big to have come through the tight entrance, he would know it wasn't a real monster, and therefore might realize that it was inexperienced. The biggest monster that could have come through the tunnel was a serpent, because its cross section was small though its body could be massive.

Dolph became a giant serpent, with phenomenal fangs. He lifted his head and issued a horrendous hiss as the dragon cleared the water. That should put the creature on notice; Dolph was almost scaring himself!

"The fish told me there was an intruder," Draco growled in dragon talk, which was similar to serpent talk; they were two branches of the great family of reptile languages. "But they said it was a bone man and an armored fossil. I think I am dealing with a form changer, here."

So much for the concealment of his nature! But maybe

he could still bluff through. Dolph hissed again and slithered boldly forward, lifting his fangs.

"Let us just find out of what you are made," Draco said, sounding distressingly unworried. He spread his wings and launched into the air. He looped once, then angled down at Dolph's head. He fired a searing bolt.

Dolph whipped his head aside. That was too close! He struck at the dragon's body, but was far too slow; Draco was past and away, leaving Dolph's fangs to snap on air.

"A bit clumsy, aren't we," Draco remarked as he looped back for another shot.

Dolph realized that this was a losing form. He was more massive than the dragon, and his jaws could crush the dragon's body if they connected. But he was slower and clumsier; he would never catch the dragon before getting badly burned.

He changed back to ogre form. "Me bash in flash!" he roared in ogre talk.

Draco was already coming in for the second pass. Dolph swung a hamfist at his snout. His ogre form was more practiced than his giant serpent form, so the fist came across more swiftly and accurately than the dragon expected. It was Draco's turn to duck out of the way as the fist smoked by him. He careened down close to the floor, and almost into the water before regaining control.

Dolph stomped after the dragon, following up his advantage. He could tell exactly where the dragon was because of the glow of fire at the snoot. But Draco flew up out of reach.

Well, there was a way to handle that. Dolph tromped over to the section beneath the nest and scooped up a handful of bones. He hurled them at the dragon.

The bones turned out to be too light and irregular to make good missiles. But he rummaged in the darkness and found a few animal skulls. These were better. He waited until Draco came in for a fire run; and heaved a skull directly at the glow.

But this time the dragon was ready. He swerved just

enough to let the skull go by, then fired. Dolph had to jump, because even an ogre was not tough enough to withstand such a burn.

He hurled another skull, but the dragon wriggled in the air, avoiding it. Draco was simply too mobile for the ogre; he had the freedom of the entire cave, while the ogre was confined to the floor. Sooner or later Dolph would get singed or toasted, and then he would be in real trouble. It was turning out to be more difficult to handle even this small dragon than he had anticipated.

Of course all he needed to do was to distract Draco until Marrow found the firewater opal; then he could change to some fireproof form and go home.

"What's that in my nest?" Draco growled, spying Marrow.

Oops! Now the distraction would have to improve, or Marrow would be toasted. The skeleton could withstand fire, but if Draco followed it up with a good bone-crunching, that could be bad. Dolph had to step up the pace.

He would have to tackle Draco in the air. He became a griffin. Griffins were fine fliers and fine fighters, and they could see well at night. Because this griffin was about twice the mass of the dragon, he had the advantage. He took off, uttering a great challenging squawk.

Draco spun about in the air, readying his shot of fire. But Dolph dodged and angled in, as adroit in air as his foe. He reached for Draco with his talons. The moment he got hold of the dragon, he would stab him with his beak, and that would be the end.

Draco whipped his snout around, blowing out fire. It was a sustained blast; it swung across in an arc to intersect Dolph's position. Dolph dived, but the line of fire followed; he could not outrace it.

Close to the floor, he became a large land dragon. He landed with a whomp that jarred him. But now he had his own fire, and was armored against fire, as fire-breathers had to be. The fire touched him and did not hurt him; instead it helped him warm up his own furnace.

Now he oriented, pumped his bellows, and let fly a bolt twice as fierce as Draco's. But it missed, for Draco had cleared out the moment he noted the new form.

Dolph stalked him, but without avail. Draco knew his cave, and could dodge endlessly. He kept disappearing behind a bank of stalagmites, then reappearing to blast at Dolph's tail. The tail was not well armored; those sallies hurt!

This just wasn't doing it. Despite Dolph's advantage of size and firepower, Draco still was getting the better of it. If Dolph made any mistake, he would lose.

He would have to make it even in every respect, by matching Draco's own type. Dolph became a firedrake.

Now two almost identical dragons confronted each other. Dolph fired a jet of flame at the other, but Draco dodged it readily—and sent a return blast that heated Dolph's tail. Ouch!

He quickly discovered that Draco's lifetime experience in this form gave him a considerable tactical advantage. Their physical equipment might be the same, but Draco's reflexes were perfectly attuned to his capacities, while Dolph had to figure things out pretty much for the first time. He was no match for the dragon in this form, either.

He dived to the floor, Draco hot on his tail. As he landed, he assumed the form of a basilisk, and whipped about to face his pursuer. This form was deadly to almost all other forms; the moment their gazes locked, the other would be dead. All Dolph had to do was keep watching the other, so that Draco could not orient on him without meeting gazes. He did not need any special training or skill for this; even his natural clumsiness with the form would not diminish this effect.

But Draco had been alert, and he sheered off the moment Dolph changed. He knew about basilisks. He looped around, then closed his eyes, oriented by memory, and fired a jet.

Dolph scooted for cover. The fire singed his tail again. Draco didn't have to see him to attack him!

But maybe he could change that. Dolph became the bat, and launched himself at the nest. By the time Draco caught up, he was on the nest, and back in his basilisk form. The dragon's treasure was all around him; let Draco blast that!

Draco sheered off again, and made several loops in the air, pondering. Then he closed his eyes again, and came in to the nest. But he did not breathe fire this time. He simply landed blind, as his familiarity with the region enabled him to do.

Marrow crowded out of the way on one side, and Dolph scuttled off on the other. Was the dragon trying to crush his tiny body with its much larger one? He could avoid that!

But Draco did not seem to be doing that. Instead he flexed his coils as if rearranging them for the night. His bright scales reflected the glow from the larger gems in the nest: the moonstones and sunstones.

Then Dolph realized what the nature of the trap was. If he saw his own face reflected in a scale, he would stun or kill himself! That was one of the few vulnerabilities of this form. Obviously Draco had dealt with basilisks before. He could only hurt himself, because his bite could never penetrate the dragon's scales, and his gaze could not hurt a creature who refused to look at him. Indeed, if Draco managed to chomp him, and spit him out quickly to avoid the poison, Dolph could be mortally crushed.

He scrambled out of the nest, jumped down, and became the bat in midair. He flew quickly across to the side of the cave closest to the underwater entrance. Then he became a tangle tree, rooted in the sludge of that region.

The dragon was already back in the air, orienting for another shot; he knew that he could look now, because basilisks could not fly. He intended to toast Dolph before Dolph could get established in some more formidable form.

But a tangle tree was no ordinary creature. It was a carnivorous plant, with thick foliage and tentacles. A blast of fire could make it wilt, but could not overcome it. Meanwhile, Dolph was extending his roots down through the water to close off the entrance, and extending his tentacles to grab the dragon in the air. The tree could sense things without light, so there was no problem about locating Draco. Of course the tree could not grow well in darkness, but this was only a temporary form.

Draco hovered just outside tentacle range. He jetted fire at a cluster of tentacles, but Dolph moved them out of the way and reached for the dragon with a longer tentacle he was growing. Draco turned and snapped at the new tentacle, which whipped clear of the teeth. They fenced that way for a while, without having much effect on each other.

Finally the dragon growled something in his language, but Dolph could not understand it; tree talk was too far removed from reptile talk. "Same to you, fried-brain," he retorted in leaf language, making an insult gesture with a tentacle.

Draco flew back to the nest. Now Dolph saw the impasse: he could withstand the attacks of the dragon, and could prevent the dragon from leaving, because his tentacles would overwhelm the dragon if he got caught. But Dolph could not get the firewater opal. Marrow could do that, but now the dragon was facing the skeleton, and it was obvious that if Marrow tried anything, he would get thoroughly chomped. Dolph couldn't help his friend unless he changed form again and went over there—but Draco had already demonstrated that he was superior in the air and on the nest.

But the dragon was not attacking the skeleton, and Marrow was not trying to get away. They seemed to be conversing. What was going on? Then Marrow stood at the edge of the nest and waved to Dolph. "Truce!" he called. "Draco offers a truce."

Dolph was able to understand Marrow's words, mainly because he knew the skeleton and could interpret the nuances. Draco was asking for a truce? Was this a trick? But in the face of this stalemate, it was worth exploring.

Dolph became the firedrake, and flew cautiously toward

the nest, ready to veer clear if necessary. "What's this about a truce?" he growled in dragon talk.

"Just that," Draco growled back. "I want to talk."

"Okay, talk," Dolph said, hovering at a reasonable distance.

"The skeleton tells me you are a prince of your kind."

"Yes."

"Then you understand honor."

"No, I'm too young for that."

The dragon was evidently discomfited. He turned to Marrow. "How can a prince not comprehend honor?" he asked.

"When he is a child who has not yet had sufficient experience of it," Marrow replied. "The learning of this is part of what he requires to become adult."

"Does this have something to do with the Adult Conspiracy?" Dolph asked suspiciously.

Both Marrow and Draco laughed, to Dolph's annoyance. "Not really, though it could relate," Marrow said. "The concept of honor is fundamental to adult dealings with others, particularly in war. Conformity to a high standard of conduct, of which integrity is integral. In this case it means that neither you nor Draco must break the truce until both of you formally agree to end it, and you will not try to harm each other in the interim. It will be as if you are friends, even though you know you are not."

Dolph considered. "Does that mean he can't toast me if I return to boy form, and I can't take the firewater opal?"

"Exactly. Not while the truce is in force."

"Then what's the point of it?"

"Draco has a pressing appointment. He wishes to attend a ceremony now, and return to finish this engagement after the ceremony is over."

"Would that be the same ceremony Chex went to?" Dolph asked, interested.

"You know Chex Centaur?" Draco asked, surprised.

"She is my friend," Marrow said. "We visited Mt. Rushmost together three years ago. She helped us out of a difficulty yesterday."

"But it's her wedding I am going to!" Draco exclaimed.

"Her *wedding*?" Dolph and Marrow asked together.

"Yes. She is to marry Cheiron Centaur. I do not want to miss that ceremony. All the winged monsters will be attending."

"I wish I could attend!" Marrow exclaimed. "She never mentioned the nature of the ceremony."

"Of course not. You are not a winged monster, so are not eligible to attend. She would not have wished to hurt your feelings."

"Surely so," Marrow agreed.

"I agree to this truce," Dolph said, assuming boy form. "I want to go to that ceremony too."

"You are not eligible either, Prince," Draco reminded him laconically.

"In any event—" Marrow began.

"But I could become eligible," Dolph pointed out. "I can assume the form of a winged monster."

"They would know you were not. Every attendee will be known to some other, and your form would be known to none."

"—this is not advisable procedure," Marrow concluded.

But Dolph was determined to go. "You would not care to leave me here near your nest, Draco, when I do not understand about honor."

Draco considered, gazing at the gems that filled the bed of the nest. "You have a point. I dislike leaving my nest unattended, in any event, and more so when there is a raider in the vicinity."

"But if I change form and fly with you, you will have no concern about that. Marrow can remain to watch your nest; he is a creature of honor."

"This is preposterous!" Marrow protested.

Draco turned his gaze on Marrow. "How can I be assured of that?"

"My parents assigned him as my Adult Companion for my Quest. They are very choosy about such things."

Draco nodded. "So I understand. The Man-King is reputed to be easygoing, but his wife would be suitable for governing dragon cubs."

"The dragon cubs wouldn't like it," Dolph muttered.

"Exactly. Not one of them would get free of the nest unsupervised. I remember my own nestling days. But I did learn how to be a dragon! I also learned not to question the judgment of such a creature, whatever her form. Marrow, will you undertake to safeguard my nest during my absence?"

"By no means!" Marrow said. "This would be a grave distortion of—"

"He agrees," Dolph said. "He can blow his bone whistle if there is trouble."

"I think perhaps he does agree," Draco agreed. "Then let us be off; there is very little time remaining. Assume the form of a dragonfly and hang on to my back; I will get there faster if I don't have to wait for you."

"But—" Marrow cried.

Dolph became a dragonfly and buzzed over to land on Draco's back, between his wings. He took firm hold with his claws, knowing that a rough ride was coming.

"Be careful!" Marrow cried as they took off. Then Draco plunged into the water. They were on their way.

8

CEREMONY

D olph closed his eyes and held his breath while the dragon forged through the water; this wasn't hard to do in this form, because his big eyes had special membranes and his breathing wasn't like that of his human form. Then Draco burst out of the cave and forged into the night air. He climbed so high that Dolph was afraid they would get burned by the stars, but the dragon knew his way and steered safely clear of them.

Draco, his elevation attained, headed south. The stars passed rapidly by, above and below them, and the great dark Land of Xanth moved more slowly, identified only by stray lanterns and natural glimmers. Dolph could see only at an angle to the sides, because of the body of the dragon, but it was enough.

"What is your Quest?" Draco inquired.

"I want to find the Good Magician Humfrey," Dolph replied promptly. He was glad to have anyone know his business, because that made it seem more important. Because he was in dragon form now, it was easy to converse.

"What makes you think you can find him, when others cannot?"

"I found a message in a secret chamber of his castle saying 'Skeleton Key to Heaven Cent' so I knew he had left it for me, to tell where he is. So we went to the key where it pointed, but all we found was a skeleton."

"There is more than one key," Draco said.

"Yes. So we sailed south to check the next, only this merwoman caught me, and she wouldn't let me go unless we got her firewater opal back, and—"

"So that's what you were after!" Draco exclaimed. "My opals!"

"Yeah. Because—opals? How many do you have?"

"Two. I'm the only one with a set of those, because they are very hard to obtain. They enhance youthfulness in the possessor, or at least the impression of it. But why should you, a prince, become a thief, when you already possess sufficient youth?"

"Well, you stole it from the merman, so—"

Draco's body shuddered and heated. "I did not steal it! I won it!"

"You mean by killing its owner?"

"I see I shall have to set you straight about that," Draco said grimly. "Obviously the merwoman did not tell you the whole story. What exactly did she tell you?"

"Just that they had this one special gem, and without it she can't get a new merman to marry her in place of the one you killed when you took the stone. So she wants it back, and she's holding Grace'l hostage until we bring it."

"Grace'l?"

"She's another skeleton, like Marrow, only female. We'll trade her for the firewater opal, and then Mela can get another husband. She was going to keep me until I grew up, but I guess I should find the Good Magician first."

"I see the way of it. So you were going to take the opal before I returned, but I came back too soon."

"Right. So then I had to fight you for it."

"Naturally. The only way to gain anything from a good

dragon is to steal it or fight for it or outwit the dragon, and I am difficult to outwit. Very well, let me explain why it is my stone, not the merwoman's. It all started about two years back, when I made a wager with Merwin Merman. He had the other firewater opal, you see, and a pair of those is worth ten times as much as either one alone, so we agreed they should be together. We had a contest to see which of us should have the set, and I won, only he reneged. He tried to kill me and take them anyway, but I killed him and got my due. So those gems are mine, fair and square, by right of wit and of combat."

Dolph realized that the dragon had a case, if this was true. But he wasn't sure it was true. "What contest did you have, and how did you win?"

"Fire, water, sand. Do you know that one?"

"No."

"Well, you count to three together and throw out a paw. Two claws means fire, because they represent the flames leaping up. The whole paw flat means water, because it lies flat. The paw balled up is sand, because it is a ball of it; you can't make a ball of fire or water."

"I guess so," Dolph said. "But what can you do with fire, water and sand? Make a bonfire on the beach?"

"It's symbolic. You put out your paws together, and each person has his paw signifying one of the three. That's how you get your winner: fire evaporates water, water covers sand, and sand smothers fire. So there's always a winner and a loser, unless you both put out the same symbol; then you just do it over."

"Fire beats water, and water beats sand, and sand beats fire," Dolph said, catching on. "But how can you be sure of winning?"

"That's the point: you can't. So it's a fair contest; nobody knows who will win a throw. That's how we decided who would have the two firewater opals: one throw. I threw fire and he threw water, so I won. But then that cheater, he tried to claim *he* had won! He demanded that I give him my opal! The audacity of it! When I informed him that he had it backwards, he grabbed me and pulled me under the surface of the sea, trying to drown me and take the gem by force. Can you imagine? He was the worst loser I ever met!"

"But I guess you didn't drown," Dolph said. "How did you get out of it?"

"He didn't know I could swim," Draco said. "It seems some folk are ignorant about that; they think firedrakes are afraid of water, just as others think merfolk can't walk on land. We stay clear of sea water because we don't like to get our wings soiled with salt; it takes forever to clean that out. But we can do it if we have to. Sometimes we're hungry, and the only thing available is saltwater fish; sometimes there's something under the water we just have to have. Sometimes we just spin out of control in a storm; then it is best to be over water, so we can make a splash landing and not get hurt. So when Merwin grabbed me like that, at first I was so amazed at his effrontery that I didn't even struggle. But when he grabbed for my opal—I had it in a pouch on a chain around my neck, ready to give it up if I lost the throw—I put my snoot in his face and toasted him at point-blank range. Then I grabbed his opal, which I had won, and swam to the surface, and took off for home. It took me days to get the salt out, and my eyes were bleary from it, but at least I had what belonged to me. To this day I still can't figure why he was such a bad loser; he had seemed to be a decent fellow, for a merman, before that moment. Had he just played by the rules, he would have lost his opal, but not his life."

"Mela thinks you just attacked him and stole the opal," Dolph said. "She thinks you're a rogue dragon."

"There were no witnesses to the event, so I suppose she can think what she pleases. But I have told it as it happened. I threw fire, he threw water, plain as two days. I am absolutely sure of that, as I am of his bad attitude. That gem is mine!"

But something was nibbling at Dolph's memory. "Mela— she said something—I think it was just a saying she used—

about fire and water. 'Sure as water douses fire'—something like that. I wonder—"

"That's backwards!" Draco growled. "I told you, fire evaporates water. Every time. You breathe fire on it and it heats and turns into steam and it's gone. When I come home and drip on the nest, I dry it out by heating it a little."

"But maybe to a merperson, who lives in water, it would seem the other way," Dolph said. "I remember something else she said, about sand displacing water—"

"That's backwards, too! Water covers sand! I'd heard that merfolk were addle-brained, and this proves it!"

"Maybe so," Dolph said uncertainly. "And there was something else she said, but mostly I remember her legs. When she turned her tail into legs, they were really quite nice."

"I dare say they would be delicious," Draco agreed, licking his chops. "Plenty of meat on them?"

"Just the right amount, I think."

"I'm hungry already!"

"Back at Castle Roogna my mother said boys weren't supposed to see girls' panties. But this was all right, because she wasn't wearing any panties."

"Right. The cloth catches on the teeth. That can be messy. Girls are best without panties."

"But what I was trying to remember—Ah, now I have it! Fire melts sand, she said. So you know, they—"

"All backwards!" Draco exclaimed. "What idiots! They think fire melts sand, sand displaces water, and water douses—" He broke off. "Uh-oh."

"I wonder whether they play that game the same way?" Dolph asked innocently. "Backwards?"

"Suddenly I very much fear they do! So that when I threw fire and Merwin threw water—"

"You mean he really did think he won?"

Draco snorted out a fierce jet of fire. "Oh, my," he hissed. "I wish I'd understood! We could have discussed the rules, gotten them straight . . ." He trailed off, his words fading into thoughts.

"When I get back, I'll tell her about the misunderstanding. Maybe that will make her feel better."

Draco choked on smoke. "Uh, maybe I have a better idea," he gasped. "I will give you the firewater opal to return to her. You need say nothing about the misunderstanding."

"Oh, sure! That's nice of you! But won't that ruin your set?"

"Some prices need to be paid," the dragon said. "Perhaps she needs to find another husband more than I need a set."

The rest of the flight was uneventful. Dolph snoozed, because he was young and got sleepy at night, and when he woke the sun was just peeking over the horizon, checking to make sure the darkness was gone. Ahead lay the broad flat peak of Mt. Rushmost, covered with bushes.

But as they came closer, and the light improved, Dolph saw that those weren't bushes, but creatures. The mesa was dotted with winged monsters! He had never imagined, let alone seen, such a variety of horrendousness! These were dragons of every size from dragonfly to appalling, and griffins, and basilisks, and sphinxes, and winged serpents, and rocs and harpies and—his mind boggled. They were all bustling about and making a commotion, but not, oddly, fighting.

"Remember," Draco hissed as they came in for a landing. "Do not revert to your human form. Conceal your identity, or your posterior and mine will be slung over the moon!"

Dolph, gazing out at the assemblage of monsters, took the warning to heart. Any of these would gladly consume him in a trice, if given a pretext, and the fact that he was a prince would make scant difference.

They landed on the strip of clear land designated for this. Fireflies marked the sides and corners, so that night flights could be accommodated almost as readily as the daytime ones. A phoenix squawked instructions for orientation and schedule, so that those coming in did not collide with those taking off. Indeed, this was a necessary precaution, for every few seconds some monster was doing one or the other. Some had evidently been designated group hunters, for they were coming in with assorted prey in their clutches, which carrion was duly torn to pieces and distributed to the hungry. Again, Dolph appreciated that this was necessary, because it would have been impossible to have every monster hunt this region simultaneously; every living thing would have been wiped out. But with rocs bringing in mundane cows, elephants, and whales, there seemed to be almost enough to go around.

There was a flurry of introductions as Draco trundled off the runway. "Draco, you laggard! We thought you'd forgotten to come!" another firedrake growled.

"No such luck, flame-brain," Draco responded. "I had trouble finding a nest sitter."

"If you just bothered to take a mate, you'd have a nest sitter!" a blue dragoness puffed.

"Stop matchmaking, Hotbox," Draco said. "When I want a wyvern, I'll choose her myself."

"Well, this is the place for it," she protested, and there was a fiery roar of laughter from the others now.

"Who's your midget friend?" a cockatrice inquired, staring through his dark goggles at Dolph.

"Keep your specs on!" Draco cautioned, not wholly humorously. A cockatrice, like a basilisk, had a gaze that was poisonous. "This is—" He paused.

Dolph realized what his problem was. They had not decided on a name for him, and could not risk his real one. "Phlod Firefly," Dolph said, drawing on a game name he had used in the past. It was his name spelled backwards. His sister, by the same token, was Yvi. They called their father Rod, which didn't bother him, and their mother Eneri, but never to her face. Grandpa Knib was a good sport, though. Now he was very glad they had played that game, because it gave him a name he was used to answering to.

"Phlod," Draco agreed with relief. "He is a prince of his

kind, so was required to attend, but the distance was too far, so I brought him."

"Still looks like a wasp waist to me," the cockatrice said. "I think I'll step on him and see if he squishes."

"I wouldn't," Draco said.

But the cocky winged lizard was already moving toward Dolph, determined to throw his small weight around. Dolph thought quickly. He did not want to give away his identity, but neither did he want to get stepped on. He had noted that the dragons here were not using their fire; evidently the truce forbade it, for obvious reasons, just as it required the cockatrice to cover his eyes. There was to be no fighting here, but apparently a little pushing around for status was all right.

Well, he could do that. Dolph simply assumed the form of a larger firefly. When the cockatrice still advanced, he became bigger yet, so that he was larger than the other. He lifted a foot.

Now the cockatrice paused, surprised. "He's bigger than he looks!"

"He grows on you," Draco said, with a discreet flicker of humor, and the surrounding monsters chuckled smokily.

The cockatrice concluded that he had business elsewhere, which was the way of bullies when they found themselves overmatched.

Now trumpeter swans sounded a fanfare. There was an immediate hush. The ceremony was beginning!

"We shall now introduce the attending dignitaries," a manticore bellowed. This monster was as big as a mundane horse, with the segmented tail of a scorpion, the body of a lion, wings of a dragon, and the head of a man with triple rows of teeth in each jaw. Its voice was oddly musical, vaguely resembling a trumpet or flute, with considerable volume. It occurred to Dolph that those triple teeth might have something to do with it. Certainly this was a loud and fearsome monster!

There was a period of ordered confusion as the dignitaries were lined up. Then the fanfare sounded again. "Komodo li Zard, Prince of the Isles of Indon Esia," the manticore fluted. Prince Komodo walked out, a dragon of moderate size with wings that were almost invisible; Dolph had to look two and a half times to see them at all. But of course they existed, because only winged monsters were here for the ceremony.

"Baron Haulass of Shetland," the manticore trumpeted, and a winged donkey trotted out.

"Duke Dragontail of Dimwit." And a formidable dragon whose serpentine tail did drag walked out.

"Smokey of Stover." This was a dragon of the smoking variety, ordinarily a landbound creature, but this variant did have vestigial wings. Dolph had never seen one quite like this before, and wondered how it had come about.

"Snagglesnoot of Synchromesh." This time a strange oily monster, with bright chrome teeth.

"Stanley Steamer, the once and future Gap Dragon." Dolph almost cried out, for he knew Stanley of old, Ivy's pet. But Stanley was almost grown now, and would soon resume regular residence in the Gap Chasm. Dolph kept quiet, for he would give himself away if he went to talk with Stanley.

"Xap Hippogryph, sire of the bride." Dolph took note of this one; he had never before seen Chex's father. Xap had the head and wings of a griffin, and the body of a horse, like a centaur gone wrong, but he was an extremely handsome creature. Dolph realized that Chem, the bride's dam, would not be present, for she was a straight centaur without wings. That was unfortunate. Presumably there would be a reception later, elsewhere, where she could attend. Dolph understood that the community of centaurs frowned on variants, so had not welcomed Chex. Thus it was the winged monsters who had adopted her. Dolph wasn't quite sure what that said about monsters, but he found that he was coming to like them better.

So it went, as griffins, chimærae, harpies, rocs, winged horses, and assorted dragons strutted onstage for their introductions—and these were only the dignitaries. The majority of the attending monsters were garden-variety, like himself in his present guise. Some were unusual, even so, such as the winged zombie dragon and the griffin skeleton from the gourd. It was impressive.

At last it was time for the wedding itself. The monsters formed into a great circle, and a rare winged mermaid sang a solo song of such great beauty and longing that every monster present seemed to wish only to cast itself into the turbulent sea, and Dolph suffered a pang of terrible regret that he had left Mela the merwoman behind. He realized that the mermaids all had some siren ancestry, and all could sing compellingly when they chose; this one's mother must have charmed a winged creature, so that the result was a crossbreed who qualified as a winged monster. She was certainly most alluring!

Then the mermaid flew to a tank of water reserved for her, for her tail got uncomfortable when dry; evidently she had wings but no ability to make legs. That was unfortunate. "Now the Simurgh," Draco whispered. "Stay low."

Dolph was amazed. He knew of the Simurgh; he had seen her in the tapestry. She was the eldest and wisest of all birds, so old she had seen the destruction and regeneration of the universe three times. She sat on a bough of the Tree of Seeds on Mount Parnassus, and governed where all of those seeds went. His mother had many rare and wonderful seeds given her by the Simurgh, but he had never heard of the great bird attending a social function.

The monsters waited expectantly; not even a growl broke the silence. Their eyes were fixed on a huge wooden perch mounted at one side of the clear area. It had been fashioned of several stout tree trunks lashed together with tangle tree tentacles, the strongest of structures.

A bright bird the size of a roc flew in from the south horizon, winging so swiftly and surely that there was no doubt she knew exactly where she was going. Her feathers were like veils of light and shadow, now one color and now another and mostly like the blue of the deepest and clearest sky. Her head seemed crested with fire, sparkling

iridescently. She was the most magnificent bird Dolph
could imagine. He had seen her image in the Tapestry, but
the reality was overwhelmingly more impressive. It wasn't
just the size or color; the Simurgh had a *presence* that manifested as she approached.

She came in and landed neatly on the perch, and both it
and the mesa shook with the impact of her roosting. She
folded her phenomenal wings, settled herself, and looked
around. Her gaze seemed to touch every monster present,
and all lowered their heads respectfully. That gaze touched
even on Dolph; he was one of the smallest of creatures,
lost in the throng, yet she saw him.

WHAT ARE YOU DOING HERE, PRINCE DOLPH?
she inquired in his mind. YOU ARE NO MONSTER!

She recognized him! She knew he was an imposter here!
Dolph started to attempt to answer, but she silenced him
with her powerful thought. THAT WAS RHETORICAL,
GOOD CHILD. HOLD YOUR PEACE, AND LEARN.

Then her attention passed elsewhere, and he could relax.
What an experience! The Simurgh had spotted him instantly amidst the crowd, and seen right into his nature. He
realized that she must have done the same for every other
creature here; she knew them all. Yet it was only a moment
before her survey was complete.

PROCEED, she thought to the entire assemblage.

Now for the first time the groom came into view: Cheiron Centaur, a handsome male with great folded silver
wings and golden hooves. His mane was neatly combed,
and his tail too; every hair was in order. He was a muscular
creature in both his human and his equine aspects, ruggedly
well constructed. He walked slowly to the centaur, then
turned to stand facing the Simurgh, his features composed.

The trumpeters played the wedding march. From the far
side an aisle opened, and down it walked Chex, sedately.
Dolph was amazed again; she had been transformed. He
had known her, hardly a day ago, as a female centaur with
wings, Marrow's friend. Now she was absolutely beautiful.
Her brown mane was so well brushed that it glowed, and

she wore a diadem of bright roses on her head that heightened the quality of her eyes. Her wings were the same color as her eyes, gray as the overcast sky, and every feather shone. Her hide glistened from breasts to flank, and there was a bow of forget-me-not flowers in her tail. Even her four hooves were as clean and bright as mirrors, sparkling as she walked.

Chex came at last to stand beside Cheiron. They made a perfect pair, he so bold and strong, she so lovely and demure.

DEARLY BELOVED MONSTERS OF THE AIR, the Simurgh thought to them all, WE ARE GATHERED HERE TO UNITE THIS CENTAUR STALLION AND THIS CENTAUR MARE IN MATRIMONY. THERE ARE NO OBJECTIONS. FROM THIS UNION WILL COME ONE WHOSE LIFE WILL CHANGE THE COURSE OF THE HISTORY OF XANTH, AND ALL OF YOU WILL TREASURE AND PROTECT THAT ONE FROM HARM. LET ME HEAR YOUR OATH ON THIS.

Suddenly there was noise, as every creature on the plateau growled assent. Dolph did not understand this, and held back; how could he agree to an oath whose effect he did not know?

YOU TOO, PRINCE DOLPH, YOU MOST OF ALL, the Simurgh thought to him alone. Her mind carried the aura of immense significance, of the tides of history surging from the past to the future and back again irresistibly, all focusing on this moment. Now he knew, without understanding, why the Simurgh had come to preside over this ceremony; it was important to the things that only she understood completely. The coming foal was special.

Dolph became aware of the ongoing ceremony; the Simurgh had not waited for his thoughts to run their young course.

... AND DO YOU, YOU FETCHING FILLY, TAKE THIS STUD TO BE YOUR MATE?

"I do," Chex agreed.

THEN BY THE POWER VESTED IN ME BY BEING

WHAT I AM, I NOW PRONOUNCE YOU A MATED PAIR. KISS.

The groom and bride dutifully embraced their foresections and kissed. The assembled monsters roared their approval.

The Simurgh spread her wings and took off. In a moment she was in the sky, and in another winging toward the horizon.

DO NOT FORGET, GOOD CHILD, her parting thought came back to Dolph. He knew he would not forget; he only hoped some day to understand.

Then Cheiron and Chex backed off together, and a harpy flew up. Dolph saw with surprise that it was a male; he had never seen one of those before. "Let me snatch your attention before the festivities begin," the harpy cried. "I am Hardy Harpy, and I am here to introduce my daughter Gloha, who will announce the gifts."

Now the child flew up. She was a beautiful little goblin girl, with the wings of a bird, obviously not of the faerie folk, whose wings were like gauze. A flying crossbreed, therefore a winged monster, though she was as unlike a monster as could be imagined. Gloha—Dolph searched his memory, and remembered that there had been a harpy–goblin romance that had almost provoked war; Ivy had been involved with that, and naturally had not told him much. The goblin had been Glory, so the mergence of Glory and Hardy would be Gloha. He had it now. Probably this was a way of allowing the goblins, who were monsters but not winged, to participate nominally.

"First," piped Gloha nervously, "from the Simurgh: three seeds." She took a breath, and seemed to lose her place, because Hardy had to whisper in her ear. "Oh, yes: the envelope, please."

A winged human skeleton stepped forward, carrying a seed packet. He handed it to Gloha, who opened it and peeked in. "The seeds of Life, Love, and Learning," she said, passing the envelope along to Chex. There was a growl of applause from the throng of monsters. This was certainly a remarkable gift! Dolph wondered whether Chex would bring those seeds to his mother Irene, for help in making them grow well. Irene's talent was the Green Thumb; she could make anything grow, instantly.

"And, and—" Gloha announced after another prompting, reading from the second envelope brought by the skeleton, "from the guest monsters here ass—ass—" Another prompt from her father. "Assembled, a vacation on the honey side of the moon. A honeymoon!"

There was a louder roar of approval. Everyone knew that the moon was made of green cheese, at least the side that faced Xanth, and sometimes it reeked pretty strong, sickened by what it saw below. But the far side was not exposed to such a sight, and remained sweet honey, as the whole thing had been originally. It was reputed to be the most delightful of all places to be, but it required so much magic to get there that hardly anyone did it. The monsters must have pooled all their available extra magic for this gift!

The skeleton brought the third envelope. "And, from the monsters of the gourd, to be delivered by Mare Imbri, a full year of sweet dreams." And as the monsters roared their approval, there was a passing flicker in the shape of an invisible horse. Mare Imbri was not technically a winged monster, but everyone knew her and liked her because of the pleasant daydreams she brought, and no regular monster could carry these, so no one protested her intrusion here.

"Now," Hardy Harpy cried, "do we want to bother with the tedium of a receiving line, or shall we let them get on with the breeding?"

There was a deafening roar: the monsters were not here for tedium. Dolph listened, excited; he strongly suspected that this had something to do with the stork. Was he going to get to see how adults summoned it?

No such luck. Cheiron and Chex thanked the assemblage, then spread their wings and took off for the moon, which was now making a special appearance by day in all its fullness, so that the happy couple could conveniently reach it. Even so, it would be a long flight, so it was indeed best that they get started.

As the centaurs flew above the throng, Chex glanced down. Her gaze fell on Dolph. Her mouth fell open in surprise. *She recognized him!* But then she looked away, and soon the couple was silhouetted by the great bright globe of the moon. Chex, sweet creature that she was, had decided not to tell on him.

The manticore returned to the center stage. "Now we celebrate!" he fluted. "Refreshments are served on the north side; plenty of carrion available! Gaming on the south side; form your groups for Dungeons and Dragons!"

The monsters dissolved into chaos as each sought its desire. Dolph saw two griffins getting together, male and female, and suddenly he knew they were going to celebrate by summoning the stork. He started to make his way over there so he could watch and finally learn the secret that had so long been denied him.

"Hey, you're underage!" Draco said, catching him in a paw. "Time to go to the games!"

Dolph stifled a bad word. Even the monsters were part of the fiendish Adult Conspiracy! What was so awful about the mechanism that no child could be allowed to see it?

They forged toward the games. But now a new problem manifested. A thundercloud was trying to crash the party! King Cumulo Fracto Nimbus had spotted the activity, and was coming to drench it to awful sogginess.

There was consternation among the monsters, who were far too crowded to take off before the storm scored and soiled their feathers and splashed mud on their clean fur. Besides that, they didn't want their celebration washed out. What to do?

"You know," Dolph said to Draco, "everyone here has wings. I bet if every monster tied down and flapped its wings, they could blow off Fracto."

"Now that's a notion!" Draco said. "I'd better relay it, because if you tell it—"

"Right," Dolph agreed. He did not want any attention focused on him!

Draco lifted his snout and sounded a fiery honk for attention. "Let's line up, tie down, and blow that fog face out of the air!" he growled. "It's time he had a lesson in manners!"

The idea appealed. Quickly the monsters organized. The biggest and strongest formed a line at the edge of the plateau, while the smaller ones got back out of the way. Three rocs were at the center of the line. Each monster dug its talons into the ground, grasping sod, roots, and rock so that it would not take off. Then the trumpet swans sounded a cadence, honking in unison. The three rocs began moving their wings, in time with the honks, and the wind gathered. Chex Centaur was able to fly by making her body light, but the rocs and others flew by the sheer power of their wings, so these generated a lot of wind.

That wind increased as they got into it. The effect was like that of a huge fan, that magic instrument that made a breeze when waved, and the anchored monsters were like a whole convention of fans, blowing hot air. That stream of wind reached out and shoved at the oncoming cloud, pushing it back.

King Fracto's foggy face clouded up as he encountered this opposition. He roared thunderously, and lightning jags shot out of his bottom. But he was a demon of the air, and the air was moving the wrong way. He could not advance against the massed draft of the monsters.

Slowly Fracto was shoved away. His visage was a fright to behold as he realized he was being bested; Dolph had never before seen a cloud as grim and dark as this. Fracto's sport had been spoiled; he could not wash out this celebration.

At last the evil cloud gave up, and drifted away to other mischief. The monsters growled a cheer. Then they dismantled their wind machine and returned to the festivities.

Dolph was pleased. He had in his small way exerted the quality of leadership that was expected of a future king, even if he couldn't take credit for it. Now that he had come to know these monsters, he liked them, and he was glad he had been able to share in this event. In addition, he had managed to settle the matter of the firewater opal, because Draco was going to give it back.

Dolph could not think of anything that could spoil his satisfaction. This had become a wholly good event.

Had he but known . . .

9

GOBLINS

Disgruntled, Marrow Bones settled himself into the dragon's nest. He did not like this at all. He should not have let Dolph go to the ceremony; the boy was only nine years old, which was young by human standards, and could get into all sorts of mischief without adult supervision. Draco seemed to be an honorable dragon, so probably would not break the truce, but there would be many monsters there who were hungry and not pledged to pass up such a morsel. Even if Dolph remained undiscovered, there could be trouble. This was to be a wedding ceremony, and centaurs were notoriously open about natural functions; suppose someone let slip the secret of stork summoning in the boy's presence? Dolph's body might not be hurt, but his mind could be irreparably changed.

Even if Dolph made it back safely in body and mind, there would still be the matter of the firewater opal. The truce was only that; when it ended, there would be battle again, and the sides seemed evenly matched. Marrow had believed that the boy could assume a form that would thwart the dragon; otherwise he would have been more cautious about this encounter. But Draco was an uncommonly savvy dragon, and this was Draco's home territory. Suppose Dolph made a mistake and got severely chomped? That would be Marrow's responsibility too. Queen Irene might be watching from Castle Roogna via the Tapestry, but her avenues of rescue would be sharply limited. She would have to send help, perhaps a man with a dragon net, but could this arrive in time? Marrow seriously doubted it. This Quest had gotten seriously out of hand!

But things had happened too quickly for his hollow head to assimilate, and the boy had gone off to the ceremony. For all the likely folly of it, Marrow could understand Dolph's interest. Chex was a fine mare, and this was likely to be a fine wedding. Obviously the stubborn centaur community would not sanction such an event, so it was up to the monsters. Marrow could not understand why the centaurs, an obvious crossbreed between the human and the equine folk, were so insistent on the purity of the species. They were similarly conservative about magic, exiling any centaur who evinced a magic talent. Yet without crossbreeding and magic, where would Xanth be? As dull as Mundania, almost by definition! Not only did the Mundanes practice neither, they believed that neither was possible. It simply was not feasible to relate to the Mundane attitude; the Mundanes just had to be left to their own drear existence.

Well, at least he could locate the firewater opal while he waited. He would not take it, of course; he had agreed to protect the nest during the dragon's absence, however sloppily the agreement had been foisted on him, and he would do that to the best of his limited ability. But when they returned, and resumed the battle, the gem would be needed. Assuming that Dolph won—and of course he had to win, because otherwise they would be unable to redeem Grace'l from the merwoman.

Grace'l. Now there was a pretty thought! Marrow realized that he had been long away from the gourd, and from his own kind; the notion of a companion skeleton was quite appealing. Grace'l had the most shapely bones he could remember. Of course she would be returning to the gourd in due course—yet she had declined when given the opportunity. Dolph had demonstrated his ability to assume the form of a gourd, so that meant that Grace'l could return home at any time. Why had she not done so?

It was most tempting to believe that she found Marrow's company as intriguing as he found hers. Marrow had been lost for a long time before being found and brought to Xanth; he had forgotten what romantic experience he might have had. His recent experiences outside the gourd had deepened and broadened and lengthened his awareness of many things, and changed his perspective, so that he was no longer truly a creature of the gourd. He knew that he would now be a poor hand at the construction of bad dreams; no self-respecting night mare would accept one of his efforts. He didn't even scare people anymore! So it was possible that he did not impress Grace'l. But she impressed him, and if she elected to remain longer in Xanth—

His thoughts were brought to a rude halt by a sinister sound. The fading thoughts rattled around in his skull for a moment before settling into a formless mass and sinking out of sight. He focused his attention on the sound.

It was a quiet tapping elsewhere in the cave. He knew it was not normal, because the bats stirred. "Did you do that, you airhead?" Brick Bat chittered.

"No, guano-face," he replied.

"Listen, bone-brain, if you weren't on that nest, I'd show you some guano! Why Lord Draco tolerates you there I'll never understand!" The other bats echoed the sentiment.

"That's because you're bats," Marrow said with satisfaction. "Are you going to investigate that suspicious sound or aren't you?"

The bat chittered something indecipherable and flew off to investigate. Marrow, abruptly nervous about prospects, resumed his quest for the firewater opal. Could something be coming to raid the nest during the dragon's absence? He had hoped that all would be quiet; he had problems enough worrying about Dolph.

The tapping continued. After a moment a bat flew to perch at the edge of the nest. "Hey, emaciated, I don't like this," Brick confided. "Sounds as if something is tunneling through the wall."

"I don't like it either, skin-wing. Do you think something caught on to Draco's absence? I could blow my whistle and summon him back."

"Don't blow the whistle!" the bat cried. "If we bring him back, and it's nothing, and he misses the ceremony because of us, he'll toast us all to ashes!"

Marrow was inclined to respect Brick's judgment in this matter. They certainly didn't want a false alarm. They were now allies in their desire to avoid trouble. "Could it be a rockworm who lost its way?"

"Rockworms don't tap, they grind."

"Better keep a good ear on it, then," Marrow decided. "Just remember, if there's trouble, we're on the same side until the dragon returns."

"More's the pity, bare-skull," Brick said, taking off.

Marrow kept searching. Suddenly he spied it: a beautiful stone that glinted with liquid fire. The firewater opal!

Then he stared. There were two of them! He rubbed his eye sockets with a bone finger, but the stones remained. He picked them up. It was true: twin opals. Which one was the merwoman's?

Brick flew back. "We heard voices. Now we know: it's goblins!"

"Goblins! Here?"

"They live deeper in the mountain, under the naga. Usually they don't come near here."

"The naga?"

"Snakes. They don't bother us, and the goblins don't bother them. Much. But if the goblins are coming here, there's only one reason."

"The gems of this nest."

"How did you guess, hollow-noggin?"

"I was fortunate, fly-by-night. Should I blow my whistle?"

The bat considered. "Maybe there's only a few of them. We could handle that ourselves. If we called Lord Draco over a minor matter, he would strip our wings and make us do forced marches over the stalagmites."

"Let's wait and see, then." It was evident that the dragon did not like to be bothered about trifles, and had ways of discouraging this.

Brick flew off. Marrow set the two opals down, and pondered the situation. If the goblins were coming, it had to be because they had seen the dragon departing or because they knew of the ceremony and had timed their raid to coincide. That probably meant they were equipped to handle the bats, who really weren't such a bad threat. Probably they did not know about Marrow, though. Could he defend the nest adequately alone?

He wasn't sure, but decided that he could always blow the whistle if it appeared that the presence of the dragon was needed. He did not want to cause Draco and Dolph to miss the ceremony; both would be angry about that.

The tapping became loud. In due course the chisels broke through the wall, down at cave floor level. Light flared out. There was no further question: goblins were raiding.

The first goblin stepped into the cave, carrying a guttering torch. The bats swarmed down to attack. The goblin cursed and batted at them, waving his flaming stick. "Bring out the hoods!" he shouted back into the hole from which he had stepped. "The vermin are making a flap."

"Vermin!" Brick retorted, outraged. "Listen, clunkhead—"

The goblins ignored him. More stepped through, wearing helmets with heavy descending flaps. They had cloaks and gloves too. Every third one had a torch, which served as a weapon as well as for light. The bats attacked, but could make no progress; the outfits were impervious to their efforts, and the fire the goblins carried was devastating to wings.

There seemed to be half a dozen goblins. They were on the floor of the cave. Marrow concluded that they were not a serious threat because they would not be able to scale the wall to the dragon's nest.

Then more goblins came, carrying long ladders. They hauled these to the region under the nest, and leaned them up against the wall. They were just long enough to touch it. The raiders had come prepared; this was an organized party.

Brick flew in to consult with Marrow. "The ruffians came prepared. Maybe you better blow your whistle now."

But Marrow had more confidence. "They don't know I'm here. Attack them as they climb; they won't be able to swat at you without letting go of the rungs. Go for their big tender feet; those aren't shielded. If any get near the top, I'll push the ladders away."

Brick gazed at him. "I am getting to dislike you less, bone-face."

"Same here, skin-snoot."

The bat departed. Soon the curses below redoubled. The goblins on the two ladders were trying to swat at their feet, and losing their balance and falling off. Those not on the ladders laughed. Fights broke out, until the goblin chief established order.

They started up the ladders again, in lines, the second goblin on each protecting the toes of the first. The bats were unable to penetrate.

"What now, bare-teeth?" Brick inquired.

"Just keep harassing them, so they have to climb slowly. Let me know when they're near the top. I want to dump as many as possible, and maybe break the ladders too."

"Beautiful! Almost worthy of a bat, that notion."

"Almost," Marrow agreed wryly, keeping his head down. He wanted this to be a complete surprise.

"Now!" Brick announced shortly.

Marrow rose up. He put his skull up against the face of the top goblin on the left ladder. "Boo!" he yelled.

"Ay-yi-yii!" the goblin screamed, appalled. He jumped

backwards, and lost his grip. He fell, crashing into the one below. The entire column bumped down the rungs of the ladder, each cursing more villainously than the last.

Marrow quickly moved over to the right ladder and did the same. But this top goblin was more nervy; he yelled "Boo!" back and started to climb onto the nest. So Marrow put a hand on the top rung and shoved the ladder to the side. It fell, slowly at first, then with greater conviction, while the goblins aboard screamed in unison.

"I think I'm in love!" Brick chittered joyously

There was chaos below. Then the goblin chief's voice sounded. "You saw a *what*?"

Marrow was pleased. He had thought he had lost his touch, but it was evident that he could still evoke a bad image.

After a time the most severely bruised goblins departed for safer territory, and new ones took their places. Marrow was not sure how many there were in all, but it was at least twenty. He thought again about blowing his whistle, but his ladder push had been so successful that he didn't see how a hundred goblins could do any better than ten. He would shove down every ladder!

But then the goblins started assembling a different kind of device. Neither Marrow nor the bats could figure out just what it was. It had some kind of webbing, and a wood section, and some kind of spring. They scurried around, gathering stones; then, with delight, skulls from the bone pile below the nest. What could they want with these?

Then Marrow found out. "Ready, aim, fire!" the goblin chief declaimed. A skull flew up and over the nest.

It was a giant sling! They were hurling things at him. This was dangerous.

"We've got to deactivate that artillery," he told Brick.

"How?" the bat asked, as a rock whizzed over, closer. The goblins were getting the range.

That stumped him. Meanwhile, under the cover of that barrage, the goblins were setting up their two ladders again.

Marrow lay low, trusting that they would not be able to hit him if they couldn't see him.

The troops swarmed up. Marrow shoved one ladder over, then moved to the second and fought with its top goblin, who was almost into the nest. Another skull sailed across, just missing him as he ducked. He managed to shove the creature over the edge, and that ladder also fell. It was getting harder, but he was still prevailing, and the goblins were taking a battering.

"Behind!" Brick chittered.

Marrow turned—and discovered a third ladder. They had used the first two as distraction while the third made it through. He charged across and shoved at the goblin who had already gotten off, pushing him back against the one just reaching the top. The little monster clamped his big teeth on Marrow's hand, chewing at several bone fingers. Marrow kneed him and finally threw him off. After a brief struggle, he managed to dump that ladder too. There was a satisfying wail as the goblins on it fell.

But by this time the other two ladders were being set up. Marrow realized that he would not be able to hold them all back. It was time to blow the whistle.

He lifted his finger to his face—and discovered that the finger was gone. The goblin had chewed it off! Whether this was sheer bad luck, or the result of goblin savvy, made no difference; his prime weapon had just been nullified.

"Blow the whistle! Blow the whistle!" Brick chittered.

"I can't!" Marrow said, chagrined. "He bit it off."

"Then think of something else! Quickly!"

Marrow tried, but his hollow head was not much for pressure thinking. All three ladders were now back in place, and another skull flew low overhead. Marrow realized that they should have the range by this time; why were the shots still missing? Then he realized that it was because they didn't want to break or scatter the gems in the nest.

That gave him the necessary notion. They had come for the Dragon's gems; he was here to guard them. But he and the bats were not the only guardians.

He stopped and grabbed a handful of gems. "Goblins!" he cried. "Do you want these stones? You can't have them. Remove your ladders, or I'll throw them away!" He held the gems in his left bone hand; with his right bone fingers he took a glittering diamond, and cocked his arm, ready to throw.

The goblins paused. The diamond sparkled in the torch-light. There was a silence.

Then the chief spoke. "He's bluffing! That stone would only land on the floor. If it doesn't break, we'll get it anyway. Ignore him!"

Immediately the action resumed. Goblins climbed the ladder, and the ones manning the sling readied another skull.

Marrow hurled the diamond across the cave. It flew in a glinting arc over the heads of the goblins, and splashed in the pool. The goblins stared, stunned.

"It didn't break," Marrow called. "But you can't get it! What do you think of that, frog-mouth?" He punctuated his jibe with a bit of finger magic.

"Get that gem!" the chief screamed, infuriated for no good reason.

Immediately three sturdy goblins dived into the water, going after the sinking stone. But in a moment there was a violent commotion. The three reversed their strokes and almost sailed out of the pool.

"What's this?" the chief cried. "Why did you quit?"

The three opened their mouths. "Yeow!" they cried as one.

Now their problem could be seen. To each posterior was attached the sharp teeth of a piranha. In a moment the fish dropped off, splashing back into the water, but the point had been made. What entered the water was not accessible.

"How's that bite you, sludge-snoot?" Brick Bat chittered from above. Unfortunately the goblins did not understand him; only Marrow could pick up on animal languages, because of his experience in the gourd. The gourd related to the thoughts of every creature, so its denizens had to understand those thoughts.

The chief considered. "But he can't throw them all in the drink," he said. "Swarm over him, grab the stones!"

Motion resumed. Marrow threw a fat gray pearl into the pool, then a topaz, but the goblins didn't stop. He hurled the rest of his handful, and picked up another. His left hand worked ineffectively because of the missing forefinger, but he could use it to help scoop up the gems.

A goblin head showed over the edge of the nest. Marrow charged it and shoved it back by brute force. The ladder toppled, to the screams of the goblins on it. Then he threw more stones into the pool. But he could see that there were far too many gems to dispose of this way in the time he had; the goblins would soon overwhelm him and get the main part of the treasure.

"Bats!" he cried. "Swoop in, grab the stones, dump them in the pool where the fish can guard them! Quick, before the goblins get them."

"Do it!" Brick Bat chittered. The entire swarm of bats swooped down, each picking up what gems its feet could hold and flying away toward the water.

The angry goblins on the ladders tried to grab at the bats, but received only facefuls of guano for their trouble. The stones were rapidly disappearing.

Marrow was meanwhile hurling gems as fast as he could. Suddenly he paused: he had just picked up the two firewater opals. Should he throw these too? It seemed a shame.

Then a goblin tackled him, and he fell back, unable to throw. Marrow did the only thing he could think of: he swallowed the stones. They popped into his head and rattled around inside his skull, where the goblins could not get at them.

"Kick that skeleton out of there!" the chief called. "Use the torches to burn off the bats! We've got the rest of the rocks!"

A goblin charged across the nest and delivered a tremendous boot to Marrow's hipbone. "Ow!" yelled the goblin, dancing around. "I broke my foot!"

But Marrow was already flying apart. He thought fast: what shape should he assume as he landed? He would not be able to reach the nest again, and in any event most of the gems were gone; the goblins would have to dredge the pool to get the best ones. Surely they would do that, so—

He landed as a rigid grid of bones, with his skull in the center and his hands and feet at the corners. He bounced on the stone, and clonked the hard heads of a couple of the goblins who happened to be in the way. The collision hurt neither him nor the goblins' heads; both were mostly bone.

"Bats!" his skull called. "Haul me into the water!"

"What for?" Brick asked.

"I'm going to be a grid guarding the bottom," he replied. "The fish will swim through me, but the goblins are too big."

"Gotcha!" Brick agreed. Under his direction, hundreds of bats came down and latched on to the bones. They lifted him up and over the water, where they dropped him with a splash.

"Take a break!" Marrow called just before his skull sank. "Rest, because *burble blub bloop!*" Too late; his skull was under the water. Magic was great for speaking, but there were limits.

The bottom of the pool was as sculptured as the upper part of the cavern. Teethlike stalagmites rose from below, and the rock curved into potlike depressions. Marrow had used the stalagmites to pull himself along as they entered. Now he did the same, grabbing on with his hands and pulling himself into place. Most of the gems should be in one major pothole here; yes, he could see them collected in the bottom. He settled down until his network covered it completely. He was anchored by the stalagmites at the rim.

"And what, if I may ask, art thou up to, misshapen man?" Perrin Piranha inquired, swimming close.

"The goblins are raiding the nest during Draco's absence," Marrow explained. "I had agreed to guard the nest, but there are too many goblins. So we threw the gems into the water where you could guard them."

"So much had I gathered enow," Perrin said. "But thy present configuration amazes me. To what purpose be it?"

"The goblins used armor against the bats. They will do so against you, or will try to trawl for the gems. This will stop them from getting them."

"Ah, now I fathom thine intent! An the goblins come, we shall guard thy network, till My Lord Dragon return."

"Good show," Marrow agreed.

It was not long before the goblins came. First they lowered little baskets on strings, hoping to scoop up gems and haul them to the surface. The fish simply chomped through the strings. Then the goblins donned protective gear complete with crude boots, weighted by cavern stones, and waded into the pool. The fish could not chomp through to tender flesh, hard as they tried. The goblins forged right on down to marrow's grid, and there they stopped. They could see the gems below it; indeed, the fish were picking up the more widely scattered gems and dropping them into this guarded hole. But they could not reach it. They stood on it and tried to lift it up, which was of course futile. Finally they waded back out to the dry part of the cave, to report to their leader.

"Melikes thy style, skeleton," Perrin said.

"Let's just hope it suffices," Marrow responded. "Goblins are determined cusses, though."

"Sooth, determined," the fish agreed grimly.

Indeed they were. Soon the goblins came down with grappling hooks, which they hooked on to Marrow's bones. The lines were too tough for the fish to bite through. Four hooks and lines were attached; then they went taut.

Marrow clung to the stalagmites as hard as he could, but the force was too strong; his grip broke, and he was hauled up and out of the water. Now he saw that the goblins had converted their sling to a pulley, and dozens of them were pulling on the ropes, drawing the grid out.

He was deposited on the dry cave floor. "Now get down

there with your baskets and bring those gems up!" the goblin chief directed his minions. "Remember, we don't have all day!"

Was it day, now? That meant that the goblins had been held in check all night. If he could hold them for the day too, the dragon would return. That was what he had to try for.

But now he was in grid form, useless here on dry floor, and he could not change form by himself. What form would be better, and how could he achieve it?

Meanwhile the goblins were busy. They were carrying the remaining gems down from the nest and putting them in a kettle beside the chief. Evidently the chief intended to see that no goblin got away with a private treasure; everything had to be gathered in one place, and then it would all be hauled away. The gems under the water would be brought up and added to that hoard. This would take much longer than the goblins might have planned, thanks to Marrow's efforts, but they already had a fair number with which they might abscond even if the dragon returned this instant. He had to find a way to dump that kettle!

He thought of a form, but the achieving of it was more difficult. What he needed was a good kick in the rear. A kick anywhere would do, in his present form, because he really didn't have a front or rear, just top and bottom sides. The bats couldn't do it; they were too small to have much impact.

Well, the goblins had kicked him before. Maybe he could make them do it again. "Hey, purple-nose, how's tricks?" he called to the nearest goblin.

"What did you call me?" the goblin demanded.

"Purple-nose!" Marrow repeated. "You must have the ugliest, blotchiest snoot in captivity! What do you say to that?"

"Hey, Itchlips!" the goblin called to a fellow. "The skull says I'm the ugliest snoot in captivity!"

"He's a liar!" Itchlips retorted. "*I* am!"

Oops! They liked the insult! Now what was he to do?

Maybe, if he couldn't insult them, he could make them jealous of each other. "No, you aren't nearly as ugly as he is," he called to Itchlips. "Compared to him, you are almost cute."

That scored. "Cute? *Cute?!*" Itchlips cried. "You emptyheaded mess of gristle, what makes you an authority, anyway? You wouldn't know ugly if your bald face was rubbed in it!"

"I'd know it if it kicked me in the tail, though!" Marrow retorted. "A pretty boy like you can't kick!"

"Can't kick? Can't kick? I'll show you!" And Itchlips gave him a tremendous kick in the shinbone.

Marrow flew up, delighted. "You're beautiful!" he called in a final sally. Then he landed in his new form.

He was a basket case, finely woven of bones, with the large ones bracing the top and bottom and the small ones between. His skull was on one side, and his hands spaced one and two thirds of the way around its top circle. He was watertight, thanks to his magic.

"Bats!" he called. "Lift me up, take me to the water, scoop up some fish. Can you do that?"

"Of course we can!" Brick said. "We can lift anything, if we can get enough feet on it." They took hold all around and hefted him up.

"Fish!" Marrow called as he lurched to the water and started to fill. "Come in! Don't let go, bats!"

Perrin and a mass of followers swam into the basket. Then the bats hauled them all up, water and all. The flight was shaky, and the water slopped, but they made it. Marrow realized that they must have some lightening magic, similar to Chem's tailflicks, for the full basket had to weigh much more than the bats did.

"Carry us to that kettle!" Marrow cried. "Dump the fish into it!"

The bats did as directed. The slopping basket swung over to the kettle and tilted.

"What's this?" the goblin chief demanded, looking up. Then he recognized Marrow, in the new form. "You again?

I'll fix you!" And he reached up to catch the rim.

"Avast, varlet!" Perrin cried, biting his fingers.

The goblin jerked back so vigorously that he fell into the kettle. Then the basket swung over, tilted, and poured out the water and fish on top of him. Perrin and his crew went to work on the goblin in a chompfest.

"Yeeoouch!!" the goblin screamed. "Get me out of here!"

The other goblins charged over to pull him out, but the piranha snapped at their squat fingers. They were unable to get hold of their leader.

"Dump the kettle!" the chief screamed. "Get the water out!" For he, smarter than the others, realized that the fish could not function well out of the water.

The minions shoved against the kettle, and it tipped over. Goblin, water, fish, and gems flowed out in a soupy mass. The fish continued to bite at whatever anatomy they could find, and the goblin continued to thrash. As a result, most of them slid down the slope and into the pool, where the other fish joined in the fun.

The goblins caught hold of their chief and hauled him out. The fish let go of his arms, legs, rear, and nose and flopped back into the water. By this time most of the gems were back in the pool, and the fish were picking them up by mouth and carrying them to the deepest and most hidden pits.

"Bats!" Marrow cried. "Pick up the kettle, dump it in the water!"

"No!" the chief cried. But the bats swarmed over the kettle, and got hold of it, and hauled it to the pool. It filled with water and sank, and the fish mounted gleeful guard over it.

"I'll get you for that!" the goblin chief yelled at Marrow. "We can't make progress until we get rid of you!"

"Lift me up, get me away from them!" Marrow called to the bats. But the goblins got there first. They laid hands on him, and batted away the bats. Marrow was captive.

"Take him apart!" the goblin directed.

This was bad. If they kicked him, he could fly apart and reform some other way. But if they simply took him apart, he would be helpless until they put him back together.

He tried to hold his form, but the goblins took apart their pulley apparatus and made levers to pry between his bones. He was tough, but not that tough; first they pried his skull loose, and then his other bones. In due course they had him all in pieces.

The chief held up the skull. "What do you say now, bonehead?" he demanded.

"I say you haven't gotten many gems, chomp-nose!" Marrow retorted bravely. The goblin's nose was swollen where the fish had bitten it.

The goblin shook the skull. "But we'll get them now, won't we, scatter-bone? Without your interference, the bats and fish won't be able to stop us." He shook the skull again. "What's that rattle?"

Marrow remembered the two firewater opals he had put in there. "My brains, you idiot!" he snapped.

"I think you have some gems hidden in there. Well, we'll get them out. We'll take your skull home and crack it open." Then he turned to his cohorts. "Take these bones and this skull down to Goblin HQ. Don't let any two of them touch each other. Then return here for work!"

Marrow realized that he was doomed. The goblins had caught on to his nature, and would destroy him and take the two opals. But by the time they did that, more of the day would have passed. Every hour made it more likely that the dragon would return. Most of the gems would be saved, for it would be very slow and difficult work recovering them from the bottom of the pool where the fish had hidden them. He had done all he could.

With that thought, Marrow had to be satisfied, as his skull was carried down into the heart of the goblin realm.

10

NAGA

They reached Mt. Etamin at dawn. "Hang on!" Draco growled as he dived for the tiny entrance. Dolph hung on, knowing the nature of the passage.

But as they swam through the water-filled cave, the fish were agitated. Dolph, in dragonfly form, could not understand fish talk, but Draco reacted immediately. He swam faster, and burst out of the inner pool at formidable velocity.

The bats were hovering. Dolph, being a flying creature, could understand them slightly. "Goblins!" they were chorusing. "Raid!" No wonder Draco had reacted; goblins were always bad news!

Draco landed at the nest. Dolph resumed boy form. Both gazed for a moment, appalled.

The nest was a mess. Its neat rim of stones had been disrupted, and all the gems were gone. There was no sign of Marrow Bones. The goblins had indeed raided.

The bats were chittering volubly. Dolph changed to bat

form so that he could understand them. Gradually the details fell into place.

Shortly after Draco and Dolph had departed, the goblins had broken in, having evidently timed this for Draco's absence. Marrow had fought them off bravely, using great imagination, supervising the bats and fish so that their efforts were far more effective. He had thrown most of the gems into the water and helped guard them there, so that the goblins could not get them. He had performed numerous acts of heroism, including the dumping of a basketful of fish into the goblins' main cache of gems, so that these had been rescued. But the goblins had finally taken him apart and carried him away in pieces. Then they had had a couple of hours to dive for the gems under water. But the fish had hidden them well, and constantly harried the goblins, so that their search was slow and unrewarding. They had in the end gotten only a few gems before they had to flee lest the dragon return and catch them. Most of the gems were safe in the water, and the fish would bring them out at Draco's command.

Draco turned to Dolph. "Your friend was a hero. He saved my treasure. Once the goblins got my gems from this cave, I could not have pursued them. Because of him, I have only cleanup to do. Therefore, in gratitude, I will give you the other firewater opal with the first. I will have the fish bring them both up now." He flew to the water, put his head under, and gave directions. But in a moment he returned without them, puzzled. "Perrin says those two opals never reached the water."

"The opals?" Brick chittered. "The skeleton put them in his head!"

"His head?" Draco asked, perplexed.

"His head is hollow," Dolph explained in bat talk. "But I don't see why he didn't throw them in the water."

"They were closing on him," Brick chittered. "He was caught with them."

"But then he went into the water," Dolph said. "Why didn't he remove them then?"

"He couldn't," Brick said. "He became a grid, then a basket, and then he was taken apart. The goblins spoke of cracking open his skull to get them."

"I've got to rescue Marrow!" Dolph exclaimed.

"I can see that he fought valiantly and well," Draco said. "But I cannot go into the goblins' caves; they are too small. I fear he is lost, and the two opals with him. Perhaps I can give you other stones in lieu—"

"I can go after him!" Dolph said. "I can assume goblin form and go where they go. I must rescue him!"

"That is not wise," Draco cautioned. "They would know you for a stranger, and quickly take you captive too. Your folks would not like that."

"I've got to rescue Marrow!" Dolph repeated with childish stubbornness.

The dragon issued a smoky sigh. "Then I must obtain for you some adult company. I assumed that responsibility when we made our truce, and I cannot let you depart alone. I shall introduce you to the naga."

"The naga? Who is he?"

"The naga are crossbreeds with your folk, who can nevertheless travel into goblin territory. They are the only creatures the goblins fear, for they prey on goblins. But they do not help strangers for nothing. They will exact a price for their assistance."

"But I have nothing to give them!"

"They will then require some service of you, which will not be inconsequential. Really, Prince, I feel it would be better for you to give up your skeleton and return to your home. I will carry you there forthwith, if—"

"No! I'll pay what the naga ask, if they can help me rescue Marrow!"

Draco made a snort of exasperation, exactly like those Dolph had noted in other adults at times, only with more heat. "Then I will introduce you to King Nabob, somewhat against my better judgment. Change form and take hold; we must go to a neighbor cave."

Dolph resumed the dragonfly form, and took hold. Draco

flew to the water, swam through the nether passage, and crawled out the upper one. He flew a short distance to another opening in the mountain, and entered.

The head of a man showed in the darkness at the back of the cave. "What brings you here, Draco?" the man inquired guardedly. "We have not abridged our covenant."

"Change form," Draco growled to Dolph. "I cannot speak their tongue well, but you can. Explain that I brought you to see King Nabob."

Dolph resumed boy form. "I am Prince Dolph," he said. "I have come to see King Nabob."

"You are human!" the man exclaimed, surprised. "What do you want with our kind?"

"Draco says that only you can help me rescue my friend, but you will ask a price."

"Does this have something to do with goblins?"

"Yes. They carried away my friend Marrow."

"One moment." The man turned about and moved away. Now Dolph saw that his body was that of a great serpent. This was a man-headed snake!

In exactly one moment another naga appeared. This one wore a crown. "Remember your protocol," Draco growled under his breath to Dolph. "This is the King."

Dolph bowed. "Thank you for granting me an audience, Your Majesty," he said. "I am Prince Dolph, of Castle Roogna."

The King studied him. "You are a long way from home, Prince. You look to be quite young, too."

"I am nine years old. I am supposed to have an adult creature with me. But Marrow Bones has been taken by the goblins, so Draco brought me here. Will you help me rescue Marrow?"

King Nabob glanced at Draco. "This Marrow Bones is a worthy creature?"

Draco growled assent.

"And this human lad?"

Another affirmative growl.

The King returned to Dolph. "You are a shape changer, Prince?"

"Yes, Your Majesty."

"Can you assume our form?"

For answer, Dolph became a naga, with only his head remaining unchanged.

"We do not challenge massed goblins lightly," King Nabob said. "We could take losses. How do you propose to compensate us for this effort?"

Dolph tried to spread his hands, but had none. "Draco said you might require a service."

The King considered. "You are the scion of King Trent, the Transformer?"

"I am his grandson, Your Majesty."

The King nodded. "That would be a decent liaison. You will marry my daughter."

Ooops! "But I'm only nine years old."

"True." The King pondered another moment. "Then you will be betrothed to her, and marry her when you come of age. She is young, also."

Dolph knew that this was problematical. His mother would throw a queen-sized fit! "Your Majesty, is there no other service I can render you for your assistance?"

"No other I desire."

Dolph knew he had to rescue Marrow, whatever the price. "Then I agree," he said heavily.

"Excellent! I will summon my offspring now." The King whistled.

In a moment a female naga joined them. She had sinuous gray-brown tresses and brown-gray eyes. Her face was really quite cute, and she had little laugh-lines around her dimples.

"Nada, meet your betrothed, Prince Dolph of the human kind."

"Hello, Prince," Nada said shyly.

"Hello, Princess," Dolph replied just as shyly.

"Seal it with a kiss," the King directed.

Nada undulated up and brought her face to Dolph's. She

tried to kiss him, but their noses bumped. "Oh, mice!" she exclaimed, embarrassed.

"Tilt your head, stupid!" the King snapped. "Have you never kissed a boy before?"

"Never, Daddy," she confessed innocently. She tilted her head and tried again. This time their noses did not bump, and her lips touched Dolph's.

It was by any standard a clumsy kiss; both Vida Vila the nature nymph and Mela Merwoman had been much, much better at it. But Dolph experienced a strange, rather pleasant sensation. He realized that he liked Nada. So he kissed her back.

She drew away. "But he has," she said. "I like him."

"So it's sealed," the King said. "Very well, Draco, you may go; we shall take it from here."

Without further word or growl, Draco backed out of the cave and was gone. Dolph was left with the naga.

The King harrumphed. "Well, let's get about it," he said. "We can't afford to be all day while the goblins march."

Dolph hoped it was all right. He did not know these folk, and worried that they might not understand the devious adult concept of honor as well as Marrow or Draco did.

"Daddy will organize whatever it is," Nada told him. "I've never been betrothed to a human prince before! Isn't this exciting?"

"You have been betrothed to others?" Dolph inquired, taken slightly aback.

"Well, no, not actually," she confessed, with a tasteful hint of a blush. "But I knew Daddy would betroth me to someone, as soon as he found a good match. He's very conscientious about things like that. We don't have enough human blood, so I sort of thought it would be to a human instead of a snake."

Because the naga were a cross between man and serpent, Dolph realized. It did seem to make sense.

Meanwhile the King had been snapping orders left and right to the naga that had appeared in the cave. Now he returned to Dolph. "We have assembled a force and de-marked an interception route," he announced. "We can catch the goblins before they reach their stronghold, but we shall have to move rapidly. It would be better if we left you behind, but I fear your presence will be necessary to reassure your guardian that we are acting in his interest. Remain with Nada; she will guide you, for she knows our methods."

"Uh, sure, Your Majesty," Dolph agreed. Adults were always so assertive!

"Get a slither on!" the King ordered. Immediately the naga set off at a rapid slide, their bodies moving efficiently along the contours of the cave.

"We'll follow," Nada said, setting off.

Dolph went with her, but quickly got tangled in his own coils. He had never assumed such a mixed form before, and had no experience with it. His human head wanted to walk, while his serpent torso wanted to slither. He could see very well, despite the darkness, because this form was adapted to it, but could not move in the manner he was accustomed to.

"Oh, that's right—you're human!" Nada said. "You don't know how to slither!"

"I sure don't!" he agreed ruefully. Actually he could have done it without difficulty as a full serpent, because the serpent-brain would have handled it. "I changed to this form to talk to the King, but it takes me a while to get used to a new form."

"I know. It took me forever to master walking," she said. "I kept falling over."

"You can change form too?" he asked, surprised.

"Of course! To human and to snake. We all can, because that's our nature. But I like my natural form best. Don't you?"

"Yes. But my natural form is human."

"Well, you can't help that," she said sympathetically. "But at least you can change to a better shape. Here, I'll show you how to slither. Just watch me."

Dolph realized that the form changing of the other creatures related to their origins. The merwoman had fish and human ancestry, so she could go either way, while the naga could assume the forms of their ancestry. They were not magicians; they had limited abilities. He, in contrast, could assume any form, regardless of his ancestry, and that was a far broader talent.

Nada undulated across the cavern. Her serpentine body flexed sinuously, and was really quite pretty in its motion. "You just sort of brace against things and squeeze forward," she explained.

He tried it, following the same route she had taken, trying to flex his torso the same way. He was clumsy but was able to move. His human brain was getting the hang of it.

The King reappeared. "What's keeping you?" he demanded.

"Just a little trouble making progress, Your Majesty," Dolph said, embarrassed.

"My fault, Daddy," Nada said quickly. "I didn't realize—"

"It's a betrothal, not a marriage!" the King snapped. "No call to get serious yet! Wait till you're of age. Now come along; we can't hold up the journey."

Dolph exchanged a glance with Nada, who made another hint of a blush. Parents were parents, throughout Xanth, and maybe Mundania too! Wordlessly they followed the King.

Dolph still had some difficulty keeping the pace. "Here," Nada said. "Go beside me, and copy my motions exactly, until you catch on. It's not hard."

Dolph joined her, so that their serpentine torsos were touching, he on the left, she on the right. She moved her head right, and he followed, maintaining the contact. Her mid-torso pressed left, and he gave way. Their bodies slid forward with surprising ease. Then her head swung left while her torso swung right, and as he duplicated the motion, he moved smoothly forward too. It was like magic! All they had to do was undulate with the right rhythm, and travel came of its own. Soon they were swaying neatly together, and making better progress.

The King glanced back. He shook his head. "Such eagerness!" he muttered. "Just can't wait for adult games! What is the young generation coming to?"

"Adult games?" Dolph asked, perplexed.

Nada essayed a third hint of a blush, almost achieving it this time. "You know. Stork summoning."

"You know how to do that?" Dolph asked, suddenly interested.

"Of course not! I thought *you* did."

"Me? No. No adult will tell me."

"Me neither. If you ever find it out, will you promise to tell me too?"

"Sure." Dolph tried to shrug, but it didn't work in this body. "And if you find out, you can tell me."

"Maybe," she said, with a cute hint of mischief. Then she turned her face, which remained just beside his, and kissed him again, briefly. This time she got her nose right. It was very nice.

The King chose this moment to look back again. "Now that's enough!" he exclaimed, exasperated. "At least wait till we have rescued the skeleton!"

They broke quickly. "He's afraid we'll figure it out for ourselves," Dolph whispered.

"Some day, some way, we'll find out what they're hiding," she agreed. "Then look out, adults! We'll tell all the younglings, and the conspiracy will be finished."

Dolph definitely liked her attitude.

They undulated onward. Thanks to Nada's guidance, he was moving along fairly well now, and was able to do it by himself. They moved into single file, following the King.

They came to a pool. "Now we can cut off the goblin detachment by using the river channels," the King said. "The gobs are restricted to the dry ones, so must take many diversions. Just hold your breath and swim; there are breathing nooks every so often." Then he plunged into the water.

"Um—" Dolph said, eying the black expanse.

"It's as easy swimming as slithering," Nada said. "Just do the same thing, and you'll move ahead. Why don't you go first, and if you falter or get lost, I'll nudge you in the right direction so you won't drown?"

That was not the most encouraging idea, but Dolph realized that it would have to do. He might have changed to fish-form and solved the problem, but he wanted to remain matched to Nada, because—well, he wasn't sure why. He took a big breath and slithered in.

To his surprise, it worked. He undulated, and forged through the water. He reached the breathing spot in plenty of time.

In a moment Nada came up beside him. "See? It's fun!"

There was barely room for the two of them here. Their heads were close together. "Are you going to kiss me again?" Dolph asked. Now he realized why he wanted to keep this form!

"Should I?" she asked, surprised.

"Well, uh, you did it twice before, when we got close."

"Then it's about your turn, isn't it?"

He hadn't thought of that. He kissed her, making sure to get the nose right. This, too, seemed to work better each time.

The King's head popped up beside them. "What is holding you up now?" he demanded. "Oh." He ducked down and was gone.

Nada laughed. "I think Daddy's beginning to regret this betrothal. If we weren't betrothed, he could tell us no. That's the rule."

Dolph was perceiving increasing advantages to the betrothal. He had never cared for mushy stuff, but this was different: it was fun. Each time they kissed, he liked her better. "All the same, we had better not delay him any more," he said. "I've got to rescue my friend Marrow."

"Of course," she agreed. That was another thing he liked about her: she never argued with him.

He took another breath and dived again. After that it was easy enough, as they went from air bubble to air bubble, following the water channel.

They arrived at a larger cave that had a path worn through its center. There were six naga, as well as the King and Dolph and Nada. "They will be arriving in two moments," the King said. "Now you younglings stay out of the action; we don't want you hurt. But when we have the situation under control, Prince Dolph must talk to the skeleton."

"A skeleton?" Nada asked, horrified.

"Marrow is a good person," Dolph said. "But he is a human skeleton."

"If you say so," she said uncertainly. "But I wouldn't refer to one of my friends that way." It was as close as she had come to differing with him.

Then the two moments were up, and the goblin column appeared. The naga had faded back behind stalagmites and were hidden, as were the King and Dolph and Nada.

The column proceeded. There were three goblin guards, followed by six goblins carrying bags of bones, then three more guards. Twelve in all. Twice the number of fighting naga. That made Dolph nervous, for her knew that goblins were ferocious fighters. Their heads were big and hard, and they seemed to have only an imperfect notion of fear. Had the King miscalculated?

"Take them!" the King cried.

Immediately the naga closed on the column. Three had assumed man form, and three snake form. The men lobbed stones at the goblins, while the snakes slithered up to bite the goblins' feet.

The goblins, caught by surprise, quickly got fighting. The guards had wooden cudgels, with which they struck at the men and snakes. But the men ducked, avoiding the blows. Each caught hold of a goblin, lifted it up, and hurled it into the water beside the path. Suddenly there were three fewer goblins in the fray.

But the six goblins with bags dropped them and opened them and fetched out long bones. They used these bones to strike at the snakes. The snakes lifted their heads and hissed in unison. From their mouths came fog, and the fog enclosed the goblins. Immediately the goblins coughed and choked, suffocated by the vapor. Three more were out of it.

The remaining goblins glared around. "There's a female!" their leader exclaimed, spying Nada. "Take her hostage!"

As one, they charged Nada. She screamed and tried to retreat, but came up against the wall behind her. It was obvious that she knew nothing about fighting.

Dolph assumed ogre form. There was room for it, in this large cave. He leaped between Nada and the goblins. His huge hairy arms reached out to embrace the entire group, and his hamfists smashed into the goblins on either side, compressing them into the center. The goblins, stunned, hardly resisted. They knew that it was futile for their kind to oppose an ogre; some of their forebears were still orbiting the moon from prior encounters, while others had been jammed through keyholes so that their heads became doorknobs. They did not realize that Dolph was not a real ogre, and could not perform such feats.

Then one of them caught on. "How did an ogre get in here?" he cried. "The tunnels are far too small!"

Dolph pounded him on the head, but it was too late. The blow did not hurt him, it only drove him into the stone floor somewhat, and the others now realized that this could not be a true ogre. They burst out of the embrace like popping corn, scrambling every which way. He was only able to catch one, whom he hurled into the water.

But by this time the naga had closed in. Each of the five remaining goblins was caught and dumped into the water. The water did not drown them, for they swam, but it rendered them helpless. They were unable to swim and fight at the same time, and the naga stood guard at the edge to prevent them from emerging. The goblins were not pleased; the water was beginning to discolor from the taint of the language they were using, and Nada was trying to stifle an appalled look. Words like that were known to be damaging to delicate feminine ears.

Now Dolph could look for his friend Marrow. He changed to boy form. "Marrow! Marrow!" he called. "Where is your skull?"

"Mmmph!" came from one of the bags.

Dolph dashed over and dumped out that bag. Several bones and the skull rolled out. There was a gag tied across the mouth. He picked up the skull and tore off the gag "Marrow, is it really you?"

"Who else would it be?" Marrow inquired curtly. "Quick, put me together before the remaining goblins catch up!"

"Remaining goblins?"

"Of course there are more on the way," the King said. "That is why we have to hurry. We don't want to fight the whole stronghold!"

"Maybe we'd better just carry away the bags of bones, and assemble them later," Dolph said.

"No, there might be some missing," Marrow said. "Just follow my directions, and this can be very quick. I regret I cannot reassemble myself, in this situation. Start with the skull bone here; next attach the neck bone, then the shoulder bone—"

"Wait, I have to find them first!" Dolph protested.

"Dump out all the bags; I'll point them out."

Quickly the naga dumped out the bags. Then Dolph carried the skull past the scattered bones. "There!" the skull said, and Dolph picked up the indicated neck bone. There turned out to be several of them, actually. All he had to do was touch the bones to the growing structure, and they snapped neatly into place. Then the shoulder bone, and the arm bones. The work got faster as the skeleton progressed and the remaining bones became fewer.

But when all the bones had been used, Marrow was incomplete. Several ribs and part of his left leg were missing, as well as his whistle finger. "There must be another bag of bones!" Dolph said. "Maybe a goblin fell behind the others."

"But how can you find it without encountering the other goblins?" Nada asked, overcoming her nervousness about the skeleton enough to approach.

"We shall have to wait for it to arrive," Dolph decided.

"This is not wise," the King said. "The main force of goblins may be much larger."

"I can become a tangle tree and hold them off," Dolph said.

"But suppose they are wary, and take another route?" Marrow asked. "I think you had better just leave me incomplete."

"No. I came to rescue you, and I shall rescue all of you. The naga can leave if they want to."

"I can't leave you," Nada said. "You are my betrothed!"

Marrow's skull turned toward her. "What?"

Then they heard the marching feet of the next party of goblins. There was no time for further discussion.

Dolph assumed the form of a tangle tree. His roots writhed across the stone, seeking purchase; his tentacles reached out to block the entire passage.

Dolph could no longer talk in the human tongue, but Marrow could. "Cluster in around the tree!" Marrow cried. "It will not attack you! Defend the tentacles from getting hacked off!"

"Watch out!" a goblin cried from the water. "It's a blubble blurb!" For a naga in man form had just reached out and pushed the goblin's head under water. Angry purple prose bubbles rose, showing the goblin's ire at this interruption.

The goblins heard. "What's that?" their chief called as they marched.

"A tangle tree," Marrow said helpfully as Dolph's tentacles reached out and grabbed the chief.

Then there was chaos, as the new goblins fought the tree. But the tangler had more tentacles than there were goblins, and soon all six of them were hanging in the air.

One of them held the missing bag. Dolph turned him and the bag upside down so that the bones fell out. Marrow limped over and picked them up, setting them in place himself. In a moment he was complete, including his whistle.

"Excellent," said King Nabob. "We have rescued the skeleton. Now who will rescue us?"

Dolph realized what he meant. If he changed back to boy form, all the goblins would be freed, and would immediately resume fighting. If the others tried to escape through the water, they would encounter all the goblins swimming there. If they just waited, in an impasse like the one he had suffered with Draco Dragon, eventually more goblins would come to overwhelm him and the naga. They were trapped!

"Perhaps I can help," Marrow said. "With a bit of help from Prince Dolph."

"But we just rescued you!" King Nabob protested. "We don't want to leave you behind!"

"You won't have to, I'm sure," Marrow said. "Kick me."

"If you insist." The King assumed man form and booted the skeleton in the rear.

Marrow flew apart, and landed in the form of a grate. Then the naga picked up the grate and set it against the entrance to the chamber where the goblins had come from. Then two of them held the grate in place, while two others fished goblins out of the water and carried them to the entrance. They pitched the goblins down the tunnel, and the grate was pushed closed so that the goblins could not return.

Two more goblins were brought. The gate was swung open just enough, and the goblins pitched through.

Before long all the goblins were clamoring on the other side, walled off by Marrow's bones. The naga guarded this gate, preventing the goblins from pulling it apart. Every time they tried, a naga in the form of a snake hissed and

belched noxious fog, driving them back. The vapor did not
bother Marrow, but the combination of bone and fog was
more than the goblins could handle.

Dolph returned to boy form. "But once the naga go, the
goblins will take Marrow apart again, and if Marrow
changes form, the goblins will charge in a mass and overwhelm us!" he cried.

"Not if you become a wood wind," Marrow's skull said.

"A wood wind?"

"Don't they have them in normal Xanth? It is a musical
instrument made of wood, that—"

"Oh. But someone has to play it."

"I have had some experience with music," Nada said.
"Perhaps I could play it."

"But you must hold it very firmly," Dolph said, "because—"

"Of course." She assumed girl form, her head unchanged,
her body bare. Dolph was pleased to note that she was his
own age, not mature. It would have been horrible if she
had turned out to be Ivy's age! She put her hands on his
arms.

Dolph assumed the form of a woodwind. This was a
living plant, for deadwood was beyond his talent. It was
hollow, with holes along its length, and a mouthpiece at
the end. Because Nada had been holding him, she was now
holding his new form.

Nada lifted him to her mouth. Her lips touched his
mouthpiece, which corresponded to his mouth in this form,
and it was like a kiss. He was delighted.

She blew, and he was exhilarated; she had such sweet
breath! Her fingers played over his body delightfully; she
had a nice touch, too.

But there was a special quality of this particular instrument. It blew out much more wind than it took in. That
was why Marrow had suggested it.

Nada lifted him so that he pointed toward the bone grid.
She blew a harder note.

Dolph sent out a fierce jet of air. It crossed the cave and

washed through the grid. "Move out!" King Nabob ordered.

The naga retreated from the grid. Nada blew another note, harder yet. This time the wind howled past the grid, holding it up, shoving it up against the wall.

The goblins were advancing from the other side, now that the naga were gone. Nada blew harder. The howl became a scream, and the wind blasted at the grid and through it, eliciting secondary notes. The goblins were blown off their feet, and went sliding back along the tunnel. Their language was so foul that it turned the air smoky, but fortunately the wind blew the sound away.

"Now kick me down!" Marrow's skull cried. "And blow harder!"

Nada walked up and made a hesitant kick at a hip bone. This turned out to be enough; Marrow flew apart, and reformed in his natural configuration.

But the goblins were charging back. Nada lifted Dolph and blew as hard as she could. Marrow dived out of the way.

The wind emerged with the sound of thunder. It swept down the tunnel, carrying rocks and sand along. It hurled the goblins so far and hard that they disappeared. Even when Nada's breath ran out, and she paused to gasp in more air, the sound of that gale carried back, rampaging onward down the tunnel.

Nada put the mouthpiece to her mouth—and Dolph reverted to boy form. Suddenly they were embracing and kissing, Nada's hands playing a tune down Dolph's bare back.

"There's no stopping those two!" the King complained, not completely annoyed.

"Ooo, you tricked me!" Nada said, no more annoyed than her father.

"I had to catch up on kisses," Dolph explained.

"Move out!" the King said. "Those goblins will be after us."

Dolph and Nada changed to naga form. They slithered

toward the water. Then Dolph halted. "But Marrow can't swim!" he said.

"Kick me into a rope, and bite my end," Marrow said.

"Bite your end?" Nada asked. Then she and Dolph dissolved into laughter.

"I'll do it!" King Nabob snapped. In man form he booted the skeleton; then, as Marrow fell into rope form, the King assumed snake form, and caught the end bone between his teeth. Then he slithered to the water and plunged in.

Already there were stirrings far down the tunnel. The goblins were regrouping! Dolph and Nada slithered quickly after the King. They did not want another session with the goblins!

It was a much harder swim, against the current, but they made it by evening. They collected in the cave where Dolph had started, when Draco brought him. "I believe we have delivered our part of the deal," King Nabob said gravely. "Now my daughter will travel with you, Prince Dolph, until you come of age." He paused as if anticipating an objection from Marrow.

But Marrow had seen the two embrace and kiss. He sighed, shaking his head, knowing that it was too late for a protest. The deal had, after all, been for his benefit.

When he shook his head, the two gems within it rattled. "We must settle accounts with the dragon!" he exclaimed, remembering. "We cannot steal his gems during the truce!"

"No problem about that," Dolph said. "He has given them both to us, one for the merwoman, the other for you, for saving his treasure. Keep them in your head until we return to the sea."

Marrow considered. "Then it seems that all accounts have been settled." He glanced eyeless at Dolph. "But your mother will be most perturbed about—"

"Well, she'll have years to get used to it, until I come of age to marry," Dolph said. He had discovered that he rather liked being betrothed. Naga was the first girl he had encountered whom he really liked.

"You must suffer our hospitality for the night," the King

said briskly, pleased that no trouble had developed. "A boy your age needs food and rest."

Dolph realized how tired he was. "I guess so," he agreed. "I hope your food is good."

Nada made a face. "It's yucky!" she proclaimed.

"It's nutritious," the King retorted firmly.

Dolph sighed. The dread Adult Conspiracy. had manifested again. Children were never allowed anything really good.

11

ISLES

In the morning, well rested and nutritiously (ugh) fed, Dolph and Nada set out with Marrow. The naga escorted them to a hidden cave aperture at ground level, and Nada bid a tearful farewell to her father, the King. She didn't seem to have a mother; Dolph hesitated to inquire about that. He felt guilty about being responsible for their separation, but reminded himself that it was King Nabob who had insisted on the deal. Dolph might have argued that he would keep his word about the betrothal, so that Nada didn't *have* to tag along with him until he came of age. But Nada was the first girl or girl creature he had really liked, and he wanted her company. So he was silent, and guilty.

Nada assumed girl form and kicked Marrow in the tailbone. Marrow flew apart, and landed in the form of a globular cage crafted of finely linked bones. Nada opened the door in it and stepped inside, closing and latching the door behind her. The naga handed her a bag of sandwiches and cookies, as well as several balls of green, blue, and orange juice.

The wind was right. Dolph assumed roc form, spread his wings, and lurched into the air. He caught the Marrow cage with his talons and lifted it. Nada waved to the naga below, then exclaimed at the marvels of flight. She had never experienced anything like this before, and was delighted. Everything was new to her. Listening to her exclamations, Dolph felt anew the wonder of it. It was as much fun having her enjoy it as it had been for him, the first time.

A flying dragon showed on the horizon. It was not Draco; the species differed. It started toward them. "Caw!!" Dolph squawked warningly. The dragon changed course. Even in dragon country, no one messed with a roc in the air. This was one reason he favored this form, just as he favored the ogre on land.

The high winds shifted to favor him, and he made excellent progress southeast. Each time he used this form, he was better at it, becoming a stronger flier with experience. Surprisingly soon the Gap Chasm came into view.

"Oooo!" Nada exclaimed, awed. "What a crack in the ground! How come I never heard stories about it?"

"There was a Forget Spell on it," Marrow explained. "It stopped folk from remembering it until relatively recently, and even now the news spreads slowly. For a time parts of it spun off in forget-whorls that caused some mischief, but now most of those are gone. Now that you have seen the Gap, you will remember it."

"Oh, goody! I don't want to forget a thing! I never knew that being betrothed could be this much fun!"

Dolph had not known it either. But he dreaded his return to Castle Roogna, where his mother would certainly have Something to Say. The fact that he liked Nada would probably make the reckoning worse, because children weren't supposed to have fun.

In due course the seacoast appeared. Dolph followed the coast south, flying lower, until he recognized the region where Mela Merwoman swam. He coasted down to the beach. Now how would they get to her underwater lair? They would have to get more air plants, and—

But then he saw two figures wading from the water. Mela, with legs, and Grace'l, with the knapsack. They had of course noted his approach in the mirror, and had come out to meet the party!

Dolph managed to stall out barely above the beach, and he dropped the cage into the shallow water. It splashed, but the water cushioned its fall so that Nada was not hurt. He was getting better at landings, too!

While Dolph changed to boy form, Nada kicked the cage in the hipbone, then changed back to her natural form. Marrow performed introductions, so that Nada, Mela, and Grace'l could tell each other apart. Then Marrow tilted his skull and knocked it with a hand bone, and the two firewater opals rolled out into his other hand.

Mela gaped. "Two?" Evidently she had not seen the action clearly enough through the little mirror to learn of this before. If the Tapestry had been watching Dolph instead of Marrow, the business with the gems might not have been shown.

"Draco Dragon realized that there had been a misunderstanding," Dolph explained diplomatically. "So he is returning your opal to you. The other—"

"Is its twin, which I am giving to you to redeem Grace'l," Marrow said. "The two make a set, far more valuable than they are individually."

"But only one is mine!' Mela protested.

"Both are yours," Marrow said firmly. "With these you should have no difficulty marrying a suitable merman." He passed the two gems to her.

Dolph kept quiet. He knew that the second opal was rightfully Marrow's, his reward for saving most of the other gems from the goblins. If Marrow had not been there, the goblins would have taken everything. Dolph had told Marrow about the dragon's misunderstanding about the firewater-sand contest, and about Draco's inexplicable reluctance to have the nature of that confusion told to Mela. It seemed that Marrow felt the merwoman should have more back than she had lost.

It also meant, he realized as he thought about it, that Mela would have no further interest in Dolph. With two opals, she could probably have her choice of all the available mermen. Since Marrow was trying to protect Dolph from what his mother would call "predatory females"— whatever that meant—this was as good a way as any.

But mainly Dolph kept silent because now he liked Nada Naga better than Mela Merwoman. He wasn't sure why, because certainly Mela's legs were more interesting, and perhaps other parts of her too, but he thought it was because Nada was a child like him, and saw things pretty much his way. Also, he was betrothed to her.

Mela stood dazed for a long moment, perhaps a moment and a half, gazing at the twin opals as they blazed brightly in her hand. Then she flung her arms around the skeleton and hugged him hard. "Oh, Marrow!" she exclaimed. "You are wonderful!"

"Um, uh," Marrow said, taken aback. "You'll bruise your flesh."

She let him go and stepped back. Sure enough, there was a skeletal pattern across her front where the bones had dented her generous flesh. "I'll survive," she said. "Is there anything at all I can do for you?"

"We, as you know, are searching for the Heaven Cent," Marrow said. "We suspect it may be on a skeleton key. Do you know the nature of the keys farther to the south? Any information would be appreciated."

"Well, I see them mainly from the underside," Mela said. "I forget whether any are skeletal, but there are some Isles of Pleasure—no, that's not it. Isles of Happiness—no, that's not it either. I really can't remember—Ah! Isles of Joy! That sounds like it. There are two or three—no, maybe five or six—I forget how many there are, but several, anyway."

"The Forget Spell!" Dolph exclaimed. "Could some of it have drifted down this way?"

Marrow nodded. "That is possible. That would account for her vagueness about the details." He faced the merwoman. "We thank you, Mela; we shall investigate those several isles. Perhaps the Heaven Cent is on one of them."

"I hope so. Don't hesitate to call on me if you need anything!" Mela stepped into the water, and her feet reverted to flukes. Soon she was gone into the sea.

"She has a nice tail," Nada remarked. Dolph realized that tails were more a part of her life than his, because of her nature. He had always found Mela's legs more interesting than her tail, for some reason, perhaps because legs were more a part of his life.

It was late in the day. Dolph and Nada shared her sandwiches and drink balls, while the two skeletons discussed prospects. "If there is a forget whorl in the vicinity, there could be mischief for us," Marrow said.

"What is a forget whorl?" Grace'l asked.

Marrow explained about the Gap Chasm and the spell that had been on it. "The original spell was disciplined, causing only the forgetting of the Gap itself, once a person departed from it. But the whorls, though much smaller, can be more intense, and cause other kinds of forgetting. By this time they should have faded in strength; still, they should be best avoided."

"But Mela suffered only slight loss of memory, about the isles," Grace'l pointed out. "That should not be dangerous."

"True. But she might also have forgotten other dangers associated with the isles. If there are dragons there, or tangle trees, or more subtle threats, we would be ill-advised to bring Prince Dolph there."

"She could also have seen the Heaven Cent there, and forgotten it!" Dolph called. "We *have* to check!"

"Yes! We *have* to check!" Nada echoed, picking up the spirit of it.

Marrow exchanged a hollow glance with Grace'l, in the way typical of adults. They were reluctant, but unable to refute this impetuous logic.

Soon the two skeletons formed two bone cabins for the night, one for each child to use. Dolph and Nada protested that they would be happy to sleep together, sharing one larger cabin, but for some reason intelligible only to adults the skeletons refused to hear of it.

Nada made a face and sighed. "I thought maybe things would be different outside the caves," she said.

"Adults are adults, all over Xanth," Dolph said. "I don't know what happens when folk grow up, but it never fails. They stop believing in the Monster Under the Bed, and start believing in nutritious food, and they join the Adult Conspiracy and all that other junk."

"Maybe something comes and casts a mean old spell over them," Nada conjectured. "I hope it never catches us!"

"We'll stop it, somehow!" Dolph said fervently.

With that resolution they had to be satisfied. They climbed into their separate cabins and slept.

In the morning Nada turned girl again, for breakfast, and they plucked and ate fresh do-nuts from a nut tree, avoiding the don't-nuts. There was a beerbarrel tree nearby, but true to adult form the skeletons objected. They had to search out wholesome milkweed pods instead, and to finish every last drop of milk in each of their pods. Yuck! Was there no end to this tyranny?

Then Dolph and Nada assumed naga form, and slithered south at a good rate. Marrow wore the knapsack, while Grace'l carried a few extra milk pods for future use. The children agreed glumly that it would have been a different story if the skeletons had had to eat. But the skeletons were independent of food, so had no hesitation in forcing nutritious food on those who knew better.

At noon they came to a signboard posted on the beach ISLES OF JOEY. They stopped and considered it.

"Is that correctly spelled?" Marrow inquired.

"Looks all right to me," Dolph said.

"But you spell the way your father does," Marrow pointed out.

"There is no 'e' in 'Joy,'" Grace'l said.

"Whoever made that sign must have forgotten how to spell it," Nada said.

"Because of the forget whorl!" Dolph exclaimed. "That explains it!" He studied the sign again. "If it really is wrong . . ."

Grace'l made a rattling laugh. "It really is wrong. Joy is spelled J-O-Y. No extra letters."

"What about 'Ile'?" Dolph demanded. "How can it have that 's' in it? Isn't that wrong too?"

"That's just the way it is," Grace'l said. "I-S-L-E."

Dolph gave up. There was no sense trying to talk sense to adults. They were constitutionally incapable of seeing the obvious.

"At any rate," Marrow concluded, "this does seem to be the region Mela was describing. We shall have to watch for isles, and explore them, cautiously."

They continued down the beach. Soon the first isle appeared, not far offshore. It looked quite ordinary, almost mundane; there was no sign of enchantment about it.

The two skeletons arranged to be kicked into their boat and sail configuration, and Dolph and Nada got in. There was a brisk sea breeze blowing in exactly the wrong direction, in the mischievous way such juveniles had, but the skeletons used their tacking magic and angled in toward the isle.

They made it safely to the convenient harbor at the north end of the isle. Here were a number of boats—large, small, and tiny. Dolph and Nada disembarked in human form, and delivered two good kicks to the key bones, restoring the skeletons to their natural forms.

They looked around. A sign proclaimed THIEVES' ISLE.

They considered that. "Are we sure we want to be here?" Marrow asked. "We are not thieves."

"But if there are thieves here," Dolph said, "one of them might have stolen the Heaven Cent, so this would be the best place to look."

A man ambled down a path. He was swarthy, and he had only one eye, and that eye flicked shiftily about. He came to the sign and dropped something on it, then approached the group. "Welcome to Honest Island! I am Black Pete, your friendly host. What brings you here?"

"Honest Island?" Dolph asked. "I thought the sign said—" He faltered, unable to remember exactly what the sign had said.

"What sign?" the man asked, his dusky brow furrowing.

The others shrugged. They did not remember any sign.

"We're looking for the Heaven Cent," Marrow said. "Do you happen to know whether it is here?"

Pete looked more closely at Marrow. "I say, old chap, you could use a good meal! Come to our traveler's hotel. There we shall relieve you of all your burdens."

Dolph was bothered by something, but could not pin it down. Certainly Black Pete was being nice enough. They followed him up the path to an elegant building almost as fancy as a palace. But as they passed through the gallant front portal, Dolph noticed that the whole front side was no more than a huge façade, a giant wall painted to look like the side of a building, with nothing much behind it. The actual building was a crude structure of logs and dried mud, with packed sand for the floor. He found this very curious, but didn't comment because nobody else did.

"Do you have any valuables?" Pete inquired, walking to the other side of the front desk. "We shall be happy to put them in our safe during your stay."

"Just the magic mirror," Dolph said. "But that's small, so there is no need to—"

"Oh? Let me see it."

Dolph dug in the knapsack and pulled out the mirror. Pete dropped something on it—or seemed to, because nothing fell from his hand. "Let me show you to your room," Pete said, leading the way out the back.

They followed. Dolph was bothered again; wasn't there something—but he couldn't remember what it might be, so he followed the others.

They found themselves outside, on a winding path. Pete led them along this, until they came to the harbor. "So nice to have had you here," he said. "I hope you enjoyed your visit. You must come again real soon." He made a little bow, then turned and departed.

Marrow looked at Dolph, perplexed. "Are we going already?"

"We must be," Grace'l said. "For here we are at the water."

Dolph and Nada kicked the skeletons, and they became the boat and sail. Soon they were on their way out of the harbor, carried by a favorable wind.

"Ahoy!"

Dolph looked to the sound. There was Mela Merwoman in her fish tail, waving from the wave. "What are you doing here?"

"Something bothered me about your journey, so I came down to see whether I could help. Do you still have your mirror?"

"Mirror? What mirror?"

Mela grimaced prettily. "Follow me to shore. I think I can help you get it back."

Perplexed, they followed her swiftly swimming body to the main beach. There she put on her nice legs and joined them on land. "There is some reverse wood here; I saw it the other day. Ah, here it is! Pick it up, Dolph, but don't do any magic."

Dolph picked up the bit of wood she indicated. "Of course I know better than to change form while holding this!" he exclaimed. "It would reverse whatever I tried!"

"What about the magic mirror?" she asked again.

Dolph's jaw dropped. "I left it on the desk at the hotel on the isle! At Thieves' Isle!"

"That's what I thought," Mela said. "I knew there was something funny about that isle, but I couldn't quite remember what it was. There have been rumors—" She shrugged. "Maybe you had better take that wood over there and see what you can do."

"Maybe I had better," Dolph agreed. He passed the wood around, and as each of the others touched it, faces lighted. Now they all understood what had happened.

"They used forget magic," Marrow said. "Black Pete dropped a bit of it on the sign, and then on the mirror, and we forgot all about them."

"But then how could Black Pete remember about the mirror?" Nada asked. "I mean, if the spot spell makes everyone forget about objects—"

"It was only a tiny bit of forget, left over from the great old Forget Spell," Marrow concluded. "Just enough to make us forget one thing for a few hours. That mirror is probably still sitting on the counter, until the forget wears off. Then Pete will find it and pick it up. It's the perfect theft! By the time we remembered it, ordinarily, we would have been so far on our way that it wouldn't have been worthwhile to return for it."

"And if we did," Grace'l added, "he would just use the spell again. What a thief!"

"But why does he have that sign out at the harbor?" Dolph asked. "That could give him away at the start!"

Marrow pondered. "Perhaps that is his way of testing travelers. If they forget the sign, then he knows the spell is working on them, and he can use it to rob them. Very crafty."

"Well, let's go back and fix him!" Dolph said. "I'll hold the reverse wood, so it won't interfere with the rest of you; as long as I remain in my natural form, it won't affect me. Then I'll give it to one of you, and—" He found himself too angry to finish his thought, knowing that it wasn't a very nice thought.

"Good luck!" Mela said, returning to the water. "I'm glad I was able to help you, after the way you helped me."

Dolph nodded. Sometimes it did pay to do nice things for other folk, even when a person did not expect any return. He had not really understood that before, but it was quite clear now.

They resumed their sea-crossing group, and returned to the isle. By the time they got there, Dolph had cooled a bit, and decided to keep the reverse wood. He could probably do more with it in his natural form than he could as a vengeful dragon.

There was the sign: THIEVES' ISLE. In a moment, Black Pete reappeared. He looked surprised when he saw them. "Back again so soon? What can I do for you?" He dropped another invisible thing on the sign.

"Oh, we'll think of something," Dolph said, keeping tight hold of the reverse wood.

They followed Pete up to his mock office. There lay the mirror on the counter, as Dolph had left it the hour before. He picked it up and put it back in his knapsack. Then he touched the reverse wood to Black Pete. "What are you?" he asked.

Pete looked startled. "I am the worst thief and rascal of these here parts," he said. "I steal from everybody who comes here, by making them forget their valuables."

Dolph nodded. The wood had reversed the man's nature, making him completely honest. His talent, obviously, was dishonesty; the man was an accomplished liar and thief. Had this not been his magic, the reverse wood would not have worked, for it had no effect on mundane things. Dolph was honest, but the wood did not make him dishonest because no magic was involved in his character. Now Black Pete was unable to conceal what he had done, because his own magic worked against him. "What of the others?"

"There are no others; I work alone."

"But there are many boats in the harbor!"

"I made their owners forget them, and now they are mine."

Which meant the prior owners must have had to swim ashore, not remembering that they had boats. Some might have drowned or been caught by sea predators. Black Pete deserved no mercy!

But he realized that there would be almost no way to return all the stolen things, for their owners were long gone. All that could be done was to post some kind of notice of warning about this isle, so that other travelers would know its nature and stay away. Or else kill Black Pete. Dolph couldn't stomach that.

"Do you have the Heaven Cent here?" he asked.

"No."

Since the man had to tell the truth, that was that. But Marrow had an idea. "We must get some of those bits of forget. They could be useful."

"Give us some forget bits, and tell us how to use them, and we shall leave you alone," Dolph said.

"Gladly!" Black Pete agreed, aware that he was getting off lightly. "I found a bunch of mustard seeds that had soaked in a forget whorl a long time. Whenever I drop one of them on something, it becomes forgettable for several hours. It doesn't affect me, because the forget spell only comes out when jogged by the fall. Here is a package of the seeds." He brought out a little square envelope.

"Thank you," Dolph said, taking the package.

They departed. Back on shore they set up a sign saying BEWARE OF THIEF ON ISLE—USE REVERSE WOOD. They left the reverse wood beside the sign. Dolph hoped that helped. It would if the travelers passed this way first, and if Black Pete didn't cross to the mainland.

They proceeded south. Soon they spied another isle offshore. For some reason isles were always offshore, never onshore where it would have been easy to reach them. Dolph wished they had the reverse wood with them, because he was now wary of these isles. Still, at least he knew to be careful.

They sailed across. There was a sign on the shore saying BEAUTY ISLE. Indeed, the isle was incredibly beautiful. It was covered with the loveliest ornamental trees and plants, and in its center was a perfectly conical mountain that shone in the sunlight. The top rose into the deepest blue sky Dolph had ever seen, and was shrouded by a mist that sported the colors of a rainbow. Dolph and Nada simply stared at it, overwhelmed by its luster.

"I do not trust this," Marrow's skull said. "Anything that pretty is bound to be an illusion."

But it was no illusion. They landed and changed forms and inspected the isle from several views. It was just exactly as beautiful as it seemed.

"A tangle tree can be pretty too," Marrow warned. "Until it attacks."

"If we find a tangle tree, I'll turn into something worse," Dolph said. But the notion bothered him, for not many things were worse than a tangle tree.

Then something worse appeared. It looked like a cross between a roc and a tangle tree, for it was huge and had giant wings and many tentacles. It charged down on them.

Dolph's mind went blank. What could he become that would scare this off?

"A wall-nut tree!" Marrow cried.

Dolph became a wall-nut tree. Suddenly his body was like a big wall formed of hardwood, with a few branches and leaves at the top. The monster smashed into this solid wall and fell flat. Little stars and planets spun in the air around its snout, showing that it had been knocked silly.

Dolph assumed the form of a similar monster. "Is the Heaven Cent on this isle?" he asked.

"There are one hundred and one and a half monsters, each worse than the last," the creature said as the stars and planets cleared. A squiggly spiral line hovered a little longer, showing that it was still disoriented. "But no Heaven Cent."

"Thank you," Dolph said. He returned to boy form. "All monsters but no Heaven Cent," he reported. "We'd better get off this isle before the next monster comes, because it will be worse than this one."

Indeed, as he spoke, there was a horrendous bellow from the lovely forest. The skeletons quickly got kicked into the sail and boat, and Dolph and Nada jumped in. They did not dare look back as the second monster charged, knowing that the sight of it would terrify them.

"There is another isle close by, to the south," Marrow said. "Shall we sail for it directly?"

"Why not," Dolph said. "It can't be worse than this one!"

He was wrong. The isle looked as awful as the other looked good. The trees on it were rotten, and the air stank. It was as if all the garbage of Mundania had been dumped there. The only good thing about it was that much of it was shrouded in noxious fog. There was a sign on the shore: HORROR ISLE.

"Why, this is like one of the disgusting settings of the gourd!" Marrow's skull exclaimed. "How delightful!"

"Theb why don't dou eggsplore it!" Dolph wheezed, holding his nose against the smell.

"Why don't I explore it?" Marrow repeated. "Thank you; I shall! It will be like a visit home."

"Me too!" Grace'l exclaimed.

"We'll wait here," Dolph said.

"Low to the ground," Nada agreed, converting to snake form and burrowing her nose in the sand.

Dolph changed to snake form, and burrowed his head next to hers. The sand helped some by filtering out some of the worst of the odor. "Mother never told me that going on a Quest would be like this!" he hissed in snake talk.

"Mine neither!" she agreed. "I hope you find your Cent soon!"

"Well, it should be on one of these—" Dolph paused. There before him was something ugly, even after allowing for the smell. It looked like a ghost, but not one of the nice ghosts of Castle Roogna. This one was huge and misshapen and had a grotesque scowl stretched across its face.

"What's that?" Nada asked, seeing it.

"It looks like a nasty ghost," Dolph said.

The ghost floated close. "Booo!" it yelled, gaping its mouth at Nada.

"Eeeeeek!" she hissed, terrified. The ghost laughed, gratified.

"But ghosts can't hurt real folk!" he hastened to remind her. "I know lots of ghosts, and—"

"I never saw a g-ghost before!" she said, trying to bury her head in the sand.

Dolph was amazed. "You never saw a ghost? That's amazing!"

"That's bliss!" she retorted. "They're horrible!"

"Boooo!" the ghost yelled again, behind her.

"Eeeek!" Nada screamed again, almost sailing into the air. The ghost guffawed.

"Now you stop that!" Dolph hissed at it.

The ghost made an obscene face at him.

That made Dolph so angry that he did something he had never done before: he assumed the form of a ghost. It was just as big and almost as ugly as the other. "Booo yourself!" he yelled at it.

Startled, the ghost floated rapidly away. "Serves it right," Dolph muttered in ghost talk, floating close to Nada.

"Eeeeek!" she screamed a third time, seeing him,

Quickly he changed back to snake form. "Hey, it's me!" he hissed. "I got rid of the ghost!"

She looked horribly relieved, which was not easy for a snake to do.

Then several more ghosts charged toward them. "Bury your head!" Dolph cried, afraid of her reaction. "I'll scare them off!" He became the biggest, worstest ghost he could imagine, so ugly it even horrified himself.

But the other ghosts floated on by, paying him no heed. What were they fleeing from?

Then Marrow and Grace'l came into view. "Hello, Dolph," Marrow called. "We have checked the isle: there is no Heaven Cent here. What a delightful place, though!"

The ghosts had been fleeing from the two walking skeletons! What a reversal! "But how did you recognize me?" Dolph asked in ghost talk.

"Oh, you're in spectral form," Marrow said. "I hadn't noticed. Of course I recognized you; you're the only prince on the isle."

Dolph reverted to boy form. "Let's get away from here! Nada can't stand it, and neither can I."

"Of course." The skeletons formed the sailboat, and Dolph held it while Nada slithered in, forgetting to change form. It occurred to him that this might be a better way to sail, so he returned to snake form and curled up with her in the bottom of the boat.

"How could you become a ghost?" Nada hissed as the wind and waves caught the craft.

"I just assumed the form, same's I do for any other creature," he hissed. "That's my talent."

"But a ghost isn't alive!"

Dolph hadn't thought of that. "I guess I can assume some un-alive forms too, if they move and act like living things. I never thought about it. When that ghost scared you, I just got so mad—" He shrugged, but of course messed it up in snake form.

"There is another isle close by," Marrow's skull said. "Shall we check it now?"

Dolph would rather have gone straight to shore and forgotten about isles for a long time. But he knew that he had to check every isle, because whatever one he skipped would be the one with the Heaven Cent, and that it would be better to check them as fast as he could. "Yes," he hissed regretfully.

The boat shifted course. Dolph lifted up his snake eyes and looked at the isle they were approaching. It sparkled like a monstrous gem, the rays of the sun seeming to be attracted to it. No trees grew on it, no brush or even grass; it was just one big scintillating rock.

"Curious," Marrow observed.

As they drew close, they saw a sign that seemed to be formed of the substance of the isle. Carved in it were the words ISLE OF WATER.

Dolph assumed boy form, and Nada became a bare girl beside him. They laughed. "How can an island be water?" Dolph asked. "The sea is water!"

Then they saw something beside the sign. It looked like a worm, poking its snout out of a hole in the rock. So the isle was inhabited after all!

Dolph assumed worm form. "Ahoy, worm!" he called in vermiculish, which was the language of worms. "Is that sign correct?"

"Certainly," the worm replied. "I am the water worm, here to welcome all to the Isle of Water. Come let me touch you, and you will understand."

Dolph distrusted this, because of their experiences on the other isles. So far nothing much good had come of their explorations there. Still, he did not want to be impolite, so he didn't make any objection. "Is the Heaven Cent here? That's all we are looking for."

"Come closer and I will answer," the worm replied.

Then the prow of the boat nudged up against the isle. The worm touched the tip—and the tip dissolved into water.

"Get out of here!" Dolph screamed, hoping the skeletons would understand him.

The sail swung about, catching the wind at a different angle, and the boat skewed away to the side. Dolph and Nada changed quickly back to snake form and ducked low to avoid getting knocked by the boom. "My elbow bone!" Marrow's skull exclaimed. "It's gone!"

"The water worm turned it to water!" Dolph hissed. "Everything it touches turns to water! That must be why this is called the Isle of Water."

"Then your Heaven Cent can't be here," Nada pointed out. "It would have been turned to water."

Yet Dolph wasn't quite satisfied. "Why hasn't the isle itself turned to water?"

"It *is* water, early birdfood!" the water worm called. Its words were hard to distinguish, because vermiculish differed significantly from snake talk, but that was the way Dolph understood it. He assumed worm form to talk back.

"But it's solid!" he called, poking his snout over the gunwale of the boat. He really couldn't see well at all in this form, but he could tell by the sound that they were leaving the worm, and therefore the isle, behind.

"It's solid water!" the worm explained.

"Ice?" Dolph asked. "It should melt in this sun!"

"Not ice! Dry water! It attracts the rays of the sun, and they dry it out until all that's left is dry water. I turn anything that comes here into more water, so the isle can grow. Come back and I will show you!"

"Maybe another day," Dolph replied wryly. What a close call that had been!

Meanwhile Nada had assumed girl form and was inspecting Marrow's elbow-prow. "You poor thing," she said. "Does it hurt?"

"Of course not," Marrow replied bravely. "Skeletons don't hurt! We have no nerves. But I will look funny without an elbow bone."

At that point the sail made a flapping in the wind that sounded very much like laughter.

Nada felt her own elbow. "I'm not used to this form, I guess," she said. "Exactly where is the elbow bone?"

Dolph realized that he couldn't find it either. He had arm bones, but not elbow bones. "Can you grow a new one?" he asked.

"In time," Marrow said with resignation.

They sailed on, their spirits somewhat dampened by the episode of the Isle of Water. But Dolph realized that it could have been worse: King Cumulo Fracto Nimbus could have shown up, and tried to turn everything wet.

"There is another isle ahead," Marrow said.

"I'm sick of isles!" Dolph exclaimed, but in his worm form all that came out was a muted gurgle, as of dirt being digested. He changed to boy form. "Let's get it out of the way, before I decide to quit this Quest and go home to Castle Roogna."

"I believe your mother thought that would happen some time ago," Marrow's skull noted.

They sailed up to the isle, which was a conventional one with rocks and trees and grass. A sign on it said FAKE ISLE. Dolph did not like the look of that any better than he had liked the reality of the prior isles. Was it actually the back of a floating monster?

They drew up to it—and through it. There was nothing there! "It's illusion!" Dolph exclaimed, relieved.

Then something bumped the boat from below. Nada

peered over and down. "Eeeeek!" she screamed in exactly the way girls did.

Dolph looked. There was a giant krakan weed organizing its tentacles for a good grasp on the boat. That was about as grotesque a monster as they could have encountered, next to an ogress. It was using the Fake Isle as a hiding place, so it could catch any creature who tried to walk on it.

There was only one thing to do. Dolph jumped into the water, changing into an even bigger krakan. "Mine! Mine!" he burbled in weed words.

"Well, now!" the krakan burbled back. Now Dolph realized that it was female, and actually a pretty attractive grotesquerie of her kind. "What say we tangle some tentacles, handsome?"

Dolph knew that even if he had been old enough, he would have hesitated to get entangled with her. But how could he turn her off without either angering her or letting her grab the boat? He couldn't think of anything.

"Uh, just a moment," he burbled. Then he swam to the surface beside the boat, assumed boy form, and quickly scrambled in. "It's a krakan, and she wants to tangle tentacles with me. What do I do?"

"Use one of the forget seeds," Marrow said promptly.

Of course! Dolph delved into his knapsack and pulled out the seed pack. He opened it and managed to draw out one of the tiny mustard seeds. "But how do I drop it on her? The water will carry it away!"

"Not on her," Marrow said patiently. "On the boat."

"Oh." Dolph felt pretty stupid. Of course it wouldn't do to have them forget the kraken; the *kraken* needed to forget *them*. He dropped the seed to the bottom of the boat, exactly as he had seen Black Pete drop them on other things.

He looked into the water. The kraken seemed to have lost interest; she was drifting away. Meanwhile, they were coming out the other side of the pretend isle. Close ahead was yet another isle; they were thickly clustered here!

They moved on toward it. This one resembled a huge cake, with chocolate sauce and ice cream piled on top, and spicy colored sugar sprinkled over everything. "Look at that!" Dolph exclaimed, his mouth watering. "Decent food at last!"

"I'm hungry!" Nada said, joining him in girl form. "Let's eat it all!"

"No, no!" Marrow's voice cried. "That is not a suitable meal!"

Dolph glanced back, but couldn't remember exactly where Marrow had gone. But he has sure that just a little cake would not hurt anything, and indeed he was hungry, now that Nada mentioned it.

A sign on the cake said FOOD ISLE. Dolph saw little fish nibbling at the fringe. They looked happy and healthy, so it was probably very tasty. In a moment they would be close enough to grab some.

"I shall have to steer away!" Marrow's voice came. "Grace'l, change your angle!"

The boom swung around. Dolph and Nada, nervous about getting hit by it, jumped into the water and splashed toward the cake. They grabbed big handfuls and stuffed them in their mouths. The cake was delicious!

Meanwhile, Marrow's voice came from the background. "This is no good! You will get sick on that food! You must get back into the boat!"

Boat? Dolph looked at Nada, and she looked at him. Both shrugged, remembering no boat. Then they climbed onto the cake, ascending toward the ice cream. Every step of the way was excruciatingly tasty!

They reached the top where the chocolate sauce and ice cream were. Sheer delight. They both crammed as much as they could into their mouths, as fast as they could, afraid that some adult would arrive and issue a firm No. They kept gobbling with the kind of desperation any person has who fears interruption, but there was no interruption. They gouged out huge hunks of sauce-dripping cake and fed them to each other. Then, between mouthfuls, they made cakeballs and threw them at each other. They hurled chocolate cherries. Then they played pie-in-the-face with huge masses of ice cream. They lay on their backs in the icing and moved their arms and legs to make angel shapes. There was chocolate all over them, instead of clothing. Nada looked as if she was wearing a mud plaster on her hair. Dolph could not remember when he had more fun!

Then, mysteriously, Dolph began to lose his appetite.

He was too full to eat any more! It was hard to believe, because he had never had his fill of cake and ice cream before, and had not realized it was possible.

Nada was looking a bit green, and she was not in her snake form. "I think—I ate—too much," she said.

Dolph concluded reluctantly that this was possible, if incredible. His belly was uncomfortably distended. Delicious food was all around him, but somehow it no longer appealed. In fact, it turned him off. "Where's Marrow?" he asked.

"I'm not sure," Nada wheezed. "The last I remember he was changing into a—I forget what. Oooo, my stomach!"

They sat side by side on the cake as the sun went down. Then Dolph had to do something private, so he walked across the cake, found clear water, and did it there. Nada went to the other side of the cake and might have done something similar. Dolph wasn't quite sure whether girls did it, but he guessed they might. After all, they ate, just as boys did.

At any rate, he was beginning to feel better, but he still didn't care for any more cake. He hated to admit it, but he really had had too much. Gorging on cake and ice cream had turned out to be less fun than he had expected.

"Do you think the Heaven Cent is here?" he asked.

"If it is, it's buried in cake," she replied. "We'd have to eat our way down to it." She grimaced. "The very thought makes me—"

"Me too," he agreed, feeling green himself. "So I guess it isn't here." He wasn't totally sure of the logic, but it seemed good enough for now.

Then, as dusk closed, Nada remembered. "Boat! They turned into a boat and—and—"

"Sail," Dolph finished. "We were sailing! How could we have forgotten?"

"The forget seed! You dropped it, and—"

"And we forgot the boat! We made the kraken forget it, but the spell worked on us too! And since Marrow *is* the boat—"

"We forgot Marrow," she said. "We heard him, but just couldn't really remember him!"

"There he is now!" Dolph said, gazing down. He waved. "Hey, Marrow! Come close so we can get back on!"

"It's about time!" Marrow's skull called back.

Dolph realized that this was a deserved reproof. He and Nada slid down the side of the cake and splashed into the water. They washed themselves off, especially behind the ears, then clambered into the boat as it came close. How good it felt to be back in the company of the adults!

"Do you wish to explore the next isle now?" Marrow inquired.

Dolph groaned. "Do we have to?"

"Fortunately not," Marrow said with the hint of a bony chuckle. "We sailed around a bit while you were occupied, and spied no more isles in this vicinity. We shall have to proceed on land for a while."

"Oh, goody!" Nada said, lapsing into her natural form and curling up in the bottom of the boat. She looked as if she had just swallowed a rabbit whole. "I don't think I'll eat again for a month!"

"Yuck!" Dolph exclaimed. "Don't say that word 'eat'!"

"It certainly does seem to be food for thought," Marrow said, satisfied.

Neither child commented. The remark was evidently intended as adult humor. It wasn't funny. Dolph changed to naga form and joined Nada at the bottom. He was still stuffed. It was easy to understand why snakes slept for a long time after eating a big meal; they couldn't stand the thought of food! Certainly *he* couldn't. If he dreamed of cake, he would know a night mare was responsible.

The boat sailed toward the mainland. By the time it got there, both children were asleep.

12

GOLD COAST

In the morning they trekked south. Nada's digestion still wasn't well, and Dolph appeared distinctly uncomfortable, but neither complained. Nada wished she hadn't eaten so much cake and ice cream, but she had seen no good way to avoid it. She was playing the part of a child Prince Dolph's age, so was guided by his actions, and he had stuffed himself the moment he had the opportunity. If she had not joined him with seemingly equal eagerness, he might have been suspicious, and she could not afford that. So she had thrown herself into it, knowing the consequence—which consequence she was now experiencing. The liability of acting like a child was suffering the pains of childishness.

It was no good dwelling on her stomach, though. So she paced Dolph as the two of them slithered along in their matching naga bodies, and turned her mind elsewhere.

She really did not like this business of deceiving the Prince. On the other coil, she understood the need. Her people's situation was getting desperate, and they had to do what they had to do to save themselves. Her father had explained it to her five years before: the goblins were not much good at anything except breeding and raiding. Unfortunately, they were doing that in Mt. Etamin. Their breeding meant that their numbers were increasing, and that made their raiding worse. The recent business with Draco Dragon's nest had really pointed it up: never before had they dared do that. But they had so many of their kind now that they could afford to keep spies at all the key places, watching the dragon, so that they could strike the moment he was gone for more than a few hours. They were watching the naga folk similarly, and encroaching with increasing nerve. Her father, King Nabob, had held them off by judicious strikes, so that it was unsafe for goblins to penetrate naga territory. But the pressure was increasing, and one year the goblins would simply overrun the naga, and that would be that.

So her father had sent an emissary to the one creature who could solve their problem, six years ago. That emissary was Naldo, Nada's brother and heir to the crown. Naldo had gone to the Good Magician Humfrey, of the human folk, and asked his Question. Then he had had to serve a year as a guardian of the magician's castle, threatening to squeeze intruders in his coils without ever really hurting them, at times quite a challenge. Thereafter Naldo had returned with the Answer, which turned out to be a shock to them all.

It was: *Marry what Draco brings.*

They had spent months analyzing those four words. They knew that the Good Magician always spoke truly, but that his Answers were sometimes subject to interpretation. There was no question about Draco: he was the Dragon of the Mountain, hardly the best of neighbors. The King elected at once to cultivate relations with Draco, so that he would bring what was required, when the time came. The deal was that the naga would never raid the dragon's nest, and the dragon would never attack the naga folk. Draco had been glad to agree, because he was unable to hunt in their caves anyway, so was losing nothing. Relations had become amicable, as they had a common enemy in the goblin horde. Draco had promised to bring them anything he thought might interest them.

But marriage—who was to marry whom? It seemed most reasonable that this applied to Naldo, since he was the one who had obtained the Answer, and he was of age. But how could they know what female the dragon would bring? They slithered around and around this matter, and chewed on it, and digested it as well as they could, and concluded that it must be a young human creature. A naga could by nature marry only one of three creatures: naga, snake, or human. The naga lacked the power to hold off the encroaching goblins forever, so that Naldo's marriage to one of their own would not seem to help. They needed an outside alliance. The serpent folk could handle goblins, but preferred to live on the land's surface, avoiding the depths of the mountain, so that too seemed inappropriate. Thus the human folk were the only real hope; they could live almost anywhere.

But not just any human folk. Ordinary humans had little special power, and were just as wary of goblins as were the naga. It had to be a princess, for two reasons: she could command many other humans, bringing the strength of numbers, and she could do magic. For this was the peculiarity of the human kind: they required magic in their royalty. Not minor magic, which they all had to some degree, but formidable magic. Magician-class magic. If a child of the King lacked that kind of magic, she would not be termed a princess, but merely an offspring. Thus a princess was, by virtual definition, a Sorceress, capable of truly potent magic. That was the type of magic that could turn aside the goblins.

Satisfied at last about the answer, they had waited. They knew that no human princess would come voluntarily to these depths; human folk were just as protective of their kin as were naga folk. The dragon would bring her. That would enable the naga to pose as rescuers, and that would dispose the Princess favorably, so that she would agree to marry one of her rank: Prince Naldo. Indeed, Naldo was quite handsome and accomplished in all his forms, a suitable match for any creature. So he held himself in readiness for the Princess, hoping to impress her, for the naga did not marry involuntarily; they had to have the union desired by both parties. The human Princess had to *want* to marry Naldo, or all would be for nothing. Because humans, like centaurs, had been known to be awkward about interspecies liaisons, Naldo knew he would have to make a good impression not only on the Princess, but on her family too.

There was just one human princess available: Ivy. She was then nine years old, and by all accounts quite cute and quite assertive, with a subtle but potent magic talent. She could intensify any quality she saw in another creature, whatever that might be. Certainly this could foil the goblins; if she saw Naldo as invincible against goblins, then he would be so. If she saw him as very intelligent, then he would be smart enough to figure out how to stop the goblins. So this was obviously the match the dragon had in mind.

Except for the matter of age. Nine was really too young for a princess to marry. She should be at least thirteen. So they knew they would have to wait for Ivy to grow up somewhat. Then she would somehow stray, and Draco would capture her, and for some reason instead of eating her would bring her to the naga. When that happened, Naldo would be ready with his charm.

The years had passed. Princess Ivy had grown. According to the reports, she was developing into a very pretty girl. They managed to conjure a picture of her, confirming it. Naldo was in love with her just from the picture and description. The goblins were pressing harder, but the naga had courage, knowing that their Answer was near.

Then Draco had come—and brought a boy. In a single flash of horror, King Nabob had realized their error. But in a second flash he had redeemed himself in the Kingly manner. He had summoned Nada, and betrothed her to the young Prince. The Answer had been implemented after all.

Nada had realized immediately what she had to do. She had been at the periphery of her brother's training, and had picked up snippets over the years. She was a princess herself, and knew the royal graces. She was also a young woman, who had ascertained to her own satisfaction that she could turn the head of any eligible male (and some ineligible ones too) she chose. Had this been an ordinary situation, she would have had little trouble.

But this was not ordinary. Prince Dolph was a child, just nine years old, while she was a woman of fourteen. Exactly the age of Princess Ivy, with whom she had always identified somewhat. Her brother had even practiced with her, letting her assume human form and play the part of a strange human princess, so that he could perfect his approaches. He was five years older than she, which was a fair differential for such a union. If he hadn't been her brother, she would have considered him an excellent match. It had been hard to see how Ivy could not be charmed. But by similar token, Nada was five years older than Prince Dolph, and that made all the difference.

Because, they had learned, Dolph hated his big sister. She bossed him endlessly, and no prince liked that. Also, girls were supposed to be more innocent than the boys they married. Boys were supposed to know everything, and the girls very little. Since it was manifest that girls were smarter than boys, the only way to get around this was for the girls to be younger. Then, after they were married, they could show their superiority. The boys were then either too stupid or too embarrassed to acknowledge the situation, so they ignored it. They did not even tell each other. That was the universal way of it. Everyone knew all about it, except the men, and of course no woman would tell. It was the mirror to the Adult Conspiracy, only in this case the victims did not know it existed until too late.

Nada was pretty sure she could handle the rest of it. She had never expected to have to play this role, but she was her father's child, and she generally had her coils in order.

She could marry Dolph and make him happy and so save her folk from the goblin menace. Except for one thing: how was she to make the little prince believe she knew less than he? When not only was she female, she was five years older?

The answer had sprung from the question. She simply had to appear younger. Thus she had reduced herself in form and attitude by six years, and assumed the aspect of an eight year old. She had always been petite in her three forms, so that was no problem. She just had to modify her human form to be undeveloped, and this was possible because it was not her natural one; she could make it what she wanted, to a degree. It had only become womanly in the past two years, so it wasn't hard to revert. In one respect she remained a child: she had not yet discovered the secret of summoning the stork. She had approached the King about that a year ago, saying "Now I am grown up; see, my body is developed. Tell me how to summon the stork." But her father had changed the subject. She regarded that as a breach of faith. It wasn't fair for the King to regard her as still a child when she was all of thirteen, and even fourteen. But now she was satisfied, because she was playing the part of a real child, and this made it easier. She had even remembered to forget how to kiss; she thought that was a nice touch.

Thus Prince Dolph had no suspicion, and they got along well. She would be satisfied if he never knew the truth, and never would she reveal how much more she knew than he. The welfare of her folk was at stake, and she would do her part. The loss of her personal happiness was a small price to pay for that honor.

But oh, she wished they had not encountered that Isle of Food! The other isles had been bad enough; she had not had to pretend her dismay when the ugly ghost had loomed, or when she had spied the kraken weed in the sea. She had had to be careful only at the outset, when they were rescuing Marrow Bones from the goblins. She had learned to play musical instruments only in the last three years, and could play much better than an eight year old. But the need for the wood wind had been great, so she had risked playing it well, trusting that the Prince would not know how much skill it required. The rest was easy: the exclamations when they were carried aloft, when they saw the great Gap Chasm, and so on. She had never before traveled like this, so her excitement really wasn't feigned. The truth was, it was fun being young again, especially with Dolph, who was a nice boy. She could be his friend, and later she would be his wife, though of course she would never love him. He was simply too young. By the time he was old enough, she would be too old. Not that it mattered; her father had explained that love was irrelevant in a marriage of convenience or alliance, and royal marriages seldom took note of it. What counted were the proprieties and the union, in that order.

"Hey! Gold!"

Dolph's exclamation brought Nada out of her reverie. She looked around. Sure enough, the landscape had turned golden.

"This would be the Gold Coast," Marrow remarked.

"Almost everything is gold, here. We shall have to cut inland to pass it by, so that there will be food for you."

"But those apples look good!" Dolph cried, slithering up to a golden tree with three bright gold apples on it.

"I don't think you should try those," Marrow said, and hurried them on.

They cut inland, and the golden vegetation faded. Of course they ran the risk of missing an isle that might be off the Gold Coast, but that couldn't be helped.

In the evening Nada and Dolph shared a potluck pie from a pie tree, lacking appetite for more. They washed in a little stream, even behind their ears, under protest. Nada remembered how she had hated that, as a child, and of course she hated it again, now, to stay in character. It really was fun in its way, being a child again, letting the skeletons assume the adult responsibilities. They were very good at it, despite their rather alien nature.

Then Marrow and Grace'l assumed their cabin forms, and Nada and Dolph settled in for the night. These bony structures were surprisingly comfortable, because the air was filtered and maintained at an even temperature, and they were safe; no hostile creatures could intrude. The skeletons were form changers as much as any other creatures were; it was that their forms were always skeletal. Prince Dolph seemed to attract form changers; maybe that was an aspect of his Magician-class magic.

Magician-class. That was a concept to conjure with. Dolph was a child, and a pretty normal example of the type, with all the fun and frustration that entailed. But his magic put him in another category. She had dreamed of growing up and marrying a Magician, without ever formulating the image; obviously she had been thinking of a human man, since there were no Magicians among her kind. Perhaps she had been borrowing from her brother's destiny, as they had perceived it; if he could marry a human Sorceress, she could marry a human Magician.

Now it had come true, in its surprising fashion. Dolph's talent was certainly all that could have been asked; he was amazing in the way he not only assumed any form instantly, but assumed its ability to swim or fly or whatever, and its mode of communication. Even a ghost! His magic was like a boulder, compared to the grains of sand of ordinary folk.

But he was five years her junior. There was the single kink in this slither, and what a kink it was!

Well, they were betrothed, and he had proved to be highly amenable to her blandishments. She would do her best to cater to his nature throughout, so that he never had a complaint. Not now, not at their marriage, not thereafter. She would be the best possible playmate, then lover, then wife to him. She was no Sorceress herself; she had no magic beyond the talents of her species. But she was a princess, and she would do what she was destined to do, the whole of her life. It was a matter of personal pride, as well as for the welfare of her kind. Her father expected it of her, and she would not disappoint him—or Dolph. Or anyone. Ever.

"Why are you crying, Nada?" Grace'l's skull asked quietly.

Nada jumped. She had forgotten that she was sheltered by a conscious creature who never slept! The skull formed the entrance, and it had turned to face inward, to speak to her. "N-nothing," she sobbed.

"It is not nothing," Grace'l insisted. "I am a woman, however strange to you. You are another. I see what the males do not. Last night you cried in your sleep; tonight you cry awake. What is your sorrow?"

"I cannot tell you," Nada said, trying to mop her tears.

"You are older than you appear, and you are unhappy. I will keep your secret."

"I'm a child! Like Dolph!"

"When you sleep, your body assumes its natural age. You are a woman. A young woman, but no child. Is this why you cry?"

"I must not say!"

"We cannot be heard. Tell me your grief, and I will tell you mine."

That brought Nada up short. What grief could a skeleton have? Her female curiosity surged forth; she had to know! Since Grace'l had fathomed Nada's own sorrow, half the secret was out anyway. "Tell me yours first."

Grace'l did not argue. She simply spoke. "I told Marrow that I had stepped out of the gourd and gotten stranded here in the real world, but that was not the whole story. I was thrown out, and I can never go back."

"But that's your realm!" Nada exclaimed. "There's no place for your kind out here! You belong in bad dreams!"

"Yes. I was exiled. It was the ultimate penalty for my crime. I cannot die; that is what made it so bad."

"What did you do, that is a crime in the realm of bad dreams? They are *supposed* to be horrible!"

"Yes. There was a troll on an isle of Xanth. His tribe of trolls raided a human village. This is the business of trolls.

They were hungry, and they needed fresh succulent children to eat. Some distracted the menfolk of the village, while others charged into the homes and distracted the women. They distracted the men by trying to kill them, but the men were too strong and managed to drive the trolls away instead. They distracted the women by trying to rape them, but the women fought with the strength of desperation and got away. Tristan Troll got into a house while this was happening and snatched up a succulent child and carried her away into the deep forest. So the raid was after all a success; they would eat that night.

" 'Oh please, Sir Troll, do not take me away from my family,' the little girl begged. 'I am my family's only child, and they will be tormented by my loss.'

"Tristan looked at her, and she was very pretty and very sweet, yet despite these flaws she was a bit like the child he had never had. He felt sorry for her family. He set her down. 'Return to your family,' he told her. 'But do not tell what I did.'

"The girl was smart enough to realize that he was doing wrong. 'I'll never tell!' she promised. Then she was away, running through the deep wood to her home.

"Thus the trolls were unsuccessful in their raid, and they went hungry that night. The human village was on guard thereafter, so no further raids were possible for some time. Tristan did not tell his fellows what he had done, out of deepest shame; he knew it had been a completely untroll-like act. Since all the rest had failed in their endeavors, they were not surprised that he had failed too. His mischief escaped undetected.

"But that night he dreamed, and the Night Stallion knew of his dereliction, for the stallion knew the worst secrets of all dreaming creatures. The stallion spent hours working up the most horrible dream for him, so bad it would require three night mares just to bring the whole of it. It was probably the most terrifying dream ever crafted for a troll, a wonderful work of art. Tristan would scream the whole night through, and be unable to wake till morning, riveted by that awful dream. After that, it was certain, he would never betray his tribe like that again!

"I had the honor to be the central figure in this dream. Tristran was afraid of many things, but of skeletons most of all. Because it was a female child he had let go, it was to be a female skeleton who haunted his sleep. It was of course a signal honor for me, my first major role, and I was duly proud. I intended to make him scream so hard and long that his tongue would fall out.

"But as I researched the details of his crime of conscience, I found it hard to build up enthusiasm. It was true that he had betrayed his tribe and caused them unnecessary hunger, but he had also averted much grief to the human family. It was of course not my business to judge him; I was only an actor in a bad dream. But when I played my part as the skeleton of a woman of his tribe who had starved because of his dereliction, and leaped out at him in the dream to send him into the ultimate abyss of terror, I faltered. 'I think you did right,' I whispered. The rest of the dream was crafted as scripted, and my default was unnoticed.

"The three night mares carried that dream to him that very night. But instead of driving Tristran Troll mad with remorse and fear, it made him only somewhat uncomfortable. In short, it bombed. The night mares were greatly embarrassed, and the Night Stallion snorted acrid smoke. He investigated the dream, and this time discovered what I had done. No wonder it had failed; I had delivered reassurance and support instead of terror. I had ruined the whole production, and made the effort of the gourd into a laughingstock.

"That was why I was exiled," Grace'l concluded. "They sent me through and destroyed the gourd after me. I was devastated, and hoped to find another gourd and sneak back. But that was foolish, and about the time that Marrow and Dolph arrived, I realized it. I assumed that Marrow would want to return to the gourd, despite what he said, or that he might have been exiled for some valid reason, so I was cautious. But now I know he is a truly fine skeleton, and I wish I could pick a bone with him, but—"

"Pick a bone? Do you mean you have a disagreement?"

"By no means! That is our way of joining in what to you would be matrimony. To pick out bones and assemble a baby skeleton. But of course I am unworthy, because of my exile, so I cannot broach the subject."

"But it is obvious that Marrow likes you, and the two of you work so well together," Nada protested. "That sailboat—"

"But would he like me if he knew my crime?"

"But it was no crime!" Nada protested. "It was a decent thing you did, for the decent thing the troll did."

"No, it was a betrayal of my kind, just as was the act of the troll a betrayal of his kind."

"But that makes no sense!"

"Perhaps not, in your terms. But Marrow is a skeleton; how would he feel about it?"

Nada, conscious of her own deception, was unable to answer. Now it was her turn to tell her grief, and she did so. "And so I cry for the happiness I shall never have, because I will never know true love," she concluded. "My dreams of marrying a handsome and magical prince will be realized, but the essence of them will be absent."

"Because he is younger than you? I do not understand."

"A girl is supposed to be younger than a boy. I could only love an older prince."

"But that makes no sense!"

Nada smiled tearfully. "Perhaps not in your terms. But I am sure Prince Dolph would be appalled if he knew."

Grace'l thought for a while. "Need you tell him your age?"

"Indeed, I need not! I shall fulfill his expectation in every way, so he will be happy. My private sorrow is irrelevant, and must not be known."

"I said I would keep your secret, but I do not understand why the age difference should be important, or why you should suffer alone for it."

"If Dolph knew, he would break our betrothal, and my folk would be lost. I would suffer far more then than otherwise, both for my folk whom I had failed, and for Dolph's unhappiness I caused."

"We are certainly of different types!"

"Why don't you tell Marrow how you feel? He would surely be glad to pick a bone with you."

"But I would first have to tell him of my crime, and then he would not."

"We are of different types," Nada agreed. "But I think we have similar problems. We both must deceive those to whom we are closest." With that she slept.

Next day they came into a glade, and were abruptly surrounded by an assortment of beautiful folk, each of whom was marred by an animal feature. The majority of them were lovely young women, dressed in white, with long fair hair. But some had dog's paws, or buzzard's feathers, or a snake's tail. And all of them had bows with strings drawn and arrows aimed. "Halt, trespassers!" their leader cried. He was a handsome young human man, except that his feet were exactly like those of a duck. "Identify yourselves!"

This was Dolph's Quest, so he spoke. "I am Prince Dolph of the human folk, and these are Princess Nada of the naga, Marrow of the gourd, and Grace'l of the gourd. Who are you, and why do you detain us?"

"We are the fee, and I am Fulsome Fee, and we mean to breed with you to revivify our diminishing stock. Each of you may pick a partner from among us for this purpose."

Dolph smiled. "We can't do that. Nada and I are betrothed, and—"

"That has no meaning for us. Whichever ones of us you select will become your permanent mate, and you will breed with that one the rest of your life. Now choose."

"And we are only nine or eight years old," Dolph concluded. "We could not breed with you even if we wanted to. We don't know how to summon the stork. As for the skeletons, they are not of your kind; I doubt the stork would come for them either."

"Your ages and types matter not," Fulsome said. "We shall simply keep you until you are of age or close enough to it, then demonstrate the mechanism for summoning the stork. We shall assume forms compatible with the skeletons. Our powers of change are limited but sufficient for this. Choose!"

Dolph glanced at his companions. "What do you know of the fee?"

"They are of the elven folk," Marrow said. "They are an old species, as old as all Xanth and Mundania both. They disappeared for a time; this is the first I know of them recently. It is considered best for other folk to avoid them."

Dolph glanced around at the drawn bows. "I can guess why. Suppose I change?"

"Nada would suffer."

Nada knew what each meant. Dolph could change into a dragon and wipe out the fee, but not before their arrows killed her. She could assume only three forms, all of which were vulnerable to arrows. She did not like this at all!

Dolph spoke again to the fee. "I am a Magician. I can change form and my powers are not limited. You must either kill me immediately or let us go. In neither case will you keep us for your purpose."

That, Nada thought, was very well spoken! Dolph was certainly bright enough and brave enough. How sad that he wasn't ten years older!

Fulsome laughed. "A likely claim! Prove it!"

Dolph became an armored dragon. Smoke puffed out as he breathed, signaling a formidable internal fire.

"Now you cannot kill Prince Dolph," Marrow said. "If you kill Nada Naga, Dolph will attack you and destroy you. Let us go our way in peace."

But the arrows were unwavering. "If that dragon moves, we shall kill the naga. If he cares for her, he will not like that."

What would Dolph do? For the first time on this trip,

Nada was afraid for her life. A nine-year-old child—he could panic, or make a misjudgment, and she would be the one to pay.

But fortunately it was Marrow negotiating now, because Dolph could not talk in dragon form. Obviously Dolph would not resume boy form while the arrows pointed!

"I repeat," Marrow said, "if you shoot Nada, you will be destroyed. Your arrows cannot hurt me or Grace'l or the dragon, but we can hurt you. All of your lives are hostage to Nada's welfare. You will not be able to increase your tribe then!"

Fulsome considered. "Perhaps a compromise," he suggested. "Let us have a fair contest, and the winner will prevail without violence."

"What contest?" Marrow asked.

"One of your number will choose companions to depart. If the other three of you are chosen, you depart in peace. If one of us is chosen, you are bound."

"But of course any one of us would choose the others of us!" Marrow said.

"Not if our folk resemble yours."

Marrow paused, and Nada well appreciated why. If the fee changed form to resemble the travelers, it would be hard to tell who was whom. But Marrow probably knew all of them well enough by now to tell. "But each of you has an animal trait. We could tell you by that."

"We have captured a drift of illusion, that will mask our animal features. It isn't much, but is enough for that. You will be allowed to talk to each, but not to touch; the one you touch is the one chosen."

"But the real ones would identify themselves!" Marrow pointed out. "That would make it no contest."

Fulsome shrugged. "Do you agree?"

Marrow checked with the others. None of them were easy about the matter, but the arrows were unwavering. Nada certainly did not want to die, and she was sure that Dolph did not want to kill the fee. It seemed better to accept the contest, and to make sure they did not lose.

"We agree," Marrow said. "I shall—"

"Not you," Fulsome said. "The naga. She will choose."

"Me?" Nada asked, dismayed. "I can't—"

"Take it or leave it," Fulsome said. "She is the vulnerable one. She cannot cheat."

"None of us will cheat!" Marrow said indignantly. "Are the fee planning on cheating?"

"The fee do not cheat," Fulsome said.

"How could anyone cheat?" Nada asked. "Everyone will be watching."

"The form changer could become a bird and fly away alone," Fulsome said. "The skeletons could find a gourd and escape."

That did not make much sense to Nada. But Marrow shrugged. "Let her choose, then."

Thus abruptly Nada found the weight on her own coils. "Don the hood while we mix," Fulsome said, putting a thick velvet hood over her head.

In a moment the hood came off. Nada looked—and blinked.

All of the folk in the glade looked just like her companions. There were about ten Marrows and twice as many Grace'ls and another ten Dolphs. There were even several Nadas, for good measure. She could not tell which were true and which were false by appearance; the likeness were perfect.

She could talk but not touch, until she chose. So she would not touch any until she was absolutely sure. She had three tries; if all were correct, then all her companions were free. But her first mistake would be her last, for she herself would be captive, along with whoever she had not yet freed.

Nada was glad she did not have hands, in her natural form, for hands had an unpleasant tendency to sweat cold and be clammy. How could she be sure of the others?

She slithered up to the nearest Dolph figure. "Who are you?" she asked.

"I am your fiancé, Prince Dolph," he replied. "Touch me and save me."

She considered that. Fiancé? Dolph had never used that term. He was her betrothed. This was one of the fee!

She approached a Marrow. She really did not know him well, so planned to guess him last. That way she might save the other two before risking herself, and if Prince Dolph and Grace'l were saved, that was certainly better than nothing. So this was just a preliminary testing; even if she thought she was sure of him, she would not touch him yet.

"Who are you?" she asked.

"I am Marrow of the gourd," he replied promptly.

"What is your last name?"

"I have none."

"Too bad," she said. "If you were real, you would know that your name is Marrow Bones."

"Oh, no!" a Dolph figure cried. "You gave it away!"

Nada was stricken. She had done just that! Now every one of the fee knew, and she would be unable to identify Marrow by his knowledge.

But maybe she could recover something from this blunder. She slithered over to the Dolph who had spoken.

"Are you the real Dolph?"

"Of course I am!"

"Then you must know Grace'l's full name."

"Grace'l Ossein," he replied—then clapped his hands to his own mouth, stricken. "I did it myself! Now you'll never pick her out, either!"

Nada was appalled. It was her error too; she should have know better than to ask the question of anyone but Grace'l herself. Now she was in trouble with two selections!

But at least she was sure of Dolph. He knew both Marrow and Grace'l better than she did. She could select him, then ask his advice on the other, and recover them all. She brought her tail around, to touch him with the tip—

"Don't do it!" another Dolph figure cried. "I gave her

full name when I introduced us at the beginning! He's a fake!"

Nada froze. Was that true? If so, she had just missed making a terrible mistake!

"I did not!" the Dolph in front of her said. "I said 'Grace'l of the gourd.' Don't you remember, Nada?"

Nada tried to remember, but now could not be sure. That meant that she could not be sure of this Dolph. She turned away.

But the Dolph pursued her. "Don't let them fool you, Nada!" he urged. "I know I can prove myself to you!"

"If you do, she's lost!" the other Dolph retorted. "You had your chance, faker."

Nada hesitated. Suppose this first one was the right one, after all? How could she risk passing him by?

"Nada, listen to me!" the nearest Dolph said. "I can tell you what questions to ask! If you don't like them, don't ask them, but don't pass me by!"

"Sure, he wants to fool you," the other Dolph said, and there was a murmur of agreement from the remaining Dolphs. "If you listen, you'll get so confused you won't be able to recognize the right one when you come to him!"

"That's a lie!" the nearest Dolph said. "You're the fakes!"

"Why don't we let her decide that?" the other inquired sensibly.

"Because she might pick wrong! She's younger than I am, and I'm just a child."

Just a child. Nada fixed on that. Of the two Dolphs, the more distant one seemed more mature—but the real one was a child, given to things like stuffing himself on cake when he got the chance. He believed she was younger than he, and in that he was mistaken—but this was also evidence of his validity. Meanwhile, that murmur of agreement from the other Dolphs rang false; they could not all be real Dolphs objecting to her deception by a false one. It was more likely the other way around.

"What questions?" she asked the closest Dolph.

He grinned. "Like what happened first time we kissed?" Excellent suggestion! She turned to the distant Dolph. "What happened the first time we kissed?"

"It was great!" that one replied. "You're a very pretty naga."

She turned to another distant Dolph. "What happened?"

"It's a trick question," he replied. "We are too young; we never kissed."

"Anybody else?" she asked, sweeping her gaze across the remaining Dolphs.

There was a chorus of answers, all different. "It made a loud smack!" "You blushed!" "I blushed!" "Your mother caught us!" "Our noses bumped!" "It was a forehead kiss."

Nada oriented on the one who had mentioned noses.

"You!" she cried.

That Dolph stepped forward. "Yes, I am the real one," he agreed. "How clever of you to ask that question."

Nada looked at the nearest Dolph. "But you suggested it!"

"I've got more," he replied. "What did your mother say when we bumped noses?"

"My mother?" she asked sharply.

"Ask him," he said, giving her a straight look.

She turned to the other Dolph. "What did my mother say?"

"I already answered one," that Dolph said. "Make *him* answer!"

She looked at the nearest one. "Well?"

"She wasn't there. I never saw your mother. But your father said—" He screwed up his features in thought. "He said to tilt your head, stupid, because—"

He never finished, because Nada slithered up to him, lifted her head, and kissed him. She had never been so pleased to be called stupid in her life!

"Gee, that's fun, stupid!" Dolph said.

She bit him gently on the ear. "That's enough of that! You proved your identity. Now help me pick the others."

"Hey, no fair getting help!" one of the Marrows protested.

"Of course it's fair," another Marrow said. "There's nothing in the contest that says she can't."

"Yes there is!" the first said hotly. "*She* has to pick, not the boy."

"Well, then," said the second Marrow. "Let's take a vote on the rules. All in favor of letting the Prince help her, raise their hands." He raised his own hand.

Only one other joined him, one of the Grace'l's.

"All opposed?" he asked, somewhat hollowly.

All the remaining hands went up.

"Guess which two are real," Dolph murmured.

Of course! "You two!" Nada called. "Come here!"

But now the fee realized their error. They crowded in, so that by the time the two real ones arrived, they were surrounded by all the fake ones. The fake Dolphs had disappeared, replaced by Marrows and Grace'ls. Nada could not tell any of them apart.

Now she was bound not to use Dolph's help. But at least she had saved him. She turned to him. "If I guess wrong, will you tell your folks I tried? My people still need—"

"I will go and help them myself," Dolph promised. "But I don't want you to guess wrong, Nada! You're the neatest girl I ever knew!"

"I'm the *only* girl you ever knew," she retorted. "Aside from your big sister."

"Yuck!" he exclaimed. "I hate all fourteen year olds! Don't ever get that old!"

She smiled, but there was a pang inside her. If he ever found out—but of course she could never tell him. At least that reminded her of her session with Grace'l. She knew she could identify the female skeleton—but she might have to betray a confidence to do so.

Maybe she could avoid that, though. "All you Grace'ls," she called. "How did we cross the water? You first." She pointed to one.

"We found a boat."

"You," she said to the second.

"We were carried across by a big bird."

"You."

"I became a sail."

Nada oriented on that one. "What did Marrow become?"

"The rest of the boat."

Naga nodded. She slithered up to touch that one.

"Don't!" another Grace'l cried. "It was a lucky guess! Out of all those answers, one was bound to be right."

They had tried that when she was about to touch the true Dolph. Making it seem that he had guessed. Trying to confuse the issue. This time Naga was not fooled. She brought her tail around.

"Last night!" the more distant Grace'l cried. "Tell!"

That made Nada pause. How could a fake Grace'l know about that? She had to check.

"Why did you leave the gourd?" she asked the closest one.

"I stepped out by accident, and couldn't get back."

Nada saw Dolph nod, accepting that answer. But Dolph did not know the truth. "You," she said, pointing to the other Grace'l.

"I—I was exiled," the other said. "Because I ruined a troll's dream. I can never go back."

"That eliminates her," Dolph said.

Nada slithered up to the true Grace'l and touched her.

"Don't," Dolph cried, too late.

"I am the real one," Grace'l said. "I did not tell you the truth, before."

One of the Marrows gave a start. Nada turned on him. "You! Why do you react?"

"I thought she wanted to return to the gourd," that Marrow said.

"We all thought that!" another Marrow said.

"How do you feel about it?" Nada asked. "You." She pointed to one of the other Marrows, not the one who had jumped.

"I'm glad she can't return to the gourd," he replied. "Now I can marry her."

"You." She pointed to another wrong Marrow.

"The same."

They were getting smarter, learning from their errors.

"You." This time she pointed to the right one.

He looked at Grace'l. "The same."

Oops! The answer had been too good! But she could refine it. "Exactly how do you make offspring? You." She pointed to the first Marrow she had asked.

"The Adult Conspiracy prevents me from answering, because you are too young to know."

Ooops, again. Sure enough, the others gave the same answer. Should she reveal her own true age, so as to be eligible for the answer? She glanced at Dolph, and knew she couldn't.

But she wasn't done yet. Only Marrow knew of life in the gourd. "Who is in charge of the making of bad dreams?" she asked the first wrong Marrow.

"No one. They're just there, and the night mares pick them up and carry them out."

"You?" she asked the second.

"The same."

"You?" she asked of the true one—though her certainty about him was diminishing. After all, the one she had believed was Grace'l had been wrong.

"The Night Stallion. He is in charge of the mares, and he directs the dreams, which have to be crafted fresh each day for the following night. All of the rest of us are mere actors, poor players, who strut and fret our hour upon the stage and then are heard no more. We—"

"Enough!" This was obviously the correct one, but Nada had one more question of him. "Can you forgive a creature who sabotaged a truly bad dream?"

"That would be difficult—" he began.

Grace'l bowed her skull. "I understand."

"—but I am sure she had good reason, and I think that

once I understood that reason, I could manage it," Marrow concluded.

Nada slithered up to him and touched him with her tail.

"I hope so," she said. "I think you have things to discuss with her."

"I believe so," Marrow said. "Thank you for rescuing us."

"I rescued myself too!" Naga reminded him. "Had I guessed wrong, I would have had to remain with the fee who tricked me."

"Where are they?" Dolph asked.

Nada looked around. All the fee were gone.

"At least they kept their word," Marrow said. "Let us depart this region promptly."

Nada was happy to agree. They headed south at a remarkably swift clip. They had all had quite enough of the Gold Coast!

13

CENTAUR ISLE

At the foot of Xanth were several small isles and one big one: Centaur Isle. All were guarded by centaurs, who made it plain that they did not want intruders in these parts.

"Chex said that the centaurs of this region were like that," Marrow said. "It is probably no use trying to reason with them."

"But suppose the Heaven Cent is here?" Dolph asked plaintively. "We have to check these isles!"

"We shall simply have to find another way," Marrow said. "Perhaps if we all think hard, we shall come up with an idea."

They thought hard, but no idea manifested. The problem was simply too much for them.

"Maybe if we thought about some other way to find an idea," Grace'l suggested.

They thought about that. Suddenly Dolph brightened. "Maybe I should change form and look for an idea!"

No one had any better notion. Dolph became a sharp-eyed hawk and flew into the forest, looking for an idea.

In the thickest part he spotted some vines with eyeballs intertwined. The eyes looked back at him. Dolph paused. Those were Eye Queue vines!

He caught a vine with his beak and pulled it free. Trailing it, he flew swiftly back to his companions.

"Eye Queue!" Marrow exclaimed. "That will almost certainly help! It can make a creature much more intelligent." He lifted the vine carefully from Dolph's beak.

Dolph reverted to boy form. "That's what I thought. One of us can use this to become smart and get our idea."

"But which one?" Dolph asked. He had fetched the vine, but he wasn't sure he wanted to use it.

"I am not certain how it would affect a skeleton," Marrow said. "Our skulls are hollow, and might simply become hollower. Our ideas might prove to be loud but empty."

"I will use it, if you wish," Nada said.

"But you're a girl!" Dolph protested.

"I'll never be as smart as you, Prince Dolph, no matter what," she said, smiling at him.

"Oh." Dolph was too flattered to pursue the matter further. Nada was way-much different from Ivy, who got so smart nobody could stand her. That was why he liked Nada so much. She was the right age and the right attitude, and she was fun to kiss. He had never properly appreciated either girls or kisses before he had encountered her. He looked forward to appreciating more with her, at such time as he figured out what it might be.

Marrow set the Eye Queue vine on Nada's head. Immediately it writhed, and sank in, the eyes disappearing. Her own eyes seemed to grow and brighten, and her head to swell a bit. "Oh, I never thought of it that way!" she exclaimed.

"You have an idea?" Dolph asked eagerly.

She gazed at him. The lids lowered across her eyes, and an obscure smile played about her mouth. "Perhaps. But I fear not relevant to the present issue."

"But maybe it is! What is it?"

"I believe I have just figured out how to summon the stork."

"Oh, tell me!" he begged.

"But I have also figured out why that knowledge is forbidden to children."

"Why?" Dolph asked, frustrated.

"It is a matter of innocence. Children stop being nice when they lose their innocence, so the adults protect them from corrupting knowledge. It may be the one decent thing adults do."

"Corrupt me!" Dolph pleaded. "I want to know!"

But she shook her had. "Not till you—till we are adult. Then we shall have been corrupted by experience, and it won't make much difference. I am too smart, now, to spoil an untainted innocence that can never be restored. It would be like treading on the sweetest, prettiest flowers."

"Oh—" Dolph searched for the worst word he knew, to express his contempt of innocence, but none were bad enough. He had to settle on the one she had used, when they had first met. "Oh, *mice*! I hate innocence!"

"Believe me, Dolph, it is better than the alternative." she said sadly. Grace'l nodded agreement.

"If I may interrupt," Marrow said. "Have you an idea, Nada, how we may search Centaur Isle for the Heaven Cent?"

Nada pondered briefly. "Yes. We shall have to go to Mundania."

"What?" the other three asked, aghast.

"The landscape of Mundania is the same as that of Xanth. But there is no magic there, and therefore no magical creatures. No centaurs on Centaur Isle. Thus we can explore the isle without hindrance, there." She paused thoughtfully. "Of course, there is a small complication."

"Yes," Dolph said dryly. "How do we get there from here?"

She smiled at him. "Why how bright of you, Dolph!" she said condescendingly. Dolph realized that there were aspects to the Eye Queue enhancement that were less than delightful. "Actually, there are several ways to do it; our problem is to determine the most feasible one."

"Wait. I don't understand!" Grace'l protested.

"Naturally not," Nada said, sounding exactly like Ivy in her more assertive moments. This was a side of her Dolph had not seen before, and didn't like. But he reminded himself that it was the effect of the Eye Queue vine, which not only made people smart, it made them obnoxious. Perhaps smartness and obnoxiousness were much the same.

"I mean," Grace'l persisted, "what's this about Mundania being the same as Xanth? I thought Xanth is where the magic is, and Mundania is where it isn't."

"Exactly," Nada said in that superior manner. "Remove the magic from Xanth, and you have Mundania. It is elementary."

"But *this* is Xanth! Mundania can't be in the same place!"

"Certainly it can. Now if we can get on to productive discussion—"

"I can think of another complication," Marrow said. "Those of us who are magical cannot exist in Mundania— at least, not in our present manner. We skeletons will lose our animation, and Dolph will lose his talent, and you, Nada, will revert to your mundane form. Do you happen to know what that might be?"

"I believe there are slightly more serpent genes in my lineage than human genes, so I would probably become a snake. But Dolph is the one looking for the Heaven Cent, so he is the one who needs his human form. He will have to go alone."

"No!" Marrow said. "He must have an adult companion!"

Dolph had never particularly liked that requirement before, but the thought of going alone into Mundania appalled him, so he decided not to argue.

"That can be arranged," Nada said. "In my human form I may appear to be a child, but—"

"I don't think—" Grace'l started.

"But snakes have briefer lives," Nada continued. "So my snake form is adult. If Dolph takes me along in that form, he will have adult companionship."

"I am not certain that is quite what is meant," Marrow said doubtfully. But he did not push the case.

"But as to how to go to Mundania, let me enumerate the ways," Nada said. "First, we could travel to the isthmus and cross into Mundania, then return to this site. But though we could travel well in Xanth by having Dolph carry us in roc form, we might have difficulty returning in Mundania. Second, we could sail out to the border of magic, which surely is not far offshore. But if we used the skeleton crew, we would be sunk when the magic went, and would have to swim back after losing Marrow and Grace'l."

"I seem to have a problem with that," Marrow said.

"Third, we could step through to Mundania right here, and return after checking Centaur Isle. But the mechanism may be awkward."

"How can we step through here?" Dolph demanded. "The magic is here!"

"By using the gourd," she said patiently. "The night mares carry bad dreams to the Mundanes as well as to Xanthians, so it stands to reason that they have direct access to Mundania as well as to Xanth; surely they would not waste time running all the way to the isthmus, crossing over, and running back to the geography they started from. They must go directly, and that is the route we must seek."

"I never thought of that!" Marrow exclaimed.

"Obviously. It is my judgment that they must use gourds, as they do to return from Xanth to their own realm. These gourds would grow within the dream community, and represent portals to Mundania, and perhaps back. So we must go to this portion of Mundania by passing through double portals. It should be straightforward enough."

"But ordinary folk can't enter the gourd," Dolph said. "All we can do is look into it and be frozen in place until someone breaks the connection. Only the creatures of the gourd can go inside."

"Not necessarily so," Marrow said. "When I was with Chex and Esk and Volney Vole, we entered through a huge zombie gourd. The experience was not completely pleasant for any of us."

"But I cannot return to the gourd!" Grace'l protested. "I am exiled from there."

"You cannot go to Mundania, either," Nada pointed out. "So your best option is to remain here."

"I can guide you to a gourd within the gourd," Marrow said to Dolph. "Then return to be with Grace'l."

"Unfortunately, I will lose the enhancement of intelligence I have reaped from the Eye Queue, when I enter Mundania," Nada said.

Dolph tried not to show his delight at this prospect. He liked Nada as an eight-year-old girl just fine, but not as a super-smart girl who acted like an adult.

They proceeded with it. Marrow led them to the place he remembered where the zombie gourd lay. The thing was monstrous in several senses: it was the biggest gourd Dolph had never imagined, and it was halfway rotten, and its peephole was big enough to admit a grown centaur.

"Now follow me exactly," Marrow cautioned them. "Do what I do, and nothing else. When you return, enter and wait where you are, until I come to lead you out; I will check every hour until I see you."

"That seems easy enough," Dolph said.

"It is not. Now remember, do what I do. Nada, you had better assume human form for this."

"Precisely," she agreed, becoming a bare girl.

Marrow jumped into the peephole. Dolph followed. In a moment Nada followed him.

They landed in a mess of rotten vines that seemed to be trying to grow down into the ground instead of out of it. Fortunately there was a path. They trooped rapidly along this path, avoiding a zombie snake that struck at their legs. They came to a region of slashing knives, but Marrow simply drew an old rusty knife out of the ground nearby and flipped it into the midst of the others. The other knives attacked it, and then fell to slicing themselves, until none were left. It was safe to proceed—but Marrow turned away, down along another path Dolph hadn't seen before. He proceeded to a green rock, and used another rock to smash it. The thing fragmented, and the chips grew hot and set fire to the ground. Soon a wooden door was revealed under the burned ground. Marrow pushed down on the near end, and the far end swung up, revealing a lighted cellar below. But instead of entering it, Marrow walked away, down a new path. This one led to a place where rats ran. Marrow kicked one, and the rats squealed and leaped into the air and became flying numbers. Marrow ignored them; he walked on to a region that resembled a great stretched sheet. He stood on this sheet and bounced. In a moment he was jumping higher and higher, the sheet adding force with each bounce. Then he sailed so high he disappeared.

Dolph had not made much sense of any of this, but now he stepped onto the sheet and bounced. Soon he was bouncing high, and then he sailed way, way up, and passed through the ceiling. There was Marrow, standing by another huge gourd. Suddenly this was adding up; here was the gourd within a gourd!

Nada sailed up through the floor, almost bumping into Dolph. "The dream realm is a perfect marvel of illogic," she remarked.

"I noticed," Dolph muttered. "But I think we're here."

"I located this gourd by exploring this region last year," Marrow explained. "I never tried to enter it, realizing that it could be dangerous for me. But if any dream gourd leads to Mundania, this should do it."

"Elementary," Nada agreed. "Now, Dolph, when we emerge, remember that I will be unable to speak to you, and you will be unable to change form. Make careful note of our location, and be on guard against surprises. If we become separated, we must return independently to the place where this gourd emerges and wait for the other. Do you have it straight?"

"Yeah, sure," Dolph agreed, annoyed by her attitude.

Was she going to be like this when she grew up? How awful it would be if she were just like Ivy!

He jumped through the peephole. There was an instant of disorientation; then he landed on the ground beyond.

He heard something land beside him. It was a snake, light below, gray-brown above, as if a hank of hair had lent its hue to that side. It was about as long from nose to tailtip as Nada had been in girl form, but far thinner.

"Do you understand me, Nada?" he asked.

She lifted her head and nodded. Good enough.

He looked behind them. There was a huge gourd, nestled in jungle foliage. This one was not rotten; it was supremely healthy. Good enough, again.

"Well, let's go to Centaur Isle," he said, looking around more widely. He discovered a pebbled path leading by the gourd; obviously someone knew of this special plant.

The stones were hard on his bare feet, so he tried to change to snake form—and could not. Right, he was in Mundania now! No magic.

He walked on the edge of the path, while Nada slithered comfortably and almost invisibly along through the grass and shrubs beside it. Mundania did not seem very much different than Xanth, so far.

Then they came to an iron gate. It was set in a wall that disappeared to left and right into the jungle. Nasty looking wire was on top of the wall; he was not tempted to climb it.

He stepped up to the gate and rattled it. Maybe he could open it and get out. But after the first shake, there was a clanging sound nearby, making him jump.

Someone came tramping down the path from behind. "Ifsf, ifsf, xibu't uijt?" a man's voice called.

Dolph tried to hide, but the tangle of bushes here was laced with nettles and thorns that scratched his skin. He had nowhere to go. Nada had no such difficulty; she vanished.

The man appeared. He was big and fat and fully clothed. Suddenly Dolph remembered that Mundanians, like Xanthians, usually wore clothing. How could he explain this?

"B cpz!" the man exclaimed, frowning. "Ipx eje zpv hfu jo ifsf?"

Dolph decided to brave it through. "I'm sorry, I don't speak your language," he said.

The man stopped. He peered at Dolph. "Uibu't Yboujbo!" he said. "Eje zpf dpnf uisphi uif hpvse?"

"If you will just please let me out, I won't bother you any further," Dolph said, knowing it was useless. Why hadn't he thought of the problem of language? How was he ever going to get out of this?

"Dpnf xjui nf," the man said firmly, taking Dolph by the wrist. "J ibwf b usbotmajpo dpnovufs jo uif mbc."

He hauled Dolph back along the path to a sinister-looking chamber. He shoved Dolph inside and shut the door. "Cvu gjstu J'e cfuufs gfudi zpv tpnf dmpuift." Dolph heard his heavy footsteps retreating.

Immediately he tried the doorknob, but the door was locked. He was prisoner of the Mundane! How much worse could this get?

Then Nada slithered in through the crack under the door. "Nada!" he exclaimed. "Can you help me get out?"

The snake slithered back under the door. After an interminably short time she returned—with a key in her mouth.

"Great!" Dolph exclaimed, taking it. He put it in the keyhole, and turned it, and it worked. In a moment the door swung open and he was out.

But what was he going to do now? He still had no clothing, and he still could not speak the strange language of the Mundanes! Even if he managed to get out the locked gate at the end of the path, he would be in trouble.

Then he heard the tramp, tramp, of the man, returning.

He ran around the building and hid. There was nothing else he could think of at the moment.

The man saw the open door and made an exclamation of disgust. Then he went in; Dolph heard him doing something inside the building.

Maybe he could run around and slam the door and lock

the Mundane in! Dolph hurried to the front, caught the edge of the door, and pushed it closed.

Then he realized that he had left the key in the keyhole. It was now on the Mundane man's side of the door! How stupid could he get!

He started to run back down the path, though he knew this was useless; the man would only catch him again. But then the man's voice called from the building. "Wait, boy! Listen to me!"

It was in Dolph's language!

Dolph stopped. If the man spoke his language, he must know of Xanth, and that meant—

"You are from Xanth, aren't you?" the man called, opening the door. "You came through the gourd? Don't run from me; I am your friend."

"But you tried to lock me up before!" Dolph called back.

There was a moment, and strange sounds came from the building. Then the man said: "Only to keep you from harm while I fetched some clothing for you. See, here it is." He held up a pile of cloth.

Dolph needed the clothing, so he decided to trust the man part way. "Stay out of sight," he whispered to Nada. Then he walked back to the building.

The man had some sort of box set up. "Fydfmmfou!" he said.

"Excellent!" said the box.

"The magic box knows the language!" Dolph exclaimed, surprised. "But how can magic work in Mundania?"

The box spoke gobbledygook to the man. The man listened, then replied in similar nonsense. It was no wonder the Mundanes weren't much, Dolph thought, because their language was ludicrous.

Then the box spoke to Dolph: "There is no magic here. This is a computer that is programmed to translate one language into the other, and vice versa. This is a task normally accomplished by the magic of Xanth, more readily, but we must make do with our relatively crude devices. I am Turn Key, the proprietor of this gateway. Who are you?"

"I am—" Dolph hesitated, but concluded that the truth probably would not hurt him, and would be a lot more honest. "Prince Dolph of Castle Roogna." But he did not say anything about Nada, just in case. If Turn locked him up again, she would still be free.

The box went through its ritual. "A prince! My, my! Well, Prince Dolph, put on your clothing, and we shall talk."

Dolph got into the clothing. It was somewhat large and loose, but would do. Meanwhile, Turn explained the situation as he knew it.

"There are few convenient connections between Xanth and Mundania. The best established is the isthmus, which leads to any part of Mundania, and any time. Any Xanthian who uses that route is magically logged in, and returns to the same time in Xanth that he departed, allowing for the duration of his stay in Mundania. The Mundanes have no such assurance; they enter Xanth only by a fluke accident, and will return randomly unless extremely cautious. Thus it is, in effect, a one-way portal; Xanthians can safely cross, but not Mundanians." He paused, glancing at Dolph. "Are you following me?"

"Oh, sure. I know about that," Dolph said airily, though actually it was somewhat complicated and dull for him. "We can go there, but they can't come here, mostly."

"An apt summation. However, there are other ways, as you have discovered. Any Xanthian who sails out far enough from the coast will revert to Mundane status, and then have great difficulty returning; that is a one-way trip."

Dolph was suddenly glad they had not tried that route. To travel into Mundania was bad enough, but to be trapped there forever—ugh!

"And then there is the gourd," Turn continued. "This is utilized mainly by the night mares and storks, when they have deliveries in this region. Mundanes don't have much magic, but they do have bad dreams, and babies. It's a horrible inconvenience for the mares and storks to loop all the way out to the isthmus and back, so we maintain this portal for them. If any get lost, it is my job to locate them and bring them back before the Mundanes discover them. Fortunately they don't realize their significance; they think the storks are wood ibises. The night mares have it easier in a certain respect, because they travel by night and are invisible, but there was this time when a mare foundered, and—but I digress. The point is, this is a limited portal, very seldom used by human folk, because they don't enter the gourd physically. Which brings us to you, Prince Dolph: how did you even know of this route, let alone utilize it?"

Dolph was concluding that Turn was legitimate, because he did know a lot about Xanth that true Mundanes did not know. Certainly he had the big gourd here, and knew its function, and had it well guarded. If the man was willing to help—well, Dolph did need help. So he decided to be candid—but still not to tell about Nada, just in case. "I am looking for the Heaven Cent, which I think is on a skeleton key. But I couldn't search Centaur Isle for it, so I am trying to do it through Mundania, where there are no centaurs. I have a friend who is from the gourd, and he knew this route, so I used it. But I forgot about the clothing and the language."

Turn frowned. "This is one region in which Mundane geography is not identical to Xanth geography," he said. "The centaurs have used magic—they do not like it in the form of talents, but do use it as a tool—to merge over a hundred little keys into one big isle. So while this is No Name Key here in Mundania, it is part of the main Centaur Isle in Xanth."

"That could make it easier," Dolph said excitedly. "Is one of those hundred keys called Skeleton?"

"Now that is an interesting thought! But I regret that I know of no such key. We have Big Pine Key, and Ramrod Key, and Little Torch Key, and Pumpkin Key and Happy Jack Key and Hurricane Key and Friend Key and Teakettle Key and Mule Key and Man Key and Woman Key and Rattlesnake Key and Don Quixote Key, but alas no Skeleton Key."

"Then I will have to search them all," Dolph said. "I must find the Heaven Cent."

"Forgive me, Prince, but I cannot allow that. With your problem of language and custom, you would soon get in trouble and give yourself away, and that would be bad for all of us. The nature of this situation must never be known to Mundanes."

"I don't care what happens, I have to find the Heaven Cent! It's my Quest!"

"I will help you locate your artifact. Then you can return to Xanth and be out of danger."

Dolph realized that there could indeed be danger, because he had no real knowledge of Mundania. He could encounter the fabulous Mundane monsters called bares who were reputed to be covered with fur, illogically. Or wails, who were said to be as big as the Xanth creature who ran along the surface of a lake while howling and leaving little prints—the prints of wails—but the Mundane variant mysteriously swam *under* the water, where no prints showed. Or rattlesnakes, supposedly carrying babies' rattles with their tails in order to scare folk, ludicrous as that was, and if the folk didn't act frightened, then the snakes would poison them. Or lions, who were believed never to lie to their victims, merely to eat them, which notion did not comfort Dolph a great deal. Certainly he had no desire to encounter any of these crazy creatures without his magic!

But all he said was, "Help me?"

"Magic is very limited in Mundania, but it does exist in mutated form. They call it—don't laugh, now—'science.' "

Dolph laughed anyway; he couldn't help it. "Silence?"

"No ell-sound in it: science. It has odd rules, and only the most trained folk can understand the more sophisticated aspects, but fortunately they make artifacts that do the magic for ordinary folks."

"Amulets," Dolph said, understanding. "That makes sense. But what's so hard to understand about 'science'?"

Turn smiled. "Let me give you an example. Suppose you

take a lamp that shines a ray of light toward another person."

"A sunbeam," Dolph agreed.

"Yes, a sunbeam will do. Use a mirror to reflect it toward your friend. That light travels at the speed of light, wouldn't you agree?"

"Of course! Everything travels at its own speed, whether it is a ray of light or a dragon." Dolph was pleased to demonstrate that he had not slept through *all* of his centaur tutor's lessons, just the dull ones.

"And suppose your friend also has a mirror, and he sends another ray toward you, and the two rays meet in the middle."

"They would pass right through each other," Dolph said promptly. "Rays hardly give each other the time of day; they are very self-centered."

"To be sure. Now suppose you hitched a ride on your ray, and your friend rode his ray. At what speed would you be approaching each other?"

Oops—this was getting into higher mathematics, not Dolph's strong subject. But he did not want to seem stupid, so he wrestled with it. It reduced to the proposition of one plus one—his speed plus his friend's speed. Now if he could only remember what one plus one was!

Suddenly, in a burst of genius, he had it. "Two!" he cried victoriously. "Twice the speed of light!" His head felt hot, but he knew he had solved the problem.

"Would it surprise you to learn that according to science, you would be approaching each other at only the regular speed of light?" Turn inquired.

"That would be ridiculous! If my friend stood still, I would move toward him at the speed of light. If he came toward me at the same speed, we would meet twice as fast."

"Science says that you would only seem to meet each other twice as fast. Actually time would slow down for each of you, so that you really did not approach each other faster than—"

"I'll never understand that!" Dolph cried. "It is non-sense!"

"Nevertheless, science says it is so, and operates on similar principles. As I said, it is difficult for ordinary folk to understand. But it works, and that is what counts."

"No wonder the Mundanes seem crazy," Dolph muttered. "Their animals and their thinking are backwards!"

"Perhaps. But a young man like you, thinking the sensible Xanth way, would have immediate trouble with Mundanes. This is another reason we protect the access. It is especially dangerous because it is a direct connection. By that I mean that a Mundane could as readily pass into Xanth this way as a Xanthian can enter Mundania, and there is no time differential. Time is the same in each realm, so a Mundane could enter Xanth, then return with the tale to Mundania and tell others, and then there could be—"

"Another Wave!" Dolph exclaimed, horrified.

"Another wave of Mundane invasion," Turn agreed. "Certainly we don't want that! So you see how important it is that this remain secret. If any Mundane caught on to your true origin, and followed you back to this garden—"

"I understand!" Dolph agreed. The man had really made his point. "Tell me how I can check for the Heaven Cent, and I shall return to Xanth as fast as I can!"

"Excellent. It happens that I have a device that can orient on particular items. I use it to locate things I have lost, which I do frequently. It functions by science, but I think is similar enough in operation to be satisfactory for you." He rummaged through a drawer. "Ah, here is one! It is verbally programmed, which means I had better set it for you, but then it will remain locked on the target. This should enable you to locate your artifact, if it is anywhere within Mundania."

"Great!" Dolph exclaimed. "Tell it to find the Heaven Cent!"

"Of course the concept has to be in its limited lexicon," Turn cautioned. "Otherwise it won't be able to work, because it won't grasp the nature of the thing it seeks. Here, let me activate it." He held up a thing a bit like a clumsy snake. "Heaven Cent," he said.

There was no reaction. The thing just lay in his hand, doing nothing.

"But perhaps if I connected it to the larger storage of the computer—" Turn said. He set the device on the table and attached two wires to it. He connected the other ends of the wires to little plug-in spots on the box that was doing the translation. "Heaven Cent," he repeated.

This time there was a *ping!* "It has locked on!" Turn said, pleased. "Excellent. Now it will work for you. Hold out your left wrist."

Dolph did so. Turn wrapped the device around it, fastening what turned out to be a strap. On the back of Dolph's wrist was a square shape with a glowing dot like an eye.

"Now Mundanes will take this for a watch," Turn said. "But actually—"

"A watch!" Dolph agreed. "Because its eye watches for the Heaven Cent! Science is starting to make sense after all!"

"Uh, yes, perhaps. It is true that the lighted indicator points toward the target. But ordinarily a watch is considered—"

"This is good enough!" Dolph said happily. "Let me follow where it points, and get the Heaven Cent!"

"Certainly," Turn said, though with a certain reservation. "But I note that it is pointing north-north-west, and there is mostly water in that direction. I doubt—"

But Dolph was already heading out, watching the watch. The path went almost in the right direction, so he followed that.

Turn sighed. "Very well, then, but I must accompany you outside. I do have a boat. Why don't we go to it now? If the indicator points toward land, we can follow it there. We will not be able to converse once we leave the translator."

The man was making sense. Dolph paused, allowing the man to turn off his equipment and follow him.

At the gate, Dolph remembered Nada. Realizing that it

might be awkward for her to follow him outside, he decided to pick her up while Turn was unlocking the gate. He stooped—but did not find her.

Desperately, he looked around. He had thought she was right with him! What had happened to her?

"Jt tpnfuijoh xspoh?" Turn inquired.

Dolph hastily stood back up. "Uh, no," he said. He would have to look for her when he returned here. Maybe she had gone to wait at the gourd.

They walked out and around, and came to a building with a boat. It was a much fancier craft than the skeleton boat, with room for several people inside, and even a roofed area.

Turn did something, and there was a noise like the growl of a dragon. Dolph jumped, but Turn gestured him to sit down. The sound was coming from a box at the back. Then the boat moved out, and Dolph realized that the dragon (or whatever) was pushing it, for there was no sail. As the man said: the science of Mundania might be based on ludicrous premises, but it did seem to work almost as well as magic.

The strange boat forged out into a channel of the sea, and turned north. Now they were headed almost directly toward the Heaven Cent! Then the channel turned northwest, bearing slightly west of the Cent. But no matter how far they went, the Cent remained roughly ahead. Dolph remembered from his experience with the magic of triangulation that this meant the Cent was far away. Of course that particular magic might not work as well in Mundania. Still, it had him worried.

That was not all that worried him. Where was Nada? Suppose something had happened to her? The very thought made him quail. She had gotten pretty uppety just before they entered the gourd, but that was because of the Eye Queue vine. Her normal self was much more likable, and he liked her very well. Very well indeed; suddenly, now, he realized how much. She just *couldn't* be lost!

After a time the channel bore north, then turned sharply to the west. Turn looked at him. Dolph shook his head; the

Cent was still far across the sea. They didn't seem to be getting any closer to it.

Turn shrugged and made the boat turn back. At this stage, Dolph was relieved, because right now he was more concerned about Nada than the Heaven Cent. They returned to the boat house, and then to the garden. Dolph looked around, but still did not see Nada.

"This is what I suspected," Turn said, back in the lab with the science box working again. "That artifact is not on any of these keys. It is somewhere on the mainland of Florida. You will have to search there."

"Somewhere where?" Dolph asked, perplexed.

"The Mundane mainland. I am sorry you could not find your Heaven Cent, but at least you have in effect searched Centaur Isle."

Dolph realized that he had indeed accomplished his mission, here. Now he had his first good notion where the Cent was. "I'll go back to Xanth," he said. "But can I take this watch? It might help."

"*May* you take it," Turn said in exactly the manner of adults everywhere. It seemed the translator had translated his words perfectly. "I am not sure it would work in Xanth, because of its scientific principle. But I have several, and it will serve as a decoration if not as an indicator, so go ahead."

Dolph decided that he really could trust this man. "I think I need to ask for your help again."

"Oh?"

"I—I did not come here alone. I came with my betrothed."

"You are betrothed? But you're so young!"

"It's a political arrangement," Dolph explained. "But she could not come here in her regular form, so—"

"Her regular form?"

"It's hard to explain. Could you set the watch to find Nada Naga?"

Turn rummaged in his desk drawer. "I have another. Just what form is she in?"

"A snake."

"A snake! You are betrothed to a snake?"

"Not exactly. Please, I'm worried about her! I must find her!"

"Snake," Turn said to the new watch. It pinged. The eye pointed into the garden. They plowed through the brush. Abruptly they came to a deep drainage ditch with slick tiled sides. Suddenly Dolph knew what had happened to Nada. She had fallen in and been unable to get out!

He jumped into the ditch, searching frantically. Then he saw her, struggling weakly in the water, barely keeping her head out of it. He reached down and picked her up. "Oh, Nada!" he breathed.

She was weak but all right. He held her up to Turn. "Meet Nada Naga."

Turn's eyes widened. "Uibu't op mpdbm toblf!" Then he did a doubletake. "Zpv nfbo uibu't zpvs gjbodff?"

"My betrothed," Dolph agreed. "Nada is a princess of her kind, but she can't take human form here. So she came as a snake, to keep an eye on me."

Turn nodded, finally understanding despite the unintelligible words. They returned to the lab. There Dolph thanked him again for his help.

Turn seemed to have some further doubts, but he did not express them. "Well, let's get you back to the gourd, and I wish you well in your Quest."

They returned to the gourd, where Dolph removed his clothing. There was no point in wearing it, since he always lost it when he changed form. Then he saluted Turn with a gesture of appreciation, and jumped into the peephole, holding Nada.

14

ISLE OF VIEW

Back in Xanth, Dolph told the story, giving Nada credit for bringing him the key to the lab so he could try to escape, but not telling how she had gotten caught in the ditch. He remembered how Draco Dragon had preferred that Mela Merwoman not be made unhappy by being told that her husband had been killed because of a misunderstanding, and he realized that sometimes there was no good purpose in telling of another person's mistakes. In short, on occasion the Adult Way made sense, though it galled him to concede this.

"So now we know how to find the Heaven Cent," he concluded. "This watch has an eye that looks toward it."

"Most interesting," Marrow said. He and Grace'l seemed oddly satisfied; Dolph wondered what they might have talked about while they were alone together. "But does it work in Xanth?"

"Yes. See, it is watching now!" He held up his wrist, and sure enough, the eye was looking north.

"Amazing," the skeleton said. "I would have thought a

Mundane amulet would be inoperative here."

"That's what Turn Key thought. But I'm glad I kept it. Now we can go right to the Cent and find the Good Magician!"

"Perhaps so," Marrow agreed, but he looked doubtful. Adults were often doubtful without reason, so Dolph wasn't worried.

They traveled north along the west coast of Xanth, suffering only routine adventures. When a dragon threatened, Dolph assumed the form of another dragon, growling it off. When a sand dune wanted to incorporate them into itself and make beautiful fossils of them, Dolph became a Bigfoot monster and carried Nada across; in this form his feet were so big that the sand could not swallow them. When a tangle tree threatened, and the jungle was too thick to allow them to pass around it, Dolph became a roc and carried the others over. Of course he could have carried them the whole distance, but was afraid of overshooting the Cent, because he couldn't use the watch while he was a roc. So they did it the slow way, he and Nada traveling in naga form, and that was nice enough. He now knew her in all her forms, and liked them all; she was such a nice girl now that the Eye Queue effect was gone. He was well satisfied to be betrothed to her.

Thus they traveled for a number of days, and no one complained. Marrow and Grace'l walked side by side, following the two naga, and seemed just as satisfied with each other's company as were Dolph and Nada.

Now they were approaching Castle Roogna from the south. Could the Heaven Cent be there? But first they had to find the Skeleton Key, and certainly that wasn't there!

The eye of the watch veered, taking them to the coast instead of inland to the castle. Dolph was privately relieved; he really wasn't quite ready to face his mother or to try to explain about the betrothal. Of course she surely already knew, having watched in the Tapestry; even so, he did not relish the encounter. He knew that she would be prepared with all sorts of Reasons why it was Not a Good Idea, Dear.

They came to the beach. There was a hypnogourd and a lovely purple flower, with a little memorial plaque set up beside them:

> BY HEAVEN SENT
> BESIDE THIS AMARANTH
> FORTY YEARS PAST
> EVIL MAGICIAN TRENT
> LANDED HERE IN XANTH
> KING AT LAST

They stared at this. What could it mean?

"Grandpa Trent isn't evil!" Dolph said.

"In the past—" Marrow began.

"What a pretty flower!" Naga exclaimed.

"—Magician Trent was known as evil, in contrast to the Good Magician Humfrey," Grace'l continued. "However—"

Dolph glanced at the two skeletons in surprise. They were getting very close to each other!

"—once Trent became King, he was no longer evil, by definition," Marrow concluded. "He had been called evil because he opposed the prior King, not because he was a bad man. Indeed, he was not a bad man, as became apparent."

"How strange that this flower hasn't faded in forty years," Nada said.

"That is the nature of this flower," Grace'l explained. "It never fades."

Suddenly something registered. "Heaven sent!" Dolph exclaimed. "This must be it!"

"You spell as your father does, don't you," Marrow remarked. "'Sent' is not the same as 'cent'—"

"But it's Heaven Cent!" Dolph protested. "I don't care how it's spelled! The watch brought us here!"

"Say, he's right!" Nada agreed. "The eye pointed this way, and—"

"Let us verify this," Marrow said, in the manner that adults temporized in awkward situations.

Dolph held up his wrist. "See—the eye is pointing right toward the plaque!"

"Try walking to the other side," Marrow said.

Dolph walked around the plaque. The eye hardly wavered; the watch was looking in the same direction it had been. "See!" Dolph said. "It—"

"Is now pointing out to sea," Marrow said. "Or to that island we see. The plaque was merely in its route."

"Uh, yes," Dolph agreed, chagrined.

"Pure coincidence," Grace'l said.

Dolph was silent. He found that he did not much like coincidence. That was a term they used in Mundania to account for magic, because they refused to believe in magic. He was sure there was good reason for the plaque being on their route; he just could not quite figure it out yet.

"That seems to be the last of the keys," Nada said. "Maybe it is the Skeleton Key. Anything you search for is always in the very last place you look; everyone knows that."

That made Dolph feel better. Nada was always a comfort. He liked her better than anyone he had known, and never wanted to be apart from her.

He paused, thinking about that. His betrothal to Nada was political, but now he realized that he really did want to marry her, when the time came. Because then she would never leave.

The skeletons formed into their boat, and they sailed across the water to the final key. A sea monster spied them, and swam over to investigate, but Dolph changed momentarily into a gargoyle whose supremely ugly puss gave the monster hiccups. That was enough; embarrassment caused the monster to retreat.

They landed on a pleasant beach, and kicked the skeletons back into shape. The island was quite pretty, with a high central ridge. The skeletons elected to walk around it, while Dolph and Nada rose to the challenge of the ridge.

When they mounted to the top, the view was impressive; they could see far across the sea. There was another sign providently displayed at the apex. "What does it say?" Nada asked. "I've got a bit of dust in my eye; I can't read it at the moment." Indeed, her eye was tearing; she had to change to girl form in order to have hands to try to clear it.

Dolph's reading was better than his spelling. "Isle of View," he announced.

Nada paused, gazing at him with her watery eye. "What?"

"Isle of View," he repeated.

She burst into tears—genuine ones, not dust-mote ones. "That's what I thought you said," she sobbed.

Dolph went to her. "Nada! What's the matter?"

"I wish you hadn't said that," she said. "Why didn't you just read the sign?"

"I *did* read the sign! It says Isle of View. What's the matter with that?"

"You're teasing me! That's not nice!"

"What's not nice about Isle of View?" he demanded, baffled.

"Because I don't love you," she sobbed.

That set him back. It had nothing to do with the subject, but it was not welcome news. He had come to like her so well that he was wondering whether love was an appropriate term. Of course he had never spoken of this to her, fearing embarrassment. Why had she brought it up so abruptly?

"And I feel so guilty," she continued. "You're such a fine young prince, and—" She lapsed into further sobbing.

"I don't know how we got into this," Dolph said. "But I guess we'd better figure it out. Are you breaking our betrothal?"

"Of course not!" she flared. "Why would I do that?"

"I don't know. But if you feel guilty—"

"Dolph, it's an arranged betrothal, you know that. It's the price my father charged to help you. You have been very good about it. I am sure we can make it work. But love need be no part of these arrangements. Why did you have to bring it up?"

"I didn't bring it up!" he protested.

"Yes you did! You said 'I love you.' "

"I did not! But now that we're discussing it—"

"I asked you to read the sign, and instead of that you said 'I love you.' Out of the black."

"The black?"

"Or the blue. Whatever."

"The sign says 'Isle of—' " At that point something finally registered. "Are your eyes clear now? Read it yourself."

Nada blinked her eyes clear and looked at the sign. "Isle of—" she echoed. "Oh, no!"

"It sounds just like—"

"Just like—oh, Dolph, I'm so sorry! I thought—"

He tried to laugh, but it didn't come out. "But if I had meant to say that, it might be true. I know I'm young, but so are you, and—"

"Oh, Dolph, please! I wish this had never—"

"I know we're only children, but if you like me the way I like you, maybe in time we could call it—"

"Dolph, I never wanted to hurt you! I didn't know you— I thought it a harmless deception, necessary in the circumstances."

He was gradually coming to understand her point. "It is an arranged betrothal, as you say. We never met before it. We might have hated each other, and it would still be a good liaison. I am a prince; I understand about these things. My Grandpa King Trent did not love my Grandma Queen Iris; he married her so she would support the throne and provide an heir. My mother Irene hated my father Dor when they were children, but she wanted to marry him so she could share the throne."

"Yes," Nada agreed faintly.

"But then Dor and Irene fell in love anyway. So sometimes it does happen. My parents were both in their teens when it happened to them. It could happen with us. We may be too young now, but when we get older—"

"No," she said, the tears starting again.

"I realize that you don't—like me now, but if—"

"Oh, Dolph, I do like you!" she exclaimed. "I think you're wonderful! But I will never love you."

"How can you know how you'll feel when you're in your teens, and I am too? Maybe then—"

"I *am* in my teens," she said.

He gazed at her, puzzled. "But—"

She took a breath, braced herself, and spoke firmly. "I never wanted you to know, but now it means too much, and I won't lie to you. I am fourteen years old."

Dolph was stunned. "That can't be!"

"I can assume my natural age in girl form, if you wish, so you can judge. I can revert to a younger form, because I've been through it, but I can't assume an older form than I am."

"Uh, yes," Dolph said. What he meant was that he understood about that sort of limit; he had never been able to assume an adult human form or adult animal forms, just big juvenile forms.

She understood him to mean that he wanted her to assume her natural age. She changed to naga form, then back to girl form.

Dolph stared. She was a completely developed young woman, not as well fleshed as Vida Vila or Mela Merwoman, but certainly old enough to communicate with the stork. In fact, she was very like his big sister Ivy.

He turned aside, appalled. He could not have imagined a more complete betrayal. She had been that age all along!

"Dolph, Dolph!" she cried. "At least let me tell you why!"

He walked away from her, numbed. "Your father needed the liaison, and you were the wrong age," he said coldly. "I understand."

She followed him. "Oh, Dolph, I beg of you, please don't

break the betrothal! I'll do anything you ask, if only you don't do that!"

He turned on her. "I may be a child, but I am also a prince. I gave my word. We made a deal. Your folks did their part. I won't break it. We are betrothed until you break it."

She sank to the ground, her tears still flowing. "Oh, thank you, Dolph! I am so grateful."

His heart felt like a stone. He hated seeing her like this, in tears, prostate, and adult. It embarrassed him, apart from the pain of the betrayal. "Please don't do that."

"Oh yes!" she agreed eagerly. "I will resume my younger form, and be your companion, anything you want! I am so happy you—"

"You are as miserable as I am, right now," he said. "Why do you want to please me so much, when you don't even like me?"

"I *do* like you, Dolph! I told you, I just don't, can't love you, and now you know why."

"Yes." She had really made her point, showing the impossibility of it. What mischief had come from the name of the isle, so innocently read!

"But if you are a prince, I am a princess. I must do what is best for my family and my folk. We need the help of your folk, and I must not fail in my part. It is not the part I would have chosen, but that is not the point. I must and shall fulfill it. The goblins—"

Dolph nodded. She was indeed a princess. He understood that aspect perfectly. She could afford to be herself only when it did not conflict with the duties of her station. The same was true for him. He had been foolish ever to think that the two of them were just children. They were royalty. Commitments were more important than feelings.

"There is no further need for you to pretend to be what you are not," he said. "Be what you are; it is better that way."

"But, Dolph, I don't have to rub your nose in—I can keep my younger guise, if you want."

"It has become a matter of indifference to me," he said curtly, and walked away again. This time she did not pursue him.

Dolph held his head high and his gaze straight forward. He came to a copse of trees that formed a concealed natural bower. He entered this, as if seeking a place for a private function. He looked around, making sure that no one could see him. Then he sat on the ground, put his head in his hands, and wept.

In due course the two skeletons completed the circuit of the isle. "There seems to be nothing of significance here," Marrow said. "Was there anything on the ridge?" Then he saw Nada approaching, and did a double take. "Who is that?"

"That is Nada, in natural form," Grace'l said. "She is older than she appeared."

"But—"

"Best we not comment," Grace'l said.

Dolph realized that she had known about Nada before, while Marrow had not. It made him feel closer to Marrow. But he said nothing about this. Instead he held up his watch and walked in the direction the eye was looking. The others followed.

The eye wavered and looked in a new direction. They were finally getting close! But when it showed by its motions that they had found the spot it was eyeing, they were chagrined. There was nothing there but brush and sand.

Dolph walked around and around in a circle, but the eye continued to watch only that one bare place. What could this mean?

They sat in a circle and discussed it. Nada assumed her naga form for this, as it was better in sand. Dolph tried to treat her as before, neither staring at her nor ignoring her, but it was difficult. If only she had been what she seemed to be, a nice girl of his own generation! If only he had not learned, the hard way, that all girls *were* alike!

"Could the Heaven Cent have been here, and been moved before we got here?" Grace'l asked.

"Then why didn't the watch follow it to its new location?" Marrow asked in turn.

"Maybe it couldn't."

"Then why does it seem so certain?" Dolph asked. "It seems to think the cent is right here."

"Maybe—" Nada said, then hesitated.

Dolph looked at her. She was still pretty, in whatever form. He looked away.

"Maybe because you got it in Mundania," Nada said. "We thought it was using magic, here, but that's really not its nature. If it is still using science—"

"The cent is in Mundania!" Dolph exclaimed. "This part of Mundania!"

"Yes!" she exclaimed. For a moment their eyes met, as they shared the momentary joy of discovery. Then Dolph averted his gaze again.

"That does seem to make sense—uh, to be reasonable," Marrow agreed. "However—"

"—we may have a problem reaching Mundania from here," Grace'l concluded. "Perhaps we shall have to seek another Eye Queue vine to enable us to figure out the answer."

Dolph remembered how Nada had used the vine before. Now he remembered a fact about the vine: it often did not generate true intelligence, but only a pseudo smartness that quickly became evident as worthless. For an example, an ogre who used it might think he was brilliant, but others would still see him as a dunce. One ogre had indeed used the vine to become smart, but that was Smash Ogre, who was actually half human; the vine merely invoked his smarter half, rather than creating intelligence from stupidity. Nada's human heritage had been evident all along; what had accounted for her increased intelligence, then?

He remembered how she had struck him at the time as like his big sister. That had turned him off, but his knowledge that her visit to Mundania would wipe out any magic not inherent had consoled him. Indeed, she had reverted to normal thereafter, becoming nice instead of obnoxious. But now he knew that the vine had in fact invoked her true nature, the know-it-all attitude of the fourteen-year-old girl. He should have taken warning then. But like the child he was, he had ignored the signal, fascinated with the notion of a girl who was not like all the others.

"The answer the last one provided turned out to be risky," Marrow said. "Only Dolph could go there in his human form, and he did not speak their language. The help Nada could provide in her snake form was limited—"

"In fact I fell into a ditch, and Dolph rescued me," Nada said. "I was a liability, not a help."

"Dolph did not mention that," Grace'l remarked.

"Dolph's a decent person," she said.

Dolph fought against a surge of appreciation, reminding himself how angry he was with her. "Let's skip the Eye Queue vine," he said. "We should be able to figure it out on our own."

They continued to discuss it, but got nowhere. The day was getting late, so they broke to find food.

"I saw a pie tree during our circuit of the isle," Grace'l said. "I can show you where it is."

"I'm not hungry," Nada said.

Dolph wasn't very hungry either, but didn't want to agree with Nada, so he went with the skeleton to find the pies.

"You know, Dolph, Nada didn't want to deceive you," Grace'l said. "She was very sad about it, but when her father told her she had to marry you—"

"I understand," Dolph said shortly.

"She cried at night, and pretended to be happy by day. She was never the child you took her for. But she was determined to make you happy."

"So I wouldn't break the betrothal!" Dolph said, his anger coming to the surface. "I would never have made it in the first place, if I had known!"

"King Nabob knew that. But the Good Magician had told

them that one of his children had to marry what the dragon brought, so when you came, they knew they had to do it. Nada believed that an innocent deception for a good purpose was all right, but she would not deceive you about love."

"She didn't," he agreed coldly.

"She is in a difficult situation, but she's a good girl."

"She is a princess." That said it all.

"She is a feeling creature. You are being cruel to her."

"What business of yours is it?" he flared.

"You agreed to the betrothal because you needed the help of the naga to rescue Marrow. Marrow was in trouble because he needed the firewater opal to release me from hostage status. Thus you were betrothed because of me. That makes it my business."

Dolph wasn't sure of her logic, but did not care to argue it. "I have to marry her. I don't have to like her."

"She had to marry you. She didn't have to love you."

Suddenly Dolph was crying, without reason, and it did not seem strange at all that Grace'l was holding him. Her bones were rounded so that they did not hurt. But nevertheless there was something strange about it, and in a moment he realized what it was. Her bones were not hard!

"You're fleshed!" he exclaimed.

Grace'l looked at herself. "Ugh!" she exclaimed. "I thought we'd left that illusion behind! Some of it must have followed me here!"

"We were talking about deception," Dolph said, wiping his eyes. "Maybe that attracted it."

"I must get it off me!" she cried, brushing at herself. The illusion was not quite as comprehensive as before, because it did not include clothing, but that seemed scant consolation to her. "What will Marrow think?"

Dolph could not refrain from smiling. "He has to like you. He doesn't have to look at you."

"Very funny!" she said severely. "This time it is worse than before; I can feel it as well as see it. Have you any notion what a turnoff something like this is to our kind?"

"About the same kind that five years age is with our kind?" Dolph asked.

"Well, I hope Marrow is more tolerant than you are!" she snapped. Then, immediately, she was sorry. "I shouldn't have said that! I apologize—"

But Dolph, stricken, had to demur. "I shouldn't hold her age against her," he admitted. "But it sure is hard not to."

"For her too," she reminded him. "That's why she can't love you."

"Yes." Dolph still did not like the situation at all, but he was coming to accept it.

They found the pie tree. It was a simple cherry tree, with no other kind of pie ripening, but that was good enough. Dolph selected two of the best and picked them. "Let's go back."

"You aren't eating here?"

"It is better to share."

"Yes," Grace'l agreed. "Even when there are problems, it is better to share."

Marrow and Nada were talking animatedly as they returned, but ceased. Marrow's hollow sockets stared. "What?"

"It's me—Grace'l," Grace'l said. "With the grace note." She plinked her finger against her smallest extra rib, and it sounded musical even though the illusion made her look meaty. "I got caught by an illusion whorl and I can't get rid of it."

"The key of G!" Nada exclaimed. "Could that mean—"

"The skeleton key!" Dolph concluded. "We had it with us all along! Then, as the others stood amazed, he proffered Nada the second pie.

"But—" she said.

"I apologize for treating you cruelly, and ask you to accept this token of amend," he said in the best princessly manner.

Her gaze flicked briefly to Grace'l as she realized the skeleton's part in this. Then she assumed girl form and took the pie. "I accept your apology and the pie, though neither was necessary," she said in the best princessly manner.

So they had officially made up. But the rift remained. They were incompatible, and no apologies could change that. How he wished it were otherwise!

"But if Grace'l is the skeleton key," Marrow said, keeping his hollow gaze away from what, to a living man, would have been considered most attractive flesh on Grace'l, "then it is a music note instead of a key for a lock. How can that unlock the Heaven Cent?"

"A magic lock that responds to music instead of to a physical key," Dolph said. "That must be what the Good Magician's message means. That Grace'l's grace note in the key of G is what will lead us to the Heaven Cent. There doesn't really have to be a lock, just that key!"

"But if the Cent is in Mundania, Grace'l can't play the note there," Morrow said.

"We can reach Mundania the same way we did before, through the gourd. Maybe it is the exit from the gourd to Mundania that the note opens."

"Yes!" Nada exclaimed. "That must be it!"

"But we have no huge zombie gourd here," Marrow said. "If we made the long trip back to the zombie gourd, and entered that, I still would not know which gourd exited here. If you exited there, you would have to travel alone all the way here, and that does not seem good at all."

"But there is a gourd just across the water, at the plaque to my grandfather," Dolph said. "We could use that—" He broke off, realizing that that would be a different matter. He could not physically enter that gourd, which meant that he would have to let his soul enter it alone, while his body remained frozen at the peephole. He did not like that notion at all.

"Also—" Grace'l began.

"You are forbidden to re-enter the gourd," Marrow concluded, remembering. "So we cannot use your note anyway."

"But you know, she doesn't look much like herself now," Nada said. "Maybe she wouldn't be recognized."

Grace'l shook her head, and her illusion curls flounced. Marrow winced, which was a good trick with his features. Dolph realized that Grace'l was now as distasteful to Marrow as Nada was to him, and for similar reason: too much flesh. But in Grace'l's case it was illusion, while in Nada's case it was not. "I wanted so much to return to the gourd," she said. "The thought of continued exile appalled me. I had hoped to find a gourd, enter, and beg for pardon for my crime and try to make amends. But now that I have come to be satisfied with existence out here, and have no further wish to return, it seems that I must. If I am the skeleton key you seek, then I will do what I can to enable you to find the Heaven Cent."

They pondered, considered, and discussed it, and decided that they would have to make the attempt. Marrow and Grace'l could enter the gourd physically, because they had originated within it; Dolph could enter it nonphysically. They knew where they were going: to Mundania right here. If there was a way through the gourd, they would find it, and the Quest would finally be done. Nada, meanwhile, would stand guard here in Xanth, and snap Dolph out of it if anything threatened.

They made the boat and sailed back to the beach on the mainland. There they went to the King Trent Memorial and picked up the gourd, which really wasn't part of it. Dolph reread the plaque, curious about its references. "By Heaven Sent, Beside this Amaranth . . ." They said the spelling of Cent was different, but he wondered. The two terms were very familiar, and the two spots were very close together. The watch had taken them right past this spot. Who had set up this monument? Who had planted the amaranth flower? He could not shake the feeling that they were overlooking something important.

"Does the amaranth grow in Mundania?" he asked.

"Of course not," Nada replied. "It's magic."

"But it might grow in Mundania, in a Mundane version," he persisted.

"It seems pointless to be concerned about it," Marrow

said. "Let's get this gourd across to the isle before darkness falls; we cannot be sure what monsters will appear in the night." He bent to take hold of the gourd.

There was a sound from the monument, as of a bell ringing. "What is that?" Grace'l asked, startled.

"An alarm!" Dolph and Nada said together. They had learned of this type of thing during their Mundane excursion.

"What would that be for?" Marrow asked.

"To prevent anyone from molesting my grandfather's monument, I think," Dolph said.

"Then we should have nothing to fear," Marrow said, relieved.

In a moment there was a stirring in the sea. Something was swimming rapidly toward them. When it came to the shallow surf, it showed as a huge ugly fish, with a tusked, piglike head. Then it heaved itself out of the froth to the sand, and Dolph saw that there were three big eyes set in its side, as well as those of its head. It had four short legs with flippers, and a set of curled horns. It proceeded toward them by bounding with considerable vigor, all four feet together.

"That's an argus!" Nada exclaimed. "We have some in our cave waters. They are mean customers!"

"But if the monument's alarm summoned it, it can't be completely wild," Dolph said. "I'd better check." He assumed the form of another argus.

The incoming argus spied him and came to a sand stirring halt. "Who are you, boar-face?" it demanded.

"I am Prince Dolph, King Trent's grandson," Dolph replied in its language. "These are my companions."

"Oh. Then you are not here to molest the monument."

"No. We admire it. Who set it up, and who maintains it?"

"That is a medium-length story, and probably uninteresting."

"No, we are interested!" Dolph protested. "I am here on a quest for the Heaven Cent, and did not know of this monument. My grandfather never mentioned it. Please tell me all about it."

"You are really interested?" the argus asked, amazed.

"Yes. I want to know as much as I can about this region and this monument. Why does it have this amaranth, and why did our touch of the gourd sound the alarm? Surely the gourd is not part of the monument!"

"Surely it *is*!" the argus countered. "Come, settle in the water where we can be comfortable, and I will tell you everything."

"Gladly! Let me just advise my friends." Dolph resumed boy form, and told the others of the exchange. "Why don't you relax until I have learned the whole story," he suggested. "It may help us in our Quest."

"But it is getting late—" Marrow said.

"I think we shall be in no danger here, even at night," Dolph said. "And I really want to know about this monument."

"It *is* his Quest," Nada reminded the skeleton. She was supporting him, as she always had, even in this hour of their alienation. Dolph noticed, and was unwillingly moved, but had no time to comment; he changed back to argus form.

He bounded with the other argus to the shallows, where the white-foamed surf rolled in. Yes, it was far more comfortable here in the water; it supported and wet his body, and cooled it, and caressed it. With the extra eyes on his sides, he could see to both sides, and above and below the surface of the water. This was a nice form!

"So you are a form changer," the argus said. "King Trent does it too, but he changes only the forms of others."

"Yes. Our talents are complementary." Dolph had learned that word because of that relation between the talents, and was proud of it. "Now, what is the story of this monument, and why doesn't my grandfather talk about it?"

"Forty years ago Evil Magician Trent came to this shore, after being exiled from Xanth," the argus said. "He had been banished because he tried to take the throne away from the Storm King, who wasn't a very good king, I understand. Twenty years after departing Xanth, the Magician found his way back, in the company of two others, Bink and Fanchon. They—"

"Who?" Dolph interrupted.

"Fanchon. The woman Bink married."

"But he married Chameleon, my grandmother!"

"There must be some mistake," the argus said, blinking several eyes. "It was Fanchon who was with him, magnificently ugly but horribly smart."

"That's Chameleon in her ugly-smart phase!" Dolph exclaimed, catching on. "She must have used a different name then!"

"No doubt. At any rate, the three of them waded ashore here, very tired, and settled down to rest on the beach. Actually they settled in three different places, but we put the monument in the center, opposite the love-lies-bleeding monument on View Isle."

"The what?"

"The monument on the isle. The one that marks the spot where the dying maiden lies."

"There's no monument there!" Dolph exclaimed. "We just explored that isle, and it's bare."

The argus sighed. "That's what happens when the warranty expires! That monument was supposed to be guarded for a thousand years, until a prince came to wake the poor girl with a kiss, but the guardian must have gotten time off for good behavior and left. Wouldn't you know some monster would steal the monument!"

"We went there to find the Heaven Cent, but there was nothing."

"Yes, the dying maiden has that. Too bad the monument's gone; the prince will have trouble finding her now."

Dolph reined his excitement; already he was learning much of value! Maybe he would learn more in the course of the argus' story. "Tell me everything!"

"Well, the three of them settled down, and naturally got into trouble, because this was a wild beach in those days. Trent looked into a hypnogourd and was hooked—apparently during his long absence he had forgotten about them, or maybe he hadn't encountered any. They weren't as common as they are today, and they mostly didn't grow where the human folk settled. Fanchon rested under a lethargy tree, and of course it made her so lethargic she couldn't move. Bink lay down in a patch of carnivorous grass, and it started rooting in him. It was only sheer luck that he woke in time, but he couldn't get up, so he started yelling. Naturally that brought every hungry monster in the area, including a harpy, a catoblepas, and me. We got into a big fight over the morsel, and Bink got away and rescued the other two. I never saw a man so lucky!"

"But what about the monument?"

"I'm coming to that. They moved on to Castle Roogna, which was then deserted, and Trent became King and restored it, and I think it's still functioning today."

"It is."

"Because this was where they landed, the Good Magician Humfrey decided that there should be a monument to mark the site. King Trent said not to bother, but Humfrey did it anyway. He used some of the magic he had collected to identify all of us who had attacked the trio, and he bound us to guard the monument."

"But Humfrey's gone! Why do you still guard it?"

"He's gone? His magic remains! We are granted life as long as the monument stands unmolested, so you may be sure we take good care of it. One day for each, the harpy, the catoblepas, and me. This is my day, and when the alarm sounds, I come quickly. The vegetables help when needed; the hungry grass and a land kraken are near, and the gourd remains here. This is a very peaceful beach now; no visitor is molested as long as he behaves."

"But what about the amaranth flower? There was no amaranth in that story."

"That was borrowed from the other memorial. When I saw that it was no longer well guarded, I feared for the flower, so brought it here. Indeed, it seems I was justified in my caution, if that monument is now gone."

"What do you know of that other monument?" Dolph had been genuinely interested in his grandfather's monument, but at the moment he was far more interested in the other one.

"Oh, that's very simple. This wounded maiden lies bleeding in a casket, and she cannot live or die until kissed after a thousand years or so by a prince. She will give the Heaven Cent to the prince who wakes her. That's all there is to it."

"But how will the prince find her, if the amaranth no longer marks the spot?"

"I wouldn't know."

"How long has she been there?"

"I think it's about eight hundred and fifty years, something like that. She has a way to go before she runs out of time."

"Runs out of time? What happens to her after the thousand years are over?"

"Well, that's the limit, you see. If no prince finds her and kisses her within that period, she will die anyway, and so will the amaranth. They are linked, you know. They live and die together. I'm sure it is an interesting tale, if anyone knows the whole of it."

"I'm sure it is," Dolph said thoughtfully.

"I had to rewrite the inscription when we borrowed the amaranth," the argus continued. "I'm a pretty good poet, if I do say so myself. I have an eye for scansion."

"Yes, the inscription is very nice," Dolph said, realizing that a bit of flattery was in order. "But I am going to have to borrow the amaranth and gourd."

"What? I just told you why they must remain here!"

"But you see, I am a prince, and I must get the Heaven Cent, which means I must rescue the dying lady, and I think I can only reach her if I use the gourd, and I think I'll find her better if I have that amaranth."

"But you don't have to take either from here! You can

use the gourd here, and go to her casket there. Distance makes no matter in the gourd."

"Why yes, I suppose I could. Very well, I'll do that." Dolph looked around. Darkness had closed while they conversed, and the shells on the sand beneath the water were glowing in pretty patterns, setting up their night lights, and the sea itself was luminescent. "In the morning," he concluded.

"You will have to clear that with the harpy; tomorrow is her tour of duty."

"I shall do that. I thank you most kindly for your interesting story."

"Quite all right," the argus said, blushing green.

Dolph returned to boy form, walked out of the water and across the beach, and reported to the others. "I learned a lot!" he said. "We can proceed from here; we don't have to take the gourd." Quickly he explained about the two memorials and the bleeding girl. "So I think I must be the Prince who will come to wake her, and that's why the Good Magician sent me here."

Nada did not comment, but she seemed pensive. It was evident that she was not completely at ease about Dolph rescuing such a maiden.

The skeletons formed their houses, and they retired for the night. "What's bothering Nada?" Dolph asked Marrow privately.

"As I understand it, a prince does not merely kiss a sleeping maiden," Marrow's skull replied. "He marries her."

Oh. "But I can't marry the maiden!" Dolph protested. "I'm already betrothed!"

"But you seem to have a problem."

"Well, sure, but we're still betrothed."

"Still, if I were Nada, I would be concerned about the other maiden. It does seem that she is the one Good Magician Humfrey's note intended you to encounter."

Dolph was silent. But he wondered, now, whether the Good Magician had known that Dolph would be betrothed to Nada before he encountered that sleeping princess.

15
GOURD

In the morning they explained things to the harpy. She was a surprisingly understanding and clean hen; the Good Magician had taught her manners. That spoke exceedingly well for Humfrey's power! Then Marrow stepped into the gourd, disappearing as he did so. Grace'l nerved herself and did likewise. For the moment Dolph was left alone with Nada. "We're still betrothed," he reminded her. "I keep my word."

"Of course," she replied.

"I have to do this. It's my Quest."

"I know."

But they both knew that their betrothal could be in peril. Suppose he had to marry the maiden in order to get the Heaven Cent? "I'm sorry about—"

"So am I, Dolph."

"Oh, mice! Why couldn't things have been as they seemed to be?"

"Because things are almost never as they seem to be. Disillusion is part of growing up."

"I never want to grow up!"

"You must, Dolph. We all must, though it hurts." She blinked. "Please get on with it, Dolph, before we both start crying."

She was uncomfortably accurate, but she did not seem much like Ivy. Dolph realized that if Nada had had magic to make herself young, she would have used it. Her age was not her fault. She had been thrown into an impossible situation, and tried valiantly to make the best of it, and almost succeeded. He could respect that. Now she was being nice despite this second threat to her position. She *was* nice; that had never been in question. "Nada—"

"Please, Dolph," she repeated, and he saw how hard she was fighting to hold back the tears. He was doing her no kindness by lingering.

Dolph sat down beside the gourd, tilted up its peephole, and looked in. For a moment there was only a blur; then he realized that his own tears were getting in the way. He blinked them clear.

He found himself in a huge building. People and creatures hurried madly in every direction, each one intent on some urgent personal business. Many were burdened by bags, cases, trunks, extra clothing, and an assortment of odds and ends. There were massive square columns supporting the ceiling, and recesses beyond the columns, and so many halls and passages and walkways that he could not even guess the extent of this room, let alone of the building. Every so often unintelligible sounds burst from spots on the walls, as if some tongue-tied monster were screaming for freedom. Surely this was the most remarkable castle in Xanth!

"What is this?" he asked Marrow, who was standing on his right and gazing across the concourse.

"This must be a new setting," Marrow said. "I never saw it before."

Grace'l was on his left, still oddly fleshed. "Have you seen it?" Dolph asked.

"No. This must be a specialized application."

"Isn't the gourd setting supposed to be fixed by the person who enters it?" Dolph asked. "Shouldn't it be one that the two of you know about?"

"No," Marrow replied. "We are creatures *of* the dream realm; our presence does not affect it. We are in effect invisible. It is the entry of a real person, in this case yourself, that determines the setting."

"But you entered before I did! How—"

"Evidently the setting knew you were coming. This is what you will encounter in any gourd you look into, with the exception of the great physical zombie gourd. That, being of a deteriorating nature, does not properly fix on the individual; it is locked into the setting it had before it zombified."

Dolph had to be satisfied with that. "Can you lead me through this one?"

Marrow seemed embarrassed. "I assumed it would be a familiar setting—the horror house, or the graveyard, or some other ordinary scene. This is so strange, I am at a loss."

Dolph had been afraid of that. "Grace'l?"

"I only hope no one recognizes me," she said. "For me, this may be better, because I am unlikely to encounter any former associates."

"You look quite unlike yourself, with that flesh on," Dolph reassured her. "You look just like a nymph."

"Well, you don't have to rub it in!" she said. "This is embarrassing enough as it is."

"But nymphs look very pretty," Dolph protested. "Men are always chasing them."

"Men are foolish," she agreed grimly. "But I suppose it is true: no one would suspect me of adopting such a tasteless disguise."

Dolph realized that it was up to him. "Well, I still have the watch. Let me see where it's looking." He peered at the band on his wrist. "That way."

The three of them looked in the indicated direction. It led through the worst of the confusion. Dolph shrugged and stepped out, and the skeleton and nymph followed.

They crossed the broad floor, guiding around the columns and avoiding the hurrying other folk. In due course they came up against a tiled wall. The eye of the watch was looking right through the wall.

Dolph remembered when the eye had led him out into the sea. He knew how to handle this; he just had to go around the wall.

They turned and walked along the wall. This brought them to a truly strange feature: a set of stairs that moved by themselves. They came out of the floor and ascended blithely through a hole in the ceiling. Other folk simply stood on these stairs and were borne upward.

Dolph shrugged. "I guess that's how it's done," he said, and stepped onto the lowest step as it slid out of the floor. It took his weight and carried him up smoothly. Marrow and Grace'l followed on the next two steps, seeming as out of place in this weird setting as Dolph himself. For one thing, the other folk all wore clothing.

The magic stairs deposited them at an upper level. They had to move along quickly to make room for the hurrying little dragon with three bags who was snorting steam as he moved, and for the buzzard bird who spread his wings slightly in his eagerness to get ahead.

Dolph checked the watch again. Now the way the eye looked was open. He walked that way—and in due course came to another wall. He followed it, and came to another set of magic stairs, these traveling down.

He sighed. He was beginning to wonder whether there was a way through this puzzle building. Maybe it would be better to ask someone.

A human man was hurrying toward the magic stair. "Sir," Dolph called, "could you please tell me—"

"No time!" the man said, hardly pausing. "I'm late! Got to catch my plane!"

"Your plain what?" Dolph asked. But the man was already riding the magic stairs down.

A woman was coming, towing two small children. "Miss!" Dolph called, "could you—"

"No soliciting allowed in the terminal, you know that!" she reproved him as she dived for the stairs.

He decided to try one more time. He spied a skeleton coming, with a skeletal bone handbag. His experience with Marrow and Grace'l gave him confidence. "Mister Skeleton!" he called. "Would you—"

"The name is Red," the skeleton informed him sharply.

"Uh, yes, Mr. Red. Would you tell me how to get out of here? I mean—"

"Why, you take your ticket to the window," Red said. Then he was gone down the stairs.

Window? Dolph hadn't seen any windows at all, just walls and stairs. Still, this was progress. "Let's look for a window," he said.

"But what about your ticket?" Marrow asked.

"I don't know what that is, but maybe I can find out at the window."

So they turned away from the magic stairs and went in search of a window. Dolph reasoned that it must be somewhere in the wall, because that was the kind of place a window liked to be. So they walked along the wall, wherever they found it.

Instead of a window they found a hall. Many people were hurrying down this, so it seemed that it went somewhere, maybe to a window. Dolph and his companions merged with the rushing throng.

They came to a chamber with several rows of seats. Beyond the seats was a window—the largest, biggest, hugest, most enormous tremendous window he had ever seen. Dolph gaped.

Beyond the window was a plain, extending way out toward the horizon. This must be the plain that the first man said he had to catch! But what could a person do with such a plain, once he had caught it, and why did he have to hurry so? Surely the plain would not fly away!

Then, in the sky above the plain, a fly appeared. It grew

swiftly, becoming a bird, and then a dragon, and then something strange: a cylinder with flat projections from the sides and fins at the back, that flew in like a roc bird with frozen wings, and came down on the plain. It made a continuous loud roar with a piercing whine at the top, and it had two gaping open perfectly round mouths at the sides, and it sent a torrent of smoke or steam or fire—Dolph could not quite tell which—from its rear. It was probably related to the dragon clan.

The wall-spots blared something unintelligible again. Immediately all the people and creatures seated in the chairs got up and walked to a door in the far side.

But they weren't going in the direction the watch's eye indicated. Dolph decided that this was not the plain for him to catch. He had to get to the Heaven Cent, and he did not want to get too close to that strange flying monster he had seen landing. It might belch fire at him without warning.

He tried following the watch's eye again, but this only led him into another wall. Obviously the Cent was beyond this building, so the best thing was to get out of the building and look for it. He consulted with the skeletons, and they agreed. Both seemed quite out of sorts in this strange environment, when they had expected to find it familiar. Dolph, who had expected the unexpected, was less at a loss. He would have found that situation interesting, if he hadn't been so concerned about finding the maiden and the cent and getting back to Xanth.

They came again to the magic stairs. This time they rode down. Now the way opened out in the right direction. The hall narrowed and the crowd compressed, the creatures as hurried as ever. Apparently this was the nature of existence here: hurry to a seat and wait.

The passage debauched into a cross passage. Once again Dolph had to turn aside from the correct direction. He turned left, and came to another big chamber girt by many stalls decorated with pictures and packages and knick-knacks and whatnots and all. Again, he would have been interested, if here for fun. Certainly, the gourd did not seem like a bad place, just a frustrating one.

He spied a great door to the outside, through which the hurrying folk poured in and out. He went out, free of the building at last. And stopped.

He was on a road, but a horrendous one. Huge boxlike things were jammed in it, nose to tail, honking impatiently. Alarmed that one might try to take a bite of him, he pressed back against the wall. But he saw that these were actually containers for people. His father had told him a tale of Mundania once, where the dragons were angular and made of metal, and the folk they swallowed didn't seem to mind.

Mundania! He must have found his way there! Now all he had to do was reach the cent.

But he discovered that the traffic of boxes was so thick and persistent that he could not get across the road, and that was the direction the watch's eye was looking. He tried walking along the edge of the road, but soon came to a corner where another road intersected, and this too was jammed with moving boxes. The folk inside them looked sweaty and harried and angry, as if this were a bad dream.

A bad dream! Of course! This was a Mundane horror, that the night mares brought to Mundanes! Probably in real life they didn't have to rush about or be confined in boxes that moved by themselves to unwanted destinations, or go docilely to the maws of loud flying monsters. But when they dreamed, these horrors were visited on them. What an awful setting this was! Worse than a haunted house or graveyard or flying knives. Dolph felt sorry for the poor Mundanes; no wonder they were so backward. The folk of Xanth would be backward too, if they could not sleep without suffering scenes like this!

The direction of the watch's eye had varied little as he walked along the road. That was its way of telling him that the cent was not really close. In fact, it was probably across the water, just as was the case in Xanth. How was he going to get to it? He hardly fancied fighting his way through all these moving boxes and then trying to cross the water without a boat!

As he stood pondering, the glass side of one of the boxes slid down. A man's face poked out. "Oooo! Gaga! Wow!" he exclaimed in a foreign language, staring at Grace'l.

Dolph glanced at Grace'l. She remained as she had been, the illusion of supple feminine flesh ruining her true hard bones, so that she seemed to resemble the barest and lushest of nymphs. Why was the Mundane staring at her and uttering those strange syllables?

"Wotta shape!" the man exclaimed. "Gimme summa that-there cheesecake!"

"What are you trying to say?" Dolph demanded, annoyed by the indecipherable words. Too bad he didn't have Turn Key's Mundane translation device here!

Now another Mundane was attracted to the scene. His box glass slid down and his head poked out. "Haybabe!" he called. "How bouta date?"

In fact, glass was descending all along the road, and heads were popping out, eyes bulging. "Gimmea kiss, Godiva!" one called. "Geta loada demboobs!" another chimed in. "Lemme geta piece ash!" another cried. All around were similarly nonsensical calls, a chorus like the screaming of harpies. Dolph and the skeletons were baffled by it all.

At this point the moving boxes went astray. One crashed into another, and another crashed into a third. Soon all the boxes were piling up, and the cries of the occupants redoubled, becoming angry. Dolph could not understand the new words any better than the old ones, but he saw ripples in the air as heat waves radiated from those exclamations, and the few blades of grass by the edge of the road wilted.

Then a solid man dressed in blue strode toward them. He ignored the crashing boxes, keeping his eyes firmly fixed on Grace'l. "Restingya her indecen exposha!" he growled menacingly. "Whatcha thinkyer doing?"

Dolph realized that action was required, because though the blue man's words were baffling, his attitude was not.

He intended some sort of mischief. Retreat was their best course.

Accordingly, he led the way back to the strange building. The blue man pursued them, waving a little stick and speaking loudly. "Stopinna nameofa law!"

They made it into the continuously hurrying throng, and were carried into the building. The blue man followed, screaming obscurities. None of the hurrying folk paid any attention.

Dolph knew that he had to get his party hidden, because otherwise the mean blue man would catch them and prevent them from reaching the cent. He looked for some place to hide.

"This way!" he cried as he spied a side passage. He caught Grace'l by one eerily fleshed wrist and hauled her out of the rushing throng. Marrow followed. They scooted around a narrow corner. Had the blue man seen them?

He had. "Halta Ifire!" his brutish voice came, and the plodding of his big flat feet was loud on the tiles.

They fled. But they came up against a door. The word SERVICE was printed on it. Dolph didn't hesitate; he grabbed the knob, turned it, and yanked the door open.

Beyond it was a set of metal steps, and they weren't moving. Good. He jumped down them, and the skeletons followed. Marrow shut the door behind.

They were in some kind of open shed, with strange equipment all around. Beyond it was a huge plain, like the one they had seen from the window. Dolph didn't like that at all; there could be dragons here!

The door burst open behind them. "Nowi gotcha!" the blue man cried, and the buttons on his clothing glinted menacingly.

They ran. In a moment they were out of the shed, and in two moments they were dashing across the plain, and in three moments they were among odd parked birds like the one they had seen before, only smaller. Each had wings that stuck straight out instead of being folded, and the strangest beak imaginable: split into two or three parts that stuck out sidewise, as if someone had smashed it to pieces. Maybe that had taught these things a lesson, because not one of them made any threatening move.

"Comebackere yoofelons!" the blue man panted, still pursuing. "Resistinga rest! Fleeing scena crime! Judge'll sendyata bighouse!"

It remained gibberish, but Dolph had no urge to discover what it meant by letting the blue man catch them. He dodged around a big bird.

There was an open door in the thing's side. Dolph remembered how the folk were in the moving boxes. Maybe they could hide in this one!

He scrambled up, and the skeletons did the same. Marrow had the wit to pull the oblong little door shut just as the blue man charged up.

But the man pounded on the panel with his mean fists. "Grandtheft airplane!" he shouted. "Never getouta tank!"

It sounded bad. Soon the blue man might break in, and they would be trapped. What could they do?

Dolph looked around. The bird had several seats in its belly, and two more up in its hollow nose. Suddenly he had a weird idea. Was it possible that this thing could move the way the boxes on the road did?

He sat down in the left front seat. Before him was a big front window that showed the whole wide plain ahead. Below it was a set of buttons with bright printed labels: START, POWER, and others he couldn't read. He pressed the first.

Abruptly the splayed nose of the bird started turning. The parts of it whirled around faster and faster, until they disappeared. Amazing!

He touched the second button. The noise at the nose increased, and the bird moved forward.

Well, now! Dolph grabbed the stick he found in front of him, for support. It tilted to the side. The bird skewed to the same side. Dolph moved the stick back, and the bird responded by straightening out. Well, again!

"I think I've found out how to move on the road," Dolph said. "Maybe I can get away from the blue man."

"You already are," Marrow said, peering out a rear window.

"Good." Dolph experimented with the stick. The bird moved whichever direction the stick was tilted. He touched another button. The bird accelerated. Soon it was moving so fast it was scary. Dolph couldn't find the button to make it slow, so he just hung on to the stick and guided the bird across the plain.

He found a long narrow road that led from the plain. Good; he wanted to get away from here, and maybe that would take him there. The bird was still speeding up; the air was roaring past it. Dolph hoped the road would continue long enough to give him time to find the right button to slow the bird.

"Look!" Marrow cried, pointing ahead.

Dolph looked. The road abruptly ended. Bushes and trees grew beyond. He would crash into them!

Desperately, he hauled back on the stick, hoping it would make the bird stop. Instead, the bird's nose tilted up, and suddenly the bird was flying. The trees passed just beneath its wheeled legs.

"Nicely done," Marrow said.

"It was an accident!" Dolph gasped.

"Oh." The skeleton seemed nonplussed.

Dolph pushed the stick forward. The bird responded by nosing down toward the trees. Dolph hastily pulled it back again.

"YOU THERE!" a voice exploded from a patch on the panel. "SMALL AIRPLANE—WHAT ARE YOU DOING TAKING OFF WITHOUT CLEARANCE?!"

Evidently the patch was talking to him. "I'm going to find the Heaven Cent," Dolph responded.

"TURN AROUND AND LAND IMMEDIATELY!!" the patch commanded, sounding very like Ivy in one of her bossier moments.

"I don't know how," Dolph said reasonably. That was generally the best way to respond to such a tone, because it made the speaker mad without actually giving cause.

The patch said something Dolph couldn't understand, but he guessed its nature, because a wisp of smoke curled up from it. Yes, his approach was working!

"Perhaps I can help," Marrow said. There followed a dialogue between him and the patch that soon got technical, so Dolph lost interest.

Meanwhile, the bird was climbing higher. It rose until it was up among the clouds, and then above them. Dolph gazed at them, fascinated.

The clouds were spaced at intervals, each one a big puff of whiteness like a fluffy pillow, with some escaping feathers of mist scattered between. Their bases were dark gray, their tops bright white in the sunlight. Dolph stared, trying to see what held them up, for it was obvious that they were too substantial to float in air. But of course this needed no explanation other than magic. He maneuvered his bird, so as not to bang into any cloud.

He peered down between the clouds. There was the ground, laid out like a tapestry. The roads looked like ruler-drawn lines, somewhat sloppily laid out. The buildings looked like dominoes. That made sense, for dominoes was a game imported from Mundania; for the first time he understood the origin of the shape of the little blocks. He saw dark circles that he realized were lakes, and solid green regions that were forests, and curvaceous contours that marked a river, complete with yellow scuff marks on the inner sides of the bends. Some parts of it were convoluted so deeply they resembled intestines, with the folds almost bumping into each other. There was a mosaic of green, yellow, and red-brown fields, with channels of slippage between. In fact, he recognized this region as the terrain around Castle Roogna, because he had studied it so often in the Tapestry.

But this was Mundania. Instead of the nice little magic paths, there were the ugly straight roads, and instead of the little roofs of the cottages there were the great square buildings. The road lines were drawn between big mundane developments, looking like spiderwebs in the crotches of trees, complete with dewlike sparkles of the glass in their windows. It was pretty, in its ugly way. Dolph was increasingly nervous about something, and finally realized what it was: he was expecting the monstrous spider to appear. One of his father's best friends had been a spider, but there were good spiders and bad spiders, and surely in Mundania they were bad.

He pulled back the stick and set the bird to climbing higher, out of the reach of any such spider. The clouds were filling in below, so that the ground was now more like the bottom of an ocean, with the clouds floating on the surface. Maybe that really was what held them up: a sea of air! Now he noticed their vertical architecture. From below they had always seemed like round blobs, but from above he saw that they were sculptured columns, far more interesting than before.

His ears were uncomfortable. He tried to scratch, but the pressure was inside. Then he yawned, and pain crackled through his ears, but they felt better. Obviously he was passing through a zone of hostile magic.

He looked down again. Clouds had filled in solidly below, so that the ground was lost. There was a second layer of clouds above the first, and the higher ones cast shadows on the lower ones. But that was the least of it. Now that the upper surfaces of the clouds could no longer be seen from below, they were free to show their true colors. Instead of drab gray, they had borrowed colors from the rainbow: red, green, blue, yellow, and striped, as well as white and black and checkerboard.

More clouds were filling in overhead. They could climb higher than he could! He found himself flying through an enormous gallery, with a quiltlike floor and curtainlike canopy. The more distant parts of the cloudscape moved by more slowly than the near parts, demonstrating that clouds, like land objects, had mastered the magic of perspective. The farther away something was, the less need it felt to move just because someone was watching, and the most distant things were so lazy they hardly moved at all. Dolph was impressed; he had thought that the inanimate near Mundania was not that smart. Mushroom clouds sprouted from the bottom level, forming little goblin faces that looked curiously up; evidently they had never before seen a stiff-winged metal bird.

Suddenly a huge bank loomed ahead; he had been so busy sightseeing he had forgotten to pay attention to where he was going. It was too late to avoid it; he had to go through it. He held his breath, closed his eyes, and braced himself for the crash. But all that happened was a slight dragging on the wings; the cloud was after all only vapor, too soft to wreck the bird. What a relief!

He emerged into a new and even lovelier vista. Elegantly hued clouds rose massively up, forming anvils whose points pointed toward blue sky beyond. Soon he would be out into open sky again, able to see everything.

"Oops," Marrow said.

Dolph looked at him. He had almost forgotten he had company! "What's the matter?"

"That looks like Fracto."

Now Dolph saw it. A small gray cloud was pursuing them. It had ugly boils on it, and a mean cast to its surface, and certainly seemed to be up to no good. That was the way of Cumulo Fracto Nimbus, the worst of clouds. "How did he get here? I mean, this is Mundania!"

"Fracto honors no decent limits," Marrow said grimly. "He probably makes just as much trouble for the Mundanes as he does for us."

"He can get pretty bad when he tries," Dolph said, remembering how the evil cloud had tried to dampen Chex's wedding. "We'd better get out of the sky."

"I have ascertained how a landing may be accomplished," Marrow said. "Perhaps we should travel to our destination and land there."

"Destination?" Then Dolph remembered. "Oh, yes, the Heaven Cent!" He looked at the watch. The eye was looking almost straight back. He had been flying away from it!

But Fracto was behind them. How could he turn back without getting caught by the evil cloud?

Dolph decided that he had no choice. He would have to try to surprise Fracto by turning around and flying right through him. If it worked, he would leave Fracto demoralized or even in fragments. If it didn't work—

Dolph suppressed that thought. He reminded himself that he was in the gourd, where reality was different; probably he couldn't really be killed here. But if he crashed, he might never get to the cent, and would fail in his Quest. He was determined not to let that happen!

He pushed the stick right. The bird moved in that direction. He pushed the stick farther, and the bird made a tightening circle. Soon it completed a U-turn, and was headed back the way it had come.

Fracto was there. The evil cloud had grown hugely in the last few minutes, and now had both a gray-black bottom and an anvil top. Sheets of lightning played about his fringes, making his face flicker malevolently. He had a giant bulbous gray nose, and glowing foggy eyes, and a mouth like the darkest of tunnels. A drizzly gust of air blew out, coating the bird with spittle. No one in his right mind would fly toward such a thing!

But Dolph clamped down on his terror and flew the bird right at Fracto. The cloud's watery eyes blinked, and his tunnel mouth gaped wider in amazement. The prey was coming right to him! There was a rumble of confusion.

Then the bird plunged into the mouth. The world turned dark, and the noises of Fracto's tumultuous digestion were loud all around. Lightning flickered inside as well as outside. Dolph had the sickly fear that he had made a bad mistake.

The awful fog closed in tightly. There was an immediate drag on the bird, and drool spattered on the front window, making the view even more dreary. Dolph felt a sinking sensation. He drew back on the stick, and the sinking stopped, but still the bird was slowing, held by the cloying slush. How long could the bird survive the digestive juices of the cloud?

There was a sudden downdraft that hauled the bird violently under. Then there was an updraft that flung it aloft as if thrown from a giant hand. Dolph felt a groaning in the wings; this was severe punishment! Fracto's gizzard was doing its best to break up the bird so that its fragments could be more readily consumed.

Then the bird shot out of the cloud's posterior. They had made it through! There were only the colorful, innocent, friendly little clouds ahead, and now the bird was heading right for the cent.

But Fracto wasn't finished. Dolph glanced back, and saw the cloud boiling madly, reorganizing for the pursuit. Tentacles of vapor were reaching out, thickening, forming new material to either side of the bird. Soon Fracto would envelop them again, and this time there would be no escape through surprise.

Maybe he could hide. Dolph pushed the stick forward. The bird dropped. It came to the nether cloudbank, then plunged through it. There was some slowing and slewing as the vapors caught at the wings; then they popped out the bottom. The disreputable landscape of Mundania was below.

Could Fracto find them here? Dolph hoped that by the time the evil storm did, it would be too late, for they would have landed at the Heaven Cent.

"You weren't fooling about knowing how to land?" Dolph asked Marrow.

"The air controller explained how," the skeleton agreed. "This isn't supposed to be our bad dream; they want us out of the air as soon as possible."

That made sense, though Dolph wondered why the gourd had put them here if it was a mistake. Maybe it was because he was destined to find the cent, and this was the only way, so the gourd had no choice about it. Just so long as they got there safely.

Fracto did find them, but now they were too low for the

storm to get a proper fix on. Dolph guided the bird lower yet. He spied the edge of the land, and the surprisingly narrow band of water between it and the Isle of View. From the boat it had seemed extensive, but it was really just a channel, as if the islands were the true shoreline. It was amazing how deceptive this perspective could be!

Now Marrow told him which buttons to push to bring the bird safely low and slow. Dolph followed instructions without question. The bird looped about and came down from the south side, touching the beach as it moved north. Sand sprayed up and the bird jerked terribly, but it managed to skew to a stop near the north end of the isle. Weak with relief, Dolph opened the door and jumped out, followed by the skeletons.

And there, ahead, was a small building. In fact it was a tomb. Flowers grew in a little garden on its top, which he knew were of the love-lies-bleeding variety. There was a solid stone door.

Dolph tried to open the door, but it absolutely refused to budge. No one could get in to the maiden or the Heaven Cent. No one without the proper key.

Dolph turned to Grace'l. "Can you open this?"

"I will try," she said.

She began tapping her ribs with her fingers. Though she looked well fleshed, and felt the same, it was illusion; her bone fingers tapped bone ribs when she did it. Her fingers seemed to pass right through the flesh of her breasts. She tapped out an ascending scale of notes, beginning with the long ribs in the center and ending with the shortest ribs down near her waist. Thus her highest notes, oddly, were lowest on her body. Finally she tapped the smallest rib of all, and the grace note sounded.

The tomb shuddered, resonating to the note. Then the door creaked open. The skeleton key of G had worked!

Dolph entered the dark opening. It was eerily cold inside. In a moment his eyes adjusted, and he saw a long box resting on a pedestal. It looked like a coffin. This would be where the sleeping maiden lay.

He heaved on the lid, and it came up. It wasn't as heavy as it looked. He eased it over to the side. The wan light from the doorway slanted in, highlighting the figure inside.

It was a girl, a child no older than Dolph. She was garbed in a simple print frock, and her light brown hair was braided on either side, falling over her shoulders. She was cute, with a few freckles, but also very pale.

"We must help her up," Dolph said. "She knows where the Heaven Cent is."

He reached down to take hold of her hands—but his own hands passed right through her body without resistance. Dolph stared, stirring her nonexistent flesh with one hand. "She's a ghost!"

"Or maybe you are," Marrow said. "Remember, you are in the gourd; your body was left behind."

"Oh, yes. But how can I get her up?"

"I think sleeping maidens are traditionally awakened by kissing. If you wake her, she should be able to get up by herself."

Dolph remembered. "Okay, I'll kiss her. I've learned how."

He leaned down carefully, and touched his lips to those of the sleeping maiden. He felt nothing, but he could see that he was in the right place. He moved his lips in the kissing syndrome.

The girl's eyes popped open. "Pi!" she exclaimed. "Xip bsf zpv?"

"Oh, no! She's speaking Mundane!" Dolph cried.

"Well, she is in Mundania," Marrow said.

The girl saw the skeleton. She screamed and scrambled out of the coffin. "Ifmq! Ju't b monster!" she cried as she hid behind the lid.

"That's no monster!" Dolph retorted. "That's Marrow!"

She peeked out at him. "You're talking sense now. You kissed me awake. Who are you?"

"I am Prince Dolph. Who are you? Do you have the Heaven Cent?"

"I am Electra. I love you. Will you marry me?"

Dolph's jaw dropped. "What?"

"I am doomed to love the Prince who wakes me, and to perish if he does not marry me. So will you?"

"But I am already betrothed!" He had known that this complication could occur; he just didn't want to accept it.

Her face crumpled. "Oh, I should have known! It's that curse! I'll die!"

Dolph was nonplussed. "You'll die if I don't marry you?"

"I'll bleed to death! I've slept a thousand years, and lost a lot of vitality, and the only way I can live is to marry the Prince who kisses me awake. That's the way it is. But the curse—"

"Do you have the Heaven Cent?" Marrow asked.

"Well, yes, but it's no good now, because it's expended. I'll have to make another. That will take about three years."

"But how can you make it if you die?" Dolph asked.

"Well, I can't, of course. Oh, if only that curse hadn't—"

"Then I'll marry you," Dolph said. "Uh, in a few years, when I'm old enough. If you'll make the Heaven Cent."

"You will? Oh, marvelous!" Electra left the shelter of the coffin lid, approached him, flung her arms around him and kissed him. This time her lips were tangible and firm. "Of course I'll make the Heaven Cent for you!" Then she pulled back. "But didn't you say you were already betrothed?"

"Well, yes. But—"

A shape loomed at the doorway to the tomb. "So!" it bellowed. "The exiled one has returned! Now pay the penalty!"

Grace'l screamed in terror.

"The Night Stallion!" Marrow cried. "He heard the grace note!"

The huge form of the stallion blocked the doorway. "You others may go. Take hold of the boy's hands, and I will send you out. But this female skeleton must remain for her trial. No doubt you will never see her again."

"We can't do that!" Dolph protested. "She made my mission possible! She opened the crypt!"

"No, go, go!" Grace'l cried. "I am lost, but you are not! Go, before you anger the stallion further!"

"I will share your fate!" Marrow said, stepping toward her.

"No! He will destroy you! None of us of the gourd can oppose him! Do not make it worse than it is!"

Marrow hesitated, obviously torn between loyalty and logic. He was no coward, as his battle with the goblins had shown, but he was also no fool. He knew he could not help, and that he had other responsibilities.

The stallion lowered his glowing gaze to fix directly on Grace'l. The flesh-illusion puffed away, revealing her bare bones. No secrets from this creature, the master of dreams! "Now, nonconformist, we shall try your mettle thoroughly."

Dolph leaped between them. "No!" he cried, facing the dread stallion. "I am not of your realm, I am a prince, and I forbid this thing! Grace'l is a good person! She should be rewarded, not punished!"

The stallion's eye fixed on Dolph. "Prince, I know your lineage. My way governs here. If you take this creature's part, you will be judged as she is."

"Then judge me!" Dolph cried. "Let the others go! I will help her as she helped me!"

"No, Dolph!" Grace'l protested. "You do not know this creature's power! I should never have come here!"

"You came to help me, and I shall help you," Dolph said firmly, not budging, though fear constricted his throat. He was a prince, and he knew the liabilities as well as the privileges of the office. This quest had shown him more of both than he had expected, but he had no choice but to honor the role he had been born to. "Stallion, try us both, or let us both go!"

"As you wish," the stallion said. His eyes blinked. Marrow and Electra disappeared. "The trial begins."

16

ELECTRA

An aged man knocked at the door of the hut. "I am looking for Electra," he said.

Electra's mother was taken aback. "My daughter is eight years old. What could you want with her?"

"She has magic. The Sorceress Tapis wishes to trade for her."

"The Sorceress!" The woman tried to shut the door in the man's face, but his toe blocked it.

"It is best to listen to what the Sorceress offers," the man said.

The woman sighed, realizing he was right. Magicians and Sorceresses were seldom good news, but they were worse when affronted. She opened the door again and let the man in.

Electra looked at him, awed at the notion of a visit from an emissary of a Sorceress. He was unimpressive: stooped, grizzled, and his beard reached almost to the floor. He carried a package under one arm. He seemed harmless.

"I am Electra," she said boldly. She had learned to be

bold, because she could only shock a person once in a day, and boldness was a better foil. Usually the mere threat of the shock was enough to stop trouble. "What magic is this?"

"Your talent, untrained, is crude," the old man said. "But properly trained, it can become far subtler and greater. The Sorceress wishes to train you, so that you will make a thing she needs. She will treat you well."

"I don't want my child to be the victim of the Sorceress!" Electra's mother protested.

"You don't want her too much with her father, either," the man snapped back.

Electra's mother fell back, dismayed. How could this stranger have learned that Electra got along with her father better than her mother did? There was rivalry and jealousy in the family, and it was getting worse though none of them wished it; but none of them had spoken of this to outsiders. The truth was that both mother and daughter secretly wished she could be rid of the other, to live with Electra's father alone.

But Electra was also interested in adventure. She dreamed of going to far places and seeing strange things and meeting unusual people. The truth was that it was very dull, here at West Stockade; about the only excitement was some distance distant, at the Gap Chasm. No one dared go down into it because of the dragon, and there was little of interest outside it. "What is the Sorceress offering?" she asked, her defensive boldness taking on a tint of interest.

The old man opened his package. "This," he said, unrolling a cloth picture.

Electra and her mother stared. It was a tapestry, with an ordinary picture woven into it, but the detail was amazingly intricate, so that it looked completely realistic. It showed a neat cottage on a beach, with trees behind bearing fruits, nuts, pies, shoes, pillows and other necessities. Pretty flowers fringed it, and a sea breeze played with the leaves. Electra fell in love with it immediately; she was very quick with such emotions.

"A picture," her mother said, unimpressed.

"For you, the picture," the man said. "For the girl, the cottage, to live in while she works with the Sorceress."

Electra's heart leaped. "That very cottage?" she asked, thrilled. "For me?"

"What's so great about a picture?" Electra's mother asked.

"It is one of the Sorceress' tapestries," the man said. "It will show a new scene every day of the week, and then repeat. You may step through to that scene, and back, if you do it the same day. You may have the use of this tapestry as long as your daughter works with the Sorceress."

"I don't believe it!" the woman said, beginning to believe.

"And you, Electra," the man said. "A companion tapestry will be with you. You may use it to return home at any time, or to visit other parts of Xanth. The Sorceress is not a harsh mistress. She will treat you very well, and you will like her. When you complete your tour with her, you will have greatly enhanced use of your talent. If you find yourself unsatisfied, you have only to use the tapestry to return to your home; the Sorceress will not try to hold you."

"This sounds like a trap!" Electra's mother snorted.

Electra had been in doubt, but this abolished it. She had never thought much of her mother's judgments, except in men. "I'll go!" she said.

Her mother opened her mouth to protest, but paused. After all, if this was a valid offer, it was a good one. If it was a trap, it was Electra taking the risk. Either way, the girl would be gone, and no fault would accrue to her mother. "If you insist," she finally said. "But I advise against it."

Electra realized that her mother was not entirely opaque. Her negative advice both protected her from blame if things went bad, and encouraged Electra to do it. Nevertheless, she was smitten by the prospect, and eager to go. "I'm ready!" she declared.

"This way," the old man said. "I shall step through, and you can follow me." He put the tapestry against a wall, where it remained, adhering by magic. Then he hefted up one foot and poked it into the picture. The foot disappeared, followed by his leg. He ducked his head, hunched his shoulders, pulled his arms in, and swung his body through the tapestry. Now only his trailing leg remained in the hut; the rest of him was in the picture. Then he heaved that leg up and through, and stood in the scene. He turned and gestured to Electra.

Electra considered. Then she ran toward the picture, leaped up, and made a ball of herself that fit neatly within the frame. She hurtled through, straightened out her body, and made a jolting but apt landing on the beach. She had done it!

She turned and looked back. There was the picture, on the trunk of a tree. Only now it showed the interior of her hut, with her mother standing there amazed. Sure enough, the tapestry was a window between the two places.

"The Sorceress is awaiting you," the old man said. "This way, please."

Electra waved to her mother, then followed him to a larger house among the trees. This was neatly painted below, and neatly thatched above, and breadfruit and honey-bun trees grew beside it, as well as—

"Are those *chocolate* milkweeds?" she asked, her mouth watering.

"The Sorceress thought you might like them," the old man said.

Now Electra *knew* she was going to like the Sorceress!

The old man knocked on the door. "Come in, and welcome!" a cheery old voice called.

He opened the door, and they stepped in. Inside was a large and bright room, with a single huge tapestry across one wall. Electra glanced at it, glanced away—and looked back. The tapestry had a number of pictures on it, in the fashion of a mural, and each one was moving. This was another magic picture!

"Do you like my handiwork, child?" the voice inquired from the side.

Electra looked toward the voice. There was an ancient little woman, with wrinkled skin and wild white hair. "Oh, yes, Sorceress!" she exclaimed.

"Call me Tapis, for we shall be friends," the Sorceress said. "Come sit with me, and we shall talk." She gestured to a stool.

Electra went and sat on the stool. "Thank you, Tapis," she said contritely. "Please, could you tell me what you want of me?"

"Why of course, Electra. But first—would you like some refreshment?"

"Let me get it!" Electra said, jumping up.

The Sorceress smiled. "Did you suppose I wanted you for a servant girl?"

"Well, yes, of course. I—"

"Not so, child. You are to be an associate." The Sorceress snapped her fingers.

A young woman appeared. She seemed to be about fourteen, and was coming into a loveliness that even a child could appreciate. Electra felt a tinge of jealousy for the beauty that she knew she could never aspire to achieve, no matter how old she ever got. "You snapped, mistress?"

"Fetch us two pods of chocolate milk, if you please, and one for yourself, Millie."

Millie departed without a word. In a moment she was back with three pods from the milkweeds outside. She gave one to the Sorceress and one to Electra. Then she gave them straws she had plucked from the straw growing nearby, and retreated to have her own.

The Sorceress poked her straw into her pod, and Electra did likewise. They drank their chocolate milk together. It was delicious. Then Millie took away the spent pods, and they talked.

"As you know, I am a Sorceress," Tapis said. "That does not mean that I am either good or evil, merely that I have great power of magic. But as you can see, I am old, and in a few more years my time in Xanth will be done. I have made many magic tapestries in my career, such as the one that brought you here, and I am well satisfied with them. The last and greatest is the Historical Tapestry you see here, which shows both the present and the past episodes of Xanth, as tuned in by those whom it respects. I intend to make a gift of this to the Zombie Master—"

"The Zombie Master!" Electra exclaimed, horrified. The Sorceress smiled again. "Do not judge a person by his talent, dear. Jonathan is a fine and able man, with a unique and potent talent. It is unfortunate that the nature of that talent discourages others, and makes him lonely. Upon occasion I step through a tapestry to have a meal with him, but of course I am not the kind of woman he needs."

"He needs a zombie!" Electra exclaimed.

"No, he needs a living woman who can tolerate the zombies. A woman like Millie, except that she is as yet too young. She has a special effect on men." She shrugged, perhaps ruefully. "At any rate, I shall give him the tapestry, but I fear he will be too generous to accept it. How do you suppose I should go about this?"

"Maybe if it didn't look quite so fancy," Electra said, frowning in concentration. "If he thought it was just a little gift, like a picture puzzle or something, a token—"

"Wonderful!" the Sorceress exclaimed, delighted. "Already you are helping me. I shall have it cut into a jigsaw puzzle, that he must assemble before he realizes its nature. By then it will be too late for him to refuse."

Electra knew that she had not suggested more than the obvious; still she was pleased with the Sorceress' reaction.

"But of course you are wondering how I would like to use your talent," the Sorceress continued. "To do that, I must explain something about myself, dull as that may be."

"You don't seem dull to me, Sor—Tapis," Electra said. "All that magic—"

"Thank you, dear. But I am, after all, an old woman, whose sunset is approaching. It is my desire to conclude my life by accomplishing what is most needful. In this manner I hope to make up for what has been a somewhat indulgent existence. Unfortunately, I do not know where or in what manner my greatest impact can be made. This is where I need your help."

"But I don't know that!" Electra protested. "I'm only a child, and—"

"You are a child with a special talent," the Sorceress said. "You are electrical; this is magic seldom seen outside of Mundania or in thunderstorms."

"Yes, I shock people, when they bother me too much," Electra said. "But then it takes me another day to recharge. I feel sort of drained until I do. So I don't shock people unless I really have to."

"Of course, dear. But you are using your talent wastefully. I shall show you how to make the magic device I need. It is called the Heaven Cent."

"Heavens to what?"

"The Heaven Cent. It is a disk made of copper, with a very special property. It sends the invoker to the situation in which he or she is most needed."

"I don't know how to do that!"

"You do not need to, dear. With your magic, properly modulated, we can fashion the Heaven Cent, and it will then do what it does. I shall use it to take myself to the site of my greatest potential service, and I shall perform that service before I expire. That is my concluding ambition, and the reason I asked you to come here."

"Ooooo," Electra said, impressed.

The following three years were wonderful. Electra had simply to carry the copper cent with her, on a chain at her neck, and to avoid shocking anyone. The cent was in a bag that contained magic ingredients which her magic caused to mix and coat it; the complicated term the Sorceress used was "electroplating." Actually it was "Electra-plating," but she was not about to correct the Sorceress on the pronunciation of her name in this connection. Meanwhile she had a remarkably easy life. Millie the maid and the old man were fine company, and the Sorceress was always pleasant. Electra had all the chocolate milk and raspberry pies she could eat; had she not been a growing girl, she might have gotten fat. She was allowed to use the picture tapestry to visit her home whenever she wished, or any other place in Xanth that the pictures showed on different days.

But mostly she just walked the sands of the nice beach of the Isle of View, so called because the sorceress made views of all kinds here, in her tapestries. The bad monsters had been driven away, so it was safe; Electra could see them in the deeper sea or on the mainland across the bay, but they never came to the isle. She also talked with the Sorceress, who was happy to converse while her old hands tirelessly performed her weaving. She had a special tree whose branches held the warp and woof, and she passed her shuttle back and forth, using enchanted thread, so that the picture slowly formed. It was fascinating.

Then a Princess came to call. She was about twenty years old, and astonishingly beautiful. She was, it developed, fated to bite into an apple, which she carried with her in an ornate little case, and it would put her into a deep sleep for a thousand years. She had also with her a nice, secure coffin, with a plush silken lining and a soft pillow, that would keep her secure while she slept. At the expiration of the alotted time, a handsome young Prince would discover her, and wake her with a kiss. Then she would get up and marry him, and live happily ever after. She looked forward to the prospect, for she had found no suitable prince in this time.

She had come to the Sorceress because she lacked a suitable coverlet. She was concerned that she would be a trifle cool during the long thousand years, so a nice warm coverlet seemed appropriate. It could not, of course, be just any cloth; she was a princess, and had to be covered accordingly. What would the Prince think, if he found her covered by just any old rag? So she required the very best, and that was the kind that only the Sorceress Tapis could make.

As it happened, the Sorceress had completed the last of her regular picture tapestries, and the Heaven Cent was not quite yet ready, so she was happy to fill in with the royal coverlet. The Princess was an interesting person, not because of any great wit, but because she was well versed in the necessary graces, and well endowed with the latest gossip of the kingdom. She knew, for example, that King Roogna was now building a massive castle to be named after him, from which he proposed to rule Xanth with integrity and vigor. But there were rumors of great restlessness among the harpies and goblins, and it was said that war between them could break out at any time. That, the Princess declared, could become very messy. She was anxious to get on her long sleep before all that nastiness erupted. She was a Princess by virtue of the bloodline of the former King, whom Roogna was replacing; since she was female and had only an ordinary talent of making that rare magic flower the amaranth bloom, there was really no suitable place for her in this framework. It was best to make a suitably graceful exit from the scene.

Electra found all this fascinating. She was now eleven years old, though she looked younger because she was small for her age; she knew that before too many more years passed she would erupt into maidenhood, and she wanted to master the maidenly manners. The princess was totally expert in these, and happy to inform Electra about even the most trifling details. Millie the maid was also interested. They formed a small class, flinging their hair about in unison, kicking their feet just so for maximum cuteness, and screaming with just the proper maidenly accent. Millie was especially good at these graces, being now about seventeen and so nicely formed that the Princess was slightly put off. It wasn't good for a Princess to associate with anyone who might distract the male gaze from the Princess herself. Still, Millie was such a nice person that the Princess was inclined to be tolerant. The Sorceress observed all this with a reminiscent smile; she was many decades past her nymphly prime, but she well understood the importance for the young women to drive men mad with inadequately-suppressed desire. It was essential, however, that the maiden seem to be completely unaware of this effect, while remaining just barely out of reach. This could require considerable finesse at times, which was why practice was so important. Innocent perfection never came naturally; it had to be acquired by hard labor.

The Sorceress had almost completed the lovely coverlet, and the Heaven Cent was almost ready for use, when they had another visitor. This was a handsome yet sinister man, compact and middle-aged, with a slightly crooked smile. "Oh, darning needles!" the Sorceress muttered as she spied him approaching. Evidently she recognized him.

Electra wanted to ask what was wrong with the man, but he was already upon them. "A greeting, Sorceress Tapis," he said gravely, evincing nuances of excellent breeding.

"What in tarnation do you want with me, Murphy?" the Sorceress inquired politely, though there was a hint that she was not pleased with this visit.

"Please, please, let us be properly introduced before we proceed to business," the man said expansively. "I see that you have here a bevy of truly lovely maidens."

Princess, maid, and Electra essayed two and a half fetching blushes. Electra's was the half; she had not yet perfected this art. But the Sorceress frowned. "If we must. Murphy, these are the Princess, Millie the maid, and Electra, all having business with me. Girls, this is Magician Murphy, whose talent is making things go wrong."

The Princess paled, Millie screamed in a somewhat unfetching manner, and Electra backed away. Maidenliness was forgotten in the face of this threat. They had all heard of the Evil Magician Murphy, the scourge of order; wherever he went, disasters developed from nothing. No wonder the Sorceress was displeased!

"Ah, I perceive that my reputation precedes me," the Magician said. "Have no concern, gentle ladies; I have no business with you. I have merely come to broach a matter to the Sorceress."

"I'm not interested!" the Sorceress snapped, her smile for once forgotten.

"Ah, but you should be. Shall we talk privately?"

"No." Electra had never heard the Sorceress so curt.

"Then I shall broach it now," the Magician said, just as if he had received the most gracious of responses. "I have come to solicit your support, Tapis."

"You shall not have it!"

"Ah, but hear me out, grand lady. You see, I wish to assume the throne of Xanth. However, there is an impediment."

"King Roogna," the Sorceress agreed curtly.

"The same; how perceptive of you. Since there are only four Magician-class persons extant, each one is important in a case like this. It is evident that the Zombie Master will not take sides; he is nonpolitical. King Roogna and I are on opposite sides. That leaves only you, Sorceress Tapis. Your support would significantly enhance my endeavor. How may I obtain it?"

"You can't. Now that is settled, please go far and quickly away."

"I am prepared to be appropriately generous. Would you care to name your price?"

"I have no price. I don't want you as king. Roogna was selected, and unless some grief comes to him, he is the legitimate monarch, and I support him. Certainly I will not act to undermine him."

"Suppose I were to marry you? That would provide you unprecedented status without responsibility."

The Sorceress choked and went into a coughing fit. When she recovered, she wheezed: "Taunt me no more, Murphy. I am an old woman, of your mother's generation, soon to die. I have no interest in being Queen, and less in marrying you. Kindly desist embarrassing these maidens with your presence. The answer is no, no, nine hundred times no, forever no, and if you persist in this insanity I may have to become negative."

Murphy frowned, and that frightened Electra. The man

was too certain of his power; his slightest malice carried horrific implication. "I trust you realize that if you are not for me, I must assume that you are against me," he stated flatly.

"I would really prefer not to be involved with you at all!" the Sorceress said. "Nor to have these gentle maidens corrupted by your presence. But if I must choose sides, then I am against you. Now, I beg of you with understated loathing, will you please go away?"

The Magician sighed with apparently genuine regret. "I shall in that case do so. But I must leave with you the curse of my nature. I had hoped it would not come to this. Are you certain you will not reconsider?"

The Sorceress looked stricken, but her words were firm. "I am certain, Magician," she wheezed.

Without further word, Magician Murphy turned and departed. The three girls breathed sighs of relief.

"The siege has just begun," the Sorceress said. "That man has laid his curse on us, and we shall surely rue it."

"But things go wrong all the time," the Princess protested. "You just have to be careful, and fix them when that isn't enough. We are forewarned." Electra and Millie nodded agreement.

"I see you do not yet understand," the Sorceress said heavily. "Then listen, my young friends, and harken to my warning, for I know whereof I speak. That man is a Magician, and his power is insidious; only another Magician could hope to oppose it, and I am too old and frail. Even in my more vigorous years I was never truly his match; that is one reason I never married. Murphy solicited a tapestry from me, to forward his evil cause, and I refused, and then there came a fluke circumstance that caused my betrothed to desert me for another woman. Then I made for Murphy a tapestry that opened onto an inferno, and sent it to him; had he used it he would have died. Thereafter he left me alone, respecting my power. But in the decades since his power has waxed while mine has waned, and my art can no longer threaten him. This we both of us know.

Now he has chosen to eliminate me, so that I cannot help King Roogna. Surely I am lost, but I shall do what I can to protect the three of you from this disaster."

She looked at Millie the maid. "My dear, you have been a good and loyal assistant, and you have fine qualities of domestic service. I shall write for you a fine recommendation so that you may obtain excellent other employment. I suggest you seek to take service with King Roogna, who is a good man and a fine Magician; he is unmarried, and his new castle will have serious need of care. Go now, this day, so that you may escape the environs of this curse."

"But Tapis—" Millie protested.

"And take with you the tapestry hanging in your room; I always intended for it to be yours. It will help you to depart without hindrance, and to travel hereafter. You have but to reach back into it after you step through it, and pull it through after you. Thereafter you will have to carry it by hand to a new location, so that you can use it again, but you know how to do this. My blessing on you, girl; you are beautiful inside and out, and will surely make some good man deliriously happy, if this misfortune does not touch you. Farewell; time is of the essence, as the curse coalesces."

Millie, dismayed, turned and walked slowly toward the house.

"And you, Princess," the Sorceress said. "I regret giving you an incomplete coverlet, but believe me, it is now necessary. You must undertake your sleep this very hour, if you are to escape; already the evil magic is coalescing. By the time you wake it will be long dissipated, so you will not suffer from it. Let us go to your coffin and be about this business."

"As you wish, Tapis," the Princess agreed, shaken.

They walked slowly toward the house. "And you, Electra," the Sorceress continued, "I regret I cannot dispense with your service this moment; you will have to help me set the lid on the coffin, so as to protect the Princess. Then I will take the Heaven Cent and use it, for it is almost complete, and you may depart forthwith. The tapestry in your cottage is yours; use it and take it with you, and never return to this cursed site."

Electra did not reply; she was too busy crying. How awful to have this wonderful existence so abruptly terminated!

They fetched the incomplete coverlet, and went to the chamber where the Princess' coffin rested. This chamber was of stone, strongly constructed, spelled to be resistant to all manner of calamities, for it had to endure for a thousand years. The coffin itself would sink right out of Xanth and into Mundania after it was sealed, so that no magic could touch it prematurely. The Princess had explained it all: there was a package of precise magic associated with the coffin. It guaranteed that her body would be preserved exactly as it was, so that she would age not a single whit, and no wrinkles would form, and all her dreams would be sweet. Only a young, handsome, unmarried Prince could find and open the coffin, and only his kiss could wake her. This would occur within a thousand years; it had to, or the spell would expire. That was the one nervous aspect: if something happened to the Prince, she would fade away, for the magic could not protect her entirely from the leaching of vitality. But the Prince would come; the spell would see to it. She would wake instantly, all her faculties complete. Then she would marry the Prince and live happily ever after.

"But suppose the Prince doesn't want to marry you?" Electra had inquired from childish curiosity.

"That is unthinkable!" the Princess had exclaimed. "He has to marry me, because that is the nature of the magic. Should he even think about being the smallest bit reluctant (as is known to occur with some men, unfortunately), I will charm him with all the virtues I have so diligently mastered. I shall clap my hands and bounce my torso, and fling my hair about, and he will soon answer to my will, for that is the magic of these things. We shall be married with suitable pomp and ceremony, and then we shall consider summoning the stork, for palaces are fine places for children to play."

"But what if you do all these things, and he still doesn't marry you?" Electra persisted. She, as a child, had few of the assets of the Princess, and fewer of those of Millie the maid. Her hair was barely long enough to fling properly, and was neither the golden hue of Millie's nor the quality dark chocolate of the Princess. She could not bounce in the right way no matter how hard she jumped up and down. Her scream was too piercing, hardly the dulcet little cry of the others. She was afraid that if she tried these arts on a real man, he would laugh. That prospect bothered her, so she sought ways to capture a man that did not depend entirely on physical endowments. This was a foolish quest, she knew, for men had no other interests, but still she hoped. If she could somehow manage to find a man who liked a lively girl, or a smart one, or who needed her talent—well, there was at least a remote chance, wasn't there?

The Princess grew serious. "I must marry him, for if I do not, I will die," she said. "The apple I bite is poison. Its first effect is to put me into a deep sleep, so deep I do not even breathe. But after I wake, that apple remains in me, and it can only be abolished by true love and marriage. So I will love the Prince who wakes me, instantly and completely, and that will suppress the poison, for love is greater than death when it is new and strong. But if he does not love me back, and does not marry me, my heart will break, and it will bleed, and I will slowly weaken and die, and it will be a most distressing tragedy. I mean, what is the point of sleeping a thousand years, if you don't marry a Prince?"

Electra had to agree that this was persuasive. And surely the Prince would love the Princess, for she was very attractive and knew exactly what she wanted.

But as they put the coverlet in the coffin, to the side so the Princess could draw it over her when she entered, there was a shudder. A stiff gust of wind was catching at the house.

Electra hurried out of the chamber and looked out a window. There over the sea was a monstrous whirling cloud whose bottom stretched down in a tightening tube to suck up water. Usually such clouds drank briefly and then drew their tubes back into themselves, their thirst sated, but sometimes they were hungry and came ashore for some sand. This one, by freak luck, was headed right for the house!

She dashed back into the chamber. "A funnel cloud is coming!" she cried.

"Murphy's curse!" the Sorceress said, looking faint. "Anything that can go wrong, will go wrong! It's happening already!"

"We must hurry!" the Princess said. "Let me take out my apple—"

But as she removed the apple from its box, a gust of wind whipped through the chamber, caught up the coverlet, and wrapped it about her head. She screamed and dropped the apple, clawing at the coverlet.

Electra ran to close the stone door, humming the key note that made it work. That cut off the nasty wind, but the roaring of the approach of the funnel cloud still grew louder. She pounced on the rolling apple and picked it up. She hurried over to the Sorceress. "Here it is!" she said, holding out the apple.

"Not to me, child!" the Sorceress protested. "To the Princess. Give me the Heaven Cent!"

"Oh." Embarrassed about her miscue, which was not at all her normal type of confusion, Electra used her free hand to lift the cent from her breast. She tried to draw the chain over her head, but it snagged on her ears.

"Be careful, child, lest you invoke it!" the Sorceress said, trying to help her.

"Oh, I wouldn't invoke the Heaven Cent!" Electra protested.

The cent flared, releasing its accumulated energy in a single flash as its plating disappeared. With shock, Electra realized that by an incredible blunder she had done just that. The cent was made to respond to the words "I invoke the Heaven Cent" when held in the hand; it recognized no other words, such as "wouldn't." She knew this, but in her confusion of the moment she had slipped. Twice in as many instants she had blundered. She, who tried so hard to do things right!

She backed away, horrified. The backs of her knees struck the low coffin, and she tumbled into it. Her flailing arm folded in at the elbow, and the apple her hand held struck her open mouth. Her jaws closed involuntarily, and her teeth bit out a piece. She tried to scream, but already the paralysis gripped her. Frightened, horrified, and immensely chagrined, she sank into the sleep that had been intended for the Princess, sent by the magic of the Heaven Cent that had been intended for the Sorceress.

Yet even then she knew that it had not really been her fault. The terrible magic of Magician Murphy's curse had made it happen. Anything that could go wrong, had gone wrong, and all three of them, and perhaps Millie too, had had their hopes and plans destroyed by this single awful surge of bad luck. An inadequate child was being sent a thousand years into the future, and she would bleed and die if she did not marry the Prince who woke her.

It seemed but an instant before she felt the kiss. She knew immediately that it was the Prince. She was a child, and ridden with guilt for the thing she had inadvertently done, but she could not help herself. The magic of the completion of the spell suffused her, and she leaped into love with her rescuer.

Then she opened her eyes and saw him. He was a boy, a child even younger than herself! "Oh! Who are you?" she exclaimed.

The boy cried something incomprehensible. Then someone said something indecipherable behind him. She looked, and saw a human skeleton.

She screamed and scrambled out of the coffin. "Help! It's a monster!" she cried as she hid behind the coffin lid.

"That's no monster!" the boy retorted. "That's Marrow!"

She peeked out, realizing that if the boy was not frightened, she shouldn't be either. "You're talking sense now," she said. "You kissed me awake. Who are you?"

"I am Prince Dolph," he replied. "Who are you?"

He continued to speak, but she was overcome by the realization that the magic had indeed worked. A true Prince had kissed her awake. "I am Electra," she babbled. "I love you. Will you marry me?" For whatever evil curse had brought her here, she had to marry him, or die.

"But I am already betrothed!" he protested.

Then she knew she was doomed. The curse still functioned, even after all this time.

The skeleton asked her about the Heaven Cent, and she tried to explain, though stunned by her doom. Not one of the four of them had escaped any part of Murphy's curse! Not the Sorceress, or the Princess, or Electra, or—well, maybe Millie had gotten away in time, but she wasn't even sure of that. What a terror that man was!

"Then I'll marry you," the Prince said. "In a few years, when I'm old enough. If you'll make the Heaven Cent."

Then she realized that the other part of the magic was functioning too: the Heaven Cent had sent her here, where she was most needed. She wouldn't die after all! She flung her arms around the Prince, who was exactly her own size.

A shape loomed at the entrance. There was a scream of terror, and Electra realized that it was not her own; there was a fourth person in the tomb, a lovely nude woman. What was she doing here?

Electra's consciousness was spinning from the suddenness of the developments, though a thousand years (or most of it) had passed in the middle of them. But she gathered that the woman was not supposed to be here, and the huge horse-shape was going to destroy her. Suddenly the woman's flesh puffed away, leaving only a standing skeleton. But Prince Dolph jumped between the stallion and the skeleton. "I forbid this thing!" he cried. "Grace'l is a good person! I will help her!"

Now wasn't that just like a Prince! He was trying to save

another damsel, even though that damsel had already been pretty garishly killed, so that only her bones remained.

"As you wish," the stallion said. Then Electra found herself standing on the beach outside the tomb, with the male skeleton beside her. Only the tomb was gone; indeed, the whole house was gone. There was nothing but sand, and a few trees, here on the shore of what was evidently the mainland near the Isle of View. More magic!

She turned—and there behind her was the Prince, seated on the sand, staring into a gaze-gourd. Beside him was a serpent with the head of a woman, watching him. This grew stranger yet!

"Princess Nada, this is Princess Electra," the skeleton said.

"Oh, I'm no princess!" Electra protested. "I'm just—" Suddenly it all became too complicated, and she started crying.

The serpent-woman changed to human form and comforted her. Electra sobbed out as much of her story as she could manage, explaining about the curse and the apple and the cent and how they had all interacted to bring her here. "So I love Prince Dolph, and must marry him," she concluded.

"But you don't even know him!" Marrow the skeleton protested.

"What has that got to do with it? I know it was supposed to be the Princess, but the magic took me, and that's the way it is. I have no choice in the matter."

Then the serpent woman, Nada Naga, explained how Prince Dolph and two animated skeletons and she herself had come here. That was similarly amazing.

"Then you're his betrothed!" Electra exclaimed. "How much you must love him!"

"No, I don't love him at all," Nada said sadly. "It is a political betrothal."

"Then you don't want to marry him?"

"I do want to marry him," Nada explained. "I just don't love him."

"But I—I do love him! And I have to marry him, or I'll die! How can you marry him, when you are of another species and you don't even love him?"

"Because I am a Princess, and I must do what is best for my folk. They will suffer grievously unless I marry the Prince and gain the help of his folk against the goblins."

"How can he marry two of us?"

Nada nodded. "I think we have a problem, Electra. But that may be academic, if Prince Dolph doesn't prevail against the Night Stallion."

Electra looked at the boy, who looked just like the one who had kissed her awake. "What happens if he doesn't?"

Marrow replied to that. "His body will remain, but his mind will be gone. His body will be an empty shell. I would have stopped him from this folly, but—"

"Maybe our problem can wait," Electra said. "First he has to win; then he can decide between us." She liked Princess Nada, but it seemed to her that her own need was greater.

They settled down to wait, eating some pumpkinseed pie together, and talked of many things.

17
TRIAL

The coffin was gone. The chamber had changed. Dolph found himself standing beside Grace'l in a room that was empty and featureless except for two doors. The door on the left was white, with the word YES printed in blue on it. The door on the right was black, with the word NO printed on it in red. Between the two was printed a question: WOULD YOU DO SOMETHING UNPLEAS-ANT TO ACCOMPLISH SOMETHING GOOD?

Dolph glanced at Grace'l, who retained her natural bone form. "Where is the Night Stallion? I thought he was going to put us on trial."

"He has his ways," she said. "He toys with folk before destroying them. He locks them in the worst of dreams and gives them the illusion they can save themselves. We are doomed no matter what we do."

"I don't know. My father Dor always said the Night Stallion was a fair-minded creature."

"But ruthless. I have done wrong, and he will make me suffer and destroy myself—and you too, now that you have taken my part. You should not have done that."

"I don't think you did wrong," Dolph said more bravely than he felt. "Nada told me about Tristan Troll and how you messed up his dream. I know the Night Stallion has a different idea, but I think Tristan was right to let that little girl go, and you were right to spoil the bad dream."

"But you didn't have to put yourself in peril because of that!" she protested. "Most people are very free in judging right and wrong, but they aren't so foolish as to get into trouble about it."

"Well, I'm just a child and I guess I don't know any better. You helped me get the Heaven Cent, and I had to help you get out of this."

"But you don't have the Heaven Cent!"

"But Electra said she would make it for me."

"Only if you married her—and you are already betrothed."

Dolph smiled ruefully. "I guess I'm not very smart with snap decisions."

Their dialogue lapsed. Nothing had happened; they remained alone in the little room. Apparently the stallion wasn't going to come after them.

Dolph turned around. There was a third door behind them, green and unmarked. He tried the knob, but the door would not open. They could not go back the way they had come, if that was the way they had come. It was hard to tell, in the gourd.

He reread the print on the wall. *Would* he do something unpleasant, to accomplish something good? It seemed he had been doing that all along, on his Quest to get the Heaven Cent! He had just sort of gotten in trouble wherever he went, and had to struggle out of it. But at least now he had the cent, almost!

"Might as well try a door," he said. He went to the YES door and turned the handle.

The door opened readily, to a room just like the first. "Stay with me, Grace'l," he said, grasping her hand as he stepped through. That hand now felt exactly like bare bones; the Night Stallion had stripped away every aspect of the illusion. "They might try to separate us, and then I don't know how I could help you." Actually, he had no idea anyway, but it did not seem wise to advertise that at the moment.

The far wall had two doors, white and black, marked with the blue YES and red NO as before. But there was no question between them.

The door behind closed after they entered. Then a new question appeared on the opposite wall: WOULD YOU EAT A LIVE BASILISK TO SAVE A HUMAN LIFE?

Dolph shook his head in dismay. "I don't know if I *could* eat a live basilisk! I mean, they can kill with a glance, and their breath is poisonous."

"I can't eat at all," Grace'l said.

"But I couldn't just let someone die, if I could save that person," Dolph concluded. "So I guess I'd try to eat the basilisk. Ugh!"

He opened the YES door. They stepped together into the next chamber.

The door closed behind them, and the next question showed: WOULD YOU BETRAY YOUR KIND TO SAVE A HUMAN CHILD?

They stared at it for a time without speaking. There was something about this variant of the question that seemed familiar, but Dolph couldn't quite place it.

Then Grace'l spoke. "That's what Tristan Troll did! He betrayed the trolls, to let the little girl live! That was why he was being punished by the bad dream!"

That made it easier to relate to. "I think Tristan Troll was right. He saved the human family a lot of grief."

"But he's a troll! They aren't supposed to do decent things!"

Dolph found the thinking hard, but he managed to forge through it. "Maybe Tristan was wrong, because of his culture, but I'm not a troll. It wouldn't be wrong for me. So I guess I would do it."

"I messed up Tristan's dream, so I guess I would do it too."

Dolph opened the YES door, and they stepped through.

The next room's wall said: WOULD YOU WIPE OUT A HUMAN VILLAGE TO SAVE A TROLL CHILD?

They stopped again, considering the implications. "We said we'd betray our kind, to save a human child," Grace'l said uncomfortably. "Isn't this pretty much the same?"

"But human beings are better than trolls!" Dolph protested. "To destroy a whole village, just to—" He faltered, recognizing the harsh parallel. Did he want to do what was right for just human beings, or for everything?

Still, even if humans were equal to trolls (ugh!), it would be wrong to wipe out a whole village just for one. He could not answer yes to this cruel question.

"Tristan Troll put his whole village in danger, because it had no other food," Grace'l said. "I thought he was right, but now I'm not sure."

"I guess the Night Stallion thought you were wrong," Dolph said. "But that little girl—"

"That little girl," she agreed. "I think of a skeletal child, and I just can't let that living one be killed or eaten."

"Well, I guess these are only questions," he said. "We're answering the best we can. We have to answer this one no."

She nodded, but her bone face looked pale, and her eyes hollower than usual.

He opened the NO door. The next room's question was: WOULD YOU WIPE OUT A TROLL VILLAGE TO SAVE A HUMAN CHILD?

"We already answered that," Grace'l said faintly.

"I guess we did," Dolph agreed, feeling miserable. He opened the NO door.

The next was as cruel: WOULD YOU KILL A HUMAN CHILD TO SAVE A TROLL VILLAGE?

Dolph felt the tears starting. He knew that this was just the other side of the last question, but it was even more painful. If the troll village needed to kill the child to survive, what was right? His certainty had been shaken. But he just couldn't say yes.

He opened the NO door. WOULD YOU KILL A TROLL CHILD TO SAVE A HUMAN VILLAGE?

Grace'l put her face in her bone hands. "I just can't do any of this!"

"I hate this!" Dolph confessed. "These are terrible questions! Why can't we have any good ones?"

"The Night Stallion never makes things easy on those who oppose him," Grace'l said. "This will just get worse and worse, until we beg him for mercy, and then we won't get it."

"Then I won't ask for it," Dolph said, fending off his own tears. "I'll just say no, until we get a better question." He opened the NO door.

WOULD YOU KISS A HARPY TO SAVE ALL XANTH?

Dolph gaped. Here was a question he could agree to! He hated harpies, but still—

He paused on the way to the YES door. Did the principle differ from that of the other rooms? It wasn't as bad to kiss a harpy as to kill a child, but it was a thing he would not ordinarily do. If he said yes, he could be back in the worse choices, just as he had been when he answered yes to the first question about doing something unpleasant to accomplish something good. That led only to trouble!

"I remember my grandfather Trent saying something about ends and means," he said, thinking hard. "He said— he said the ends did not—did not justify the means. I never knew what he meant. But now—"

"Is it right to do something wrong, to accomplish something good?" Grace'l asked, phrasing it more neatly than he had been able to. "I always thought it was, but now I think maybe it isn't. I messed up that bad dream—"

"No!" Dolph cried. "The Night Stallion is making you think his way, to think he's right to punish you, and I know that can't be right, because what you did was nice. I'm not going to say it's bad to be nice!"

"But maybe—"

"No! I won't do this any more! These are bad doors!"

Dolph turned and wrenched at the handle of the door behind him, the green one without a YES or NO. To his surprise, it opened. "Come on!" he said, grasping Grace'l's bone fingers. "We're getting out of here!"

They returned to the prior room, and Dolph crossed to the green door. It opened. He hauled the skeleton through.

Before long they were back in the first chamber. Dolph tried its green door, the one that had been stuck before—and it remained stuck.

His flurry of hope collapsed. They could not after all escape this way.

But he refused to admit defeat. "These doors are bad!" he proclaimed. "They all ask—ask the wrong questions. They all make us do something bad for something good, and that's wrong. The—the end does not justify the means!"

He tried the green door again, wrenching at the handle, expecting failure—and this time it opened without resistance. "Come on!" he cried, delighted by this surprise. He took Grace'l hand again and hauled her through.

Before them was a vast chamber, filled with creatures. Dolph blinked, unable to assimilate it all at a glance.

"The court is now in session," a voice boomed. It was the Night Stallion, speaking from a lofty desk at one end of the chamber. He wore a black cloak that covered all of his body below the head, and looked impressively sinister. "The participants will take their places."

He glanced to the side. "Defendant," the Night Stallion said.

Grace'l stepped forward. "Grace'l Ossian," she said faintly. She took her seat at the separate table the stallion indicated for her.

"Counsel for the defense."

No one stepped forward. The stallion's eye fell on Dolph, and suddenly Dolph realized that this was *his* job. He stepped up. "Prince Dolph," he said as boldly as he could manage, and sat at Grace'l's table.

"Members of the jury: introduce yourselves and stand for challenges."

A line of creatures came from the central throng. The first was a dragon. "Draco Dragon of Mt. Etamin," he growled clearly, then shuffled onward to find a place in the jury box. This was an enclosed platform with a dozen places, suspended by four stout cables at the corners so that it hung from the ceiling. It was only a human handspan above the floor, and swung gently as the dragon's weight came on it.

Dolph was amazed. How could Draco be here, and how could he speak the human language? Then he realized that this was the gourd, the realm of dreams; anything could happen here. Draco was probably here in dream form, just as Dolph himself was. In dreams folk could speak and understand whatever the dream said they could; it didn't have to make sense.

"Counsel for the prosecution has approved all the members of the jury," the judge said. "Counsel for the defense may challenge now. Half are from Xanth, and half from the realm of dreams; that ratio will be maintained regardless of challenges."

Oh. Dolph wondered who was handling the prosecution. But right now he had to be sure the jury was fair. He knew just enough about the process of justice to know how important this was. So he had to question the prospective jurors and object if any were too bad.

He was surprised that Draco was a juror, but that could be all right. He didn't worry much about logic, just about making sure of the dragon's neutrality. "Draco, you remember how Marrow Bones saved your gems at great risk to himself, because he was a decent person. You must understand how important it is to be that way." The dragon nodded, interested; he certainly valued his gems! "Well, Grace'l is Marrow's friend, and she is a lot like him. She did a thing at great risk to herself, because she is a decent person. She saved Tristan Troll from being tormented because of the decent thing *he* did, and then she came back to the gourd to help me complete my Quest, and she got caught, because of me. Do you think a person who helps me like that should be punished?"

Draco nodded no. One down. "No challenge."

The next creature swam up. It was a small silvery fish, almost round in outline. "Perrin Piranha," he announced, and swam to the next place in the jury box.

Dolph remembered that fish! He was the leader of the water guardians near Draco's nest! He might be satisfactory as a guardian, and he had helped Marrow fight the goblins, but how could he serve on a jury here?

Then he realized that the little fish would know nothing of Grace'l or her crime. Therefore he, like Draco Dragon, was an objective party. He would learn about Grace'l in the course of this trial. But how would a bloodthirsty fish react to the messing up of a bad dream? Dolph was worried. This was, after all, a hanging jury; the jury box turned slowly, slowly in the air as the weight in it shifted.

A little bird was next in line. No, it was a bat. "Brick Bat, and what's it to you?" he snapped as Dolph glanced at him, and sailed smoothly to the third place in the box.

Worse yet! Brick Bat might have been a good cave guardian for the dragon's nest, but he was a mean creature who could decide against a nice person like Grace'l just for spite. Who had selected this jury? Unfortunately, he knew: the Night Stallion, who was also the judge. This boded ill indeed!

"Perrin Piranha and Brick Bat, Marrow Bones helped you to save the gems from the goblins. Grace'l Ossian would have done the same. Can you blame her for being that way?" The little fish and the little bat looked thoughtful; they might not be convinced, but they were doubtful. That was good enough; their savage little minds were not closed. "No challenge."

Next came a surly-looking goblin. "Itchlips Goblin," he gritted, and stomped to the box. Dolph did not know this one, but he knew that *any* goblin was bad news, for anything. If this had been one of the goblin horde who had raided the dragon's nest and taken Marrow apart—and, considering the other jurors from that engagement, this seemed likely—he would have a grudge against all skeletons, especially any who were close to Marrow.

"Itchlips, if the trolls raided your stronghold and abducted someone dear to you, wouldn't you want it to be someone like Tristan?" The goblin looked startled; he hadn't thought of it quite that way. "And if Grace'l is punished for being nice to Tristan Troll, then no one else will dare to do what he did. So your loved one—" Dolph made a throat-slicing motion. The goblin flinched; he was having a second thought. "No challenge."

A handsome young man with flat duck feet came up. "Fulsome Fee," he said, and took the next seat in the box. Dolph was chagrined again. That was the leader of the folk who had tried to force the members of his party to interbreed with them, to revivify their waning stock. Nada had foiled them, but surely Fulsome carried a grudge against Dolph and his friends, Grace'l included. What could be worse than this?

A buxom woman garbed in green leaves, whose reddish brown hair fell to her feet walked up, her body swaying in a manner that caused even the nonhuman folk to watch with interest. Dolph had seen that walk before! In fact, this was—

"Vida Vila," she said, and undulated on to the hanging jury box, her hair waving along behind her. She was the nature nymph whose tree Marrow had threatened to chop, and who had then wanted to marry Dolph, because he was a prince. She had turned out to be all right, in the end, and though Dolph was not yet versed in the fine points of adult female anatomy, he was sure that hers could serve as a model for study. But he had gone on to become betrothed to not one but two other girls, and if Vida learned about that, she might turn into a bear and attack him. He was distinctly nervous about having her on this jury.

Still, he remembered how protective she was toward children. That could count in his favor.

"Fulsome Fee and Vida Vila, I hardly need to talk to you about the importance of preserving children," Dolph continued. "Grace'l is being punished because she cherishes children; you know that. I know you can't support that." He saw that he was correct.

The box was now half full, with no really good jurors for his purpose. But they weren't really bad, either. What would the rest be like—the ones from the gourd?

The next juror stepped up: a woman who looked like nothing at all. "Onoma Topoeia," she said, introducing herself, and as she spoke she looked exactly the way she sounded, which was rather strange.

Ono! Dolph thought. *She's going to change her mind every time anyone speaks!*

"Onoma, doesn't it seem odd to you that a person should be punished for doing something decent?"

"Nothing seems odd to me," she said, looking oddly like nothing. "Everything looks just the way it sounds."

Dolph found it impossible to relate to her. He didn't know where she stood. But if he barred her from this jury, she might be replaced by something worse. He decided to gamble that she would not be too bad.

Next came a pig, towing a block of ivory almost as high as himself. It had been partially carved, and was evidently to be a statue of a female pig. "Pyg Malion," he said, and trotted on to the box. Vida and Onoma had to help him haul up his ivory; evidently he planned to work on it during dull periods of the trial. Was that good or bad for Grace'l, Dolph wondered, and dreaded the answer.

"What is it that you are sculpting?"

"Galatea, the loveliest of pigs. I love her."

"But she's just a statue!" Dolph protested. "An ivory statue, and not even finished yet."

"Neither is your case," Pyg retorted.

He had a point. Dolph decided not to challenge.

The following creature looked so completely stupid that

Dolph wondered how he had ever qualified for jury duty. "Ignore Amus," he said dully, and blundered on to the box. Dolph liked him no better.

"Do you think a woman should be punished for—"

"I don't know nothing about anything," Amus said.

"Then how can you vote on it?"

"I'll just vote the way everybody else does. That's what I always do."

Well, if the majority voted Dolph's way, this creature would be all right. Better to let him be.

But worse was coming. This was a big, heavy-bodied animal with broad horns who looked twice as stupid as the prior juror. "Oxy Moron," he lowed with light heaviness.

"How's that?" Dolph asked.

"Oxy Moron. I'm stupidly clever. I like routine contrasts and bright darkness."

"Uh, about the defendant—"

"She's a nice meanie."

"But—"

"And you're a smart fool."

Yet again Dolph pondered, and yet again decided to leave well enough alone. This creature just might be making sense.

Dolph could not even attempt to categorize the last two jurors. They seemed to have no fixed forms.

"I am Synec Doche," the first said. "You may address me by any of my parts, or any part by the whole, small-foot."

Dolph's head was spinning. He couldn't understand any of these folk! He went to the last.

"I am Meto Nymy," the man said. "You may describe me by any of my attributes, loser."

Baffled, Dolph retreated. How would these strange folk vote? He could not tell. "No challenge," he said.

The hanging jury was complete: twelve odd creatures. How they would decide Dolph could not say, but it did not look excruciatingly good.

"Counsel for the prosecution," the stallion said.

A new figure emerged from the throng. Seeing her, Dolph almost fainted. "Princess Ivy," she said clearly.

His sister! His snooty fourteen-year-old-sister! Of all the times and places for her to show up, this was the very ultimate worst! How bad could his luck get?

Bad luck? No, he realized. This was the gourd, where the Night Stallion ruled. This was the realm of dreams, and the stallion was the master of bad dreams. Grace'l was on trial for the way she had messed up a bad dream, so now she was suffering her own bad dream, and Dolph was in it with her. Luck played no part in this; the Night Stallion was crafting the slowly closing pincers of the worst of dreams. A dream from which neither the defendant nor her counsel could wake. A dream whose end would be—what?

Dolph had been nervous before, and afraid. Now he was terrified. Grace'l had tried to warn him of the stallion's power; now he appreciated the nature of that power. The stallion had only played a game with him, giving him irrelevant doors to agonize over, while setting up this horrendous trial. And was the jury also irrelevant because the decision had already been made? No, he could not accept that! But how was he to change the outcome and save Grace'l from destruction? For he knew this was what conviction would mean. He was alive; he would wake when the dream was done. Grace'l would not.

His terror remained, but his thinking caused it gradually to change from the urge to cower to the urge to fight. There was no way that he, a mere child, could hope to fight the power of the Night Stallion. Not here, not in the stallion's bailiwick. Not by the stallion's rules. Yet he had to try. This was not bravery on his part, but desperation. Grace'l was all bones, but she was a good person, and he had to help her somehow.

"The defendant is charged with spoiling a duly constituted dream," the judge Night Stallion said, "and with violating her exile. How does she plead?"

"Oh, I did it," Grace'l said unhappily. "I—"

Dolph jumped up. "She doesn't mean that!" he exclaimed. "She pleads Not Guilty!"

"But I did—" Grace'l said. "I wouldn't try to deceive—"

"Not Guilty, by reason of—" Dolph paused, his inspiration failing. Of course she was guilty; not only was this a rigged trial, she was bound to lose even if it was fair. But that was like the doors with the impossible questions: either answer was just more trouble. He had to get her out of that kind of choice, between guilt and guilt. He had to find a way to make it all right.

The entire court was frozen, awaiting his plea. The jury was watching him, and so were all the creatures of the audience, and the judge, and his sister. All waiting for him to say something really stupid. So that Grace'l would wish she had come here without him.

"By reason of—" Still he was stalled. What could he say to make it better, when none of these creatures were on his side or Grace'l's? That the ends did not justify the means? They would turn that right around, and prove that the end of sparing a decent troll did not justify the means of messing up a well-prepared dream. That the end of finding the Heaven Cent did not justify the means of violating Grace'l's exile? That was the cruelest part of it: by their definitions Grace'l was wrong on both counts, and he could not counter those definitions. Yet still he knew there was something wrong, and that she should not be punished for her decency. How could he make that clear?

"That it just wasn't like that," he concluded miserably.

The judge frowned. "The defendant pleads Not Guilty by reason of that it just wasn't like that," he repeated tonelessly.

There was a snicker from the audience, echoed in the jury box. Ivy sniffed disdainfully. He had blown it, as she had known he would.

"Prosecution?" the judge inquired.

"We intend to prove that it was too like that," Ivy said promptly. "That foolish skeleton messed up a perfectly good dream, and then came back to gloat about it. Off with her head!"

The audience applauded, and several members of the jury nodded. There was a statement with guts!

"Make your case," the judge said.

"The prosecution calls as its first witness Truculent Troll," Ivy said, reeking with confidence.

A tall, ugly, mean-spirited troll came up to the witness stand. "Do you know what will happen to you if you don't tell the truth?" the stallion asked him.

The troll quailed. "I'll tell anything you want, honest!" he said quickly. "I swear!"

"Witness has been duly sworn in," the judge said.

Now Ivy started in, in the way she had. "Truculent, are you from the same village as Tristan Troll?"

"That blankety bleep?" Truculent exclaimed, enraged. "You know what that mule-bottom *did*?"

"Just answer the question," the judge warned.

"Yes, I'm ashamed to say I'm from that village."

"And what did Tristan Troll do?" Ivy asked.

"He tried to wipe out our village! He had a tasty morsel, that we all would have shared, and he let it go! We nearly starved! We had to tide through on crottled gleep! I still get sick just thinking of it!" Indeed, the troll looked ready to retch. An orderly sidled near with a basin, just in case.

"Your witness," Ivy said with a smirk at Dolph.

His witness? Dolph had no idea what to do. He sat there stupidly.

"Counsel for the defense, do you wish to cross-examine this witness?" the judge asked.

Dolph looked at the troll. "He does look pretty cross, but I guess not." There was another titter through the audience, and he realized that he had blundered again in some way. So he reversed himself. "Uh, I mean, yes, I'd better. Troll, what was this tasty morsel you say Tristan let go?"

"A female homo-sap juvenile," Truculent said gruffly.

"A what?" Dolph asked, thrown by the description. He had thought it was a little girl.

"A human brat."

"Do you mean a little human girl?"

"That's what I said, idiot."

Dolph saw a reaction in the jury box. It was Vida Vila. He remembered that her kind was protective of children. Maybe he had something here after all. "You were going to cut up this little girl and roast her?"

"Naw, we don't use knives. We just tear 'em apart and chomp 'em raw."

Draco Dragon was salivating, but Itchlips Goblin was looking unhappy. Fulsome Free seemed angry, and Vida Vila was outraged. He was scoring! This jury did have some scruples.

"Thank you," he said politely. "That will be all." For the first time he suspected he might have a chance.

The troll departed. Ivy, grimacing for some private reason, called the next witness: a little boy.

"Little Boy," she asked, "are you from the human village that the trolls raided that night?"

"What's it to ya?" he responded.

The Night Stallion twisted his horse lips into a frown. "How would you like a dream like this?" he inquired of the boy. A picture appeared over the boy's head, showing a giant hairbrush descending.

"YesIam!" the boy said instantly.

Dolph realized that this trial was no joke, in this respect. The witnesses were expected to answer without being irrelevant or sassing the members of the court. Was it possible that the verdict was not already sealed?

"And do you know the girl who was captured by the trolls?"

"Yeah." The boy was about to say more, but he glanced at the judge and changed his mind.

"What kind of a person is she?"

"A nerd. A real dope. And bossy too. You know how girls are."

Dolph had to clap a hand over his mouth to keep from laughing. That boy really knew his stuff!

But Ivy played it with a straight face. "So the village would have been better off without her?"

The judge glanced at Dolph. "Do you have an objection? That calls for a conclusion on the part of the witness."

But Dolph, getting smarter, had been watching the jury. The question had angered several members. His side was better off with it, because Ivy was doing his job for him.

"No objection," he said.

"Yeah, sure," the boy said. "She was a pain! I'm sorry she came back."

Ivy realized she had made a mistake. "Your witness," she said, ending it.

Dolph approached the boy, who was younger than himself. "So you don't like that little girl?" he asked.

"That's what I said!"

"Do you like any girls?"

"Of course not!"

"So you'd be glad if the trolls carried them all away and ate them?"

"Gee, that'd be great!"

Dolph looked wisely at the jury and nodded. Several members nodded back. The boy had been revealed as a brat. "No more questions."

Ivy, disgruntled, called her next witness. "Mare Frigoris."

A black female horse trotted up, seeming quite solid. Again, Dolph reminded himself that this was the gourd; the night mares lived here, and so were as solid here as anyone.

"State your name and occupation, please."

The night mare did not actually speak; instead she projected a dreamlet into the minds of the listeners. In this little dream she had the form of a pretty black woman with her black hair in the form of a ponytail. "I am Mare Frigoris, after whom the Sea of Cold on the Moon is named. I carry bad dreams to those who deserve them."

"How long have you held this position?" Ivy asked.

"Three hundred years."

"You are then an experienced carrier of dreams?"

"Yes."

"And do you take pride in your work?"

"Of course. It is a great and necessary profession. I take my work most seriously."

"And were you the designated carrier of the dream for Tristan Troll that night?"

"I was."

"Did you have any reason to doubt that it was a quality bad dream, suitable for the occasion?"

"No. It was presented in a package. In fact, the full effort was so important that it required three night mares to handle it. I was the first: a position of honor."

"And did that dream occur as scheduled?"

"No." The black maid in the dreamlet frowned. "It was a disaster, and a sore embarrassment to us all."

"Exactly what happened?"

"A critical part was to be played by a female skeleton—"

"The defendant?"

"Yes. But instead of scaring the dreamer as she was supposed to, by playing the part of the skeleton of a female of his tribe who had starved to death because of his dereliction, she—" Here the dreamlet maiden faltered, appalled by the enormity of the betrayal.

"Take the time you need," Ivy said sympathetically. "Tell us in your own words exactly how that wretch ruined your work of artistry."

The dreamlet girl recovered her equilibrium. "It was so subtle, so devious, I didn't catch it on my initial review. All of the dream was correct, guaranteed to keep the victim screaming in his sleep until he was more horse than me."

The audience and the jury burst out laughing at the pun. "Order in the court," the judge said indulgently.

"Then why didn't it work?" Ivy persisted.

"Because of those few words she whispered at the beginning of her part," the black mare girl explained. "She told the troll 'I think you did right.' Then he knew that it was only a dream, and that even those who had come to torment him didn't want to. He no longer took it seriously,

and he hardly suffered at all. The entire night's dreaming
was ruined!" Here the mare girl broke down, and was unable to continue.

"Your witness," Ivy said smugly.

What was Dolph to do with this witness? There was no
question of the facts; Grace'l had certainly done the deed.
"No questions," he said.

"The prosecution has no more witnesses," Ivy said. She
needed no more; she had made her case.

The facts were clear enough. Dolph realized that his only
chance was to change their interpretation. Surely the jury
would be able to appreciate Grace'l's motive, once her side
was stated. He knew just the person to make this clear.
"Mela Merwoman."

Mela walked up. She had her legs for this, and they were
just as pretty as they had been before.

"Mela, are you acquainted with the defendant?"

"Yes, I got to know her well when she was at my lair."

"What kind of a person would you say she is?"

"Well, of course she's not alive; she is formed of bones.
So I don't know whether it's fair to judge by—"

"Make an effort," Dolph said, in the curt courtroom manner that seemed to make the best impression. He didn't
know much about trials, but he wasn't stupid.

"I'd call her a really nice person. She cares about people,
and she always tries to do what's right. Her friend Marrow
is that way, too; he—"

"You say she cares about people," he interrupted, knowing that they could not afford to stray from the topic and
fudge the point. "But she is not alive, not truly human. How
could she care about a human child?"

"She cares about anyone who needs caring about," Mela
said simply. "There are some living folk who don't care."
She looked darkly at Draco Dragon. "Grace'l is a nonliving
person who does care."

He saw Vida Vila reacting in the jury box; she was unlikely to vote against Grace'l after this. Fulsome Fee was

nodding agreement too; he had a concern with children, for his folk needed more of them.

"So if she had to punish someone who had saved a child from harm, would you say that she was justified in—"

"Objection!" Ivy cried. "Conclusion on the part of the witness"

"Sustained," the judge said.

But Dolph had made his point; more heads in the jury were nodding. It had been no accident that Grace'l messed up the bad dream for Tristan Troll. She had done it because of the way she felt about people. How could she be condemned for that?

"Mela, if *you* had to play a part in a bad dream, like the one Grace'l—"

"Objection!" Ivy cried. "Irrelevant, immaterial, and misleading!"

"Sustained."

Well, it had been worth a try. "No more questions," he said.

Ivy had no questions; Mela could only make Grace'l look better.

Next he called Tristan Troll. There was a stir in the audience; this was a daring move! But Dolph knew he had to be daring, if he was to fight his way to anything like an even chance for Grace'l.

"Tristan, why did you let that little girl go?" he asked. "Please tell this court in your own words, with as much detail as you need." He knew this would be a touching story.

"Objection!" Ivy cried. "Irrelevant! We don't need to know why, just that he did it, and what the defendant did then." Naturally she did not want this touching story presented.

"This is the act that started this whole thing," Dolph said. "We have to have it straight, because the bad dream was what got Grace'l in trouble. How can we judge her, if we don't know exactly what caused her to do what she did?"

More members of the jury nodded. They were not inflexible at all; he was winning them over! He had surprised himself by his logic; he might have a better mind than he had suspected.

"Overruled," the judge said. For a moment Dolph was disappointed, thinking that he had lost the point; then he realized that it was the objection that had been overruled, and he had won his point.

"I had always thought of the human folk as mere animals," the troll said. "Just so much flesh waiting to be caught and eaten. But when that little girl spoke to me, and told me how bad her loss would make her family feel, I thought of my own little cub troll, that I always wanted but never had, and I remembered how lonely it was without her, and I didn't want to do that to anyone else, not even human folk. So I let her go. I know it was foolish, because trolls never spare humans, nor humans trolls, but that was the way it was."

Dolph figured that was enough. Anyone on the jury who had a child would understand. "Your witness."

"But you knew you were doing wrong, didn't you?" Ivy asked the troll. "So that you deserved punishment?"

"Objection!" Dolph cried.

"I withdraw the question," Ivy said with a smirk. She had done her damage, regardless of the answer. "No further questions."

Finally Dolph called the little girl as a witness. She came to the witness box, and she was impossibly little and cute.

"Do you understand what the trolls intended to do with you, before Tristan let you go?" he asked her.

The little girl burst into tears. Fulsome Fee looked angry, and Vida Vila almost jumped out of the jury box. Neither of them liked the abuse of children.

"Your witness," Dolph said.

"No questions," Ivy said quickly. She did not look comfortable.

That was it; there were no further witnesses. It was time for the counsels for the prosecution and defense to make their summations, before the jury decided. This was where it all came together—or apart. Dolph's hands were sweating; he had no idea what to say.

Fortunately, Ivy had to speak first. "All this business about nice skeletons or sorry trolls or sweet little girls is irrelevant," she said. "Skeletons are supposed to be scary, and trolls are supposed to be mean, and little girls aren't necessarily sweet." She whirled on Dolph. "Do you disagree?"

Dolph, caught completely by surprise, choked. Ivy was her own best example!

"You the jury have to consider just one thing," she continued savagely. "Did the defendant do what she was supposed to do? You know she didn't; therefore she is guilty. That is all there is to it, and you know it."

Ouch! At one nasty stroke, she had negated all of Dolph's witnesses. How could he counter that? Grace'l *had* messed up the dream, and that was all that the denizens of the realm of dreams cared about.

Then he remembered that he couldn't win if he accepted the gourd's definitions; it was a fixed game. He had not gotten anywhere he wanted to go when he kept opening doors with questions he didn't like; he had only escaped that trap when he rejected that whole business. He had to break out of those definitions. There might not be much of a chance, that way, but there was no chance at all the other way.

He had to get through to each member of the jury, to make that person or creature vote his way. To make a really effective summation that would move them all.

"Well, uh, er," he said, "You know it just isn't right to punish a person for being nice. The ends of making bad dreams don't justify the means of—" He stalled, confused. What point had he been trying to make? He couldn't, in this pressure situation, get it straight. Ends and means— but it was gone. "That's all I have to say." He returned to his table, chagrined.

Ivy looked across at him. "Brother, you blew it," she said sneeringly.

He was already aware of that.

The jury consulted. Dolph looked at Grace'l. "I tried," he said, near to tears again. "I really tried."

"I know you did, Dolph," she said. "It isn't your fault that no one can win a trial in the dream realm."

The jury straightened. "Have you reached a decision?" the judge inquired.

"We have, Your Honor," Draco said.

"What is your decision?"

"Guilty."

Dolph had been discouraged, fearing just this result. But now that it had happened, he was outraged. "But it isn't fair!" he cried. "She's so nice, and this is all so mixed up!"

Ivy turned toward him. He could tell by the mean set of her mouth that she was about to say something ungirl-like.

Then, without warning or interim, he was in a courtyard. Grace'l was standing before a pocked brick wall. There was a blindfold around her skull.

"Ready!"

Dolph looked toward the voice. There was a squad of ten centaur archers, now lifting their bows and nocking their arrows in unison. The centaur commander stood to the side, where he could see both the squad and the target—which was Grace'l, across the court.

"Aim!"

Ten bows oriented, and ten strings drew back as ten terrible arrows were aimed at the condemned creature.

"Wait!" Dolph cried, running out into the middle of the court, between Grace'l and the firing squad.

"This is highly irregular," the centaur commander said, frowning.

"But you can't execute her just because she messed up one bad dream!" Dolph protested.

"Indeed we can, unless she recants and swears never to do it again and makes up for it by being twice as mean as the others in future dreams."

"I can't do that!" Grace'l cried, appalled.

"She can't do that!" Dolph echoed.

"I thought so. She is recalcitrant. Move aside, or you will share her fate," the centaur commander said curtly.

"She did what she did because the dream was wrong!" Dolph said. "She's a nice person, and she just couldn't participate in an unfair punishment. How can you, centaurs, known for your fairness, do this thing? How can you execute a person you know is right?"

"We do not make the rules, we only implement them," the commander said. "For the final time: move, for we are about to fire."

Dolph backed up until he touched Grace'l. He turned and put his arms around her. "I defended her, I share her fate!" he said. "I believe as she does: that dream was wrong!"

"As you wish," the centaur said. He turned again to the squad, which had remained immobile during this exchange.

"I'm sorry, Grace'l," Dolph said, his tears flowing. "I tried, I just wasn't good enough!"

"You were good enough," she said. "It was a lost cause from the start. We know we are right, even if they don't accept it. At least you tried, and I thank you for—"

"FIRE!"

Ten arrows shot toward them, each one unerringly aimed. They struck together. There was an explosion of light.

They stood in a tiny chamber, before the Night Stallion. "Are you satisfied?" the stallion asked.

Dolph, dazed, couldn't answer. He seemed to be still alive. Grace'l seemed intact, the blindfold gone.

"We are," a chorus of voices replied.

Dolph looked. One of the walls had fuzzed out, and beyond it was the jury box, with the twelve creatures present.

The stallion focused on the skeleton. "You have been found guilty of being too nice for work in the crafting of bad dreams, and your constancy under duress has been verified. You are therefore barred from this type of employment; henceforth you will work exclusively in good dreams. Since there is small call for your specialty in those, you are hereby granted leave in Xanth until a call arises for an animated skeleton in a good dream. Depart with our favor; you are indeed a good person."

Grace'l was almost speechless. "But the trial—"

"Was to ascertain the exact nature of your belief. You might have interfered with the dream because of laziness or carelessness or confusion. It was essential for us to know, if you were to resume work in the gourd. Had you remained beyond the dream realm, none of this would have been necessary."

"But the execution—"

"We had to ascertain whether your position was firm, rather than merely a pose to elicit sympathy. When you maintained it even at the end, we knew that you truly believed in goodness."

"But Dolph—" she said.

"Ah yes, Prince Dolph." The equine gaze oriented on Dolph. "You showed your values. You defended her as well as you were able, and, given your age and inexperience, this was creditable. You remained consistent even at the end, putting your life behind your belief when your words failed you. You will one day make an excellent King of Xanth. Meanwhile, you will be treated with due respect in the gourd. Whenever you enter, the first denizen of the dream realm to spy you will proffer any help you need to find your way around or to accomplish something. You have proved out, Prince Dolph, and we of the gourd salute you."

Then the remaining walls dissolved, and the entire courtroom reappeared. The audience burst into applause, which was joined by the jury, and the witnesses, and the squad of centaurs, and even Ivy who no longer looked mean at all. She had done her best to provoke him, to make him say something he did not believe in, and she did not look unhappy that she had failed. In losing his case honorably, he had won it.

Dumbfounded, Dolph tried to speak. But as he opened

his mouth, the entire scene dissolved, and he was on the sand of the beach of the shore of Xanth, looking up from the peephole of the gourd. Grace'l was beside him, and Marrow across from him, and Nada and the new girl, Electra.

He realized that he had saved Grace'l, and found the way to get the Heaven Cent, but still had formidable problems to handle.

18

CHOICE

Next day they fashioned a huge basket of vine and driftwood; then Dolph became a roc and carried it the short (for a roc) distance to Castle Roogna. The folk there were expecting him, of course, for the Tapestry had remained tuned, and King Dor and Queen Irene and Ivy were all outside waving as he circled down. He made a good landing, and reverted to boy form.

Then there was a happy chaos, as everybody met everybody whom he or she had only heard about or seen on the Tapestry before, and the rest of the day disappeared in whatever.

Marrow and Grace'l and Nada and Electra were given rooms in the castle, and night shut things down. Dolph found it odd, trying to sleep alone in his room on his soft bed with only Handy his bed monster for company; he missed Marrow's bone home and the near presence of the others. He couldn't sleep; everything was too fresh.

There was a quiet knock on his door. "Yeah?" he called, hoping that maybe Marrow was there.

It was Ivy. Oh.

"Dolph, I just wanted to tell you," she said. "I had the strangest dream yesterday. It wasn't even night time! All about this big strange trial, and—"

"I know. I was there."

"Well, my job was to—I mean, it seems awful mean, but I had to prove that your skeleton friend, Grace'l Ossian, was—"

"I understand."

"I really thought you did a pretty good job, but in the dream I couldn't say that. I had to—"

"I know."

"I mean, she *is* a very nice person, and it was really bad what happened to her because of that dream. But now—"

"Thank you." This was awkward, and he didn't like it.

"But that isn't really what I came about," she said.

Of course it wasn't. She was too devious for that. Dolph waited.

"I know you have this problem about—about Nada Naga and Electra. You can't marry them both. I can see how awkward it is, Nada being so much older than you. For you, and for Nada too."

"She's your age," Dolph agreed. Had she come to gloat about that?

"But of course her folk need our help with the goblins, and she's a princess, so she's doing it. And you made a deal, so you're doing it. But the way it worked out—"

"Yes." Now it was coming; he could see her working up to it. Certainly he had gotten himself into a picklement.

"Well, I thought if you had a way to get out of it—"

"A Prince does not break his word," Dolph snapped.

"But if she didn't have to marry you, to make that liaison and get help, then—"

"But she does. We both know it."

"I think there is another way, Dolph."

She was going hit him with something that would make it even worse. He knew it. That was her way. He just wanted to get it over with. "What?"

"If another liaison was made, so the naga could get the help they need, then she wouldn't have to marry you, and you wouldn't have to marry her. The deal would not be broken, because it wouldn't matter anymore. Especially if we helped the naga sooner than it would have been with you."

"That could only be done with another marriage," he pointed out. "And she's their only daughter, and I'm the only—"

"I could marry her brother," Ivy said.

"Son," he continued. "So there isn't any other way to—" He did a double take. "What?"

"Prince Naldo Nada," she said. "He was going to marry me, only you were the one the dragon brought, so she had to fill in. That's where the trouble started. It was probably that mean Magician Murphy's doing, somehow. She didn't want to deceive you, Dolph, any more than Grace'l wanted to get you in trouble in the gourd. It just happened that way, and she had to make the best of it. She's really a very nice girl, you know."

"I know. But—"

"So if I married Prince Naldo, then the liaison would be good, and your betrothal to Nada could be dissolved by mutual agreement. He's a handsome man, in his human guise, so it wouldn't be so bad, and—"

Dolph saw that it was true. That *would* honorably eliminate the need for him to marry Nada. Yet he was still astonished. "But why would you—"

"I told you: because it's a good way out. Nobody loses, and nobody gets embarrassed. And you won't be in that picklement anymore."

"But do you love Naldo?"

"Of course not! I don't even know him! But that doesn't matter; I'm sure that in time it would happen. Good things can come of arranged marriages. Our grandparents—"

"I remember. But I mean why would you do something like that when you don't have to? It's my problem, not yours, and—"

"Because I love you, you idiot!" she flared. Then, after a shocked pause: "Oops! I didn't mean to say that."

Dolph felt a wash of heat like that of a dragon's breath, passing through his body without hurting it. "You can take it back, then." But now he remembered all the little things Ivy had done for him through the years, such as showing him how to get cookies from a high shelf by becoming a slug and climbing up to them, and covering for him when he accidentally broke something, and telling him secrets while not blabbing his own secrets. In a hundred little ways she had shown how she cared, if he had ever thought to notice. In the heat of their frequent arguments he had forgotten such things, but now he recognized them as tokens of the deeper reality. Love was not confined to adults, or to folk of different backgrounds; it had its family forms too.

She sighed, and he saw with surprise that there were tears on her face. "No, I can't. Because it's true. You may be a brat and all that, and we fight all the time because that's the way it's supposed to be between siblings, but you are my brother, and I do love you, even if it isn't proper to show it. I'd die for you, Dolph, if I had to, and marriage isn't nearly as bad as that. So there's no need to make a big mushy thing of it. You've got a problem I can solve. I can help you, and—"

"And I love you," he said. "I guess I just couldn't face it, so I pretended I hated you. But when I saw you applauding in that dream, at the end, I felt—"

"That was the only part of it that was real, really," she said. "I hated being so mean to you, when it counted, but the Night Stallion said—"

"I know. And I tried to believe that all fourteen-year-old girls were terrible, and then when Nada turned out to be—"

"Her age really doesn't matter. I like her; she's a true princess. So now I can do you both a favor—"

"I don't know. Let me think about it, Ivy."

"But what's to think about? I told you I'd do it."

"Just hug me," he said, unable to hold back his tears any longer.

"Oh." She hugged him, and he hugged her, and they both cried, which was foolish, because they were not unhappy.

In the morning he met privately with his parents, King Dor and Queen Irene. "As you know, we have been following your adventures," Dor said. "We have noted your problem with Princess Nada and the girl from the past, Electra. We can understand how you would wish neither to abridge your agreement with Nada, nor allow Electra to perish, even if she were not needed to fashion the Heaven Cent you seek. It is an honorable dilemma."

"Yes," Dolph agreed.

"Certainly they are both nice girls," Irene said. "We would not wish either of them to be hurt. But you are very young yet, and even when you are grown, you cannot marry both. It is necessary to dissolve at least one bethrothal."

"Well—" Dolph began.

"As it happens, we believe we can alleviate this problem," Dor said. "As we see it, Electra is the better match for you, because she is closer to your age and she loves you, and of course she is human, quite apart from the business aspect. We realize that this love is the result of magic, but that kind is as valid as the other kind. It is also true that she will die if she does not marry you, and this spell is so deeply ingrained that we cannot alleviate it. The betrothal keeps her alive and well, but were it broken, she would fail rapidly. Certainly we would not want this to occur."

"True," Dolph agreed. "But—"

"So we believe the betrothal best eliminated is the one with Nada Naga," Irene explained. "She is older than you, and does not love you, and is only partially human; it is a purely political liaison. We need only to discover a way to break it off without hurting any parties or causing any political repercussion."

"I'm not sure—" Dolph began.

"So we have decided to extend our help to the naga folk regardless," Dor continued. "We shall arrange to send magical weapons from the castle arsenal that they can use to hold back the goblins, and we will show them how to use these, and if that is not sufficient, your mother will go there and grow some plants that will have an effect. We shall do this without the requirement of any marriage. The marriage is only a means to an end; the end is the alliance between our folk, and that is the end we shall serve. This shall be accomplished well before you come of age to marry, so—"

"No," Dolph said.

Both looked at him, surprised. "This is not enough?" Irene asked. "In that case, you have only to say what you consider—"

"No, I don't want to break the engagement. I want to marry Nada."

"But Dolph," Dor said reasonably. "If you break off with Electra—"

"I know. So I'd better keep that one too."

"But you can't marry them both!" Irene exclaimed.

"Why not?"

Dor and Irene exchanged a parental glance. "Son, we've been trying to explain—" Dor began.

"Yes, you have," Dolph said. "You have been explaining how you will organize my life for me, as you have always done. But you haven't been listening. Ivy wants to help too; she says she will marry Prince Naldo."

Both parents jumped; evidently this was the first they had heard of this. "I really don't think—" Irene started.

"In the gourd, in the course of the trial, I had to find out how to fight my own battle or a battle for another person," Dolph said. "To do that I had to get to know my own will and to understand the doctrine of ends and means. You are proposing means to the end of breaking my betrothal to Nada Naga, but that's no good, because I don't want to break it. I want to make my own decision, based on what I truly want and believe is best, even if it doesn't make much sense to you. When I become King I will have to do that, and pay for my mistakes. It is never too early to learn that kind of discipline: responsibility for my own situation."

"What is it you really want?" Dor asked, nodding with a certain surprised approval, though Irene was grim.

"I want to marry Nada. She's a good match for me, and a princess, and I love her. So I thank you and I thank my sister for your efforts, but they are not needed. I'm staying with Nada."

"But she's five years older than you!" Dor exclaimed.

"The same age as my sister," Dolph agreed. "What does it matter? I learned last night that there's nothing wrong with that age. What counts is the relationship. She's a really nice person, and I love her, and I know she'll make a good wife. I'm glad to help her folk fight the goblins, but even without that, I want to marry her."

"Dolph, you are only a child!" Irene protested. "You can't begin to know what love is!"

"I am only a child," he agreed. "I have no idea how to summon the stork, or any of the rest of it. But I know what love is."

Both of them shook their heads in the way that adults had. "You only think you know," Dor said. "I realize that your feeling can seem very important, now, but—"

"Give me the test of the roses," Dolph said.

They were stunned. "Oh, my child, my little child!" Irene breathed. "What are you saying!"

"The roses," Dor said with equal dismay. "Those are not for you!"

"I think they are," Dolph said. "Because they will make you listen. Give me the roses, today. If they do not vindicate me, then you can break my betrothal to Nada."

The parents exchanged another significant glance. "So shall it be," Dor agreed.

The roses grew in a special courtyard by themselves. There were five bushes, and each grew roses of a different color: white, yellow, pink, red, and black. Each represented a different type of emotion: indifference, friendship, romance, love, and death. They were enchanted, so that a person could pick only a rose of the appropriate color; any other would stab his hand with its fierce thorns.

There were seats around the outer fringe of the court. The roses grew in a circle, and within the circle was a pentagonal tile just big enough for one person to stand without being scratched by the thorns on any of the bushes. No one could walk to that tile on the ground; it was necessary to descend to it by a rope ladder hanging from a balcony. The roses were seldom actually used to verify feeling; they were normally admired from a safe distance. The only person who could approach them safely was the gardener, who loved them passionately. Their mixed perfume wafted through the castle, making it pleasant throughout.

Dor and Irene sat at one end of the courtyard. Ivy was near them, and then Dolph, Nada, and Electra. Marrow and Grace'l completed the rough circle. All were solemn.

"Prince Dolph has asked for the test of the roses," Dor said. "He will pick roses for Electra and for Nada, and then they will pick roses for him. The betrothal that has no Red Rose of Love on either side will be dissolved without prejudice, and appropriate arrangements will be made to honor all related commitments." He glanced around, obviously not sanguine about this, and Irene was tight lipped. "Electra?"

Electra stood, smiling. She walked to the ladder under the balcony and climbed it with alacrity. She looked and acted no older than Dolph, though she was eleven. She was a cute girl, and her two brown braids whipped around as she moved.

She reached the balcony, then got on the ladder and climbed down to the central tile. She stood there amidst the roses, waiting. The bushes swayed, brushing gently by her, not scratching; they were orienting on her, for this was part of their magic.

Dolph approached. He circled the bushes once. Then he

reached for one, and plucked a yellow rose of friendship. He held it up, showing it to everyone; then he held it by his face and addressed her. Her smile did not falter; she had known he did not love her. It was a situation she hoped to change, by the time they both came of age to marry.

"I do not love you," Dolph told her. "But that is no fault of yours; I only met you yesterday, and I hardly know you, but I'm sure you are worth marrying. You will die if I don't marry you, and I need you to make the Heaven Cent so I can find Good Magician Humfrey and complete my Quest, so I will marry you. It will be seven years before I am of age to marry, and by that time I should know you very well. So don't be concerned because I don't love you; there is plenty of time for that to change, and even if it doesn't, I will do what I must to save you, just as I did for Grace'l. Meanwhile, we can be friends." And the rose he held assumed the merest tinge of pink.

He tossed it to her. She caught it, and held it. "I know," she said. "You are a prince. If it hadn't been for Murphy's curse, it would have been the Princess who slept, and you would not have been betrothed before. You are very nice to handle this mess so graciously."

"I don't think the Princess would have been much interested in a nine-year-old boy," Dolph remarked with a wan smile.

"She would have slept a few more years, until you were a man, and then she would have been the answer to all your wildest dreams. She was perfect."

Dolph remembered something. "You told us of Millie the maid! Did you know that she arrived here too? She was a ghost for eight hundred years, and then she recovered and married the Zombie Master."

"He's here too?" Electra asked, amazed.

"Of course they're older now, and have grown children, but you could visit."

"I must do that!" she exclaimed, clapping her hands girlishly and flinging her braids about. She was remarkably fetching when she did those things. "I had hoped Millie escaped the curse, but it must have caught her and killed her, but now the curse is gone from her and she can be happy. Oh, I'm so glad!" Then she turned pensive. "But I wish I knew what happened to the others, to Tapis and the Princess, after I ruined both their hopes."

"I watched them on the Tapestry," Ivy called. "After Castle Roogna was finished, King Roogna came and talked to them, and they went with him. The Sorceress saw to the furnishing of the castle, making it nice, and you know it really needed it, because the King just wasn't much of a hand at that. And the princess—well, after a while she married the King."

"But she was of the line that preceded his," Electra protested. "They didn't like King Roogna much."

"I guess that changed, because the King liked her, and he needed a wife who knew how to do things the royal way," Ivy said. "They looked pretty friendly the last time I tuned them in; you can come and watch with me, if you like."

"Oh, yes!" Electra exclaimed. "I guess the Sorceress found where she was most needed after all, and the Princess was willing to settle for a king if she couldn't have a prince. So maybe Murphy's curse didn't do them as much harm as I thought. I'm so glad! An awful burden is gone from me." And she clapped her hands again, and made a little skip with her legs that Dolph noticed. She was going to have good legs when she grew up.

Then Electra put the stem of the rose between her teeth and climbed the ladder to the balcony. Soon she was on her way to join Ivy; it was evident that the two were going to get along well. Electra would surely be a good companion around the castle, because she possessed many of the traits that Dolph had thought Nada did. And of course she would be making the Heaven Cent, so that he could finally complete his Quest and find the Good Magician. He did not regret being betrothed to her.

But now it was time for the serious business. "Princess Nada," Dor said solemnly.

Nada got up, walked to the up-ladder, and climbed it as readily as Electra had, though she was in her mature lady form. She reached the balcony, and transferred to the rope ladder. It swung as it took her weight, and her skirt flared, showing her legs. Dolph was unashamed about looking, for he knew it was his right as her betrothed. She did not need to wait until she grew up to get her legs nice; she was there already. Of course there was no reason why she shouldn't be, since this was not her natural form, merely her natural age; she would hardly assume an ugly human form. He had become a fair connoisseur of legs in the course of the Quest.

She landed on the tile, and the rose bushes touched her, zeroing in. In a moment they settled; they were ready.

Dolph approached again. He circled, then stopped at the red bush. He touched a stem, and the thorns fell from it, as they had for the yellow rose. He picked a fine red one, and held it up so all could see its brightness and that his hand was unscratched.

There was a little squeak, as of almost-concealed dismay. It was Irene, who had thought he could not pluck that color rose. She had thought him too young. Dor, too, was surprised, but none of the others were. The young had known better than the old, and the skeletons had understood better than many humans. Love knew no barriers of age.

"I love you, Nada," Dolph said. "You are a princess, and you are a fine person, and you are beautiful, and I want to marry you. We have had good times and bad times together, and I thought you were a child like me; to see you adult is strange, but it doesn't matter. I came to know you as a companion, and I liked you from the start. But I know it is a political liaison, a betrothal made for business purpose, not really of your choosing. I know you are prepared to do what you must to make it work, and that that will make you become the very best wife it is possible for a woman to be. But it is no longer necessary for you to make this sacrifice. My folk will help your folk regardless, and my sister will marry your brother instead, if you wish. So you can be free, without hurting your people."

He paused, nerving himself for his conclusion. "I love you, Nada. But I know you do not love me. I would not make you suffer. I would not make you marry one you did not love, or wait seven years for your own fulfillment. I promised not to break our betrothal, and I shall not, but you may break it if you wish. I would not have my joy at the expense of yours. I want your happiness more than anything else."

There: he had said it, as he had rehearsed it during the night, and he had not stumbled or spoken inelegantly. But though his voice had behaved, his eyes had not. Nada was blurring before him, and he knew the tears were running down his cheeks. He had garbled his summation at the trial, but this speech had been even harder to make.

Then Nada spoke, and her voice shook, and he realized that she was crying too. "You have made a very generous offer, Dolph, and I think I knew you would do it, because I have come to know you well. When I revealed my deception to you, and begged you not to break the betrothal, you were hurt but constant; you did not break it. I cannot break it now. I see how fine a person you are, and I know that you will be even better when you mature, and it is not in me to reject you though you give me leave to do so. You are a prince, and a fine person, and I liked you from the start, and I know you love me and will make the very best husband, when you come of age, and I will wait for you, if you do not change your mind. Perhaps when it is time I will be able to meet your generous love with my own."

Dolph stared at her through the blue of tears. *She had not done it!* She had not taken the easy way out. She was letting the betrothal stand. "Oh, Nada," he whispered, and the rose he held became so bright it seemed on fire. Then he tossed it to her, and she caught it and held it, accepting it and what it signified.

Then she climbed the ladder and was gone from the tile. Dolph found a hanky and wiped his face. He had thought the dilemma of the double betrothal would be solved at this point, and that he would now be grieving while his parents relaxed. He wanted only to prove that his love was real, before it was damned. To establish the principle, by making his own decision. But, as with the decision at the trial, the outcome was reversed, and Nada would after all marry him. Instead of grief he had joy—and instead of a solution, he still had the problem of two girls to marry.

"Dolph," Dor said.

Oh, yes—the other part of the test of the roses. In a daze Dolph walked to the ladder, climbed to the balcony, and down the rope ladder to the tile. The bushes touched him as his vision cleared. They had to know him, so that they could tell whether he was the true object of the emotion indicated by the color selected by the one who picked a rose. The roses were very specific; they could not be fooled by a person who loved but loved not the one on the tile.

Electra approached. She walked without hesitation to the red bush, and picked a red rose, and tossed it to him. Then she returned to her seat without a word. She had proven her case, and vindicated her betrothal. She was not a princess, but that did not exclude her. She was exactly the kind of girl who was right for him; indeed, the spell of the Heaven Cent had brought her to where she was most needed, both as a person and as a talent. Except for Murphy's curse, that reached even this far into the future to mess it up. Could that have been the reason that he, rather than Ivy, had come to fulfil the naga's Answer? Dolph knew it would have been much easier for Ivy to marry Naldo, and for him to marry the ancient Princess, or Electra. Everyone would have been conveniently settled. Instead he had met and loved Nada, and though he could see in this the operation of a curse against Electra, he still loved Nada. He almost had to smile: if this was all the power of an eight-hundred-year-old curse, what a powerful curse it had been! Even with knowledge and the means to nullify it, he could not bring himself to do so. Whatever could go wrong, had gone wrong—and he would not have it otherwise.

Yet what of Good Magician Humfrey? He had left the message that had sent Dolph on the long additional loop of the Quest. Surely Humfrey had known about the complication on the way! Why, then, had he done it? Where was the Good Magician now? Dolph's Quest had really solved nothing, only generated a horrendously difficult situation where someone was bound to be badly hurt. Or had Murphy's curse messed up even the Good Magician's perception? No, that seemed unlikely; probably Dolph had messed it up by himself by misunderstanding the nature of the skeleton key and looking in the wrong places, and by letting himself get captured by Mela Merwoman. The rest had followed from that.

Now Nada approached. She walked slowly around the bushes. She paused at the yellow bush, but did not reach for it. Instead she went on to the red bush.

"Don't try that one!" Dolph said with sudden alarm. "I understand about you, just as Electra understands about me."

"I have to, Dolph," she said.

She put her hand to a stem—and screamed, jerking her hand back. Bright red blood was flowing from a terrible slash. The magic thorns had struck her.

Nada stared at her hand, and at the blood, seeing the proof of what she had hoped was not the case. She did not love Dolph, even though she wished she could.

Her face crumpled. Then she stepped toward the black bush, the one with the roses of death, and reached for it.

Dolph dived from the tile. He plunged through the bushes and tackled Nada, bearing her away from the black rose. They fell together to the ground, clear of the bushes.

"You should not have stopped me!" she cried. "I could have taken that one!"

"I know you could have!" Dolph agreed. "You wanted to die for me! To free me! *But I don't want to be freed!* Promise me never to do that again."

"I know," she said, and kissed him. "I promise. I think one day I will be able to take the red rose."

Then the others were around them, and Marrow was helping Dolph to stand, and Grace'l was helping Nada.

"There's not a scratch on him!" Irene exclaimed. "How could—?"

"Our son has proven himself again," Dor said. "The roses understand true conviction."

"But he's only nine years old!"

"Old enough," Dor said. "They all are."

"But he can't marry both!"

"There will be seven years to work that out," Dor said.

Dolph, holding Nada, turned and gestured to Electra. She came to him, and he held them both. Seven years seemed like a very long time. In Xanth, with magic, anything could happen, and usually did.

PIERS ANTHONY was born in Oxford, England, in 1934, lived in Spain for a year after the Spanish Civil War but emigrated with his family after his father was arrested by the Franco government (apparently by mistake). Since the age of six he has lived in the United States and now resides in Florida with his wife and their two daughters.

Mr. Anthony published his first story in 1963, after eight years of trying. His first novel, *Chthon*, was nominated for both the Hugo and Nebula awards for the year 1967. Since then, he has had over 60 books published—including such classics as *Macroscope, Cluster*, and the Incarnations of Immortality series—and eleven of his books have been *New York Times* bestsellers. The first novel in the Xanth series, *A Spell for Chameleon*, earned him the August Derleth Award in 1977.